THE
PASSION
OF
WOMEN

a novel

SÉBASTIEN JAPRISOT

Translated by Ros Schwartz

CROWN PUBLISHERS, INC.
New York

Published by Crown Publishers, Inc., 201 East 50th Street
New York, New York 10022. Member of the Crown Publishing Group.

Originally published in France as *La Passion Des Femmes* by Editions Denoël in
1986. Copyright © 1986 by Editions Denoël. This translation published in Great
Britain by Martin Secker & Warburg Limited.

CROWN is a trademark of Crown Publishers, Inc.

Manufactured in the United States of America

Library of Congress Cataloging-in-Publication Data

Japrisot, Sébastien, 1931–
    [Passion des femmes. English]
    The Passion of Women: a novel / by Sébastien Japrisot; translated
by Ros Schwartz.—1st ed.
        p.   cm.
    Translation of: La passion des femmes.
    I. Title.
PQ2678.072P3813   1990
843'.914—dc20   89-48546
                                                                                    CIP

ISBN 0-517-56940-X

Book Design by Shari deMiskey

10 9 8 7 6 5 4 3 2 1

First American Edition

"And if he left off dreaming about you, where do you suppose you'd be?"

"Where I am now, of course," said Alice.

"Not you!" Tweedledee retorted contemptuously. "You'd be nowhere. Why, you're only a sort of thing in his dream!"

LEWIS CARROLL

Contents

8:15 P.M.

S UDDENLY THIS OBSTINATE YOUNG
man tells himself that he's going to move, and he does.

He heaves himself up from the sand and stands once again, his right hand clenched over the abomination staining his white sport shirt.

As far as he can see, despite the sweat—or tears of exhaustion—running down his forehead and blinding him, the beach is empty, and so is the ocean.

It is the moment, as the afternoon draws to a close, when the sun is round and red above the horizon, when all that is left on the sand is a child's forgotten ball, also red, as is the stain on the white sport shirt, that moment when hotel dining rooms are already beginning to accommodate the first murmurs, the first clatter of chairs being scraped back, when forgetful children in unfamiliar rooms demand their ball, full of sorrow that it is bedtime, but when, far from the living, on the vast deserted beach, all that can be heard is the cry of the sea gulls and the breakers.

This obstinate young man—that is how he describes himself when he talks about himself—staggers along the beach, doubled up over his wound, and he knows neither where he has come from nor where he is going, but only that he must keep going, one step at a time, for as long as his legs will carry him, until he collapses again.

How many times has he already collapsed and gotten to his feet? He remembers lying on his stomach on the sand, right at the beginning, during a never-ending bad dream. The sun had been higher and had burned him. He lost consciousness; he drifted, motionless, through a universe of fetuses, but he could feel the sun burning his back, and that slimy thing against his chest. And then, the very second he was about to open his eyes, a cool and soothing image had shot through him; he would have liked to hold on to it, but it had escaped him.

Now—one step at a time, his whole weight thrown forward—he realizes that the beach is sloping down toward the foam on the waves, that he must move away or he will sink into the water the next time he falls, and that will be the end.

This obstinate young man is going to die in any case, he tells himself. Already, the fires of hell are consuming him. He can no longer run. He can no longer walk. If he stopped for a second—but he mustn't—if he could look about him, through the sweat and the sand, he would see that nowhere is there help at hand, or within reach, that he is alone, his chest has been smashed in by a volley of gunshots, that his life has been ebbing out through this wound for too long, and that the best—or the least stupid—thing to do is to retrace his steps so as not to drown.

He does not turn around, he uses his last strength to cut across the beach, climbing up the slope, reeling like a drunkard, and he falls again.

At first he is on his knees, frantic and breathless, and he uses his hands and elbows to help him put a few more yards of sand between himself and the ocean. And then he knows that he will not advance any farther; he overbalances and lets himself fall on his back, his eyes open.

Even the sky is empty.

In an hour, in two hours, thinks this young man with an awesome imagination—that is how he describes himself when he talks about himself—the moon will rise to that precise spot where its image will be doubly reflected in my dead eyes.

But perhaps not, he tells himself. In an hour, in two hours, the tide commanded by the moon will have already covered me and the waves will have carried me out to sea. They will never find me—or

I'll be found by a fisherman, God knows where or when, somewhere between here and the Americas, who will catch me in his net among a shoal of mackerel that will have practically devoured me.

He closes his eyes.

He tries to recall the pleasant image that had come into his mind when he came to earlier, just before raising his hand to his chest and discovering that dreadful thing. He cannot.

If the tide carries me off, he tells himself, they'll look for me, they'll question the people who knew me. For months, perhaps years, until they'll have to give up hope of finding me alive. I'll be that adventurous young man they'll talk about in hushed tones, who disappeared one ill-fated summer evening, from the beach, leaving no trace except for the froth on the waves.

He struggles to raise himself up on one elbow to make out his footprints, to assess how far he has come. The sand, churned up all day, remains unfathomable. He clearly remembers a child's ball that was lying not far from him, when he started walking the last time, but it is as if the ball had been a figment of his imagination, or it is out of sight, in a hollow, miles away or a stone's throw.

Lying on his back, breathing gently, he closes his eyes again. He is not in pain. He is not really afraid. He wonders how much longer he will feel his heart beat beneath his hand. And if he will be lucky enough, before everything stops—his heart, the sun's descent, and the whirl of the galaxies—to see that image again, which he liked and which eludes him. And who they will question when those lousy mackerel gobble up his brain. And the truths, the false truths, and the lies that will further complicate the distressing mystery of his death to the *rat-a-tat* of the worn keys of a court clerk's typewriter.

And then, just as he sinks into the future to exercise his awesome imagination, this adventurous young man smells the scent of oleander wafting over him, he hears a laugh, and suddenly the forgotten vision shoots through him again, luminous as it had been the first time, so soothing, so real that he is forced to believe it is a sign from the heavens.

Rushing toward him in a great blast, a young girl with fair hair, dressed in white muslin, perched on a swing, her arms and legs bare, her face sunny, overwhelming in her happiness. And when, at the end of her flight, she dives backward and fades away, another appears, piercing the splendor of summer, sensual as a Gypsy, her eyes blackest black, her heart the most passionate, and she comes and goes to be replaced at once by a third, with the curves of a whore and a pert little face, the swish of her petticoats impregnated with the honey taste of oleander.

As for him, his heart beating more heavily each time, he counts four of them, he counts five, and goes into raptures over a blouse revealing a golden breast, or a flash of thigh glimpsed above a silk stocking, and he could count six, seven, ten, coming and going on a swing, without any of them fading away, without ever forgetting the first, her swanlike neck, the poignant suppleness of her waist, or her golden gaze.

If I absolutely have to depart, I may as well go with this image in my mind, thinks this young man as he lies on the sand protected by a lucky star.

For that is how he most often described himself.

Emma

I HAD JUST TURNED TWENTY-FOUR.

I was an illustrator in an advertising agency—the advertising world was less glamorous in those days—that overlooked the port of Saint-Julien de l'Océan. I was not very experienced but everybody agreed that I was pleasant and of good character, obedient to my superiors and conscientious in my work. I married the personnel manager.

For our honeymoon, we were given ten days' leave in August, and we planned to drive around Spain. My fiancé, Monsieur Séverin, had bought and converted an old van that had served as an ambulance during the war. I mean the First World War, of course. Behind the front seat were two bunks with our bedding, and the space underneath housed cupboards. There was a washbasin with a little water tank and there were cooking facilities. My fiancé had repainted the outside himself, a dirty yellow color that he pompously called "artistic yellow," but as he had never created anything artistic with his own fair hands, you could still clearly make out a large red cross on either side.

The wedding reception was held at the Hôtel des Bains, with a jazz band and games where the winner gets a kiss. I think I was happy, except that my fiancé—I mean my husband—went from table to table, glass in hand, talking loudly as always, and I felt a little anxious because we were supposed to be leaving at nightfall and he was not the sort of man who would allow me to drive.

At about seven or eight o'clock, more and more guests went into the kitchen, clowning around and starting to eat all over again. We took the opportunity to slip away. I kissed my parents, who looked away to hide their emotion. I was leaving them for the first time. My husband had no family except for an elder brother whose ear he had bitten during an argument over a horse, years back, and they were no longer on speaking terms. As far as I can remember, the horse had died long before we got married.

All day, I was very careful with my beautiful white dress, which both my mother and grandmother had worn as brides. A lady from Ré, who was highly thought of for her skill with the needle, had altered it to suit modern taste. I have kept a photograph, taken on the steps of the church after the ceremony, which I enclose with my statement so that you can see for yourselves what a wonderful dress I wore, despite our modest means, and also—that's right—to show you what I looked like at twenty-four, just a few hours before the events that shattered my life. I will not ask you to return this photograph to me. I never had the courage to throw it into the fire, because my parents are in it, standing next to me, but I cannot look at it without crying.

> The black-and-white postcard-size print shows Emma as a rather tall, slim young woman with fair hair. She has a good figure and eyes that are probably blue. Her face is smiling and melancholy, and her dress, made of lace and satin, is indeed very beautiful. Her thick hair, piled up on her head, is held in place by a circlet of orange blossoms, and her forehead is framed by carefully dressed curls. Her husband, Séverin, in gray tails, is a stumpy man of forty with a pointed face and a conceited bearing.
>
> (From the notes of Marie-Martine Lepage)

We set off and it is unlikely that anyone noticed our absence. I was relieved, because throughout the reception I had been dreading the jokes and innuendos that would be sure to accompany our departure. I was easily shocked in those days.

My husband, who had exerted himself considerably, had long since removed his jacket and tie. He flung them onto one of the bunks in the van as he climbed into the driver's seat. I looked exactly the same as I had that morning, except that I had let down my hair and was holding my headdress in my lap.

Saint-Julien de l'Océan is a seaside resort at the end of a peninsula known as La Pointe des Amériques. Its renown is eclipsed nowadays by that of Fouras and Marennes, but in those days it had a population of a thousand souls in winter and no less than five thousand during the holiday season. The highway to the mainland was bordered by oyster beds giving way to pastures surrounded by marshes. I recall a huge red sun followed us as the evening mist stole over the expanses of water.

We had not left the peninsula when night fell. Drowsy from the wine, my husband only managed to stay awake because of the jolts. I dared not say anything to him, for he was a man who would flare up at the slightest remark, and also because I was so used to being his subordinate. Finally, he placed his hand on my knee with proprietary determination and shouted—he had to raise his voice to make himself heard—"We're going to spend our wedding night here, while I'm still up to it!"

He parked the van away from the road, at the entrance to a pinewood. We climbed down on either side to get into the back, which he called the "love nest." The moon had risen, it was almost full, and the sky was studded with stars. I lingered outside for a moment to enjoy the coolness and listen to the night birds.

When I climbed in, Séverin had lit a spirit lamp and changed into the pajamas he had bought for the occasion, sky blue with yellow and black stripes, the breast pocket embroidered with his initials. He said, with a sly, conceited air, "I've thought of everything." He opened a cupboard under one of the bunks and took out a bottle of sparkling wine he had saved, and two metal tumblers. I did not feel like it, but I drank a little wine to avoid an argument. Then, as I sat there on one of the beds, without looking up or saying a word, he sighed. "All right, I understand." He lit a cigarette and got out of the van to go for a walk while I undressed. As I closed the doors that he had left open, I saw him go over to a nearby bank and sit down.

I unfastened my dress and carefully slipped it over my head. No doubt the rustling of the material in my ears prevented me from hearing any other sound, for I suddenly found myself being bodily seized as a rough hand was clamped over my mouth. I did not even have time to think it was my husband playing an idiotic joke. A muffled, breathless voice, which was not his, ordered, "Be quiet! Don't move!" My heart felt as though it would leap out of my breast.

The arms clasping me pushed me backward and almost lifted me off my feet. In the lamplight I glimpsed a tall young man whose face was hidden by a beard. His head was shaved and he wore a loose, collarless shirt. He reeked of the marshes. Crushed up against him, I guessed from the noise that he was bolting the van door.

Then he murmured feverishly, "If you do as I tell you, you won't come to any harm." He was leaning over me, his dark eyes looking into mine. I didn't know how to make him understand that he was suffocating me, but he must have read from my expression that I was too terrified to put up a fight, and he removed the hand that was over my mouth. Without allowing me the time to recover my wits, he dragged me, panting and half-naked, toward the front of the ambulance, saying, in the same muffled, feverish voice, "You drive. We're leaving." He blew out the lamp in passing. I wanted to answer, and it was the truth, that I barely knew how to drive, but he broke in, "Do as I say or I'll kill you!"

I clambered over the back of the seat. He stayed behind me, one hand gripping my neck. I couldn't remember what to do to start up the van. I groped about and found the ignition. As I hurtled along in the dark, it was the man who stretched an arm over my shoulder and switched on the lights.

As I turned the wheel with all my strength to get back onto the road, I heard the bottle of sparkling wine and the beakers clatter on to the floor. My panic-stricken gaze caught my husband silhouetted outside. At the sound of the engine, he stood up, barefoot, rooted to the spot, and although I couldn't make out his face, his terrible immobility conveyed how thunderstruck he was. He was, God forgive me, the very picture of the poor devil abandoned on his wedding night, in his pajamas and in the middle of the countryside.

We drove toward the mainland. Bellowing in my ears, the man was growing impatient. I was going as fast as I could, but our van, with its "reconditioned" engine, would barely do more than forty.

At the end of the peninsula, a ninety-foot bridge spans a silted-up sound that the water covers at the equinoctial tide. Well before, the man made me stop and switch off the headlights. I turned around to look at him. He was sitting on the bunk where I had left my dress and was removing his boot laces. His shirt and trousers, of the same coarse cloth, were spattered with mud.

He tied the two laces together to make one, then, with the suddenness of a cat, he bounded to his feet and yanked off the little chain I was wearing around my neck. Although it didn't really hurt, I was unable to stifle a cry. He raised a large threatening hand to me. "Shut up!"

After which, his shaved head touching the ceiling of the van, he removed the gold medallion hanging from my chain and threaded it onto his shoelace. It was my first piece of jewelry, my christening present. It was an engraving of the Virgin carrying the Infant Jesus. Despite the lack of light, the man was very deft with his hands. "There," he said, "that'll look more natural."

He ordered me to hold up my hair. He slipped the lace around my neck, the medallion in front, and I could feel him tying a slipknot. He pulled to show me. His bristly beard against my cheek, forcing me to keep my head back, he told me in an almost friendly whisper, more terrifying than any shouting, "We'll be meeting people before long. You'd better be up to it. One slip and I'll break your neck. Snap!"

We drove off again. I can't tell you the state I was in; words fail me. I wished I could have woken up. The scenery speeding past on either side of the road, which I had known all my life, was as foreign to me as a nightmare landscape. I was cold and I was burning.

The bridge stood out sharply against the sky. At the entrance shadows moved about, carrying lamps. Headlights were switched on. I slowed down. I could sense the man crouching against the seat behind me and his shoelace tautened under my curtain of hair. He asked me, "How many of them are there?" His voice was incisive and trembled no more than his hand. As I approached, I counted seven men. I told him so.

In the beam of my headlights and theirs, I saw that they were soldiers in sky-blue uniforms, with guns and helmets, and that they had put up a double roadblock. The one in charge was coming toward me with his arm raised to stop me. I knew him by sight from having seen him in town. He was a strapping fellow with a rugged face, black hair, and the squashed nose of a boxer: Chief Warrant Officer Malignaud.

And Malignaud had recognized my husband's van. He came up to my door saying, "So you're Emma?" We were lit by the harsh beams from the roadblock, which made the shadows very dark, and he, too, seemed unreal.

He said, "A prisoner has escaped from the citadel. You didn't see anything unusual on the road?" My head jerked slightly back, caused by the shoelace around my neck, but it could have been surprise. I said no, and even, without so much as a tremor, "We haven't seen anybody."

All I was wearing, as I sat at the steering wheel gazing up at him, was a slip that was too short and white stockings. Without being able to make out his expression under the shadow of his helmet, I knew that he was looking me up and down with some suspicion. He asked, "Where is your husband?" I said, "In the back. He's asleep." I lowered my eyes. My heart was thumping so loudly you could hear it. I don't know what I really wanted at that moment, for him to discover the man behind the seat or for him to step aside and let us through. I felt that he had shifted his attention to inside the van, but fleetingly, and was dwelling on my bare shoulders and thighs again without leaning any farther forward toward my door. Finally, he murmured, without my understanding what train of thought had led him there, "Of course, it was your wedding night." And he stepped aside.

Once more in the full glare of the lights, he waved the soldiers to open the roadblock for me. He said, steadying his voice to hide his embarrassment, "Take care, Emma. The man we're looking for is a monster." After some hesitation, he barked, "Rape and murder."

I opened my mouth, perhaps to ask his help, but the man behind the seat had guessed it, and a tug of the shoelace, stronger than the first, made me throw my head back and close my eyes. Chief Warrant Officer Malignaud, I now know, took that for the reaction of a young bride still traumatized by her first embrace, and regretted having distressed me more than was necessary. I started up the van again, I don't know how. I drove past the blue soldiers, through the narrow gap between their covered van and their barbed-wire barriers. Two or three of them raised their lamps to see me, and one of them, noticing the white tulle bows decorating the old ambulance, even cried, "Long live the bride!"

On the bridge I gathered speed.

A moment later the stranger sat up behind me and I felt the shoelace slide around my neck. He said as he freed me, "You're a good girl, Emma. Behave yourself and you will soon be safe."

I heard him rummaging about in the cupboards above the mattresses, and suddenly he appeared at my side, clambering over the back of the seat, holding a jar of my mother's preserves. He began to eat, at first with his fingers, then by pouring the contents of the jar into his mouth by the glassful. I couldn't see what it was, I couldn't smell it either, so strongly did he stink of the marshes. He chewed without speaking, his eyes on the road, as composed as a lawyer, and as I was looking at him in spite of myself, while I drove, he made me turn away by pressing a grubby forefinger on my cheek.

When he had emptied the jar, he wound down the window and threw it out. He said, "I haven't had anything to eat since yesterday morning, other than a few oysters I was able to steal. I crushed them between two stones." Then, abruptly, "There's a crossroads coming up. Turn right, toward Angoulême."

A weak feeling of relief had come over me, after the roadblock, which left my nerves shattered, my mind blank. It took me a long time to choose my words before I dared speak. I knew that as soon as I opened my mouth, the tears I had so fiercely held back would gush out of my eyes and show him how weak and silly and at his mercy I was.

To allay suspicion, I concentrated on scanning the darkness beyond the headlights more intently, and said, "Why don't you leave me here and carry on alone? You'd go faster if you drove."

I couldn't keep my voice from pleading and my eyes suddenly misted up with tears.

He replied, without even looking at me, "You're talking nonsense. I don't know."

We drove deeper into the Charente region, which he knew well, or had studied on a map before escaping. I did not speak again and he did not emerge from a deceptive drowsiness other than to tell me which road to take, without ever telling me where we were going. I gradually realized that we weren't going anywhere. He seemed preoccupied solely with driving through sleepy villages, with disturbing their silence. There was little traffic in that area at night, at that time, especially on the little roads I took. We didn't meet more than two other cars, but both times, on seeing them coming, he reached over to the steering wheel and sounded the horn like a maniac. Then he sank back into his seat with a satisfied sigh.

He did not have a watch, and neither did I, but he had a better idea of the time than I did, for every now and again he could lean out of the window and see it on the pediment of a church. At one point, having studied me closely, he said, in a curiously gentle voice, "There, in half an hour we'll stop somewhere you can sleep."

We never got that far. A few seconds later, on a forest road, the engine spluttered a bit, then fell silent. The fuel tank was empty. We were on a slight slope and the man shouted at me to drive on. Farther down, he made me turn abruptly on to a dirt track that plunged into the woods. I thought, as my headlights swept about, that we were both going to be killed. When the van finally came to a stop, jolting me out of my seat, the man was furious. He accused me, I imagine, of not having warned him that the fuel tank was nearly empty, and I would have had plenty to reply to that—in the first place, I knew nothing about it—but was so exhausted that I couldn't even hear what he was saying anymore. I only had the strength to lay my head on my arms, on the steering wheel, and fall asleep.

I felt as though I was being shaken at once, but when I opened my eyes, it was daylight. The man was standing on the other side of my door with alert black eyes, several days' growth of beard on his chin, his bald head, and his mud-spattered convict's uniform. The nightmare continued.

He told me that I had slept for three hours, and so had he. I looked around at the "love nest." Everything had been flung untidily on the floor—the food, the clothes, my saucepans, everything. I looked at him through tears of rage, but he did not flinch. He said, as if it were the most natural thing in the world, "I needed money, for the gas." I shouted, "Couldn't you have asked me?" He smiled, and I was surprised to see that he had very white teeth, teeth that didn't suit him. He said, "There were plenty of other things I was looking for but couldn't find. Except this." And he suddenly held up in front of me my husband's razor, the blade exposed. I recoiled in the seat, in spite of myself. He closed up the instrument, very slowly, and said, "Come on, get out."

The early-morning sun streamed through the trees. I shivered in my short slip. We went to the rear door of the van; I was all numb.

There, he asked me if I was hungry, or thirsty, or if I wanted to pee. I told him I wanted to put some clothes on. He answered in a neutral voice that "That's not possible." I gave up the idea of arguing. I told him, swallowing my pride, that I did need to be alone, for a few minutes. He pointed to a thicket. "There! And remember, I can run faster than you!"

Then, when I came back, he gave me a beaker of lukewarm coffee and two bars of chocolate. He stood in front of me and did not take his eyes off me, but I didn't look up. I stared at his shoes, which he had laced up again. I wondered how long he would keep me prisoner, how long he would go around in circles until he was caught.

When I had swallowed my last mouthful, he led me under the trees. It didn't occur to me that he wanted to kill me—he wouldn't have bothered giving me coffee—but all the same, I was becoming increasingly anxious.

He stopped at the foot of an oak tree from where I could still see the van. On the ground, there was a large ball of material that he had picked up, and that looked familiar, and suddenly I realized what it was: he had torn up my clothes to make himself a rope. And why else would he need a rope than to tie me up?

I leaped backward; I screamed. For the first time I wanted to run away. The heels of my shoes sank into the soft earth, and I hadn't taken three steps when I was pinned to the ground, and I soon changed my mind. A knee on my stomach, a nasty glint in his eye, he said, "Don't ever do that again! Ever!" Then he brutally dragged me to the oak tree and tied me to the trunk, my hands behind my back; all the time he was doing it, I cried. I had lost a shoe and he took off the other one and threw it a long way away. Lastly, he gagged me with what was left of a sheet and that terrified me more than anything else.

But this was not the end of my ordeal.

Straightening up, he recovered his breath and looked at me for a few seconds without saying anything. And then he gave a funny sort of smile, and there, in front of me, he raised his hands to his ears and suddenly, without a grimace, he tore off—yes, tore off—all the skin from his head!

I screamed inside my gag and closed my eyes.

When I was brave enough to open them again, he had not budged. He was testing the elasticity of a rubber skullcap, something that looked like a football cut in half—and that is precisely what it was. His hair was pulled back and plastered down with glue.

He said, "I'm as crafty as a barrel of monkeys, you'll see."

And he left me there.

I saw him get into the van. He stayed in there for a good while, without my being able to hear what he was doing from where I was. I did everything I could to loosen my bonds, but other than by uprooting the tree to which I was tied and taking it with me, there was no way I could escape.

At last the man reappeared and took a few steps toward me—or he was playing another trick on me and it was someone else. He had shaved and washed, and his hair, with blond highlights in it, tumbled over his forehead. He had changed into a white sport shirt, a pair of summer pants that he had lengthened by letting down the hem, and a pair of moccasins, all of which he had stolen from my husband. He was holding one of those old gas cans that they put in the woods, full of grain for the pheasants. He looked like a driver who had run out of gas, like anybody else. I hated him.

He said, "There's a village not far away. I'll soon be back."

But I thought that it was Sunday and that he wouldn't find gas so easily.

I watched him walk away and disappear. I didn't cry. I mustered my strength to uproot the oak tree.

I remained tied to the tree for a long time.

The sun was climbing through the foliage and I was hot. The birds were singing at the tops of their voices. A golden pheasant crossed the little clearing where I was standing. He only glanced at me and continued on his way, busy with his own problems. I tried not to think about snakes, man-eating ants, and beasts that don't even exist but that nourished my fears when I was little.

By that time—eight o'clock, 8:30—it must have been ages since my husband had raised the alarm, even though he was in his pajamas and barefoot. There was no mistaking a van like ours, painted "artistic yellow," garlanded with tulle like a wedding cake. I was sure that they had pinpointed our whereabouts to within a few miles. All the local police would be scouring the countryside. Who knows, perhaps they were searching the surrounding forest and would appear any second. All I had to do was breathe through my nose, which is very healthy, and wait quietly.

I did have one misgiving, just one, but one that I could not put out of my mind. My husband had not seen the man enter the "love nest." He had only witnessed the untimely, incomprehensible departure of the van, with me at the wheel. What had he concluded, in his narrow mind, stupid beyond belief? I knew him well enough to say that he had quite simply thought I had run away, because I didn't love him—he knew me well enough to know—and because the prospect of a wedding night with him disgusted me. And in that case, I could picture the rest as clearly as if I were there. Too vain and full of himself to go and confess his misfortune at the first house with a light in the window, he had walked along the roadside, hopping from one foot to the other until he reached Saint-Julien de l'Océan, where he had gone home, keeping close to the walls. At three o'clock in the morning he had gone to bed, exhausted and vindictive, plotting the revenge he would take on my return, convinced that I was such a silly goose that I wouldn't go anywhere other than to lie low at my aunt's for a day or two. Then he had gone to sleep, and at that moment was still asleep, as were the police.

I ended up despairing when, suddenly, a twig snapped not far from me. There were other sounds, which I listened to, my heart in my mouth. Somebody was walking through the thicket. All I could do was groan, from under my gag, but never did any piglet grunt with such ardor. Only my legs were free, but I kicked out furiously in all directions. Tears of frustration and hope filled my eyes.

A moment later a gamekeeper appeared in the clearing, a real gamekeeper, with a mustache, a peaked cap, boots, and a double-barreled gun. He froze, openmouthed, when he saw me. Then he came over to me with measured steps, crushing twigs underfoot. He said, incredulously, "You poor lady!" I moaned all the louder under my gag so that he would hurry up and release me.

He leaned his gun against a felled tree trunk and took out a large checked handkerchief to mop his brow. It was only after replacing his cap that he bent over me. First of all he tried to find which knot he should untie first to rid me of my bonds, and in so doing—how shall I put it?—he saw me as I was: a twenty-four-year-old girl, half-naked, my hair disheveled, unable to shout or struggle, staring imploringly at him.

I saw him change his manner even before he changed his tune. He repeated, hypocritically, "You poor lady!" And so saying, he slid a clumsy hand between my thighs, amply revealed by all my kicking, exclaiming with malicious delight, "Mmm! It's as soft as down in there!"

I tried with all my strength to kick him away, and his cap fell off, but he couldn't care less about his cap, or my kicks, or my muffled screams, the filthy swine, his beastly hands wandered all over my body, inside my underwear, growing bolder every time I jumped, until I was exhausted, breathless, and had given up fighting him off. On the brink of fainting, I saw him calmly undo his belt. I realized that I was done for. I closed my eyes.

Just then I heard a thud. I no longer felt the maniac's weight on top of me.

The escaped prisoner from the citadel was there, holding the gamekeeper's gun by the butt, and the gamekeeper was huddled on the ground clutching his head.

The rest didn't take more than a minute.

The escaped prisoner kicked the gamekeeper hard in the ribs, saying to him, "Get up, you bastard!" The other raised himself onto his knees, still holding his head, and groaned, his eyes closed, and seemed to be in great pain. He managed to stand up, but he was livid, and from the way he was holding his chin, I thought his neck was broken or even worse.

The escaped prisoner pointed the gun at him. He said, without mercy, "Now, I'm going to count to three. When I get to three, I'm going to kill you!" And so saying, he shouted, "One!" The terrified gamekeeper staggered off into the thicket, groaning in pain, his head in his hands. When he could no longer be heard, the escaped prisoner kicked the cap lying on the ground and sent it flying.

The birds were singing again, peacefully. He put down the gun and bent over me. It was the first time I'd got a close look at him since he had spruced himself up, and I would actually have found him good-looking if it hadn't been for the circumstances of our meeting and the emotions I had just been through. He lowered my gag. I said to him, in sincerity, "Thank you."

I had forgotten—or almost—the sorry state to which my underwear had been reduced and that I was even more naked than before. It was his eyes that reminded me. Instead of freeing me, he stared at me in a way that suddenly revived my anxiety. I could sense that he saw me as I was—a girl of twenty-four, etc., etc.—and I asked him, in a flat voice, "What are you planning to do?"

His only reply was to replace my gag.

Very, very slowly, he caressed one breast that the gamekeeper had exposed and said, "It's true that it's as soft as down." And yet he did not seem to be mocking. It was as if he were fascinated. I realized, again, that I was done for. I closed my eyes.

He didn't go far. He untied my bonds, at first without a word, with a gloomy air, then he said, "I haven't had a woman for six long years, but I'm not the sort to take one by force."

Once I was freed, he helped me to my feet. Aching all over, I had only one thought and that was to keep on my slip, one strap of which had broken. I no longer dared look at him. He picked up my shoes and gave them back to me.

I followed him meekly to the old ambulance. He was holding the gamekeeper's gun in his right hand and, under his other arm, his makeshift rope. He had left the can full of gas behind the van. No doubt he had returned right at the start of the battle—since he had overheard my attacker's loathsome phrase—and had crept noise-lessly up to the gun before intervening. Had he arrived a little later, would he have shown himself immediately and risked being caught, or would he have let me be raped in front of his eyes, thinking only of getting his hands on the gun? I remembered Chief Warrant Officer Malignaud's words: this man himself had raped and killed.

As he poured the fuel into the tank, he said without turning around, "Go and get changed, we're leaving."

I climbed into the devastated "love nest." I managed to retrieve a clean pair of panties, but had nothing else to wear other than my wedding dress, the only one he had spared when making his rope. Tears came into my eyes again, but I controlled myself. I had been through too much to continue behaving like a bleating sheep; I wanted to be cool and calculating. I would find a way of turning the tables soon, and then he would pay for everything and more.

I washed myself with the flannel and some cologne. There was no water left in the little tank: it was there, in a little waterproof bottle, that my intelligent husband, who feared Spanish thieves more than any others, except for the Italians, had hidden the money for our trip.

I was just fastening my wedding dress when the escaped prisoner joined me. He had violently kicked out everything that cluttered the floor, followed by everything that was lying on the mattresses, by the armful. I cried out, although I had vowed to myself not to be surprised at anything, "For goodness' sake, they're looking for you, they'll find all that!" He replied, "I hope they do." So saying, he closed the doors behind us. I had to hitch up my skirts once again to clamber over the seat.

We filled up with gas at a country hand pump worked by a woman who was at least a hundred. Unbidden, she listed all the local people she suspected of belonging to the fifth column, adding for each one, "Oh, but I've got my eye on him, I have." When we left, she said, "Make the most of your husband while he's young; after that they send them to the trenches and the fun's over."

Later the escaped prisoner ate the rest of my mother's preserves—with a spoon, this time—and half a sausage sliced with the razor. I ate the other half as I drove. We had nothing to drink, and later still we pulled up by a fountain at the entrance to a village. The only thing I remember of this village was the peal of its church bells. They chimed midday. Having quenched our thirst and filled the little tank, without seeing a soul, we ripped off the tulle decorations from the van and the man told me to turn the van around. By way of explanation, he declared, "We've gone far enough."

Setting out again in the opposite direction, I gave up even trying to understand when, at the first crossroads, he made me turn to the west, toward the ocean we had fled. He sank back in his seat, looking pleased, and said, "My name's Vincent. When we get back to the peninsula, I'll let you go." I thought I had misheard, or that he was mad. I said, "The peninsula? You want to go back to the peninsula?" He replied, "It's the only place where they're no longer looking for me."

I must say that from that moment, despite the crazy intricacy of his itinerary—"I was born in July," he said, "I move sideways like a crab"—and despite what happened subsequently, we never stopped driving toward the Atlantic.

I drove under a fierce sun, which made us wind the windows down. I was constantly brushing my hair from my eyes. We hardly spoke. Sometimes I looked at him, hoping that he would fall asleep. He no longer frightened me so much. He no longer smelled bad. He watched the road, his elbow resting on the door, his legs out-stretched, relaxed as if he were on vacation.

At one point he asked me, "Have you heard of the citadel?"

It is a tiny island without a name, off the coast of Saint-Julien, entirely enclosed by ramparts built under Richelieu. It was besieged during the Wars of Religion, and according to the tourist brochures I was given to illustrate, the real d'Artagnan had lost an arm there, in the course of a battle. I faithfully believed this for a long time, until I counted up all the arms and legs that the poor boy had lost elsewhere, according to the brochures for Brouage, La Rochelle, and Ré, and the thought of him meeting a dog in the street in his final state was just too awful.

In more plausible times, the citadel had become a maritime prison and, since the war, a military jail. When I was little and grown-ups talked about it in front of me, because my existence was so insignificant they forgot my presence, they called it "Limbo," and several times I also heard it called the "Rattrap," for even the rats couldn't escape. But what about crabs?

I answered the escaped prisoner: "The agency where I work is in the port of Saint-Julien. I've often seen the boat that takes food to the prisoners." He remained silent for a long time, then he said, "The best thing in the citadel was the cinema once a month, and twice at Christmas."

Later that afternoon he wanted to stop. We were in the middle of the countryside, not a house in sight. I left the engine running while he got out, and my heart started to beat faster. He said, "Make the most of it, too." I replied that I didn't want to go. He picked up the gun to get out. He simply raised the two barrels and pointed them at me. I got out.

When we had gone farther, driving into the sun, he said, as if he had heard my thoughts, "What good would it do for you to run away? We'll wait until it's dark to enter the peninsula and nobody will see us. I'll leave you at the same spot where I captured you."

I answered him, my eyes misty with sincerity, "I promise I won't try and run away. But you know very well I'll be questioned. How do I know you won't kill me?"

He shrugged. "I don't give a damn if they question you." And he withdrew into his silence.

An hour later, in a vineyard-covered valley of the Charentes, I missed a bend. On purpose.

I can recall fleeing, frantic, barefoot, through a leafy vineyard shot through with the purple glare of the sun, my wedding dress hampering my legs. I had to hitch it up in order to run.

I ran from one row to another, pushing back my hair, which was clinging to my face, listening, hearing nothing but my own breath, then I rushed deeper into the labyrinth of greenery, convincing myself that the man was lying unconscious amid the debris of broken windows and dented metal, and that I wasn't going to be cut down on the spot by a gunshot I would not even hear going off.

I don't know how long I ran like that.

And then, unable to go on, staggering about, my chest burning, my head lolling, I felt almost relieved when, caught by an ankle, I fell onto the clods of earth. He was on top of me, pinning me down, furious. He, too, was out of breath and he looked at me with eyes full of hatred, but I didn't care, he could beat me, or kill me, I didn't care, I was totally exhausted.

He said in a breathless but angry voice, "You haven't understood a thing! Not a thing!"

We lay there for a few long moments getting our breath back, one on top of the other, silent, looking into each other's eyes.

When we got back to the ambulance, I realized that we would not be able to go anywhere. It was lying across a ditch as if planted in the earth among the vines, and the rear left wheel was not touching the ground. The escaped prisoner's door was swinging, all twisted, the windshield was smashed to smithereens, and the seat was lying on the ground.

I had no recollection of the "accident" except for the noise and the fact that I had clutched the wheel with all my strength before I skidded. I have even less idea how I got out of the cab.

The man—Vincent—had a gash on his forehead, one of my fingers was hurting, my white clothes were spattered with earth, and that was about all my exploit had achieved. I even retrieved my shoes—one was under the steering wheel, the other in the road—and he recovered the gun, intact, from the ditch.

We hid among the vines until dark, in case anybody came poking their noses in, and in fact a bicyclist did come past, his hips swaying from side to side on his creaking bike, but either he wasn't nosy or he was nearsighted, and he continued on his way without stopping.

Under the full moon, we climbed cautiously into the van, after we had both rocked it to make sure it was tilting at the best angle. Inside, everything was riveted to the floor and there was little damage, but it was difficult to stand up.

Once the mattresses had been put back, Vincent sat on one side, I on the other. His anger had worn off long ago, but he was determined not to let me see. He said in a surly voice, "Tomorrow we'll find someone to get this old heap back on the road." I hadn't uttered a word since he had caught me, but I, too, needed to talk, so that I would feel less lost. I didn't know what about and I didn't want him to snub me. In the end, all that came into my head was: "I prefer you with hair." Contrary to all my expectations, he laughed, a short but happy laugh. He explained that in the citadel, with the complicity of the prisoner-hairdresser, he had worn his false shaved head for two months so as to better deceive his pursuers after the escape. I asked him how he escaped but his face darkened again and he simply answered, "I can't tell you that, Emma. It might still be of use to a comrade."

I looked in the cupboards to see what food we had left and I found a piece of bread, cheese, and some chocolate. While we ate, I inquired whether I might ask him a perhaps indiscreet personal question. "Try, we'll see." That morning he had told me that he hadn't had a woman for six years. But before, when he was free, had there been a woman in his life?

He got up to drink from the tap of the little tank, hanging on to the washbasin to keep his balance, and I thought that he didn't want to answer. But as he sat down, in the milky light that came through the open door, a far-off look in his eyes, his voice gentle with nostalgia, he dropped his facade and confided in me.

"The woman I loved most, the true woman, the first," said this young man with a faithful heart, "was my grandmother.

"She was small and vivacious, as poor as southern Italy, as honest as her flashing eyes, and always dressed in black, because she wore mourning for my grandfather right up to the end. Summer and winter alike, she never went out without her umbrella—black, of course, with an ebony handle inlaid with mother-of-pearl.

"It was she, when I learned to read and write, who came to wait for me, in the evening, outside the primary school of La Belle-de-Mai, in Marseilles, not far from the Boulevard National, where I was born.

"At first, practically every day, in the din of school letting out, bigger boys used to gang up on me on the pavement, tear up my book and hit me, but I was already tough and I faced them with my fists, deaf to their insults: 'Macaroni! Muckworm! Go home, dirty dago!'

"The moment came when I would be overcome by numbers,

paralyzed by too many hands, but it was the moment, the most exhilarating of all for me, when my grandmother always chose to appear in the sunlight, crossing the road like an exterminating angel, her eyes sparkling with pleasure at punishing the wicked. She soon dispersed them, stabbing their legs with her umbrella, pursuing the ones who were slower to run away, frozen with fear, and shouting: 'Little fascist! Next time I'll smash your skull in and your own mother won't be able to find your brains!'

"Then she would take my hand and walk off, defiantly eyeing the women who were there and who carefully avoided intervening. She would say, 'Do you mind!' And the two of us walked down the sun-drenched street, with the noble gait of children of San Appolinare, in the province of Frosinone. I was proud of my grandmother and her umbrella and, believe me, by November, I was respected."

The escaped prisoner fell silent, his elbows resting on his knees, his gaze lost in his memories, and I dared not break the silence. I was afraid of betraying my emotion.

I could see him in the moonlight almost as if in broad daylight. I had guessed he was thirty, the night before, but he was probably younger. I liked his hands and his voice, and even—why not say so now?—this moment of my life when we were together, in a van stuck in a ditch, as far from my home as if I were on another planet.

I leaned forward and murmured confidently, "Someone who has such reverence for his grandmother cannot rape and kill." He bowed his head, looking gloomy, but he did not reply.

Later, after standing at the door of the van for a long time looking at the night, he picked up the rope he had made and apologized: if he wanted to sleep, he had to tie me up. I told him I understood.

I let him tie my wrists and ankles as I lay on my back. He went and closed the doors. I heard him lie down on the other mattress. At last, in the dark, he said—and I was waiting, waiting for him to say it—"I was unjustly convicted."

What a shock he had, early the next morning, when he saw my bonds on the floor and my bunk empty. He got up so suddenly that he lost his balance and slid to the bottom of the floor. He thought, The traitress! He was convinced I had gone off to expose him.

He jumped out and ran around to the front of the van. He

stopped in his tracks, his hair all tousled. I was standing there in my dirty wedding dress in the company of a mustachioed farmer holding a wagon horse by the bridle.

I said to the farmer, "Here's my husband. It was our honeymoon trip."

The fellow had not uttered a word when I had gone to find him in his farmyard. He had listened to me, shaken his head with a scornful snort, and gone off to harness his horse. In heavy corduroy trousers, pulled in at the waist by a wide flannel belt, his collarless shirt rolled up to the elbows, he gave a fearsome impression of rancor; he seemed to bear a grudge against the whole world.

He looked Vincent up and down, as one looks at a worthless tree, and let out the same snort he had given me. After that he went up to the van and glanced over it. I asked him humbly, "Do you think you'll be able to repair it?" I am still waiting for the reply.

The horse pulled the ambulance to the farm, his head down. Vincent helped the man handle a jack and they hoisted the van up onto blocks. They took off one axle. I was sitting to one side, on a stone seat, and I watched them.

The sun was high and hot when a girl about my age, with black hair that was even longer and thicker than mine, appeared in the doorway of the house, bare-legged and wearing a housewife's apron that was outrageously or calculatingly unbuttoned, and nothing else. She had obviously just gotten out of bed. I thought at first she was the farmer's daughter. Yawning, she said, "Come in. My husband can manage on his own. Anyway, he hates people watching him work."

> One notes the expression "outrageously or calculatingly unbuttoned." From this point, Emma's testimony differs greatly from that which she gave the police immediately after her escapade, and even, at the end, actually contradicts it. Evidently, with time, not having much to fear in revealing the ambiguity of her behavior, she is more sincere here in her account of the events than she is in her prejudices.
>
> (From the notes of Marie-Martine Lepage)

By midday, the taciturn fellow had taken off all the bent parts from under the ambulance and straightened them out with great blows of the sledgehammer on a forge burning in the farmyard. Vincent's clothes and my wedding dress and underwear hung drying in the sun on a clothesline a few yards from him.

My so-called husband and I had washed in turn, in the living room, and the young farmer's wife, Elise, had lent us each a sheet to wrap up in. We were sitting on either side of a big oak table and she cooked us a chicken she had just slaughtered. Without asking us, she had put on a twenty-year-old phonograph, with a copper handle and horn, which was playing a fashionable bolero, "It's No Use Trying, It's Possible," over and over again. Anyone would have thought it was her only record. She only had eyes for Vincent, who returned her stare. A little earlier, with precautions that were absolutely ridiculous, she had cleaned the cut on his forehead with peroxide and ruined a roll of bandage in order to stick an inch of it in the right place.

She was, I have to admit, a lovely specimen, but poisonous. From behind, Elise had a wiggle to make you giddy. From the front, she was sheer provocation. She did her utmost to show off her thighs through the slit of her apron.

Bringing the chicken to the table, first she served Vincent, whom she called "my lovely man." She brushed against him so brazenly that in the end I could not refrain from saying, "Aren't you ashamed of yourself? With your husband outside!" And she turned a gaze full of hypocrisy to me and answered in a voice full of ingenuity, "I haven't done anything wrong. It's clear that you don't love your husband. Well, I don't love mine either. So?"

Thereupon, without taking any further notice of me, she began to dance barefoot to the rhythm of her bolero, her arms uplifted, her lips moist, her black Gypsy eyes looking deep into Vincent's, and she said to him, "Do you know what I would like to have been? That girl, you know, who danced for a king. There's a prisoner in the dungeons, she's crazy about him, but he doesn't want her. . . ."

Vincent watched her and listened to her, a chicken wing in his hand, looking like the cat that swallowed the canary. "And I would dance and dance," she said, "until they brought me his head on a silver tray. . . ."

I don't remember, perhaps he clapped.

After having eaten well, and also drunk a good deal of the wine the farmer made from his grapes, Vincent encouraged me to lie down in the conjugal bedroom that Elise offered me—it was the only other room apart from the living room—for the fellow was still banging away outside and the repair was likely to take some time. It was quite plain to me that the two of them were trying to get rid of me, but I didn't say anything, and in any case, what could I say? That I had been lying all day, that they should call the police? And then, it was true, I was tired, and I had had enough of the phonograph and this girl's performance and of the ugly taste of what today I have to call jealousy.

Once alone with the door closed, I sat on the edge of a bed so high that my feet didn't even touch the ground. I felt even smaller and more helpless. I told myself that it was forgivable for a man deprived of women for "six long years" to succumb to the charms of the first one who offered herself to him, that I had plenty of things to hate him for, but not for that, and that besides, if I had wanted to, last night in the van, or even the night before in the forest, I wouldn't have had to go to much trouble to bewitch him as well as she had: one look, and I was done for. But all my fine reasoning was no help: I could hear their whispering on the other side of the door; I was well and truly betrayed. And then I couldn't hear them anymore, and that was worse. I rushed so fast into the room to have a look that I lost half the sheet that was covering me. They were no longer there. I resigned myself to closing the door and I was returning dejectedly to sit down when a stifled cry, from outside, had me running to the bedroom window. Through the slits in the closed shutters, I saw that the back of the house overlooked the vast vineyards. Draped like a Roman emperor, Vincent was pursuing Elise among the vines. I could hear their laughter above the farmer's relentless hammering.

Before he even caught her, she had already completely unbuttoned her red apron. She simply let it slide off her. She did the same with his sheet. They looked at each other for a few seconds, both of them naked, then they threw themselves at each other and fell, entwined, on the soft earth, guffawing all the louder.

I couldn't see them anymore. I took a chair and climbed onto it. I think they were fighting, that they were smearing grapes all over each other like children. Through the shutters I could sometimes make out a leg or a head appearing through the leaves. What I saw, or guessed, when their laughter stopped—too bad if you think I'm perverse—tormented me and fascinated me at the same time. Worst of all, I began to hear Elise's shameless moans, as if beaten out by the blows of the hammer coming from the farmyard, and gradually they adopted its rhythm. Women aren't supposed to be particularly affected by such a sight. You know as well as I do that it's bound to be a man who said that.

I had the strength, despite everything, to tear myself away, to leave the room. Wrapped in my sheet, shoes in hand, I went into the farmyard to recover my clothes, which were dry. The farmer, at his forge, didn't even look up. He hammered and hammered, streaming with sweat, amid huge showers of sparks, and from time to time, as if to reply to some idea that was bothering him, he let out his strange scornful snort.

The van was ready to go by the end of the afternoon, minus the windshield and the broken door.

Vincent paid the farmer with my husband's money. He immediately sat at the wheel and then I understood that he had not brought me with him as a driver, but as a hostage. That did not demoralize me any more than I was already. Even if he had admitted to me that his grandmother did not exist, I wouldn't have opened my mouth.

He didn't say much either before we reached the peninsula, other than to tell me to move closer to him because the cab was open on my side and he was afraid I'd be jolted out of my seat. I didn't budge. Gusts of warm wind made my hair fly in my face and deafened me. I felt as if it were cleansing me of everything.

We made a stop before the bridge, the sun in our eyes. Apparently the roadblock was gone. Vincent still jumped into the back and took out the gun, which he had hidden in a cupboard. I had to take the wheel again. He said, "I know very well what's bothering you, Emma. I hope it doesn't make you do anything stupid." It was a plea.

We crossed the stretch of water without seeing anybody. Immediately afterward, he made me turn off the main road, along which we had come two days before, and take the coast road. Bathers were cycling home. Children attending a summer camp were walking silently along the roadside, exhausted by the pure air.

We stopped in the dunes, above a deserted beach. We jumped down onto the sand. Vincent, taking off his moccasins, asked me to wait for him, he wanted to go and reconnoiter. I watched him walk away, in a sport shirt and trousers ironed by the farmer's wife, toward the yellow rocks where I often used to play as a child and which were called, I don't know why, "The Crowns." Perhaps he had asked me to wait purely to delay the moment when I would go to the police. Perhaps, on the other hand, he would leave me one last chance to be able to tell them that I had escaped. I didn't want to ask any questions. I waited for him.

When, sitting on the dune in my wedding dress, I saw him coming back, the sun was a red ball just above the horizon and there didn't seem to be any other sound in the whole universe but the cry of the sea gulls and the noise of the breakers. Vincent dropped down onto the sand next to me. Putting his moccasins back on, he said, all excited, his eyes sparkling, "There's a big white yacht anchored in a creek, behind these rocks. If I manage to get on board, it will take me far away, to the ends of the earth. They'll never find me."

He saw a tear roll down my cheek. He murmured, disconcerted, "Whatever's gotten into you?" I said, without moving, without looking at him, "Take me with you."

He shot up like a jack-in-the-box. He cried, "Do what?" He was at a loss how to tell me I was mad. All he managed to say was, "What about your husband?" Looking him in the eye this time, I repeated, very softly, "Take me with you."

He shook his head in irritation but, I realized, it was only a facade to hide his emotion. In the purple light, he told me straight: "You're twenty-four, Emma." As if I didn't know. And then he walked toward the van, which was parked a little higher. As he opened the rear door, he shouted, "Why do you think I've respected you until now? I wouldn't take advantage of your innocence for anything in the world!" And so saying, he vanished into the "love nest," perhaps to get the gun, which he needed more than he did me.

I stood up, my fists clenched, and walked over to the old ambulance. I leaned against the chassis so as not to see his reaction to what I was going to say, so as not to show him the rage inside me, which choked my voice. And I confessed the truth to him.

Let's talk about my innocence.

Other than my elementary-school certificate and the diploma from an art school in Royan, it was the only thing I had when I had applied to the agency, a year earlier, and when Monsieur Sévérin, the head of personnel, had taken me on. He was a man with a pointed nose and an authoritarian gait, who would get on his high horse to appear taller. I had passed him sometimes in Saint-Julien, but without paying him any more attention than he deserved, which is to say none at all.

From the first week, he always found an excuse to keep me behind after the others had left in the evening. It was a sketch to be corrected, an illustration to be redone, or any other excuse he could think of. At first he was content to compliment me on my dress, on the color of my eyes—which was enough to make me feel ill at ease, for he always tilted my chin to look at them—but he soon became bold enough to give me a pat on the bottom, to brush up against my breasts, claiming that he had no ulterior motive because he was double my age.

I did not dare complain, but each day I was more anxious as going-home time drew near, and at night it was an obsession that kept me awake. I had nobody to confide in. I was too shy to have friends and my parents wouldn't have understood. To them, Monsieur Sévérin was an honorable man, whom they were flattered to greet in the street and who, in any case, deserved our gratitude since he had taken me on.

One November evening, with the rain beating against the windowpanes, he grabbed me by the waist and tried to kiss me. This time I struggled, but the more I tried to extricate myself, the more determined he became in this hand-to-hand fight, with no regard for my clothes. In the end I scratched his face.

I managed to get to the other side of my worktable and put it between us. On it stood the only light that was still on in the artists' room. Monsieur Sévérin was breathing noisily, his face crimson, and as I adjusted my clothing, I noticed with horror, on his cheek, the four marks I had made were bleeding.

When he was able to speak, he said in a nasty voice, "Dirty little tease! You know it won't take me long to have you fired." He took from my table a drawing for an advertisement that I had just finished. Without even looking at it, he tore it into four pieces, which he dropped on the floor, saying with a hyena laugh, "No good!"

The next day, the day after that, same scenario. He snapped at me, in front of the others, to stay behind and finish my work. And when we were alone, he came to torment me. Little did my pleas matter to him, he hugged me to him, lifting up my skirt, drooling obscenities into my neck, and I had the greatest difficulty in the world getting away from him. Then he would tear up my drawings and say, "No good!"

I threatened to go and get the boss himself, who unfortunately never came to the office. He simply laughed spitefully: who would be believed, him or me? I would be taken for a hysterical girl, that was all.

I don't know if people could still understand today; it was the time of the economic slump, strikes, unemployment. My parents, who had me very late, were old and had no resources. I was afraid I wouldn't be able to find another job. One evening I allowed him to undo the front of my blouse and lay me on my back on the drawing board. While he took me, standing between my dangling legs, like an animal, the pain didn't matter, I was crying with shame.

Innocence?

For months, every evening, at the office or at his house—because once you start . . . isn't it so?—I lay on my back, on my stomach, or stood on all fours, giving in to his every wish.

By the time I was twenty-four, I had as much innocence as a doormat.

"The bastard! Oh, the bastard!" Vincent exclaimed, pacing up and down inside the van, wild with indignation. He sat down to calm himself. I drew near, wiping my cheeks. One thing disconcerted him: "And you married him?" I said sadly, "He demanded it. To have me all to himself. Besides, you know what it's like, in small towns."

"The bastard! Oh, the bastard!" Vincent was off again, even louder. I couldn't resist, I threw my arms around his neck.

"Precisely! Avenge me! Let's punish him!"

I got so carried away by I don't know what magic that I found myself straddling his knee. I kissed him, I pressed myself up against his body, I caught myself sliding my hand inside his sport shirt. How soft his skin felt, and how nice it was, at last, to want to love! Heaven forgive me, I forgot my shame and moaned in his neck, "Please, please do to me what you did to that Elise!"

Still disturbed by my secret, he shied away a little and fought against his own desire, but very soon my mouth found his, he held me in his arms, and I felt him abandon himself like a flood that has been held back for too long. In a kiss during which the whole world spun around with us, we toppled over and fell across the bunk. A hand on my back unfastened my wedding dress. Another, deliciously possessive, was finding its way up my thighs. I realized I was done for. I closed my eyes.

Almost at once, unfortunately, Vincent sat up, his eyes staring, listening. He asked me in a dull voice, "Did you hear?" I didn't understand what. With burning cheeks, my dress around my waist, I listened with him. We couldn't hear anything except the breakers. And yet he said, with terror, "The dogs!"

He shot up and shouted, ripping off the bandage from his forehead: "They've found me! They're surrounding me!" He looked about him as if deciding which way out to take, then his gaze returned to me. For a fleeting second I saw him overcome with sadness and regret. He murmured, "It's probably for the best. Goodbye, Emma."

As he moved to turn around and face the open door, I cried, "No!" and tried in vain to clutch his legs. I fell from the bunk; he jumped out. In a glimpse of my destiny, I saw the gamekeeper's gun on the mattress. I grabbed it before rushing after him.

He tripped in the sand as he tore down the dune, losing his lead. I shouted as I ran down toward him, my hair in my eyes, "No! Vincent, I beg you! Stop!" He did not stop. He didn't even turn around. I pulled one of the triggers. I don't remember wanting to. I lost my balance perhaps, hampered by my unfastened dress, slowed by my high heels, and the random shot rang out into the red sun. It was the first time I had held a gun. The report made a mass of sea gulls fly up from the shore and astonished me as much as it did Vincent.

He faced me, his eyes round, silent. Still advancing, I implored, "You can't just leave me! Not after what I told you! It's not possible, you understand!"

By now, far beyond the dunes, in the pinewoods stretching inland, we could clearly hear the barking of a pack of dogs.

Without taking his eyes off me, Vincent had begun inching back toward the yellow rocks. He shouted, horrified, "They're going to hang me, don't you see? You crazy woman, you'll have me hanged!" He moved backward faster and faster, waving his hands desperately in front of him to make me point the gun away. I saw in his eyes that he wanted me to disappear, that he wanted me not to exist, and I pulled the second trigger. Through my tears, I saw him fall on his back, flung backward by the shock, his chest spattered with blood, and he fell, arms outstretched, onto the sand.

I stood there transfixed with horror, gun in hand. Suddenly there was silence everywhere. No more barking, no more sea-gull cries. I couldn't hear my own breathing.

I don't know how long this emptiness lasted.

When I found the strength, I turned away from what I had done, I ran back to the van, and I fled a long way from there.

That is what happened. What I was able to say at the time, to the police or to Chief Warrant Officer Malignaud, is of no value, except that I didn't know, and I still don't know, why I fired. Perhaps so as not to have to kill myself.

The rest you know better than I do, and what has become of me is of no interest to anyone, but I want to answer your questions to the end, even though I find the last one sadly offensive. Vincent never spoke to me, during those two days when we were on the road, of either an inheritance or a will. I would have remembered. The only possession I was aware of, other than his charm, which was fatal for both of us, is this flat, gold ring, which he wore on his left hand and which you think I didn't notice.

I did notice it, in fact, and from the minute he kidnapped me, when he clamped his hand over my mouth. I talked to him about it later; I was astonished he had been allowed to keep it during his years in prison. My reply will be his: he told me only that it was his grandfather's wedding ring, that his grandmother had given it to him a long time ago so that she would feel less of a widow, and that to remove it, they would have had to cut off his finger.

Belinda

WHEN IT HAPPENED, I WAS AL-
most twenty-four. It was in August, and I was born in September, on the twenty-eighth or the twenty-ninth, nobody was ever sure. I was found as a baby beside my dead mother, in one of those beach huts where they store deck chairs and air mattresses. She had given birth all alone. I had been bawling for yum-yums for such a long time that I couldn't go on anymore. So, on the birth certificate they wrote twenty-eight or twenty-nine; they weren't too bothered about details. All the same, I've had my name in the papers twice in my life, and that was the first time.

For twenty-four years, I kept out of trouble. An angel. When fame struck me again, I was turning tricks in a whorehouse, a very ritzy one, with a very nice class of clientele. Vases full of flowers, cost a fortune. Private bathroom with turquoise tiles and all the taps made of silver. Bedroom with a four-poster surrounded by net curtains, to be romantic and to keep the mosquitoes out. And my balcony overlooking the ocean. It was called "The Queen of Hearts." If you haven't been there, you haven't been anywhere.

I'm as honest as the day, busy as a bee, and as sweet as its honey. Once, when I was still in Paris, I took lessons to learn how to speak properly. A three-week fling, a present from my angel of the asphalt, the fastest operator that a young girl making her First Communion could meet at the Gare Montparnasse. He was there when I arrived from Brittany. Not that I'm Breton, my beach hut was in Nice. I had been on a trip to Perros-Guirec to see an old friend from the orphanage who was twiddling her thumbs and wanted me to come and live with her. Her name was Justine, pronounced Desdemona. I had called her Demon ever since she had become my heartthrob. It was she, one Sunday afternoon in the dormitory, who made me come for the first time. She was as chubby as I am long, and so naive she needed an alarm clock. When all had been said and done, and I'd tried out her man after a spin around Perros-Guirec in a front-wheel drive, I knew there was no future for me, so I left. The horoscope in *Bonne Soirée* said that Libras were losers until next time, but Libras have good equilibrium and I hadn't even set foot on the platform in Paris when the love of my life relieved me of my suitcase and was already telling me so.

The love of my life, from the minute I set eyes on him, and during the four years that followed, he was the only one, he was unique, the tornado of my nights, the highlight of my days: Beau Masque. He was so ugly it melted your heart, a head shorter than me but stocky, and he never kept still, even when he was asleep. A real bundle of nerves. I was actually sixteen at the time, eighteen on my emancipation certificate, and he was not much older, at least at first. I later read, on the receipt from an old paycheck when he was a cable fitter, that he was hiding six extra years from me. When I told him, because bees sometimes sting, *smack-thwack*, forehand-backhand to teach me arithmetic! He brought color to my cheeks, did Beau Masque, but I needed it, that winter, to walk up and down the Rue Delambre. It was colder than an Eskimo's behind. The wine froze in the shop windows. I swear it did. If you didn't live through it, you haven't lived through anything.

In February the bourgeois shut themselves up in the warmth, the workers were being killed in the streets, and I went for whole afternoons at a time without opening my legs. That was when Beau Masque preferred to invest and had me take private lessons to teach me to speak as I do now—at 238 Boulevard Raspail, in an attic overlooking the cemetery. My teacher—I've forgotten his name— was a very clean retired man, always wearing a tie and a celluloid collar. He used to tell me, "A subject, a verb, an object, full stop."

And also, about his sad life, his wife killed at thirty under a carriage, his son the year before, both buried beneath his dormer window, and the war, the war. To pay for the lesson, I did the best I could in his armchair, when it was time to go, but he never went through with it to the end, he cried noiselessly over his memories. Beau Masque, who boasted he owed nobody anything, offered him money, or somebody else instead, but the old man wouldn't accept.

When I had finished learning, we flew off like swallows to my part of the country. We lived in Cannes and in Beaulieu. I did the hotel bars, the foreign businessmen's pleasure parties. It was all right, no more. As for Beau Masque, he was pissed off with all that sun. He would have liked me to be a lady, in a posh joint with the job security of a typist in the civil service and a cigarette holder like Marlene Dietrich. The last straw was that he nearly got caught.

Not by the vice squad, worse. He had told me that he had been declared unfit for military service. Something to do with his heart. When he made me come, immediately afterward I put my ear to his heart, in case it acted up. Regular as the subway. He had been lying, of course. One evening he came back to our room at the Hôtel des Tamaris in Beaulieu, deathly pale. He told me to pack our bags. A clairvoyant had warned him that the French army was hot on his heels. He was about as unfit for service as a military cadet. At twenty he hadn't even turned up for the physical. Honestly. Since then, the color sky blue brought him out in spots and he had his cards read so as to be the first to know in case of trouble.

That was how we ended up heading for the southwest and I started at the Queen of Hearts, not far from Saint-Julien de l'Océan, on a peninsula of dreams and pinewoods, the Pointe des Amériques. In January the air is heavy with the smell of mimosa. It's the sky of the south with oysters as a bonus. I lived there in heavenly bliss for several months, until they caught Beau Masque once and for all.

I remember the wonderful Sundays, before he was a soldier. He lived in Rochefort, where he had his comforts, but he could come and see me, in his white car, as often as he wanted. He wanted to twice a month, rarely more, and he never came inside the Queen of Hearts. It was not for a man and he might have met officers in civilian clothes among our guests. Besides, although Madame was very kind, she refused to see him. He had schemed to get me a job there. She only accepted top-notch young ladies, ones who knew how to conduct themselves, spouting "notwithstanding" and "the fact remains that" on any subject from that day's newspaper, ones who could slip away to the toilet with the delicacy of the Duchess of Windsor—in short, well-bred girls who had been to exclusive nursery schools, while by the end of my studies, I hadn't climbed any higher than the bar stools of the Carlton, and even then only for two evenings, before they decided I lowered the tone and heartlessly kicked me out.

But I've already said: I'm a good girl, not snotty, not nosy, always even-tempered, and to be totally honest, you could have measured me all over with a tape measure, you wouldn't have found an inch too much or too little. Notwithstanding the fact that she found me a teeny bit uninhibited, Madame soon adopted me as one of her own daughters. I allowed myself to be dressed as she wished, I was less careless with my language, I stopped swinging my charms like the harlots of the Rue Delambre, in fact I was more and more what Beau Masque had dreamed of, cigarette holder and all. The fact remains that she still didn't want to meet him. The Sundays when he took me out, he waited for me in the garden.

He took me to lunch on lobster cooked in Sancerre in the smartest restaurant in Saint-Julien, Le Grand Large, where he had the table placed on the terrace, facing the port. In the afternoon, a walk. I can still picture him, in a white alpaca suit, white shoes, his straw hat on his head, his Havana in his mouth, his nose turned up like a king. I walked a yard behind him, contented, under a great tunnel of palm trees alongside the ocean, in a silk suit matching his, ditto the wide-brimmed hat and a parasol to protect my lily-white complexion. Of course he sometimes had his worries. He would wheel round and shout, "We're fed up to the back teeth, look at us! Just look at your mug!" He would imitate Minnie Mouse's dumb look. He would shout, "I'm pissed off, shit!" And *smack-thwack*, forehand-backhand to calm his nerves.

But I knew that deep down he loved me. Sometimes we drove in his sports car to the creek of The Crowns. You only saw people there at the height of the summer. We would slip on our bathing suits with straps, as was the fashion at the time, and he taught me to swim. He couldn't swim himself. He cried as if his lungs would burst: "What would I do in a shipwreck? Swim, for Christ's sake! Jesus, look at this idiot! Swim, I tell you! Stop drinking!" Finally, nauseated and tired, he would say, his voice three octaves lower, "Shit!" and shove my head underwater so that I would drown faster.

When he brought me back to the Queen of Hearts, it was heartrending for me. He didn't even get out to kiss me. He sat at the wheel of his convertible Bugatti, cold as the previous winter, mean like you would not believe. He always dropped me at the door, at the bottom of the garden. That door, I can still picture it. It was made of varnished solid wood, very nineteenth century. Just beside it, on the wall, there was a copper plaque, no bigger than my hand, depicting a playing card. Nobody would ever have thought it was a brothel.

I cried. I would walk around the car so that he would speak to me again. I would say to him, sweet as the honey that I am, "You'll come back on Sunday, won't you?" He would remove my fingers from the lapels of his jacket and reply, dusting himself off, "We'll see, we'll see. . . ." And I knew that I would agonize during the interminable days, and I cried all the more. I said, "Will you think of me?" And he answered, "Of course, of course," and he would sound his horn to put a stop to my whining. He had never been demonstrative, except to teach me how to live, or in the beginning, in the dingy hotel room in Montparnasse that he had made me rent.

At the Queen of Hearts the only resident man was an affectionate twenty-year-old boy, who did everything: caretaker, cook, barman, piano tuner, shoeshine boy, fire extinguisher, the young ladies' confidant, and the apple of Madame's eye. He wasn't tall, or strong, but he had learned to fight like the Japanese. Apparently, one evening before my time, he flattened five undesirable characters single-handed, before anyone could blink. He was known as Jitsu, and he always wandered around barefoot, in a fine cotton kimono jacket and trousers, a headband across his forehead and his waist pulled in by a wide black belt.

It was he who opened the door for me when Beau Masque hooted. Through my tears, I stared after the car until it reached the gate, more miserable each time, and then Jitsu would put a comforting arm around my shoulders and take me inside, saying in a voice heavy with all the sympathy in Charentes, "Come, come, Mademoiselle Belinda, don't get yourself in such a state."

But the rest of the time I was reasonable; my optimistic nature got the upper hand again. I told myself that Beau Masque must have been a saint to waste his Sundays teaching me to swim and that he was a million times more flattering, even with his faults, than the shoal of mackerel I had known, including my girlfriend at Perros-

Guirec's Johnny-come-quick. Well, that's what you tell yourself when you're infatuated; you're not fussy over one clout more or one kiss less, if you're a sucker like me.

How but how on earth could I have imagined that this light of my life would end up being court-martialed and imprisoned for life?

First, the marines caught him at home, in Rochefort, but he wasn't sent into the marines. After well and truly softening him up for three months, they stuck him in the infantry, in Metz. He wrote to me:

My dear Georgette,

That's my real name.

> *I'm not fooling around anymore. I'm keeping my nose clean. The grub isn't brilliant. Send me parcels and money. If you can, get some nude photos taken of you. I've got a buyer. I jerk off when I think of you.*
>
> *Your poor Emile*

That's his real name.
Then he wrote:

> *My darling wife,*
>
> *I'm licking boots to get myself off sick. A buddy from the Bastille tells me we're being sent near home. Don't forget my dough. They liked the photos. Do some more. Tell the photographer to get a good shot of your ass. They all think of you when they jerk off.*
>
> *Your poor soldier*

They sent him to a Rennes hospital, for two toes that he had gotten his friend from the Bastille to crush with the butt of his rifle. He wasn't able to go on the marches anymore. I was proud of his courage, and what he had to endure to get closer to me made me weep into my pillow. He wrote:

My dear,

I nearly died. The grub is shit. Don't forget my dough.
I'm scared that Hitler will go to war and that they'll
even send the disabled to the slaughterhouse. The last
photos were lousy. For this place, try and look
lecherous. You should play with yourself, that lot can't
control themselves.

Your beloved darling

That's not all, and there were worse. Beau Masque wrote to me
every week. On Thursday or Friday mornings, Jitsu would bring the
envelope to my room, with a big smile. Notwithstanding the stin-
giness of the style—anyone would think he was the one who had
taken in my teacher's lessons—and the spelling mistakes that had
been corrected, I found his letters very beautiful, I could sense the
sorrow they concealed. Of course, all the girls wanted to read them,
but I never allowed them to, except for Zozo, the black girl, because
of that business of the photos, which made me go crazy.

My photographer, an old man with glasses who did weddings and
local schools, was even more out of his depth than I was. Despite
the price I paid him, which I never told Beau Masque, for the poor
thing would have had the additional worry of bringing ruin upon us,
he thought this work was idiotic and his heart wasn't in it. Zozo, a
superb, supple girl from the colonies, had done this sort of posing
when she landed at Marseilles. She advised me as best she could
and I even got a whole set that I thought was really dirty, but we tore
them up, it wasn't worth it anymore: the minute Beau Masque was
up on his eight toes, he had rushed out and raped a novice at the
game—at least that's what he was accused of—and this time, his
head was on the block.

You can understand why I fell ill. I was carried half out of my
mind to my room and given injections for two weeks to make me
sleep.

When the doctor who took care of us, Monsieur Lauzey, pre-
scribed that I convalesce, on my balcony looking out over the ocean,
Madame told me that Beau Masque had been imprisoned for the
rest of his life.

*   *   *

First of all, he was put in a fortress in Lorraine. He wrote to me:

My poor, poor Jo,

*I am xxxxxxxxxxxxxxxxx. xxxxxxxx the Good Lord
xxxxxxxxx. xxxxxxxxx fate. Forget that xxxxxxxxx.
xxxxxxxxxx crash xxxxxxxxxxxxxx my life.*

Your xxxxxxxxxxxx

After that they censored everything. I received blank letters with blacked-out lines.

I had started working again, but I didn't feel up to it. My smile was enough to break your heart. They gave me money that I hadn't earned, that I was sure the other girls took from their share to give to me. I cried all the more, I felt as soft as fudge.

I have never been able to pray, even at the orphanage where it was the devil's own job to wake me up after Mass. But everybody including Madame told me it might help Beau Masque, so I went to see the Virgin one Sunday evening, at the church of Saint-Julien. I lit a candle for him. I told her that my man wasn't bad, that he had put me in a brothel that I'd never even have dreamed of when I was little, that he taught me to swim at The Crowns, and that it was all the more difficult for him as he couldn't swim himself—all those things. I cried so hard that I ended up seeing tears on her cheeks. I asked her to forgive me for being a whore, but it was my vocation, I was sure she understood.

The very next day, believe it or not, they transferred Beau Masque to the Rattrap, a citadel on an island just opposite Saint-Julien. You could see it if you climbed to the top of the lighthouse. I had to trudge up the two hundred and twenty corkscrew stairs every Sunday, with opera glasses lent to me by one of the girls. I couldn't see much, just the stone walls and black holes, but it was better than nothing. On Friday evenings I went to the port with Jitsu to watch the departure of the boat that took provisions and wicker to the citadel. Now, my angel was forced to make baskets. I often tried to have myself a soldier, to give him a parcel, but none of them would ever do it.

I was able to see Beau Masque once, just once, and I didn't know it was for the last time. Thanks to Madame, as always. She had had a word with a young officer in tails who knew the nephew of a general, and this general, who had the ear of the major in command of the citadel, couldn't sleep at night for the love of a beauty from the bourgeoisie of Surgères who blew all her husband's money—he was a leather merchant—at the casino in Royan. I gave five thousand old francs to this woman to help her pay her debts. A few days later in the kitchens where we spent our afternoons in casual clothes, Madame handed me my pass with a great deal of sighing. She had never approved of the extravagances I went through for Beau Masque.

I hadn't seen him for two years. I was nineteen. During the crossing, which lasted three quarters of an hour, I stood at the prow of the boat, heedless of the spray. I was dressed in black from head to foot, like a widow.

They showed him to me in a big corridor shut off by an iron gate. We sat on chairs on either side of the bars. I was expecting to find a skeleton, but he was the same as before, and even pinker and plumper. He told me in fact that he was well fed and that he licked everyone's boots to get the leftovers; I could drop the subject. They had shaved his head, which made him look more mature and more virile, but he got annoyed and told me to drop that, too, that he curled his pubic hairs to make up for it.

They gave us twenty minutes and permission to kiss each other twice. He hadn't kissed me yet. He barely looked at me, he was so busy keeping an eye on his guard, who kept ten paces from us. He leaned forward, all feverish as the time flew past, and talked to me in conspiratorial tones. I leaned forward, too, until my forehead touched the bars, but I couldn't hear half of what he said.

It was clear to him that I wasn't pleased with what he had done. He whispered, "Shit, I tell you it wasn't me! You know me, I can have all the broads I want. Why would I go and take one by force?" I told him, "You took me by force the first time." He answered, "You're different, I loved you." Of course, I was moved, I let him give me his sales patter. It was more or less the same as usual: "Work! You understand? Work! It'll take dough to get me out of here." I didn't know what he had in mind, but I didn't dare ask him, perhaps for fear of being overheard by the guard. Besides, he told me himself: "You earn the money, the rest is my business. I'll find a way of letting you know." I had been advised not to touch him through the bars, otherwise the visit would be ended, but as it was over anyway, I placed a hand on his, batting my eyelids to let him know he could count on me.

He walked off down the corridor, the way he had come, without a kiss. I realized that he was only thinking of himself and that even if he got out of this booby hatch, nothing would ever be the same as before, and I wouldn't be either. Our ways were parting. During the return crossing, I tore off my hat veil, I let the wind blow on my face. I wasn't even sad. A little empty, that was all.

But don't think because I didn't love him anymore that I was going to leave my man destitute. I'm no kept woman. That very evening, under the crystal lights of the Queen of Hearts, in a long ivory dress with a plunging back, slit to the buttocks, my hair up in curls à la Garbo, wearing all my jewels and my lips provocative, I became the Belinda of the good old days again and Madame opened the champagne.

From this moment, and for four years, I devoted myself entirely to my nights and to saving up to help Beau Masque escape. I thought about him less and less, and it's true, I sometimes even had a crush on someone else and came in the arms of another, but never, may the Virgin who heard my prayers strike me dead, never did I break my promise to him.

I was dressed like a princess, surrounded by affection and luxury, protected from the worries of the world. I was so happy during this period and each day was so like the others that I can't piece together any memories. A sail drifting past out at sea, white and blue, which I watched from my balcony. A masked ball. A Charleston: "Don't Touch Anything Before My Mummy Comes." Giggling in the kitchen, over our midday breakfasts. A train journey to go and visit my Demon, who was dying in Bagnolet. I arrived too late. Paris, one evening, with the lights of the Exhibition. Another time, a week in Cassis, near Marseilles, with a ship owner. Madame had wanted me to accompany her. And also the pranks with Vanessa and Savenna, the twins at the Queen of Hearts, when we hadn't learned to tell them apart yet. Paid holidays. The Spanish civil war. The lighthouse that I didn't go up anymore.

And then, one morning, Jitsu found a letter with no stamp in the mailbox on the gate. It was for me. It read:

Mademoiselle,

I've got something important to tell you from
you-know-who. He needs thirty thousand. If you can
manage more, it's better. I'll wait for you this evening
at seven o'clock by the Menauds lock. I'll be the
fisherman with a red scarf. Greetings.

Madame, who kept my money at her bank, went to get the sum
in the afternoon. I could manage more but she said, "If you give a
cent more for that creature, I'll give you back the lot and you can
pack your bags."

It was the beginning of August. It was still broad daylight when
Jitsu drove me to the lock in the black Chenard belonging to the
Queen of Hearts. The fellow with the red scarf was sitting all alone
at the edge of the canal, his legs dangling, with a long fishing rod to
make him look like a fisherman. He didn't get up. He told me to put
the cash, which I had wrapped up in newspaper, in his fish basket.
I wanted to know what was going on. He had darting eyes and his
cigarette butt trembled in his mouth as if he were running a great
risk. He said, "I was with Beau Masque for three years, and I don't
want to go back there." Then he said, "In a few days, he's busting
out. He doesn't know if he'll be able to see you for a long time. He
forbids you to move." I asked him how I could be sure that he had
been sent by my man and that he wasn't going to keep the money
for himself. He replied, "If you had put it in the basket like I told
you, you'd already know." There wasn't a hint of a fishbone in the
bottom of the basket, but a wrapper from a packet of Army cigarettes, folded in four. Beau Masque had written:

Jo,

If we don't see each other again, remember that your
Emile is happy in a far-off land thanks to you. Be
careful not to say anything because if I'm nabbed, I
know someone who'll do you in. For sure.

I thought that to be honest, it was for the best. If he had written
something less disgusting, I know what I'm like, I'd have moved
heaven and earth to help him even more. Now I was rid of him. I tore
up his note with my fingertips and threw the pieces into the canal.

What I've just told you, which is the story of my life until my fate caught up with me, ended one Friday. The following Friday, toward evening, we heard the sirens of the citadel wailing. I could hear them from my balcony.

I sent a friend to find out what was going on, a blonde with blue eyes who had the blood of the Czars in her veins from her mother and the accent of a Montmartre street urchin from her father. At least most of the time. Sometimes the Slav blood veered toward the Viking, Montmartre had a whiff of the Auvergne, but who knows. We called her Michou and the clients called her Ninotchka. She returned not long after, with the news: in town, people were laughing at the soldiers who were running all over the place; a prisoner had escaped from the Rattrap. Who? How? Nobody knew. She said, before leaving my room, "Believe me, you'll never see him again." I replied, "So, I'm cured of the burn."

The next day, nothing. The day after that, Sunday, no more than the previous day, except that I was down in the dumps all day, I don't know why. Beau Masque, who never dipped his feet in a basin of water without screaming bloody murder, I imagined him lost among the marshes of the peninsula, more wretched than a dog. And then I thought of the first time we met, of other silly things. It's quite something to ask the name of a guy who was born with a lopsided mug, with eyes that are obviously not the same make, and for him to reply, "Beau Masque, they call me Beau Masque." I didn't even smile. It wasn't possible. As for his smile, it was painful. Whenever I hear someone talking about a half smile or a lopsided grin, it still gives me the shivers.

The fact remains that on Monday afternoon, I went out to buy a bottle of perfume I had ordered—I used to wear *Quelques Fleurs* by Houbigant in those days—and the hairdresser, a spiteful little minx whom I have to mention again later, unfortunately, was giving her clients a rundown in her shrill voice, wiggling about in a way that even the dumbest of my sisters of the Rue Delambre would have been ashamed of. Yackety-Yack, they called her when they talked about her behind her back, and Madame Bonnefoy, or Bonnifay, I can't remember, to her face. In short, the time it took to go out and come back again, perfumed for the rest of the summer, I learned that they had removed the roadblocks on the peninsula and that my petticoat chaser would be wooing the Spanish girls from now on. To say I was relieved is an understatement. I was as light as a feather. I had difficulty stopping myself from blowing away.

The shock that brought me back down to earth arrived that very evening, just before midnight. I was just done with a client and was freshening up in the bathroom. That was when Jitsu walked into my room without knocking, with disaster written all over his face, to inform me on behalf of Madame that Beau Masque was downstairs in the kitchens, badly wounded. I stopped only to slip on my black silk negligee. I hadn't even finished doing it up before I was rushing down the main staircase. Downstairs, in the reception room, they were waltzing, in evening dress, under the chandeliers. I crossed the entrance hall, Jitsu at my heels, and I went down to the kitchens.

It was one of those lovely old-fashioned kitchens with copper pans and scrubbed floors like on a boat. In the middle there was a heavy walnut table, polished every other day, with matching chairs, and they had pulled out one of those chairs for my prisoner. Michou, Zozo, and Madame were standing around him. On seeing him, I stood rooted to the spot. He was exactly as I had expected, dirty, with no strength left and an ugly brown bloodstain that had dried on his chest, but one detail left me speechless: it wasn't Beau Masque.

Luckily for what followed, or thanks to fate, Madame spoke first. She asked me, suspiciously, "Is that your petty pimp?" She had never seen Beau Masque other than from a distance, from a window, when he used to come and wait for me. As I didn't reply, she said, "Prison has changed him a great deal."

The man on the chair I had never seen before in my life. What struck me first was the look he shot at me, a pleading look. It wasn't difficult to understand, even for an ignoramus, that he was scared to death that I would betray him. A lot of things happen, in three seconds, in black eyes like that. Before I had collected my wits, I heard myself say, "Take him up to my room."

Zozo and Jitsu supported him under the arms to help him walk. I saw that he was tall, with broad shoulders and storklike legs. He was wearing a sport shirt, a pair of trousers, and moccasins that must have been white once. I reckoned he was about thirty. Madame said, "Use the service stairs, please." She had already picked up the telephone to call the doctor.

They helped the stranger up to my room, one stair at a time, and settled him on my bed. He didn't complain, but I could see that he was in pain. I was alone with him for a good fifteen minutes. He had closed his eyes. He didn't say a word. Neither did I.

When Monsieur Lauzey, our doctor, had finished his business, I was on the balcony, looking at the night, my head all in a spin. He came to join me, buttoning up his coat over his pajamas. He said, "I've removed all the lead I could find in his body. He's robust. In two days he'll be on his feet." I sensed that he wanted to tell me something else, but he was a very discreet man. If I was sheltering the runaway from the citadel, what business was it of his? He simply added, "Don't worry, it was only buckshot."

As soon as he had left, I closed the door behind him and leaned against it, facing the four-poster bed. The wounded man had opened his eyes and was sitting propped up by two pillows, a huge dressing around his bare torso, and was already looking a lot better. I asked him harshly, "Who are you?" He replied, "An accomplice of Beau Masque's." I went over to him, drawing aside the netting, already gentler: "Have you seen him?" He lowered his black eyes with eyelashes a mile long: "Three days ago, when he escaped."

I sat on the edge of the bed, waiting for him to say more. I can still picture him. He had a clean face, and stared at me for a long time before speaking. I could sense that he was somebody beautiful and unobtainable. I swear it. In the end, I was the one who looked away.

"Last Friday, when the citadel sirens were wailing everywhere," said this intrepid young man, "I cut a football in half and stuck it on my head to make me look like a jailbird. I put on my leather jacket, my motorcycle helmet and goggles, I got onto the big-engined English bike that I'd been dreaming of for nearly fifteen years, and went off hunting all over the peninsular, to find your lover before the soldiers tracked him down.

"No doubt you're wondering how I knew about his escape. I'll tell you that sometimes I sit at the table, on misty nights, with a strong beer and all the regrets of my lost childhood, that I like talking of my grandmother or listening to others talking of their grandmothers in those circumstances, but no matter how little attention I appear to be paying, I am always able to recognize the whisper of betrayal, the murmur of treason, the sigh of ignominy.

"In the back room of the Neptune, that bar on the port that never closes, one evening of great loneliness, I overheard the drunken discussion of two strangers. There was only a thin, grainy glass partition between us, but they didn't take any notice of me and I wasn't able to make out their faces. All that I can tell you about the one who was baring his soul was the anguish I heard in his voice and the scarlet red I could see around his neck through the glass, probably a scarf. He talked of being on the run, of a stolen boat, of corrupt guards. He talked about a prisoner whose smile was a wound. He talked about you. He said, 'She's a tall girl with sea-blue eyes, a silken body, who cuts across our lives like a dream, for our money and for love of him.' He regretted, in fact, having promised to help a certain Beau Masque, and all he wanted from his drinking companion was encouragement to break his word. That's the whole story. When the sirens went off on Friday, I did what someone I had never seen ought to have done but, I knew, never would.

"I sped along on my racer till I reached the edge of a wood that this man had mentioned. It is inland, surrounded by vineyards and pastures. The air was mild, the sun was slipping down behind the trees. I waited for nearly an hour, leaning against my bike, tormented by the idea that I was mistaken, that this was not the meeting place. And then, in the silence of the twilight, a commotion broke out, so muffled at first that I didn't know where it was coming from, but which soon grew louder through the woods. It was the dogs.

"Almost immediately, amid the crackle of dead branches, parting the last thickets, the fugitive with a shaven head appeared in front of me. Sweat was streaming down him and he was doubled up from choking. He dropped to his knees when he saw me. As far as I could tell, this human wreck had no more than two minutes' start over the pack that had been set on his tail. I threw him my leather jacket, my goggles, and my helmet. I said, 'Hurry up. Give me your clothes and put on mine.'

"We undressed without a word, we even exchanged shoes. The barking was getting closer. While I finished becoming him and he me, I said, 'Take my motorbike, I'll give your pursuers the slip.' Standing up now, having recovered his breath, Beau Masque looked at me with incredulity and gratitude. He exclaimed, 'I'll never forget what you've just done, never!' I replied angrily, 'I'm not doing it for you, you bastard, I'm doing it for Belinda; you call her your wife and you've shut her up in a brothel!' He stood glued to the spot, his ugly mouth open in amazement, and then he was overcome with terror again and he leaped onto the bike. Before stepping on the gas, he turned toward me and yelled, his eyes bloodshot, 'In that case, the woman's yours, comrade. You've paid for her.'

"He roared off across the fields, to get to any dirt track or road that would take him far away from there. And I, in a shirt soaked with his sweat, in a pair of trousers that were too short, wearing prison boots, I waited until he had disappeared, wished myself good luck, and ran as fast as I could in the opposite direction, through the woods, pursued by the howling of the dogs."

I swear I was a little at sea when the poor boy had finished his story, especially as he looked at me with peepers full of adoration. My heart melted. I said, "So you knew me?" I was absolutely sure that I was seeing him for the very first time that night. He replied, with an embarrassed air, "I've often followed you without your knowing, when you go into town, but I've never dared speak to you."

I was even more moved. I took his hand. It was feverish and soft. I asked him, "Who shot you?" A little sigh, and he said, "A bride on her honeymoon. After hiding in the marshes for a whole night and day, I forced her to take me in her truck and suddenly—"

Suddenly shouts and a commotion on the ground floor made us both jump. He sat up in bed, staring at the bedroom door with anxiety. I signaled to him not to move and I went to the staircase to see what was happening down below. Horrors. Sky-blue soldiers, helmeted up to their eyeballs, had invaded the big drawing room. Holding their guns, they were pushing the girls and the clients back under the chandeliers, urged on by the voice of a brute with a fearful look in his eye, standing in front of the spectacle with arms folded: Lieutenant Malignaud. Anyone would have thought we were in a henhouse.

Never had such a disgrace fallen on the Queen of Hearts within a hooker's living memory, alive or dead. Madame was beside herself. I saw her cling to the officer's arm, crying, "For goodness' sake, Lieutenant, you know our reputation!" And he freed his arm abruptly and replied louder than her: "Precisely!" She sank onto a sofa, clinging to the faithful Jitsu, who wouldn't have been frightened by twelve war veterans and who comforted her as best he could: "Come, come, Madame, don't get yourself in such a state!"

When hearing Malignaud shout to his men, "Search the whole damned place!" I didn't wait to hear any more. I was back in the room in three strides. I got the injured man out of my bed, picked up his sport shirt and moccasins while he slipped into his trousers, and I led him as fast as if he were well to the only part of the house where we could successfully hide a tall beanpole, marked with the Indian tika for having met me in the street. Luckily, it wasn't miles away; all we had to do was cross the corridor.

On the other side of the corridor, almost opposite my room, stood a lovely painting signed by the artist inspired by another earlier artist, depicting *Truth Emerging from the Well*. The title was etched on a golden plaque in case anyone didn't know it. I swung the masterpiece around and turned the little key in the little door of the little storeroom that was behind it. Not a single piece of furniture, and exactly four paces around the room. We had christened this place "the cell" because recalcitrant girls were locked up there, at least in the old days, when there were some.

My protégé's terrified panic when he saw what awaited him can't be described in words, in any language. If you haven't seen it, you haven't seen anything. I caught him by the arm and pushed him into the poky little closet. I could already hear heavy boots climbing the stairs. Before locking the door and putting the broad and her water tank back in front of it, I felt sorry for him, he looked as though he were being buried alive, and I whispered, "Come on! It's only for a few minutes!"

He spent the whole night in there. At one minute to eight in the morning, we were all still packed into the big drawing room, Madame and Jitsu too, some lying down, others sitting, our eyes open out of habit. They had allowed the clients to leave and put out the lights. Lined up in a single row, leaning on their guns, the soldiers who were guarding us had fallen asleep on their feet. The dreadful Malignaud marched up and down, far away in his gloomy thoughts, and his boots creaked. At eight o'clock on the dot, he flung open the curtains. Outside, it was a lovely summer's day. He let out a long sigh and said, defeated, "All right, then. Let's go. Parade in the garden."

There were ten of us girls at that time, like the Ten Commandments, and nine were already tucked up in bed when the troop stepped out of the door. I stayed with Jitsu, at Madame's side. Before following his men out, the lieutenant stopped in front of her and showed her the palm of his right hand, stained dirty brown. He remarked, nastily, "It's blood, but not mine! The bastard whose tracks led here, I sincerely hope that by now he's dead!" Then he looked Jitsu up and down and said, "As for you, just wait until you're in my regiment, I'll keep your nose to the grindstone."

The fact remains that he left, with all his men, and I was able to free the captive. Gray, he was gray. When I put him back in my bed, fully dressed, with three blankets, he was shivering and his teeth were chattering. I had Jitsu bring him up some coffee. I had to hold the bowl so that he could drink. He stared into space with crazed eyes.

After a long while he calmed down and gave me a feeble sort of excuse. I was still wearing a black silk negligee. He let his head sink onto my thighs with a great sigh. He murmured, "I've got to explain to you. . . ." He picked absentmindedly at a slice of bread and butter.

"When I was six or seven, I can't remember," this young man said bitterly, "my monster of a father abandoned my mother without a penny. We still lived in the Boulevard National, in Marseilles, where I was born. My mother had to send me to boarding school in order to work.

"It wasn't far, in a suburb known as the Trois-Lucs, but I remember it as being the back of beyond. I probably measured everything according to the distress I felt at being separated from my mother. I saw her for a few hours on Sundays, and the first hour was poisoned by the apprehension of the last. She came by bus to fetch me at midday, and she brought me back before sundown. When she left me, at the school gates, I cried as if I was never going to see her again. A despair that was so deep, so persistent, for I felt it inside me day and night; I don't think I've ever felt anything so strong since. Even today, all I have to do is think about it to feel just as I did then. The wooden arch over the gate, which creaked when the mistral blew. The paint is all flaking; all you can make out, in gray letters on a faded background, is SAINT SINS SCHOOL. The gravel drive leading up to the buildings and the quadrangle surrounded by plane trees. I have fair hair. I am the same height as the door handles. In my right hand I am holding the little suitcase that contains my clean laundry, marked with the number 'eighteen.' There's a vegetable garden, somewhere, and I hold my nose so as not to smell the tomatoes. I have hated tomatoes since those days, I can't explain why. I eat anything, as long as it's not tomatoes. I can't eat a piece of tomato without being sick.

"In my class there are two windows on either side of a wood stove, black desks with china inkstands, a rostrum with a table and cane chair that squeaks every time the schoolmistress moves. I am in the front row, with the little ones, almost facing her. She is the head-master's wife, but she's a lot younger than him, she looks like his daughter. She always dresses severely, she has a pretty, severe face with very deep blue eyes. Her long black hair is pinned up in a bun and, sometimes, a lock escapes and falls on her cheek. She raises her arm to put it back in its place and you can see that her breasts, underneath her blouse, are round and full. Some boys call her 'Titties,' but most of them call her 'Mommy Long Legs' because she's even more intriguing below than on top.

"While we do our homework, she reads, her forehead resting on one hand. She is cut in half by the tabletop and her legs seem to belong to somebody else. They never stop moving. And she crosses them, and she uncrosses them, then she crosses them again. The only sound in the classroom is the scratching of quill pens and the squeaking of the chair. The schoolmistress's stockings are always smooth, and we'd like to be able to see right to the top. It is unlikely that at that age I was motivated by anything other than curiosity, but I stare fixedly at the schoolmistress's legs as I munch a piece of bread and butter that I have saved from breakfast. I would like to see more and more, and often, helped by the tightness of her skirt, the ploy works and reveals a little bare flesh, or the whiteness of her panties. At other times I was hypnotized to the point where all it took was for my neighbor to prod me with one finger and my head would fall on my desk and I would be asleep.

"Things never end so well. Without fail, Mommy Long Legs would look up from her book and, with that ferocious eye, dark as the watery depths, realize at once where mine was gazing. She sits up straight, yanks her skirt down, and pronounces my sentence: 'Aren't you ashamed? Wait for me in the corridor after the study hour.'

"The corridor is the entrance hall. It is paved with black and white tiles, like a chessboard. Beside the front door, opposite the headmaster's office, there's another very narrow door that we never talk about without lowering our voices: the punishment room. It is in there that toward five o'clock, when the others are playing ball in the quadrangle, the schoolmistress pushes me, murmuring in my ear, 'So, you like looking up my skirt? You like it?' And just before locking me in, when she is just a sinister shadow against the light: 'We'll see if you still like it as much tomorrow morning!'

"The punishment room," this young man said sadly, finishing off his bread and butter, "was a square one pace long and one pace wide, like yours, without a skylight, without a light, with nothing other than the darkness. I didn't cry, or plead, I was already too proud to give Mommy Long Legs that pleasure. I imagine, for terror is my only memory, that I sat there huddled in a corner, and that I forced myself to think of my mother, of my grandmother, of my monster of a father who had left, who, if he had known about my plight, would certainly have come back to set me free. Or I must have convinced myself that I was growing and growing in the dark, the way other people's hair turns white overnight, and that to everyone's amazement, I would smash down the walls and escape. But monster fathers never come back again. And all the nights and all the days it takes to grow higher than the door handles, everyone knows, is a long time."

That was how he caught that nasty claustrowhatsit. I was overwhelmed with pity, when he shook me up a bit more: "You know, every day, she would punish a different pupil. I'm sure she showed us her legs on purpose." I said, indignantly, "A schoolmistress! My poor, poor darling!" And I realized that I was hugging him to me and that I was stroking his hair as I would have done with a child. I'm repeating myself, but too bad: I was getting on to twenty-four, and he was pretty close to thirty. It's funny, in a way, that I was the one to comfort him. And yet I was happy like that, I would willingly have gone on all morning.

After a while I realized he was falling asleep. I supported him so that his head would be resting on the pillows and switched off the bedside light. In the bluish daylight that filtered through the curtains at the window, he stretched out a hand for me to hold. He murmured, "You are so good to me, Belinda." I was getting used to the half darkness; I could see his eyes and all the emotion in them. Without weighing up the pros and the cons too much—it makes you mean—I simply replied, "As Beau Masque gave me to you, I'm your woman."

That was all for the moment. Almost immediately, his hand in mine, he fell into an exhausted sleep. I watched him sleep for a long time. When it came to looks, I had come off better for the swap, but it would have been hard to find someone uglier than Beau Masque. As for the rest, I still didn't know anything about him, except that he was born in Marseilles, and that he didn't like tomatoes, and that he wore a wide, flat wedding ring on his left hand, but that didn't stop him hanging around cafés on his own until morning, eavesdropping on the secrets of bogus fishermen. He didn't spend all his bread trying to get into an impossible position, like Beau Masque, but all the same he must have been going to live through all sorts of disasters in his dreams; I could tell from his breathing, and from the way he winced. I drew back the blankets to give him a peck on the chest, just above the dressing. His skin was soft, I liked his smell. I slid my hand down to his belt. To be honest, I wanted to go lower, and to touch him, without waking him, perhaps to do more, without his knowing a thing, and I would have watched his face to see if his dreams changed. Just hesitating for a moment made me go all you-know, so I made myself get up. I tucked him up carefully, after sneaking a blanket from him, and went to sleep on my sofa.

The fact remains that from that day, as I've already said, I was his woman.

By two o'clock in the afternoon he still hadn't woken up. I went down to the kitchens to find the others. Madame was still all upset by the events of the night before, especially by having had the troops in her establishment, but when I told her, and my voice quavered, that we couldn't throw Beau Masque out into the streets, that he would get caught pronto, she looked me squarely in the face and said, "Beau Masque or anyone else, a man on the run who seeks sanctuary in my house is as sacred as in a church. Who do you think I am?" And I must say that to the end, everyone held their tongue, not only Madame but also the nine girls, not forgetting Jitsu.

That evening, before going down to the lounge to receive our first gentlemen, black Zozo, Michou, Magali, and the twins came to watch the wounded man dine in my four-poster bed—all dressed up to the nines and squawking like parrots, they were so excited at meeting, at last, the man who had made me suffer so. I had found him a pair of black silk pajamas, with silver buttons and frogging. I had shaved him, combed his hair, and manicured him; he looked like a prince surrounded by his court. As he ate, still with a voracity that made your heart ache, he answered their questions without a sour note, he described the prisons he hadn't known as if we were there. I felt myself blush with pride, I puffed up like a balloon. Except that he winced when they called him Beau Masque, and I was afraid the others would notice. As soon as they had gone out, each one taking her leave with a great deal of fussing, I asked him his real name. He told me, "Antoine." And after swallowing: "I prefer Tony, it's classier." I thought that was as good a starting point as any to ask him the question that had been bugging me all day: "And are you married?" He looked at his ring and answered, "Oh no. That's my grandfather's wedding ring. My grandmother gave it to me when he died." I was delighted, I can't deny it. I said, "I'll tell the others not to call you Beau Masque anymore for safety's sake."

After the bed had been cleared of the remains of his meal, I snuggled up next to him and kissed him properly. Right away, I wanted him to make me come. But I was dressed to go downstairs, I could hear the music below, and I didn't want to bother Madame again with my moods. I said, "My darling, my Tony, my love, be good, you're the death of me, you're creasing my dress, please, wait till I come back, have pity on me"—a right little madame who would have been killed off even in a pulp novel. In the end, I tore myself away from him, but I don't know whose legs got me down the grand staircase, mine had completely turned to jelly.

I didn't work that night, we hadn't had time to organize another room for me. In any case, after the scene of the previous evening, I wasn't the only wallflower. It even took several weeks before the clients who had been so well treated had the heart to come back. I had two or three dances, I listened to advice on stocks and bonds from a banker taking the waters at Saint-Trojan, on the Ile d'Oléron, I smoked a packet of Turkish cigarettes as I watched the large hand of the clock over the bar go around—in short, I was in no hurry for the party to end. At midnight, which according to Madame was unheard of in any establishment since the Carpentier–Dempsey match, we shut up shop without covering our overhead.

I got undressed and had a wash in the bathroom, and slipped between my nuptial sheets without waking up my betrothed. I gently undid his pajama buttons one by one, and untied his belt, and satisfied my desire of the day before. I don't know if he was pretending to be asleep to humor me, or whether he was only aware of my hand and mouth in the depths of a dream, but he didn't open his eyes or make the merest suggestion of a movement and I was already dying. And then he held me in his arms and rolled me over on the bed, and by the time day broke behind the curtains, he had made me die so many times that I didn't have the strength left for anything, but I was still moaning. Believe it or not of the whore that I am, we had coffee together, a bit later, sitting opposite each other at the little table by the window, and I was embarrassed, in broad daylight, like a ninny who's just been deflowered. Then he took my face in his hands so that I would look at him, and just from his shining eyes, his smile, I knew it wasn't a crush, it wasn't a passing fancy or a fling, but that big thing that everyone talks about from hearsay, because a friend's sister-in-law's aunt thought it had happened to her—until the next time—and now it was happening to me, Miss I've-been-everywhere-done-everything: watch out, and the floodgates, when they gave way, it was Niagara Falls. I swear it was. As he was too emotional himself to think of moving the cups out of the way, so we drank salty coffee.

Then, for three weeks, I was walking on air. Dr. Lauzey removed his dressing. Jitsu drove me to Royan to buy some clothes for my convalescent patient. I filled the trunk of the Chenard and piled the backseat high. A black dinner jacket and a white dinner jacket, which he needed, I'll tell you why in a minute. A dozen shirts. Jersey sport shirts. Sweaters Made in England. Shoes Made in Italy. Six pairs. Two casual outfits, three about-town suits, one made of white alpaca to stop any of my friends who were jealous from saying that I didn't treat him as well as Beau Masque. I'll skip the details of the ties, the thin socks, the handkerchiefs, all silk. I'll skip the hats, including a Maurice Chevalier boater. I'll skip the pajamas, the dressing gowns, the bathrobes as thick as rugs, the Cartier wristwatch, cigarette case, and lighter, the forty-carat cuff links, tiepin, and signet ring. Jitsu ran from the shops to the car, his arms full of packages. The more I bought, the happier I was. I had taken a fat wad of bills with me to pay for it all, but in the end, I had to sign credit slips.

It was no joke getting all that upstairs when I got back; we all had stomachaches. Tony spent the next day playing at modeling. One of the girls, Lulubelle, set up her sewing machine in our room and did the alterations. A right dandy, my dear, and he liked everything except the signet ring, which I ended up selling to Madame so that she could make a present of it to Jitsu.

Now I'll explain why Tony needed dinner jackets. The first afternoon when he was back on his feet, when there was nobody downstairs, he visited the drawing rooms with me, and was in ecstasies over the luxury and the baroque decor, but what thrilled him most of all was the grand piano. He sat down at it, as if it was the most wonderful thing he'd ever seen, cracked his fingers, and began to play. When I say play, it's because my vocabulary would fit into an overnight bag; it gave me goose pimples. One by one, the girls who were still in their rooms appeared openmouthed at the top of the stairs, while the others came belting up from the kitchens. Despite the fact that he was playing classical, *"Sur un Marché Persan"* ("At a Persian Market") sort of thing, and that you had to hum him popular tunes, you can guess the rest. Until then, the only one who used the piano was Magali, who could thump out a few tunes, or the twins, on busy evenings. For music, we had the latest record, with a whole battery of loudspeakers behind the drapes, but Madame, who was very particular about furnishing, said that there wasn't a famous establishment that didn't have its grand piano and besides, it was a good place to put the gladiolus.

And so Tony became our pianist, which got rid of one headache, since now my room was free during my work hours. Everybody, including Madame, was happy, and it was much more fun for him than being at loose ends or climbing up the curtains of the four-poster. As he was born difficult, and at first he fretted over living off my money, it also gave him the satisfaction of being able to say that by playing the piano he was earning his board and keep. Although I had the means. During that period when love made me radiant, every night I brought in more than a typist earns in a month, all in three tricks, by picking and choosing. All it would take was for a hedgehopper to land, aiming at the girls, and I would bust the piggybank (???).

The hardest thing with Tony was to stop him from going out. He kept saying, "But it's Beau Masque they're looking for, not me!" To hear him talk, he could even step outside the door and find himself face-to-face with Lieutenant Malignaud—whom he called Malignoble—and the latter would go right on walking without taking any notice of a merrymaker who had just got his rocks off or more likely had been thrown out before he'd even said hello. I said to him, "What about the bride you kidnapped? She might still be in town!" And he replied, rolling his eyes to the heavens that I could be so dumb, "She was someone capable of killing me, not turning me in." Maybe. In any case, Madame and the girls were utterly convinced that he was Beau Masque, and I couldn't imagine them calmly continuing their game of rummy if he said, with his finger on the brim of his hat, "Ciao, I'm going out for a breath of air." Even if only half of them had enough between the ears for the penny to drop, and two of them nothing at all, there was still Zozo, Michou, and Madame, who would smell a rat. But try talking sense into a claustrowhatsit.

At first he made do with the balcony. He would count the clouds, the boats lying high and dry at low tide, he would fill his lungs. After five minutes, he'd come back and lie on the bed, his head cradled in his arms, even unhappier than before. He didn't feel like smoking, or drinking, or reading the story of a film, or talking, even less like having a romp. A bear.

And then, one evening when the sun was all red on the horizon, he climbed over the balustrade and let himself hang above the garden. I pleaded with him. It was too high for him to drop down without breaking something. He mumbled something I didn't understand and let go. He fell into the border without doing himself any more damage than would a cat. He looked at me from down there with one finger on his lips, and he went off, keeping close to the walls, to live his life.

I quickly slipped on a raincoat and some shoes, not even any panties, and I raced down the stairs four at a time. I ran haphazardly through Saint-Julien, and then down to the port, and I went into the Neptune and the other cafés to see if he was there. He wasn't anywhere. I turned back and I began running aimlessly again, praying to the Holy Virgin like crazy.

I found him when it was dark, when the holiday makers were sitting down to supper, sitting on the edge of a fountain all by himself and lost in thought. I didn't go up to him. I watched him without moving for a minute, just for the pleasure of seeing him. I think he was floating an empty matchbox in the water. In the end, he became aware of my presence, on the other side of the square we were in, and came over to me, his hands in his pockets, kicking a pebble. I flung myself at him, I told him I had been afraid that he had left for ever. He laughed, kissed my hair, and hugged me very tight. The words I hadn't heard when he jumped over the balcony were: "Find a rope so that I can come back in."

We strolled to the end of the pier, our arms around each other's waists, without meeting many people, and as he realized I wasn't wearing anything under my raincoat, he walked faster and faster as we approached the lighthouse. He pinned me to the wall in the dark porch, and I wrapped my arms and legs around him, below that huge light sweeping the ocean, and my heart was thumping, thumping.

We went back to the Queen of Hearts the easy way: through the door. When Jitsu opened it, he revealed nothing more than his usual smile. I must say that he wasn't blind and that he had seen the real Beau Masque more closely than the others. He had known something fishy was going on from the first evening. As for Madame, she was in the kitchens. I left Tony and went down to find her without getting changed.

She was in tears. She was chopping onions. She didn't even look up to see who had come in. I said, "Madame, I lied to you. Tony isn't Beau Masque." She replied, without even looking up from what she was doing, "Thank you for telling me. It's an open secret. I think even Magali knows." Magali was the thickest of the lot of us. As Madame didn't add anything, I asked her, in a much lower voice, "Are you going to kick him out?" Sigh. "Have I kicked him out? Well, then?"

After a moment, sensing that I couldn't bring myself to move, she said, "Go and get dressed, you'll be late." I went back to the stairs, but I couldn't stop myself from asking, "Why didn't you?" She answered in a tired voice, "Would you have let him go alone? So?"

The matter never came up again. Life was a dream and I dreamed twenty-four hours a day beside my man. I can still see him, sitting at the piano under the bright lights of the big drawing room, in his white dinner jacket, his hair plastered down like George Raft, a relaxed smile disclosing his pearly teeth, as beautiful as an ad. His eyes sometimes met mine across the swirling of a waltz and it was as if we were alone in the world, guardians of a mystery that belonged to nobody but us. In short, I was madly in love with him. Even when I was in bed with someone, I thought about him, I concentrated to hear the music from downstairs, going "Ssh!" if my athlete felt talkative.

The best time was in the early hours of the morning, when the clients had left and Jitsu switched off the lights. We just kept one light on the piano, and in that little circle of light, for the few of us who stayed to listen to him, Tony, in his shirt sleeves, with blue and gold armbands above his elbows, a cigar in his mouth, a bottle of bourbon in front of him, would play those black American tunes full of nostalgia. My favorite piece was "I'll Carve Your Name on All the Trees," and he played it as if it had been written for me. I stood behind him, my hands on his shoulders, proud that he belonged to me, and sometimes, because something or other would set him off, he would confide his secrets to us, in a voice that went with the music.

He would say, "The first woman I loved, the very first, was when I was nine years old, in Marseilles, when at last they took me away from that boarding school I was always running away from and sent me to a Jesuit school. I remember, it all began one winter morning, at the very moment when the shadow of our teacher, who was pacing up and down the classroom, his hands in the sleeves of his cassock, fell over me. . . ."

Rouen, February 1431

As on each day when there was a hearing, the prisoner was freed from the heavy block of wood fettering her legs, but the chains that were never removed from her hands and ankles were left.

Pushing her out of her dungeon, to the sarcastic comments of their round-helmeted accomplices, two of the English guards, armed with pikes, pushed her ahead of them along the long subterranean passages.

She walked courageously, tall and upright, in dark, masculine attire, her face still childlike under her short hair, dragging her irons across the cobblestones. Around her neck hung a cross, the type made in Lorraine, the polished metal of which reflected, every now and again, in a sudden flash, the flame of a torch hanging on the wall.

Once again she climbed the stairs of bitterness. She saw the door of the tribunal of infamy open. As she entered this room, which they had chosen in order to keep her better hidden from the eyes of honest people, it took her a moment to grow accustomed to the daylight, and it was a pitiful sight to see the wretchedness in which the cowardly guards kept her. Nevertheless, alone at last, she boldly walked the last steps that brought her face-to-face with her judges.

Grouped around the ignoble Bishop Cauchon and his damned soul L'Estivet were at least forty assessors—the number varied each day—as well as men of arms and men of the cloth, all intent on her downfall out of their fury at having feared her when she was in battle, or for the powerful Cardinal Winchester's money. All except one, whom we will talk about shortly.

That day, made cautious by the replies she had given at the previous hearing, the bishop did not question the girl himself, he had someone else ask her the treacherous question that could be her downfall: "Joan, are you certain that you are in a state of grace?"

To which she replied simply, in the soft, penetrating voice that had once given strength to the gentle Dauphin: "If I am not, may God make me so. If I am, may God keep me so."

A long murmur ran through the audience at these words. L'Estivet was unable to conceal his confusion and Cauchon his anger. A little astonished, but regaining her spirits a little from having given such a good answer, Joan looked about her, and it was then that her eyes encountered for the first time the feverish gaze of the only ally she had in the room.

It was the fourth hearing, on February twenty-fourth, and as far as I knew, a Saturday, said this young man with a good memory. The moment the girl's eyes, which were not blue as people claimed, but the color of hazelnuts flecked with gold, rested on me, I understood that my life belonged to her, that I would never cease defending her and keeping the vow I had made on my sword.

For the time being, I had to wait, and the impatience, the grief I felt for her, enraged me. When they asked her age, she answered, "About nineteen years old." That was also the age I gave myself. I saw myself as tall and sturdy, as I am today, but poorly clad, as one can imagine a boy brought up fatherless, who had traveled on foot from his distant Provence, with no other worldly goods but the sword mentioned earlier, with no other comfort but the motto engraved on the blade:

AD MAJOREM DEI GLORIAM

Having arrived in Rouen, which was full of Englishmen and Burgundians, two days earlier, I managed to slip into the square with the monks, my face concealed under the large hood of a coat, like Errol Flynn in *Robin Hood*. At night I slept in the castle, sitting in a dark corner of the courtyard, eating whatever the servants gave me.

I saw Joan again at the next interrogation, and once again she noticed me. Then I came there every day, mingling with the crowd, and although I could never be in the same seat, she was able to find me at a glance. Her expression conveyed the trust she had in me, and although I was still of little use to her, seeing me seemed to be a help in itself.

Alas, from March tenth, under some lying pretext but with the sole aim of tormenting Joan even more, the vile Cauchon moved the location of the hearings. I learned from the various rumors that he would interrogate her in prison henceforth, with only two assessors and two witnesses.

Parted from her, I was even more aware of the danger she was in than before. Throwing caution to the winds, I forged a note signed by the bishop: he allowed the prisoner to receive a visit in her cell from a canon who would hear her confession. That same night I knocked on the door of the dungeon in whose bowels Joan was imprisoned. When the guard opened up, having glanced over the letter, he stepped aside to let me pass, and I understood that I was in God's hands. I went down the steps, and putting my faith in Him, I arrived directly in the damp passage leading to her cell. Five armed guards watched the poor girl day and night, never leaving her a moment's peace, but I was aware of that, as was everyone who lived in the castle, and I had chosen to arrive at the hour when there were only three of them, the other two having gone to get the soup with the five helmets.

Once again I showed the counterfeit note. Gripping my sword under my cape, I listened to the guards palavering for a long while, without understanding their gibberish, for at the time I only knew our language and a little Latin. But I said that the heavens were with me. The one who had the keys opened up the cell in the end, undoing several locks, and suddenly I found myself standing before the girl, her self-appointed champion.

How can I ever forget that moment? Imagine a dark room, with stone walls oozing damp, and no other furniture but a rough wooden bed, no other light than a narrow vent level with a courtyard where no one ever ventured. The young girl from Lorraine, in the masculine clothing which I had always seen her wear, and encumbered by her chains, was standing beneath this vent, her beautiful face raised toward the only sliver of sky that she could see. Turning around at my entrance, she greeted me with a smile of immense relief. I understood that she had never given up hope that I would come.

I flung myself at her feet, without paying any heed to her guards, and cried, "Joan, to come before you, I have transcended the abysses of time. If you go by appearances alone, I haven't even been born yet. I shan't be born for another five hundred years, but I am tormented by your misfortunes to such an extent that I even forget that I myself have suffered solitary confinement and desertion by my nearest and dearest, and I want, contrary to all human reason, to save you!" Far from being offended by this speech, Joan raised her chained hands to my shoulders: "Softly, softly, my lord," she said. "My voices have already informed me of what you have just told me. Go, do God's will."

Upon this order, I kissed the cross with a double horizontal bar that clung around her neck and I stood up, throwing off my monk's cape and revealing my sword to the dumbfounded guards. The narrowness of the cell prevented them from attacking me at the same time or from wielding their pikes correctly. I had soon managed to split open the head of the first one, who died from having exchanged his hat for some broth, and to pierce the heart of the second through a hole in his doublet. I reeled for a moment under the weight of the third, who yelled his head off to raise the alarm, and whom I swung over my shoulders in a desperate effort. He ended up impaled on my sword against a wall that was already spattered with blood, and that is how I left him.

I did not waste a second in grabbing the keys from the one I had killed first, and released Joan from her irons. While I was doing that, on seeing the massacre, she took pity on the souls of her tormentors, saying, "I pleaded on their behalf, but let them go to the devil!"

We left the cell. We were immediately faced with the problem of knowing which way to run. Joan put her soft hand in mine and said, "Let us go boldly the way I was led so many times!" And we set off at a run through the network of corridors beneath the castle. Just as well for us, for we were hardly a lance's throw away when we could already hear a large number of Winchester's soldiers rushing down the stairs to the dungeons. As well as the din of their weapons, the fury of the dogs they brought with them made my blood run cold.

It was a long time before we regained our breath, turning left, then right, in a maze of corridors, lit for a fleeting second by the flame of a torch, and I could sense, courageous as she was, the woman I loved more than anything in the world growing weaker as she clung to my hand.

And then suddenly there was an intersection, and on one side of it we could make out a distant opening into the night, wide enough for a girl's body, and I paused, trembling with anxiety. I had the impression we had put some distance between ourselves and the barking and unruly tumult of the soldiers. I said to Joan in a choked voice, "Go that way. Don't worry about me, I beg you with all my heart. I shall shake off your pursuers." Her sad, beautiful face said no, no, but I took the liberty of pushing her backward and she retreated down one corridor, I down another.

One last time we looked at each other. She said, her voice husky with tears, "My kind companion, my sweet heart, may God, Master of the Universe, watch over you. Already overwhelmed with all the requests I've made for our people, the good and loyal French, may He still grant that I see you again in His kingdom of heaven."

She turned around and fled, her huge shadow sweeping the walls. Then, choking with tenderness and despair, I wished myself good luck and began to run as fast as I could in the opposite direction, pursued by the howling dogs.

By the time he got to the end of his story, Tony had stopped playing the piano for some time. I can picture us all as if we were still there. That night, standing around the lamp were Zozo the black girl, Magali, Michou, and the twins—in short, the regulars—plus Madame, who had come to join us, and even Jitsu. Our emotion made us hold our breath. For a while the only sound was the ticktock of the clock above the bar. My throat hurt from holding back the flood; the others too. At last, Vanessa and Savenna murmured in unison, "Then what?" Tony looked up at us with eyes that were still lost in the Middle Ages. It took time for the question to sink in, then he said, "Then? Then the English didn't want to lose face. *They burned someone else!*" And he slammed his hands down on the keyboard and nearly deafened us for life.

Despite an assuredly remarkable memory, it is doubtful whether Belinda was able to reconstruct her lover's story on her own, at least in the terms in which it is presented above. From having, on another occasion, heard the story myself and from the same lips, I have taken the liberty of combining my memory with hers, in order to reproduce it as faithfully as possible.

(From the notes of Marie-Martine Lepage)

The fact remains that I was crazy about him, to the extent that I was already sinking to the level of a greenhorn: a wedding ring, a little thatched cottage, a hand-knitted layette, a post-office savings book, and all that. He didn't exactly jump for joy when I allowed myself to daydream out loud, but he didn't beat me either. Beau Masque would have killed me.

I gave myself another two years, without balking at the opportunities of looking at the canopy over my bed, before I would say farewell to the girls and set up in business as an honest woman. I didn't need to sound out my Tony to know what would make him happiest. A movie theater somewhere, or rather two, to give him somewhere to walk to; otherwise he would let himself grow fat in a reserved seat. He was as crazy about movies as I was about him. Every afternoon, as soon as he was able to go out, come rain, wind, or hail, he would go to see a movie. As there was only one theater in Saint-Julien, he had to put up with seeing the same movie three times in three days. It was lucky that in those days there was still a double bill. I swear, without having seen them, I know them by heart: *The Crowd Roars* with Robert Taylor, *Ramona* with Don Ameche and Loretta Young, *Marie Antoinette* with Norma Shearer, *Marked Woman* with Bette Davis, *They Made Me a Criminal* with John Garfield and Luise Rainer as a Chinese girl, the Dead-End Kids, Dorothy Lamour and Ray Milland in a thing on a desert island; if I had time, I could write a book about it. In the early hours, when we went up to our room, nothing more to be said, he always serviced me real quick, but as soon as it was over he would launch into telling me about his films, over and over again, saying, "Are you asleep?" if I closed one eye. The next day I had bags under my eyes.

In my free time, I looked after his suits, I ironed his shirts until there wasn't a crease, I polished his shoes, I ran into town when I saw that he was about to run out of shaving cream or cigarettes, I did everything a woman should do for the man she loves. Result: I was blissfully happy. I couldn't swear that one or another of the girls had never thought of stealing him from me, perhaps he even let his gaze dwell on Lulubelle's thighs or Michou's tits, but it was harmless; I would have had to be pathologically jealous to believe he was the sort to abuse my hospitality. Besides, when I say he used to look at what he shouldn't, I'm exaggerating; he could hardly blindfold himself every time he met a naked girl in the corridor. It's all very well being in a classy establishment; I may as well have bought him a white stick and a little dog right away.

No. Except at the movies, he was never seen with anyone else but me. On Sundays he would take me to lunch at the Grand Large, like Beau Masque, and we sat almost at the same table. We had lobster in Sancerre, everything the same. In the afternoon, a stroll beneath the palm trees, along the seafront. I would walk three feet behind him, perfectly happy, with a silk dress and matching parasol and wide-brimmed hat, only the color was different. Tony preferred me in pastels. He pulled me along in his wake like a king his queen, him in a white suit and boater, with swaying shoulders and a Havana cigar; just looking at him made my knees turn to jelly.

Besides, someone who hasn't experienced it could never believe that to do the same things, in the same places, with one Lothario or another would be so different, like day and night, chalk and cheese, hot and cold. And it's nothing to do with time. I lived with Beau Masque for two whole years before the state snatched him from me. With Tony, the way I'm going on, anyone would think we were heading for a golden wedding anniversary. Poor old us. From beginning to end, the whole thing lasted four weeks, twenty-six days to be precise; I later had the time to count them.

Tony also taught me to swim. He knew how. And it was even bang in the middle of a session that things changed. I didn't realize it right away, and yet a weird old storm was brewing in the sky that afternoon, as though it was doing everything it could to warn me.

We were both in the room, me on my stomach on a stool, in skimpy panties and patent-leather court shoes, doing breaststroke movements the way he had shown me, and he was judging the effect from his armchair, smoking his cigar. From time to time he said, "Smoother. Gently." He never raised his voice, he never got angry. So I was rowing like a galley slave, displaying my arms and legs, my back arched, my chin in the air, my eyes gazing into the wonderful future when I would at last be able to do something else on a beach other than get sunburned, when suddenly there was a clap of thunder outside, so loud that I almost went sprawling. Tony replied, "Come in!" I thought it was a joke, but the door opened and all the rotten luck I can possibly have deserved in my life invaded the room.

It was Jitsu, accompanied by a girl I've got to describe, otherwise the rest won't be believable; people'll think I've got a screw loose.

General appearance: a country bumpkin, and even the complete country bumpkin, the typical country bumpkin, the caricature of a country bumpkin. In fact, she came from a farm, you couldn't invent someone like her. Hair: dirty. Very dirty, because she had masses of it, and black as a Gypsy's. Her eyes: you couldn't see them; she stared at the floor as if she only had one thing in mind, to be swallowed up by it so that you couldn't see anything of her at all. Age: anything from twelve to eighty? She had no makeup on and wore an old, shapeless coat that was too big for her and hid the rest, except her feet. In fact, she was three years my junior, I later discovered. To complete the picture, espadrilles that she'd have been better off swapping for something out of a rubbish dump, a granny straw hat, a boiled cardboard suitcase that looked as if it had been tied up with string and boiled, and out with the handkerchiefs. She was a real Little Orphan Annie; it was pathetic.

I stayed on my stool, like a statue of a frog, but Tony bounded across the room, looking all excited. He spouted a heap of thank-yous to Jitsu to take his mind off being pushed outside, and he leaned up against the closed door, whether to stop Jitsu from coming back in or to prevent the darling from running away, I don't know. As I was still watching all this goggle-eyed, he said, clearing his throat, "This is Salomé. She's someone who did me a favor, and for me, that's sacred!"

I got up, tits bared, a little wary all the same, and went over to get a better look at her. She kept her eyes fiercely fixed on the floor, standing there like a chrysanthemum that hasn't got long to live, but Tony suddenly grew a bit bolder, and then not just a bit: "I wanted to give you a surprise. She'll be your stand-in, she'll make money for us! You know what, Belinda? We'll be able to buy our movie theater sooner, all you've got to do is teach her!"

I was flabbergasted. Even my friend from Perros-Guirec's pimp had done things in style when he wanted to chat me up; he drove me around in his front-wheel drive for three hours, bought double ice creams, showed me the photo of his poor mother, acted as though butter wouldn't melt in his mouth so well that in the end, when I said no, I actually took myself for a virgin. Tony, I have to say, had not shown much enthusiasm until then for taking over the loot, it was even a real pain trying to slip a couple of louis in his pocket when he went out to the movies. Seems as if it's a sudden urge, or that the more ignorant a man is, the more nerve he's got.

In any case, I hadn't come back down to earth before he was already saying, "Good. Now, if you don't want to, we won't have her." Sharp, petulant, incomprehensible as a letter from the bailiff.

He went over to the wardrobe, just like that, took out a white sport shirt, the pants and moccasins he wore that first evening, and there they were, all on the bed. I said, "What are you doing?" The only reply was the rain beating on the windows like a drum. He took off his terry-cloth bathrobe. He slipped on the pants. I repeated, as if it wasn't obvious, "Tony, please, what are you doing?" He looked at me as he did up his fly. "Thank you for everything, Belinda. I shall always regret losing you. But I can't live in this . . . this . . ." He couldn't find a filthy enough word. He said, "Not for two, three years, or even longer! I can't! I can't!" Shit. There were tears in his eyes, I swear there were. He turned around to put on his sport shirt. I could interrogate the clod standing there with my eyes till the cows came home, to try and understand what was happening to me, but she didn't move a muscle, she stood there like a lump. She could have said the first thing that came into her head, that she didn't want to cause any trouble, that she had just dropped in for a chat, for a pee, but not a word. And you see how sneaky he was. His back to me, with that voice of a guy who doesn't believe it but you never know, he said, "But I fixed things up nicely. As soon as the Bonbonnière was free, I thought of Lison." One translation of that, I understood: the Bonbonnière had been Estelle's room; she was a funny girl who had left us, feeling very sorry for herself, the Sunday before, to go and work in Le Havre, where she had a baby with a wet nurse. The other riddle wasn't difficult: the shy clodhopper had a real first name like everyone else, and it was Elise.

I went over to him, I put my arms around him from behind. My forehead on his shoulder, I asked him sweetly, "Who was Salomé?" He understood that I was prepared to argue; he sat down all smiles on the edge of the four-poster. He said, "A dancer in the Bible. She wanted the head of a guy who yelled in the desert and who ate grasshoppers. They made a film about it." And immediately afterward: "You only need to whisper a word in Madame's ear, she doesn't refuse you anything."

I looked at this Lison, I walked slowly over toward her, racking my brains as quickly as I could. Under her coat, she looked about as well made as a sack of potatoes; I wouldn't have bet a penny on her chances. And besides, I thought I was cunning, too. I leaned over to see her eyes from below. They were black, stubborn, silent. I asked her, perhaps just to hear the sound of her voice, "And what do you think about all this?" And then, let idiot be my epitaph, she's the one who got the better of me. She answered, without batting an eyelid, so quietly that it sounded like a breeze, "I've always dreamed of being a whore."

I went over to lie on my stomach on the stool again and I went on practicing the breaststroke so as to look busy, and then I stopped and sighed. "If she's only a stand-in and she splits everything three ways, we can try. Let's say for a week."

Do I need to paint a picture? The massacre didn't take long. The words were barely out of my mouth when the poor creature finally looked up out of the corner of one eye, just one, and gave the sharpest, most hypocritical look ever seen. When she took off her coat, I swore I would never buy another potato without taking it out of its sack and I advised Tony to go for a stroll. When I got her out of the housewife's apron she was wearing underneath, next to her skin, I had my first doubts as to the kind of favor she could have done for a pianist who wasn't blind. Never mind my generosity: the bath, the shampoo, the lavender soap, my *Quelques Fleurs*, my makeup, even my toothbrush. When I offered her some underwear, she said, "Thank you, I've got some." She undid the string around her suitcase—with hands, let it be said in passing, that hardly bore the marks of working on a farm—and she unpacked a ball dress made of silk chiffon, the same color as Lison's skin, with high-heeled shoes to match. Once dressed, she was still stark naked. I asked her, "Where did you get that?" She said, "Someone on the way." And as I wanted to chat a little, and for her to wait until the next day at least to make her debut: "We'll have to put the boss in the picture. I'll manage fine by myself."

I swear, men are dumb. Tony must have been dumb to imagine that degenerate needed educating. From that first evening, the clients who came out of her room—I refrain from saying her screwing parlor out of respect for poor Estelle—looked as if they'd just seen the devil. They came downstairs toward the bright lights keeping close to the walls. She turned her nose up at nothing, you hear me, nothing, neither the manner nor the number. At least once a night, she went upstairs with a threesome, and Madame, who managed to persuade a regular to confide in her after a lot of pleading, told Zozo the black girl and me, "There are things I didn't even know existed!"

What's more, I'm sure of it, Lison wasn't pretending to be in seventh heaven. You only had to look at her when she appeared at the top of the big staircase after the battle, in her long, transparent chiffon, her eyes sparkling and her hair still damp on her forehead, prouder than an empress. As for me, a shiver ran down my spine. After remaining terrifyingly motionless for a moment, she would come downstairs step-by-step and move among the people without seeing anybody, as if magnetized by the piano. If Tony wasn't already smoking, I could bet my rotten life that she would take a Camel from the pack in front of him, light it with the Cartier lighter I had lovingly chosen in Royan, and smear lipstick over more than half of it before putting it in his mouth. And all that, of course, with airs that made me puke, because someone once said that she looked like Hedy Lamarr, and knowing full well that I never took my eyes off her.

Then she would whisper in the guy's ear, without missing a chance to rub herself up against him, and he would suddenly start playing another tune. He would strike up a sort of bolero that she had brought in her skull along with her evil spells, "No Use Trying, It's Possible," and she would begin dancing all by herself in front of him, for him, and everybody would make room to gawk at her. She raised her arms, spread her legs, wiggled her belly and her ass, and shook her black mane: the effect that created, it's not up to me to say; it was unlikely that I'd be turned into a hat stand, but even as a woman, even though I'm hopeless at catechism, I found her as filthy as sin.

If I say I was jealous, nobody would believe me. She did everything she could to drive me crazy. When she came into my room to give Tony her earnings, she called me "the Old Girl." Twenty-four years old next month, I pointed out to her. She replied, "I meant 'the Veteran.'" Sucker that I am, I flew at her, I pulled out a handful of her hair. If Tony hadn't stepped in, she'd have ended up bald. Then—it was on the third day—she called me "the Old Whore," but why bother to answer an idiot? With her, it was perfectly simple, if you didn't call her Salomé, you were talking to somebody else.

The fact remains that she purposely handed her money to Tony, not to me. All her money, in fact; avarice was the only fault she didn't have. She retorted, the first day, because he insisted, and so did I, that she keep a third for herself as agreed: "It's already wonderful that I'm being fed for doing nothing." Honestly. But that didn't stop her from asking how much I'd earned, just to emphasize that she'd brought in more dough. There was a lot I could have taught her, firstly that novelty wears off faster than you can use up a roll of toilet paper, but I'm not vulgar, and in any case, her money went into the same bank as mine; it would be the same color when I retired from the game. She may well turn so many tricks at once that people will begin to mistake her for a dartboard; that day will come sooner rather than late.

But then, it wasn't her stupidity that made me mad, it was the change I noticed in Tony, without being able to do anything about it. During my arguments with her, he didn't know what to do with himself. When we were alone, he avoided my eyes. If I kissed his neck, like her, he moved away. In bed, let's forget it. I didn't dare make a fuss. Every morning of that shitty week, I cried into my pillow before falling asleep.

On the day before the last day, my head was in such a spin I felt like banging it against the wall. I asked him, "Tony, my Tony, if there's something bothering you, even if you have to hurt me, tell me what it is." He pushed me away, without being brutal, simply with a deep sigh: "Be a good girl, Belinda. You make me tired." I said, "You see, you don't love me anymore!" He replied, without looking at me, "It's not that. I can't stand this room, this house anymore. I'm tired of everything." I retorted, "Even your Gypsy?" He gave me a look I had never seen before, a spiteful look, but it only lasted a second. He shrugged and said, "Leave Salomé alone, she's not to blame. I'm trying to tell you that I'm not made for this sort of life."

With these words, he went out to see that afternoon's movie. Later I was overcome with suspicion: supposing he had pretended to leave and had come back up noiselessly to join his Lison? I went to the door of the Bonbonnière. I couldn't hear anything. I opened the door. She was lying naked on the bed, her chin in her hands, looking at the stills of one of the movies Tony had talked about. I don't know if she had even learned how to read. She looked up, and as my thoughts were probably written all over my face, she said snootily, "He isn't here. He wouldn't be that stupid." I left, but that last phrase haunted me until the next day. I went over all the places where they could meet outside the house.

People will wonder: the week was up, why didn't I ask Madame to throw the floozy out? I did. Madame gave me exactly the same reply as when it had been a question of my future: "Would he let her go alone? Well then . . ." So I began to cry on a chair in the drawing room, and Jitsu, terribly sorry about all that, kept saying, "There, there, Mademoiselle Belinda, don't get yourself in such a state."

And then came that afternoon of horror. I was already no longer myself. I lay prostrate at the foot of the bed, without washing, without doing my hair, in my black silk negligee. I filled an ashtray with cigarettes that I had stubbed out as soon as I lit them. Tony had gone out, supposedly to see *Marie Waleska*. It was the movie he had seen the day before. He said, as he got ready, "There's nothing else on, and I'm suffocating here." At the last minute I noticed that he was wearing the pants and moccasins he had worn on his arrival, and the same sport shirt. He said, "I feel comfortable in these. I'm still allowed to dress as I please, aren't I?" And he had slammed the door so as to leave on a bad note, because afterward you have fewer regrets for being so rotten.

By the hour when everybody at the Queen of Hearts was already getting dressed for the evening, he had not come back. Beyond my balcony, I could see the big red ball of the sun descending over the ocean. I couldn't bear it any longer. I went to have a look in the Bonbonnière. Salomé wasn't there. I went down to the lounge. It was deserted. I went into the kitchens. Nobody. I was shivering from head to foot. It felt as if everything was going too fast, that it was too late to stop things. I opened a cupboard. I took out the rifle that Jitsu used in the winter to shoot ducks. I found the cartridges next to it.

I went into the garage. I looked inside the Chenard. Then I walked around the garden, perspiring and freezing in my black negligee, clutching the rifle. I was blinded by tears. I went out of the gate and crossed the road. I wandered around the pinewood for a while and the dunes that stretched between the Queen of Hearts and the ocean, then I don't know how, I was suddenly sure I knew where they were. I ran, losing my slippers, wanted to pick them up, then thought, screw it.

I ran down to the long, deserted beach. I walked in the sand toward a hut made of planks and wattle, where, in the high season, they sold drinks and chips. The whole sky was red. I staggered as if drunk, I was fighting back my tears. When I reached it, I wiped my face with my forearm. I think I didn't want them to see that I was crying. I also think I asked the Virgin to stop me from creating a tragedy and she begged me to throw the gun far away, but I could hear muffled noises inside, and I kicked the door down.

Tony was there all right, just like in the unbearable visions my jealousy invented, but the woman who was in his arms, and whom he was impaling standing up, that crimson, bleating artificial blonde, wasn't Salomé. You'll never guess who it was. I didn't recognize her right away myself: Yackety-Yack, the hairdresser from Saint-Julien.

They hadn't bothered to get undressed. Her dress hitched up to her navel, she was still wearing her wide hat, and her Sunday-best panties were caught around her ankle. As for him, pants undone, he was supporting her buttocks with both hands so that she could enjoy it more. Rooted to the spot, they looked at me as if I'd been let loose from hell. That's what I probably looked like.

I shouted, "Get out of here!" He obeyed me with a shifty, mocking grin, and as he shut up shop, moving as far away from the gun as he could, he shouted, "Listen, it's not at all what you think!" As for the other bitch, I took no notice of her. I don't know at what point she ran away, or in which direction. I only had eyes for Tony. He retreated across the sand and I followed him step-by-step, and his face, through my tears, was just a pale blob against the red sky.

I shouted, "Can't you see how you're hurting me? Can't you see it?" He waved his hands frantically in front of him to stop me from shooting. Begging me, he called me Emma. I swear he did. He didn't know who I was anymore. He thought he was in the same nightmare as the month before.

I yelled, "Belinda, dammit!" And I shoved the barrel of the gun into his chest. He almost fell. Panic made him say whatever came into his head. "All right, all right. Have it your way. But listen to me! Ten minutes ago I didn't even know that broad!" He held his left hand out to me to show me his wedding ring. "She was only bringing me news of my wife!"

I froze. "Because you're married as well?" He nodded; he, too, was glued to the spot, and I think he even attempted an idiotic smile, as if saying that to me made everything all right, absolved him from everything. I fired. He fell backward, his legs and arms strangely twisted, his chest covered with blood. I'm sure he was dead before he even touched the sand. He didn't shout, or if he did, the sound was drowned in the noise of the shot. If someone did shout, it seemed to me that it was a long time afterward. Perhaps the hairdresser, running as far away as she could, perhaps just the sea gulls. I don't know. Perhaps me, inside.

I can't tell you either how far from the water's edge I killed him, or whether the tide was low or high, no details like that. And it would be pretty daft to think that it occurred to me to move the body so that it would be washed out to sea. I wouldn't even dare touch it. I looked at him, lying at my feet, my mind a blank. I looked at him and I was cold. That was all.

Then I told myself that my life was over. I hugged the rifle, and as I didn't know where to go or what to do, I went home.

Zozo

THAT'S NOT WHAT HAPPENED AT ALL.

First of all, he wasn't called Tony, or Vincent or whatever. His name was Francis. He was a student.

Second, Beau Masque was never in prison. No chance of that, he was such a home bird. True, he was called up, but at the same time as everyone else. I heard he was a corporal. After that I didn't hear a thing.

To crown it all, I'm not black. Every whorehouse had to have a black girl in those days, but there were more brothels in the Charente than there were girls in Senegal. So they used to paint me with a walnut-stain mixture every morning. I even had rather a sweet little kisser like that, all you could see was my teeth.

So either Belinda's lying or I am. I wonder where on earth she got all that from. She must be blabbing to get attention, or else there's some money to be made—she always was a penny-pincher.

The Queen of Hearts, for example—the chandeliers, the concert piano, the clients in tails, the champagne, and the petits-fours— never saw anything of the sort. It was a nineteenth-century villa, degenerate-bourgeois style, with more brambles in the garden than palm trees. You caught your foot in them on the way out. And we couldn't go out when we felt like it. Only for the decarade, which means every ten days, and even then . . . It wasn't Paris, or even Nantes. After we'd had a little drink at the port, sticking our tongues out at curious onlookers who stood round gawking at us, there was nothing else to do. I got so pissed off that I preferred not to go out. I'd stare at my white body in the mirror to get to know myself again, but that got boring. There was nobody waiting for me outside. I didn't even know the man who sold me in the first place; that's what happens to fallen women.

I've seen a few brothels in my time and that one was no worse than any of the others. At least, when you opened your window, there was the good smell of the sea. You knew everyone there—the notary, the chemist, the butcher. Fathers brought their sons along when they were old enough. The drawing room smelled of furniture polish. The famous piano was a reject from the auction rooms; it was thrown in for free when we bought the clock for over the bar. It was always whatever time you liked, it had lost its hands. You see how well I remember. A piano upright as the law, full of wood-worm, it had been painted white to jazz it up. It had lost so many teeth it could no longer even bite. It was opened for the twins when traveling salesmen dropped in. They'd dress up as little girls, with white socks, and bows in their hair, and play the first exercise from the Pink Manual with four fingers. Depressing. We consoled our-selves with sparkling wine. For the regulars, it was the white wine from the local cooperative. *Les Caves du Soleil*, it said on the label. We never served anything else.

And as for Madame. I must be dreaming. She left the idle life of the colonies to become a brothel keeper in Périgueux. Then she came into an inheritance from her brother, a dealer in Pineau, the Charentes liqueur. She was still in her thirties, and not bad, except that she dressed like a whore to throw people off the scent. She wasn't a bad woman, but she had her good days and her off days. On the good days, she ignored us completely.

Belinda's stories really give me the creeps. I'm not for hanging nutcases, but if ever I bump into her again, I'm keeping out of her way. Otherwise it makes me laugh, like all the rest—fairy-tale dresses, rooms with net curtains and steambaths. Luckily you never come across anything like the joint she describes, otherwise we'd all have to deliver our own mail: there wouldn't be a single girl left at the post office to sell stamps. Another thing, so that nobody dies ignorant. There weren't ten of us at the Queen of Hearts, there were seven, like the Seven Deadly Sins: Belinda, seeing as that's what you call her—to us she was Jo, or Georgette—Michou, Magali, the twins, and me, plus Lison, who came later.

Lison had left her husband, a blacksmith twice her age, because he didn't speak to her anymore. Why he wouldn't speak to her she didn't say. I never saw her dance anything but the tango, the fox-trot, or the waltz, with tiny steps, like the rest of us. No better, no worse. She was a pain in the ass on slack evenings, because she always wanted to poke her nose into your business when you were in the middle of things. Apart from that, she was a good girl. More than once she and I went up together with a client whose eyes were bigger than his belly. Never any trouble over sharing the honors.

As for Georgette, nobody wanted anything to do with her. She got everyone's back up. I'm not aggressive but I didn't like her airs and graces when we were with the john. She'd make us waste ages just haggling over the price. She was a good-looker, with green peepers that would drive a priest to drink, but she was stuck-up and spiteful as well as stingy. If you could round up all the girls who were there in those days, they'd say the same.

Now, at that time—ah! I'm getting there. Belinda doesn't half go to a lot of trouble to mix up the years in her story. I only heard of one breakout from the citadel during my time there. It's true that the soldiers came and searched the house. In the middle of the night, correct. But either I'm the one who's gaga or the uniforms and puttees were khaki, not blue, as I remember. Blue had been abolished long before.

In my opinion, although anyone can be mistaken, it was a few days before the war, at the end of August, in the year of the mobilization. I remember blue-, white-, and red-striped posters. Poland, the Maginot Line, that's all people talked about. All our customers left, so did Jitsu.

And he was another one—what a nasty piece of work. Vicious as the clap, he made holes in the walls to spy on us in the nude. He used to dress in Japanese clothes with a headband around his forehead like in Georgette's fairy tales, but when we gave him a clip around the ears to teach him some manners, he would cry. As for the thought of him standing up to a man! He cried even more when he left for the army. The day before, we drew lots to see who would give him a fond farewell. Magali drew the shortest straw. He was in and out so quickly that she didn't feel a thing. He was so disappointed that she did the necessary so that at least he'd have something to remember. Afterward he used to write her letters that were enough to make you take out fire insurance. I don't know if he used to enjoy Madame's favors. Perhaps she had her perversions, too. So you see, I do have a memory for dates.

I was getting on to twenty-three. I arrived at the Queen of Hearts before any of the others. Sixteen years old, without protection, and I'd already known two brothels. I took everything in my stride, except for my little black ass, which looked funny. Always happy. Small tits and matchstick thighs were in fashion. I got on all right, never any trouble. I felt a bit lonesome sometimes, but everybody has their troubles and it's best not to dwell on them. I can't think of anything more to say about myself. Oh! Yes. My name's Suzanne. I don't know why zey called me Zozo.

I saw Francis for the first time on a weeknight, around midnight. He stayed at the bar. Madame poured him a glass of white wine or something. The place was crowded. She left him standing there, without boasting about the virtues of any of her girls. We were all already hitched. I noticed him because he was very tall and new. His hair was plastered down and he had a side part, a tight suit, a still little collar, and a string tie. After that I didn't look at him anymore. He must have left while I was turning a trick.

Two or three days later he came back. It was a Friday, our worst evening. We latched on to the ones who weren't sure, especially when the end of the holidays coincided with the beginning of something else, even if we didn't know what, and it wasn't hard to figure out that our little sisters in the East were going to have more work than us. At around eleven o'clock, Madame had collared the young man at the bar—anyone would think it was for herself. A waste of energy. He didn't take his nose out of his glass and kept his back to the room. He paid and left. I was in the middle of harpooning a skipper from Saint-Julien, otherwise I'd have cornered him before he got to the door. He didn't look like a turkey. I told myself that perhaps the girl he wanted wasn't available. The first time, they often came with a set idea. I looked to see who was missing. We were all downstairs except Georgette.

The next evening, same scenario, moth-eaten suit, end of the bar. Madame winked at me to look after him. Just as I was about to join him, he gave a sidelong glance at the part of the room where his beloved was laughing her head off on the knees of a shop owner. She was twanging the elastic of her suspender belt like you wouldn't believe. I said to the handsome mysterious stranger, "Do you like Belinda?"

He was like a kid caught stealing cookies. For a moment he refused to look up from his beer.

"Why don't you ask her?"

Sweet as anything. No answer.

"Hey! I'm talking to you!"

He made a little pout, a mixture between a smile and a look of embarrassment, or vice versa. At last I heard the sound of his voice. It was soft, a little husky.

"I don't dare. And besides, she's never alone."

"Do you want me to ask her?"

"Oh no! That's the last thing I want!"

I forgot to press the matter. I asked him if he'd buy a drink. Then, little by little, because he didn't thaw easily, I found out that he was twenty-nine and that his name was Francis, that he studied in Paris something that I didn't care to ask him to repeat, and that he was particularly fond of American movies and mild cigarettes. In spite of himself, he gazed after Belinda's gams as she led her john toward the staircase. I may as well mention in passing that the staircase wasn't at all like she said. It was made of decrepit wood, and it had been painted to look like imitation marble. But what does it matter? With a friendly index finger, I turned my rascal's head toward my African beauty.

I said, "Look, it's unnatural, a big boy like you staying downstairs all the time. Don't you like me?"

I showed him my lovely snowy smile. His wasn't bad either. He shook his head in protest, ashamed at his audacity. I was wearing one of my two favorite outfits. Which was lucky because I didn't have any others. The first was the usual short corselet with mid-thigh stockings, but white, for contrast. The second, the one I was wearing that evening, a two-piece in red raffia that barely covered my treasurers, with matching anklets. A real chocolate delight. Depending on whether they threw me peanuts or not, it was a choice between Tarzan's floozy or Josephine Baker. Except that I frizzed my hair. In short, as my friend was taking a nosedive back into his beer, I leaned over to persuade him from underneath.

"Come on, come upstairs with me. You know that black girls are very sensitive?"

He wagged his chin to say yes. Without looking at me. He was red, bright red. I was expecting him to kick up a fuss for another two hours. Not at all. He drew himself up to his full height, gulped down his beer in one go to give himself courage, and forward.

In the room, just a glance around him, surreptitiously, and he sat on the edge of the bed, his gaze riveted to the floor. To put him at his ease, I closed the window and drew the curtains. It had been terribly hot that day. I made the most of every lull to dive into the washbasin. By the end of the afternoon, I had to be restained. But what does that matter. I took off my flopper-stopper and my grass skirt. My student wouldn't have been out of place at a wake. His hands between his knees, still in his jacket. I had to force him to take it off one sleeve, then the other. I had one doubt. I asked him, so softly that I could hardly hear myself, "You have been with a woman before?"

He simply shook his head. He closed his eyes, he was so ashamed.

"What about your wedding ring?"

"It was my grandfather's. A family heirloom."

I thought it wasn't the best bait for catching girls, that he'd have done better to leave it in a drawer.

He cried out as if he'd been stung: "Never! You'd have to cut off my finger to get it off me!"

Suddenly I saw his eyes at last. Dark, timid, with something in them that wasn't completely all there. The eyes of a kid.

When the regulars brought us their sons to learn a thing or two, I occasionally deflowered one. I did my best because of the present but I didn't like it much. To be honest, I've always preferred mature gentlemen who know how to play their cards. It's less messy and more instructive. As a rule, beginners were given to Magali. She had the knockers and the chubbiness for it, and she liked making them come; you could hear them from downstairs. I have to say, she gave them their money's worth. The whole works, all in one go; when they left, they were set up for life.

But he was nearly thirty, it wasn't the same. I was flabbergasted, that's for sure. He was a good-looking lad, in a way that became fashionable later with Gérard Philippe, he had both arms and legs, he was intelligent because he was studying something—I didn't understand what. And gentle into the bargain. It made you wonder how the hell he could have slipped through the net of all the horny little bitches who can't see any further than a family allowance book.

It does indeed make you wonder. Without wishing to influence anyone's judgment with a personal remark and one that is somewhat embarrassing to my modesty, I have to say that on this particular point Zozo's testimony is, if not a direct lie, at least rather naive. From having met the man she calls Francis well before she did, I think she allowed herself to be taken in by his ploy to get her to take pity, which was consistent with his nature, for he would stop at nothing in order to seduce, even saying that he was unattractive.

(From the notes of Marie-Martine Lepage)

It's true, I had decided to wise him up as quickly as possible and forget about the whole thing. I asked him if it was the room that turned him off. It, too, was all white, for contrast. It was a far cry from the plushness of the other bright spark, but it wasn't ugly. There were a load of knickknacks on the walls to give it a colonial look.

He shrugged, that was all. Then I asked him if it was my body he didn't like, if he was inhibited by exoticism. I said, "It's not hard to remedy, you know. All it takes is three minutes and a bit of soap. Why won't you look at me?"

He swiveled his gaze, but just long enough to see that I wasn't wearing a crinoline. He nodded to show that he liked me. He let out a great sigh.

I knelt on the bed, beside him. I caressed the nape of his neck. I said, "I like little Francis."

"Please don't call me that. Call me Frank, it sounds more virile."

"All right."

I started unbuttoning his shirt. He all but did it up again as I went. To take his mind off the fatal moment, I talked to him: "Perhaps you're thinking too much about your studies?"

"I never think about them."

"Put your hands on me."

He did.

"In ten years I've taken two exams. One in Latin, one in Greek."

"Lower."

He did.

"I'm only good at Latin and Greek. The rest, nil. I'm still in the first year."

"Don't you want to stroke my breasts?"

He did.

"All my school friends have already settled down, married with children. I don't listen to their advice."

"Lie down."

I did the rest.

Fate is quite something. I had never been bowled over by anyone, black or white, and it had to happen with him. Of course, it can happen with certain clients that I forget to count the flies. There are times when despite yourself, you can't help it. But that hadn't happened more than four or five times since I'd been a hooker—in other words, it hadn't happened more than four or five times ever. What's more, each time, no matter how hard I gritted my teeth to hide my plight, the john noticed. I was ashamed to see the cunning glint in his eyes. Afterward I would never go up with him again. I preferred to imagine him and give myself pleasure on my own. A whore has her pride. In any case, it was definitely something other than that kind of mistake that happened with Francis. He clawed at my heart, as they say in books. As soon as he kissed me on the lips, I was done for. I never allowed the others to do that. With him, it happened naturally. When I realized, we'd already been smooching for some time.

Afterward we laughed. About everything—about him, about my lisp, even about nothing. I was afraid one of the girls might hear us as she walked down in the corridor; I told him to "Ssh" or I closed his mouth, and we guffawed even louder. Then we started all over again. He learned faster than with his studies. I had almost forgotten that time passes. When I saw what time it was, we got dressed quickly. I let him go down first so that the girls wouldn't see us together. You can't fool even the naivest of women about that. Even from behind. He wanted to kiss me again as he left the room. I let myself go. I was happy.

All the next day my heart was heavy. That evening I felt choked every time a john came into the drawing room and it wasn't him. I'd heard that screwed-up guys had ended up in the slaughterhouses of North Africa for less than that. I was afraid he wouldn't turn up. I was afraid Madame would look at me if he did turn up. But he'd told me he'd come, and he's one of those rare guys who keep their word.

Luckily, I didn't see him arrive. I was upstairs with a summer-camp instructor. When I came down, Francis was waiting at the bar, in the same place as usual, staring into his beer. I was wearing my white corselet and stockings. I was in a state in case he didn't like me anymore, but Madame signaled to me that he had already booked me.

In the bedroom I was even happier than the day before, and I think he was, too. He loved my white stockings on my black skin, except he would have preferred it the other way around. I kept them on. To tease him, I said he was a little lecher. I saw that he didn't like me saying that. I gave him a load of cuddles to make it up to him. Like in a song that was around at the time, "Melancholy but Not Sad," he said that I didn't understand him, I didn't understand him. The first woman he had loved, the true, the only woman, was his mother. She was very young, very beautiful, and very blond. Of his father, he said, "My monster father." It was in Marseilles, in a dago district. When the monster had abandoned her, with him, six or seven years old, on her hands, without a penny, she had no choice but to work.

Francis said, "She sent me to boarding school but I can't blame her, she had no choice."

Even so, he was as miserable as a dog. He only saw her on Sundays. She would spend a long time in front of the mirror dolling herself up for the walk.

"She would take me to the zoological gardens, at the top of the Boulevard Longchamp. She bought me biscuits and pivolos."

I had no more idea than anyone else what on earth pivolos were. I didn't dare ask him. It was probably a popsicle of some sort. But what did it matter. He watched his mother in her silky underwear slip on her stockings and look at her reflection critically. She would ask his opinion. He would rush toward her and nestle up to her stomach and hug her very tight. She was the most beautiful woman in the world. What am I saying? She was all women rolled into one, the beautiful, the ugly, the good, the bad, the smell of milk, the fragrance of flowers. He hammered it home, as if I was dumb.

"You understand, stockings, lace—it's lovely and feminine, I've never been able to forget that. It's femininity I love, I'm not perverse!"

I told him he wasn't perverse. I would have told him he had a halo above his head if it made him happy. What fascinated me the most in his stories was watching his eyes and his mouth. He could have told me anything. I was goofy about him. Even the first time, you understand. I wished he could have seen me as I really was, white, with soft hair, and then a whole load of stupid things that you think of the minute you're alone. My day off was due the following Thursday. I couldn't stop thinking about it.

He came back a third evening, then a fourth. Madame had kept quiet about him always choosing me and about me staying up there for double the time, but it was close. On Wednesday, just before he showed up, she took me aside behind the bar. My walnut stain must have turned a pale coffee color, I was so anxious.

She said, "Tonight I'll leave you alone, but after that I can't. All the others have noticed. If you carry on, I'll have to denounce you. And I wouldn't like to."

I protested feebly, for appearances, but she snapped back that she'd been on the streets before I was born and not to take her for a greenhorn. She unfolded a fifty-franc note before my eyes. She said that Francis had given it to her the day before.

"Do you want me to spell things out? It's one of the ones I gave you last week!"

As I kept my mouth shut, I didn't even ask her how she'd spotted the miserable few notes she'd let me have; she put a fake sisterly arm around me and said, "Look. You know what we call what you're doing? Giving your savings to a john to pay for the trick? Well, it doesn't have a name. The girls who've done it in the past haven't come back to tell the tale!"

She thought I was horror-stricken, that I was going to have a good cry, and that that would be the end of it. Poor Madame Shitface. Even at twenty-three, even hardened to everything, you don't give a damn what you have to pay to be happy, or to even catch a glimpse of what happiness is. She repeated that she'd let me have Francis that evening. And I was standing there thinking that the next day was my day off. I couldn't see any further ahead than that. The guy who'd had me last time, I didn't know any better than I'd known the one before him. Tomorrow no Tom, Dick, or Harry was going to take away from me. At last, someone would be waiting for me outside, somewhere, with that pang of anxiety that I had felt, and just the thought of it made my heart thump like it would burst.

Life is long and kind, as Francis would say. Troubles pass, like everything else, they leave no more trace than the spring rains. To prove it, I'm still here to talk to you. And that Wednesday evening, in his arms, I laughed as I'd never laughed; I knew I was lucky, whatever happened.

I don't want to talk about it, except for one thing: for the holidays, he had rented, on the other side of the Pointe, an old wine store-house buried among the thickets, and that was where he was going to wait for me the next day. A whore through and through, but I felt as fresh as Danielle Darrieux in a movie; my first date—I haven't forgotten it.

On the dot of nine, I was at Yackety-Yack, the hairdresser's. I had my mop straightened, first the top, then the bottom. The change showed me a bright and breezy kisser in the mirror. I wanted even more rouge on my cheeks and more lipstick. It's unbelievable how dumb you can be, but what fun it is. At eleven o'clock, I bought from the Chic Parisian, opposite the church, undies that'd just kill you, silk stockings, a little bra to let my rosebuds peep out and blossom in the open air. For fear of forgetting a detail of what I'd rehearsed a hundred times in my mind, I'd written everything down on a piece of paper. A Veuve Cliquot, and another one so that it wouldn't be a widow, a pack of Camels and the homemade choc-olates from the pâtisserie Estanque, in the port. When the clocks chimed midday, I was hanging about a hundred yards from my beloved's house, under a tree on which I carved his name with my nail file, wearing a sky-blue dress that spread out like a saucer when I spun around. He had said two o'clock. At the last minute, the very last, I punched the tree to stop myself from crying; I said, Suzanne, you devil, Suzanne, you devil.

Well, that's how it is.

What happened next, I don't want to tell you either. We stayed together until it was dark, until after midnight, and finally, until dawn. He took me back to my place, I accompanied him back to his, and we were off again. We hadn't kissed enough. We still had everything to tell each other. I can't remember how we managed to part. The sun poking its nose out like a crab louse. The truck taking away the garbage and all dreams. As he left me outside the rusty gates of my hostel for young ladies, Francis grabbed me with both hands under my dress, lifted me higher than him to make me laugh. He said, "Don't ever forget me." I didn't laugh. I swore I wouldn't.

That afternoon, at around five o'clock, he turned up in the drawing room, his suit as shabby as ever, his tie just as stringy, but with that look of someone who's been drinking instead of sleeping. Before I realized, Madame stepped between him and me. He shouted in her face, "You, get out of the way or I'll smash the place up!" There were three souls in the room, like every Friday, but they weren't there for a fight, nor were the girls, and nor was Madame. Francis grabbed my hand, I was disguised as a bush girl, and we headed for my room. He had something to tell me.

First of all, he scrubbed me from head to foot with carbolic soap. He kissed every part of me as it became white again. Between two pecks, he poured out the most unbelievably tangled story. He had almost reached my toes when I was able to grasp the thread of it: at boarding school, when he was a little boy, he had had a very nasty teacher.

I said, "I know. You used to peep up her dress without wicked thoughts, you just wanted to see her pussy."

"Wait, wait! This morning, would you believe, I met that woman here, in the port!"

I didn't fall over backward. And yet it's easy to do when you've got one leg on the edge of the washbasin and you're having your toes scrubbed. So as not to appear to have lost interest in his childhood memories, I said, "She must be old now."

"But that's the thing! She hasn't changed!"

He had seen her coming out of a café. Slim, dark, navy blue eyes, a tight raincoat, holding a bag, twenty-five years old. I pointed out to him that he was the one coming out of the café. My opinion was that he must have been in a fine state. I didn't put it like that, but I got the general idea across.

Not at all. After leaving me, he was a bit sad, but he hadn't gone for a drink. He never drank in the morning. He'd had a light coffee and two slices of bread and butter.

Fine. He had followed the woman from a distance, as far as a seaside villa with a large garden and a wooden sign over the gate. When she had disappeared into the house, he had gone up to it to read what was written: SAINT AUGUSTIN'S SCHOOL. *That was exactly what his boarding school in Marseilles had been called!* Afterward, of course, he had gone for a drink. He needed to refresh his spirits.

Without ever having spoken to her, I knew this woman. She had moved to Saint-Julien three or four years earlier, with her husband. I hadn't had a chance to see the husband. The day school started, wanting to find a ball that the kids had thrown onto the roof, he had taken a nosedive into the cemetery; that's what you get for being nice to brats. She had weathered the shock and carried on running the boarding school alone.

Before Francis talked to me about it, you can guess how interested I was in all that. She was about the age he said, it was true. Twenty-four, twenty-five. A bit starchy, a bit churchy, but not bad—depending on your taste. In any case, my student was in a right state over the whole thing. He gave me the towel after drying only my back. He paced up and down the room rubbing his hands together.

"I made inquiries," he said. "She comes from Marseilles. The kids call her Mommy Long Legs like we used to. Fate plays some hallucinatory tricks, extraordinary!"

I asked him what it meant. It was the right word, for sure. I'm not a whiz at math, I never learned to do anything except open my legs, but if the hussy was already twenty-five when he was seven, she couldn't be younger than him now that he was getting on toward thirty. Halluci—what was the word?

It took more than that to deflate him.

"In fact, she must be forty. She looks twenty years younger, that's all. It's perfectly common. And vice versa, by the way."

Fine. Supposing she really is his schoolmistress, getting on toward fifty without a wrinkle, without an ounce of fat, a phenomenon. Supposing she is. So what? He paused for a minute in his pacing up and down. He looked at me with that little smile that says so much more than words. Then he went and lay down on the bed, his neck resting on his hands, his ankles crossed.

Looking at the ceiling, he said, "During the vacation, she lives alone. So I've got a plan."

When someone keeps you hanging about, I don't hurry them. If they see that you are calmly putting down your towel, that you're doing your hair in the mirror, looking as eager to hear the rest as a three-legged pedestal table, it comes much faster.

He asked me, "Have you heard about that prisoner who escaped from the citadel?"

I'd have had to be deaf not to have heard.

"Well, I'm going to pretend I'm him!"

Well, it was beyond me. Run for your life. I must have had eyes as big as saucers when I went over to him. And yet he didn't look any crazier than anyone else. He was pleased with his idea. He was thrilled. If one day someone does a painting of the guy who's found the answer to all his problems, he should be lying on the rayon bedspread of a room in a brothel, his hands behind his head, a strand of hair over the right eye, wearing creaseless pants, his legs crossed. In the corner, a poor girl who's just heard that everything's changed, the earth is no longer spinning, now she's flying around on the end of a kite. As long as they're not stingy with the Charenton yellow, the straitjacket gray, and the gilding on the frame, it'll be a prizewinner.

"I want to get into her house," ranted Francis. "I've got it all set up: the grubby shirt, the boots, a mean look. I'm going to make her die of fright for a whole night, perhaps longer!"

He needed treatment, I don't even have to say it. I did say it to him though. He sat bolt upright as if I were a viper and I'd just bitten him. He shouted, "Do you know what that meant to me when I was little? It's sacred!"

So saying, he let his whole body sink back onto the mattress, his hands in the same place to support his pig head, deaf to everything. For a while, I kept my trap shut. I sat down beside him. He hadn't shaved. His hair was tousled. His eyes drilled through the ceiling.

To be honest, now that I was all clean, all fresh, I would have preferred something else to discussing the trials and tribulations of schoolboys. But we had had our fill the day before. I told myself that he couldn't have built castles in the air any higher than a pile of saucers. He had a bit too much to drink, that was all. So had Michou. And even Magali, who was the biggest chump of the whole crop. When it had worn off, a good night's sleep and he'd be laughing, he would swear blind he hadn't thought a word of all that.

After a quarter of an hour, I asked him sweetly for a ciggie, to find out what was going on in his mind. He rummaged in his pants pocket, he even lit one for me. Not that I liked it, but the atmosphere became less strained. He rested his cheek on my stomach, gave me a kiss, and sighed a couple of times. I asked him softly, very softly, so as not to bother him: "What are you thinking about?" In the same tone, as if we were discussing the weather, he replied, "If she's still got a punishment room, I'll lock her in it."

For the hour that he stayed with me, perhaps longer, he carried on ruminating like that. And then, as he left, his jacket over his arm, he kissed me and said, "If all goes well, I'll see you tomorrow." Stiff, solemn. Anyone would think he'd just received his marching orders. That's what I was planning to tell Madame, anyway, to explain his bursting in like that.

To him I just said, a little sadly but nicely, "Listen, Frank. If you do that, you're getting involved in some stupid prank and even you don't know what it can lead to."

I was not far wrong; nobody, unfortunately, will contradict me, but I could never have imagined the madness it turned into.

There. I've said all I had to say. All that I've said, I saw and heard. It's up to you if you don't believe me and prefer the crazy ramblings of that nutcase, Belinda. Do know what occurred to me? This business of an inheritance that you were talking about, Georgette must have picked it up somewhere while her ear was stuck to a keyhole. I wouldn't put it past her and that might explain why she went to the trouble of making all that up. But what does it matter.

At the Queen of Hearts I was the only one who knew Francis. He flashed through my life quicker than a dream. Counting on my fingers—no need for my toes—I knew him for precisely seven days. I didn't even have time to find out that he played the piano.

You know, as does everyone else, I was to see him one more time, but at a moment when he was no longer himself, when I was no longer myself, neither white nor black, neither Suzanne nor Zozo, and I haven't the heart to remember it. All the more so because there's someone else who'll tell it much better, with big words and no lisp. As for me, it came over me when I was a little girl, after the terror I had of setting fire to the house. It was in Saint-Ouen, close to the gasworks. A little more and I'd have blown up the whole district. That's what it leads to, having parents who are barely fourteen and who go out and enjoy themselves at all the local dances instead of watching over their brat in her cradle.

Caroline

I WON'T TELL YOU THE DAY, OR
the month or the year. Nor where the thing happened to me. If this
account falls into the hands of people who know me, I don't want
them to be able to make any connection with the person I have
become. I have suffered too much to have all the mire surrounding
me churned up again.

Let's say that it was late one summer, somewhere on the Atlantic
coast, in a little town like so many others, with its fishing port, its
church, and its gossip. I was twenty-five. I had been a widow for
four years. I won't talk about my husband either, first because his
memory does not deserve to be sullied, and second because I'd have
very little to say, having only known him for a few months.

I continued running the boys' boarding school we had set up
together on my own. During the school year, I was helped by a cook
and another schoolmistress. We had up to twenty pupils, mostly
problem children. The oldest was under ten. During school vaca-
tions, I administered injections to the local people so as not to
remain idle in the empty house.

It was a Friday, as it was getting dark. On finishing my usual
round, I visited the hairdresser, Madame Bonnifay. I didn't like her

very much, she was a scandalmonger. When I was shut in the dining room at the back of the shop with her, she gossiped about all her clients who were of the age to have sexual relations. She was truly obsessed with these things. I think she also derived a perverse pleasure from making me feel ill at ease. From natural modesty and from my upbringing, I was her exact opposite, but she never tired of bringing the conversation back to what was for me the most incidental aspect of my widowhood. She refused to believe that thoughts of the flesh did not bother me. I was young, pretty, shapely, I don't deny, but does a woman have to be ugly to be honest? I confided as little as possible to her, certain that my words would be bandied about, deformed, in her salon. Her nickname was Yackety-Yack, and no wonder. I had made the mistake, once, of expressing surprise, in confidence, that she did the hair of one of those residents of those houses of lust that could be found in those days in even the most remote provinces. Since then, the hussy insolently looked me up and down in the street; I preferred to cross to the other side.

What's more, Yackety-Yack herself was not considered a model of virtue. Try as I might to remain deaf to gossip, our cook told me some hair-raising stories about her. One night, *on all fours on the rocks.* Another time, in a beach hut, *screwing a man standing up.* And worse, which I won't go into. It was public knowledge that the hairdresser's husband had so many horns on his head that he could no longer go through doors.

The evening in question, the whole town was talking of nothing but the escape, a few days earlier, of a prisoner from the Rattrap, a jail off the coast from us. Despite the searches and roadblocks, he hadn't been captured. He was the subject of Yackety-Yack's conversation as she pulled her pants down. I mean during the time it took her each time to lie on her stomach on the edge of a divan and delay the injection in every way she could think of. Unbelievably squeamish the minute my syringe approached; it was always the same song and dance.

"Please, not hard! Don't hurt me! Don't hurt me!"

She was a radiant blonde, men probably found her appealing. When she exhibited her white behind like that, arched with apprehension, I couldn't help thinking that in the same place, in the same posture, and perhaps with the same words, she probably sometimes presented herself for attacks that were formidable in a different way.

I would coax gently, "Relax. Don't tense up."

She would turn her round, imploring eyes to me, but it was not pity that suffused me. It was a feeling of sweet revenge. I could at last punish her for all those moments when she delighted in my embarrassment and heightened it with her insinuations. I kept her in that state of terror for a good minute longer, waiting until her eyelids closed, screwed up with torment, until her face was buried in her arms, until she almost wanted the unavoidable jab, her whole being refusing and begging for it at the same time, and I would deal the blow. Her cry, strangled in her throat, was one of stupor and abandon. Her whole body would collapse on the divan, panting, ridiculous, her dress hitched up, her panties around her garters, and then, at length, I would inject my venom into her body, at my leisure, in spurts, down to the last drop.

Then, back on her feet with great difficulty, adjusting her clothing, she would whimper a bit. I would assert that in my whole life I had never seen such a firm behind, and she would calm down again. She was silly rather than spiteful and, I have to admit, not at all vindictive. She picked up the conversation where we had left off. This time, as she rummaged in a drawer for money to pay me for her pain, she was hot on the heels of the escaped prisoner again.

"Do you know how he managed to get through the roadblocks? In a van belonging to someone from here, in the middle of the night. And do you know why the van wasn't searched? Because it belonged to a couple on their honeymoon. The military are so tactful! All the same, I've got my own ideas on the subject."

I didn't care to hear them. It's obvious that I only asked out of politeness as I accepted the offer of a chair to sit on.

"There's only been one marriage this month," she said, lowering her voice. "That of Monsieur Séverin and his graphic artist, Emma. I did the girl's hair for the wedding myself. Wonderful hair. But what a job it was. I had a field day. In any case, they bought an ambulance from the Great War for their honeymoon trip. Dirt cheap, I know, it was my husband who sold it to them. And in the evening they set off. Only there you go!"

Silence. She was brilliant at keeping you on tenterhooks. I mean her other listeners, because all I wanted was to rush home.

"Yes, then what?" I said out of politeness.

A glance at the door. She came closer, a hand on my arm, almost whispering, "The same night, someone I know saw, with their own eyes, old Séverin come back to town alone. Lucky you're sitting down: he was barefoot and in his pajamas!"

I confess I didn't grasp the impact of this revelation immediately. I knew Monsieur Séverin by sight—he was in advertising and worked for an agency in the port. I had also seen his fiancée in the street, a stuck-up creature who wiggled like an eel and wore see-through dresses to get attention. I would have liked to give her a jab, and watch her lose her airs and graces. I had heard that they had been lovers for months when they got married. My cook had even, in my presence, made a remark that was supposed to be funny but that made the color rise to my cheeks: endowed as he must be, old Séverin couldn't do her much harm. I had read in a book discovered by chance in our attic that small men, on the other hand—But never mind that. It is a matter, I am sure, of personal taste, and I had very little experience on the subject.

In any case, Yackety-Yack only kept her mouth shut long enough to savor my bemused air, then she added, "I've got something up here, I have!"

She tapped her finger against her temple. Another glance in the direction of the door. Her perfumed face was practically touching mine.

"Don't you understand?" she asked. "That night the escaped prisoner was on the same road as them. He kidnapped the bride in the van. Since then, old Séverin's been holed up in his house, but as for her, nobody's seen her!"

"Come, come, he would have run to the police, he'd have lodged a complaint!" I retorted.

"Too proud."

"They probably had an argument on the way."

She made a gesture that told me I could think what I liked, and pressed the money for the injection into my hands. The bill probably made me regret my harshness toward her a little, and I restrained her arm as she made for the door. To please her, I asked her to go on.

"But what do you think? Why hasn't she come back?"

"Too proud. The man who kidnapped her hadn't seen a woman for six years. Do I have to spell it out? Besides, perhaps he strangled her as soon as he was safe, and the ocean'll wash her body up."

You can imagine the frame of mind I was in when I left the salon. I've already told you, I didn't particularly like Emma, but I was still a woman, and sensitive. I had seen her coming out of church, on her wedding day, so fresh, so fair. It was myself four years earlier, right down to the color of the hair. Toward the evening, I had also seen the bright yellow truck pass our house, decorated with white tulle. I pictured her dreadful wedding night. The van parked on a country lane, in the moonlight, miles from anywhere. She inside, naked, perhaps tied up. What she must have suffered before he killed her. And have accepted, her face tearstained, in the slim hope that he would let her live.

Halfway home, I didn't have the courage to walk through the port, where men sitting drinking on the terraces of the bars always followed me with their eyes, undressing me. Some even whistled. Generally, wearing a tightly belted beige trench coat that I always wore whatever the weather, I was content to walk faster. That evening their lust would have repulsed me. I preferred to go via the station, where I knew there were soldiers. Of course, they, too, watched me with heavy, silent persistence. But they were the army, the one that was supposed to be the bravest in the world; I knew I was safe from impropriety.

When I crossed the square, there were a dozen of them in khaki, their guns at their feet, silhouetted against the setting sun. I remember an orangey red light softened the shadows, setting aglow the station walls. I knew the man in command, sitting on a bench apart from the others. He was a tall, robust man, in his prime, with virile features, his hair salt and pepper at the temples: Captain Malignaud. He had come to my husband's funeral. He never failed to greet me when he saw me in town, and sometimes we would converse politely about this and that. He was said to be taciturn, strict with his men, but it was purely on the strength of his qualities that he had risen in the ranks, and I confess I found he had great presence. He said "Good evening" when he saw me, and as I had no urgent matters to attend to in my empty house, I went over to him. He had a geological survey map spread across his knees.

After a few formalities, I asked him, "Well, Captain, haven't you found your runaway prisoner yet?"

I told him it was the talk of the town, and that it seemed natural to broach the subject with an officer in charge of the search. Malignaud, in fact, was not surprised. I simply noticed his expression harden.

"We're watching the roads, the stations, and the beaches," he said, folding up his map. "I'm sure that he can't have slipped through the net! The bastard's still there, hiding out somewhere!"

He had raised his voice, thumping the paper with the back of his hand. I ventured, "Anyone would think you had a personal grudge against this man."

"This man?" he cried. "He isn't a man, he's an animal!"

Then, ashamed of letting himself get carried away in front of a woman, he removed his peaked cap and made room for me on the bench. I sat down next to him. Our faces turned toward the purple sun, he murmured in a dull but calmer voice, "I have never told anyone of the memory which torments me, Caroline. May I call you by your first name? It will be easier for me to tell these things to a friend."

"Many years ago now," began the captain, "we were stationed in a village in the Arles region for the fourteenth of July. As staff sergeant, I was staying with the mayor, a farmer who found me a mirror image of himself. This rank had been conferred on him at the Chemin des Dames, and I was born a peasant. I say it with no shame whatsoever, for I later pulled myself through the higher school certificate purely by dint of my own efforts.

"This hardworking man had no sons, but he did have an eighteen-year-old daughter who was young and pretty, purity itself: Pauline. Watching her come and go from the house, throwing grain to the hens, sewing in the evenings, always nicely dressed and modest, was a new pleasure for me. Already in my fortieth year, having nothing but contempt for the garrison girls, I dreamed of Pauline as a youth dreams of an angel. However, her air of embarrassment when I came off duty, certain furtive looks which I caught her giving me from behind her work, indicated that she was not indifferent to me.

"The eve of the village fete, after supper, there was a fireworks display, and the family, with the exception of Pauline, who was clearing the table, went out to watch. Convinced that I wouldn't get another such opportunity to speak to the dear child for a long time, I lingered at the table, in my sky-blue uniform, smoking a cigarette, finishing a glass of wine, and as she prepared to clear away my place I took her hand and kept her by me. She lowered her eyes, intimidated. It was easy to tell that she had never come across such boldness. Although I was as perturbed as she was, I told her how much I liked her, with all the sincerity of the French soldier.

" 'Pauline, I don't have a daughter, but if I did, I would have liked her to be just like you.'

"She replied softly, without daring to look at me, in a voice that smelled of lavender and rosemary: 'You are very kind, Sergeant.'

" 'Pauline,' I then said, 'stay as you are, pure and innocent. When my enlistment is over, despite the large and unfortunate age gap between us, I shall ask for your hand.'

"For a split second she raised toward me eyes that had a some-what startled expression; it's perfectly natural. She immediately recovered her reserved air. We didn't exchange another word, but believe me, only modesty prevented her from accepting on the spot. I have often relived that scene in my mind, during the years that followed. She and I, alone in the dining room, the cracking of fireworks in the background, the shouts of admiration from the family outside, the sweet warmth of her hand in mine, the blue gaze that had met mine for a moment. . . .

"Pauline.

"I was never to see her alive again," the captain went on in a faltering voice.

"The next day, after a banquet at the town hall which duty obliged me to attend, I went to the village square, decked out with colorful flags and invaded by a joyful crowd. I thought I would find her there, dressed in a typical Arles costume, smiling under her white lace headdress. I would have watched her dance to the sound of the fifes and tambourines. Perhaps I'd have danced with her. I was as happy as a conscript under a summer sky. I sought her for a long time, everywhere, jostled by couples locked in embrace, taunted by bumpkins who'd had too much to drink, without the faintest premonition that before evening, my life was to be shattered at a stroke.

"It was the hour when the sun remains suspended like a great ball of fire over the scrubland. A corporal came to inform me that something nasty had happened at the farm. He didn't say what, but my heart was full of Pauline, I could only think of her. I took a few men with me and we drove to the mayor's house in a truck.

"The dreadful sight awaited me in the farmyard, on the barn doorstep. Pauline was lying on the ground, like a contorted doll, wearing nothing but a short blouse in shreds. The visible side of her face was stained with earth, blood, and tears. Blood was everywhere, on her poor, naked body. My first gesture, when my frozen heart began to beat again, was to remove my jacket and cover her. Nothing of this girl, who had never been profaned during her lifetime, should be profaned after her death, even by the gaze of my soldiers.

"But may the monster who did it burn forever in hell. She had been profaned, assaulted, degraded for hours on end, until, no longer able to bear the shame that was being inflicted on her, she had thrown herself from the top of the barn through an opening, to escape her torments!

"We found the monster at the very scene, sprawled in the straw, overcome by wine and his own uncontrollable bestiality. He was a private from my company, unruly, deceitful, with all the vices of the Italians in his blood, a bully like those of his race but cowardly enough to attack a defenseless girl, concealing his laziness, his lust, and his drunkenness under an air of hypocrisy.

"I will hold my tongue. I hate the monster so much—I've always refused to call him anything else—I've been pursuing him for so long, his extermination my only hope of reward, I tremble at the thought, as you can see.

"When he was dragged before his victim's body," the captain continued after a long silence, "I couldn't stop myself from lunging for his throat. It was madness, and my soldiers restrained me. He didn't recollect a thing, or at least that's what he claimed. Dazed and tousled, he seemed unaware of what was happening to him. In the distance you could hear the blare of the dance music. The family had not yet been told of the tragedy. The mayor was perhaps dancing with his wife. When I recall these things, when I picture the murderer barefoot in the farmyard, his hands tied behind his back, his collarless shirt open, showing his chest, like a condemned man before his execution, I say to myself that it mattered little what would have become of me; my men should have let me act as his executioner.

"Instead of that, his court-martial judges, perhaps indoctrinated by the politicians, said they were touched by his youth—dammit, had he been touched by Pauline's youth?—they wanted to take into account his inebriated state at the time of the crime, they granted him life. I was in the witness stand. I did not know how to suppress my fury. The minute the trial was over, on learning that he was to be imprisoned here, in the citadel, I requested a transfer.

"It was hard to obtain and took a long time. I went back to studying in order to write letters, I waited humbly and patiently at every level, right up to the minister. At last, after two years, I obtained a post in this town as warrant officer. It wasn't, as I had hoped, a transfer to the prison itself, in the monster's stench, where I would be able to embitter every hour of life which he had stolen from my beloved Pauline and me. And yet this was already balm to my suffering. Will you believe me if I tell you that I have often climbed up to the top of the lighthouse armed with a telescope? I could only see high gray walls, black loopholes, but I knew he was there, and my hatred was intact. Will you also believe that after so many years of uneventful service, my heart leaped in my breast when I heard there had been a breakout? The minute I heard the sirens, I knew it was him.

"That was more than three weeks ago. At the beginning I thought he had given me the slip; I won't tell you under what circumstances, for the reputation of a young and honest wife might suffer. For a brief moment during the night, he had been very close to my revolver. I could have killed him point-blank, but he slipped through my fingers. But the workings of his mind are unpredictable. Anybody would have thought that having gotten through one of our roadblocks, at the entrance to the peninsula, he would lose himself on the mainland, make for Spain, or Italy, or somewhere. Well, he didn't. He got through the roadblock so that we would stop searching for him here. His plan was to escape by sea. Luckily, he hasn't been able to do that so far. He's lying low somewhere, in town perhaps. I won't tell you, I'm not allowed to, where he found sanctuary until now. Believe me that it's a place well suited to his character, and it's only due to his lies and women's weakness that he has obtained the help he needed.

"But it will soon be dark, Caroline. You ought to go home. When we've caught him, whether I kill him this time with my own hands or whether a firing squad takes care of him, all the mystery surrounding his escape will become clear. And you will judge for yourself whether his abject stubbornness in perverting innocence is not that of a monster."

I reached home at twilight. The silence was broken only by the cries of the gulls and the sound of the waves. I was distraught. All the way home through a maze of narrow white streets, I kept hearing Malignaud's words and imagining the young girl from Arles's suffering. I couldn't stop visualizing horrendous scenes, violent sex, vain tears. I ran across the garden, unable to banish them from my mind. Pauline at the mercy of her attacker in the straw, Emma on the floor of a truck decked out for her wedding—everything became confused. I do not know how long I struggled with the three locks on the front door, but the minute I was inside I closed the door behind me, leaning on it with all my weight, and bolted it, as if I were being pursued by a swarm of wasps.

I switched on the hall light. I recovered my breath. The house was warm and comforting. I was relieved to hear the ticktock of the pendulum clock again and I inhaled the pleasant smell of furniture polish. I put my bag and my keys on the Chinese console table as I did every day and hung my trench coat on the varnished walnut coat peg, glancing at myself in the mirror. I saw nothing but a hazy turmoil in my eyes. I adjusted my hair. I wore it in a bun to conform to people's expectations of a boarding-school headmistress. After my evening bath, my hair was entitled to a hundred brush strokes, the whole length. It came down to my behind. It was brown and shiny. I only let it down when I was alone. In class I also wore spectacles, which I didn't need at all, with ordinary glass lenses, purely to make myself more ugly. People are so stupid.

What else did I do? I probably adjusted my skirt belt and smoothed a fold in my white blouse with a large collar. Then I made my way to the kitchen, which was always open when I lived alone. I switched the light on as I went in, without knowing that I was turning the light on hell.

He was there, hidden behind the door!

I could feel his presence behind me even before he grabbed me and clamped a hand over my mouth to stop me from screaming. I saw the knife he had snatched, a horrible carving knife. My legs gave way under me.

In a strangled breath, I heard in my ear: "If you value your life, keep quiet!"

I did nothing to defend myself. I wasn't capable of it. He held me against him for a few seconds, without moving, then suddenly he thrust me toward the table in the center of the room. I clung to it to keep my balance and turned around as best I was able.

He was the man they were talking about in town, at least judging from his height and the color of his eyes. But how can I explain? He didn't look like the shameless brute you would expect. He was certainly tall, with broad shoulders, but slim, almost thin. A heavy lock of chestnut hair fell over his forehead. I had heard his head was shaved smooth. Even beneath a beard of at least two days, his features were fine and intelligent: black eyes, a long straight nose, a dimpled chin, and, when I saw them, very white teeth. Above all, I had the feeling at that moment that in his grimy shirt and trousers, knife in hand, he was as frightened as I was.

"Do you know who I am?" he asked in a hoarse voice. I nodded. I tried my utmost to regain my composure.

"I've searched the whole house. Haven't you got any firearms?" I must have betrayed a slight hesitation, but either it escaped his notice or he put it down to my nerves. I shook my head.

"Show me your tongue."

Without thinking, I showed it to him. I must have been out of my mind!

He simply remarked, "Well, you can talk!"

I made an effort. I managed to produce a thin squeak that humiliated me even more. "My husband didn't want any guns in the house. With the children, you never know."

"How long ago did your husband die?"

"Four years."

He looked me up and down. Insolently. He felt more at ease since I had shown him my tongue.

"Have you got a fancy man?"

I shrugged indignantly.

"So how have you managed for four years?"

I was even more indignant but was unable to withstand his gaze. I retreated along the table. Without moving, he closed the door.

"When I ask a question," he said, "I like to get an answer."

"I have nothing to answer."

A little sigh. He advanced toward me, casually, toying with the knife. I retreated step-by-step, until I bumped into the wall.

When he was very close, he said, "I haven't had a woman for a long time."

It wasn't the knife that frightened me most, but his black eyes, what I read in them. I moved to the side. All he had to do was lean one arm against the wall to bar my way. He was as quick as a cat.

"You know what I'd like?" he said in a sugary voice, which was more terrifying than anything.

At the same time, with the tip of his blade, he delicately opened my blouse to see my skin. I was as if paralyzed. My temples were throbbing. I could picture myself having my breasts bared with the knife, one button at a time. Then he would slash my slip straps with one stroke without my even feeling it. He would caress my bare breasts. He would kiss them as he held my shoulders, pinning me against the wall, powerless.

I stammered, closing my eyes, "I beg you, not that. . . ."

A silence, then I heard him shout, "Not what? I'm hungry, dammit!"

People will laugh as they read these lines. It serves me right for being so naive. But I promised to tell the whole truth, even if it was to my disadvantage. And put yourself in my shoes: what woman, shut up with a man whose brutality, vices, and infamy were common knowledge, would not have feared, every second, that she would be raped?

> Teacher she may be, but here, Caroline uses the word "naïveté" instead of "hypocrisy," "truth" instead of "connivance." Of the seven mistresses, or at least so they claimed, whose testimonies I have recorded, she is in fact, and by far, the most hypocritical, if not also the most complacent: in this respect I think she is beaten by a formidable rival who does not encumber herself, as we shall see, with either serpentine twists or a complicated past. Even so, it is still true that the scene in the kitchen, which was certainly extremely unpleasant when she experienced it, makes one laugh when she embroiders it with her fantasies. The same causes produce the same effects, and my only difficulty was that of choosing at which point in her story to take the opportunity of making that comment, and I shall not come back to it.
>
> (From the notes of Marie-Martine Lepage)

And so I heated up what was left over from lunch, beef olives, or "headless swallows," as they are called in Provence. My mother had taught me how to make them; I ate them readily and they had the advantage, when I was alone, of lasting for several meals. While I was setting the table, the escaped prisoner washed his hands at the sink and splashed his face. I made no attempt to run away, he would have caught me before I could unlock the front door. I made the most of the opportunity to think.

The telephone was in the hall. There was little chance that he would allow me to call for help. The little window in the toilet on the ground floor. It was high, I didn't know if I would be able to reach it by standing on the seat. The kids preferred to slip through the barred cellar window. The key to the cellar was with the others, on the key ring sitting on the Chinese console table. But the whole plan seemed like a Chinese puzzle to me: get hold of the key ring, find the right key as I ran down the corridor, open the cellar door, lock it behind me, gallop down the steps, reach the window, contort myself to get through the bars, and all that to find him most likely waiting outside, impassive, armed with his knife. No. I didn't have to leave the cellar. I could shout. There were enough villas close by for someone to hear me. If I couldn't think of anything else, I could try my luck.

As if he could read my mind, he said after drying his face with the tea towel: "Stop fretting, I'm too far ahead of you. I've pulled out the phone wire. I wore myself out dragging an old wardrobe in front of the basement window. You won't go upstairs without me. And even wee-wee, I don't mind keeping an eye on you."

So saying, he stuck the big knife in the wooden table, sat down, and held out his plate for me to serve him.

"You'll see, Mommy Long Legs," he added, "I wasn't born stupid, as my grandmother was always telling me."

Of course it wasn't his vanity that startled me, or that he was ruining a table that had seen worse, but that he knew the nickname my pupils had given me.

"Why do you call me that?"

"If your food is good, I'll tell you."

I filled his plate. That made me hungry. I set my place opposite him. When I was sitting down, I saw that he ate greedily, with his hands. He sucked the sauce from his fingers. As he looked up at me, he stopped dead.

"What's the matter?"

"Do you eat with such vulgarity on purpose?"

He wiped his hands on his shirt, looking more annoyed than contrite. I thought that he was going to pick up his fork, but not at all. He grabbed the one I was holding, bent it in two, and threw it on to the table.

"You," he said, "would rather not eat than be as vulgar as me."

And he continued eating as he pleased. A pig. When he had finished up what was on his plate, all the sauce cleaned off with his forefinger, there was no need to do the washing up. He threw himself against the back of his chair and admitted that it was good.

Then he stared at me for a long time, without moving. I returned his gaze. I could read in his eyes a contentedness full of melancholy, very strange. They say that even animals have a soul.

Then, with a short laugh, he leaned toward me and said, "It's crazy! You're the spitting image of your mother!"

Of course I could have wondered why the poor woman should come into it, but he didn't give me the time.

"Saint Sins School!" he shouted triumphantly.

I think that the shock I felt in my heart was as great as the one I had had on arriving home. SAINT SINS SCHOOL was all that remained of SAINT AUGUSTIN'S SCHOOL on my parents' gates, in Marseilles. The other letters had flaked off.

I asked, probably rather pale, "Do you know Marseilles?"

"I was born there, fathead."

"And my parents' boarding school?"

"I ran away from it."

"What's your name?"

He brushed back the rebel lock that hid his eye.

"Edouard. Call me Eddy, it's friendlier."

He pulled a cigarette, which was all crumpled, from his shirt pocket. He rose, pushing back his chair, to go over to the stove for a match. I flung myself on the knife stuck in the kitchen table. The blade was plunged in deeply and I wasn't able to dislodge it.

"Wait," he said, "I'll show you."

He calmly recovered his weapon and slid it into his belt. A little sigh. He suddenly took me by the shoulder and propelled me toward the door.

"That's enough of the small talk! Forward march to the bed-room!"

I lost my balance on the tiled hall floor. He caught one of my arms and I was being propelled once more, this time toward the staircase. My skirt hampered me as I went up the stairs. Walking ahead of him, I felt like a streetwalker.

He made me go into my bedroom with no further ado. The shutters were closed. He also shut the door, fastened the latch, and wedged a chair under the handle. I said to myself, You've got to shout for help, too bad if he kills you! You've got to shout!

I couldn't.

Once again I was pinned to the wall. Only my bedside lamp was lit. The man's huge shadow moved. I saw that I was lost. He was going to throw me onto the bed. He would tie my hands on either side with the curtain loops. He would rip my blouse. No, he would gag me, he would remove whatever was in his way with a sadistic gentleness, taking his time, like someone who has nothing to fear: my white slip, my straight, navy blue skirt. He would slide my white lace panties down my legs and would stretch me out to tie up my ankles as well. He would make me suffer the dreadful caresses of his hands right inside my thighs, where the skin is softest. . . .

No, he wouldn't waste time playing with me, he had the whole night for that. He would put the bolster and the pillow under my hips right away, and raise me up from the bed with one powerful arm to open me up to his overwhelming lust. Then, reveling in my tears, contemplating me as I lay entirely offered up to him, he would rip off his trousers and I would watch with horror the monstrous penis burst out before penetrating me, perhaps tearing me, right to the depths. I refrain from describing the changing images in my dazed mind during those few seconds. There is no woman who, without having gone through my ordeal, hasn't imagined it at least once as she lets herself go, in morbid anticipation.

However, and most fortunately in the circumstances, my attacker was as Captain Malignaud had said: unpredictable. Just as he approached me, his face no doubt sardonic against the light, all that I was capable of uttering, in a voice that was no longer mine, was "What are you going to do to me? Tell me, what are you going to do to me?"

It was a long wait for the reply. Did he take pity on me at that moment? Was he impressed by the straightness and the dignity that I forced my whole body to maintain?

He said, "If you calm down a little, nothing."

But immediately afterward, like taking from a thirsty kitten the saucer of milk that has just been put in front of it: "In any case, not right away."

He flung the knife down on the bed.

"Just try touching it again," he said. "Just you try."

Then, as if I weren't there, he started removing his shoes, his socks, and his dirty shirt. His torso was more robust and muscular than I would have imagined. As he undid his fly, he looked at me and stopped.

"Would you mind looking the other way?"

I obeyed like one of my pupils being made to stand in the corner. I heard him opening the wardrobe with the mirror. I glanced over my shoulder in spite of myself. For a split second I saw him completely naked. He had slim hips, firm buttocks, paler than the rest of his body. He had a very beautiful back, I have to admit, which opened out in a triangle up to his broad shoulders. He didn't have an ounce of fat on him; that is why he was so quick and seemed thin in his clothes. His chest, without being fleecy, had enough hairs to cover any scars . . .

> "A split second!" The time our little bitch allowed herself would make a camera jealous. Her back and front description makes me wonder, but I would not allow myself to amputate her testimony by so much as a comma, firstly because I haven't done so for any of the others, but above all because her absurdities, here and there, are very revealing about the schoolmistress and her tendency to disguise the facts, or, of course, the scars.
>
> (From the notes of Marie-Martine Lepage)

His stomach was flat and hard and his arms accustomed to prison labor. His penis, if you will excuse someone who is almost a nurse talking about it as naturally as about any other member, seemed neither longer nor shorter, nor fatter nor thinner than the penises of the men I had glimpsed, except that it was proportional to his size. Anyway, I've read in this book that I came across by chance, and as I mentioned earlier, that you can't go by a penis at rest; some triple in size and even more under the effects of desire. It's terrifying.

I didn't have time to see what he was doing, but I understood. In the wardrobe there were clothes that my husband had worn little, or not at all. I don't know why I kept them. Perhaps because I can't bear to throw out new things, or because I had hoped I was pregnant when he died. What I felt, at twenty-one, alone in a practically strange town, isn't relevant to this affair. Suffice it to say that my husband was fairly tall, too, although much older and different.

In any case, it seemed once and for all that the escaped prisoner could read my thoughts, even when I had my nose pressed to the wall, for he suddenly asked, "How old was your husband?"

"Forty-nine."

"How did you get on with him?"

"We got on well."

"Even in this bed?"

I didn't reply. I heard a brief snicker, but that was all. When I was allowed to turn around, he had slipped into a pair of summer pants, a Lacoste shirt, and moccasins.

"It's not the best there was," he said, "but I prefer white, it gets dirty quicker. That way, you get changed all the time, you're always impeccable. It's the Jesuits who taught me that. I was knee-high to a grasshopper."

He stifled a yawn.

I didn't feel anything seeing him in my husband's clothes. Well, not as much as I thought I would. And, except for his beard, he looked just like anybody else, he was less frightening. Before he even said it, this time, I knew he was going to do his clairvoyant number on me.

"You wouldn't by any chance have a razor for shaving your legs?"

"I don't need to shave my legs."

He picked up the knife from the bed and tested the blade with his thumb, looking more than obvious. He placed it in his belt. Then he rolled his dirty clothes and boots into a ball and threw them under the wardrobe.

"There's a grindstone in the kitchen," I told him.

I wanted to add that if he had to slit my throat, I'd prefer him to do it in one go, but I stopped myself in time. He would have become suspicious if he saw me in a joking mood. He had just reminded me himself of what I had desperately been trying to remember ever since he had captured me: where the hell my husband had hidden his gun when we had moved in four years earlier.

As he was finishing shaving at the kitchen sink, the hall clock struck eleven. He couldn't stop yawning. He stared wide-eyed. No doubt he hadn't had any sleep for a long time. I kept quiet and remained motionless on a chair, hardly eager to help him keep awake. He washed his face with the taps on full blast, rinsed his mouth, dried himself, dried the knife, and contrary to all expectations, carefully cleaned the sink. I presume he did it automatically after the discipline of the prison. Finally, he took out of his pocket the bunch of keys that he had seized to lock the kitchen door. Without his beard, he didn't look thirty.

As I had expected, he made me go upstairs again. My embarrassment at knowing he was behind me, ogling my behind and what my skirt revealed of my legs at every step, had not diminished. He sensed it, as he sensed everything; he made it worse with one of his typical remarks—too disgusting for me to repeat.

However, I felt less anxious as we entered the bedroom than I had the first time. He would probably tie me to the bed, but I doubted that it was to rape me. He wouldn't rape me before he had slept. He would keep me intact until he woke up, perhaps even without undressing me, to make use of me in the fullness of his strength. That meant that I would have several hours in which to get rid of my bonds, take the gun from under the wardrobe, and God willing that the weapon was loaded, become a murderess myself. If it wasn't loaded, if it wouldn't work after four years of neglect, or if, at the last minute, I couldn't find the courage to kill a human being in his sleep, I would have the chance to frighten him, to hound him out of the house, or to run away myself.

But I had underestimated him. He didn't take me to my room, where I thought he would lock us both in, but to the pupils' dormitory. It was, in fact, several adjoining rooms with the partitions knocked out. Twenty little mattresses without sheets or blankets. The surprise, the disappointment at being away from the gun, made me exclaim without thinking: "But we'd be more comfortable in my room!"

"We?" he said. "Did you think we were going to sleep in the same bed?"

He put on an air of horror mimicking mine. What's more, I saw the beginnings of a smile, which showed his white teeth and left no doubt that he was mocking me.

"Unfortunately, there is a window in your room, Mommy Long Legs. I want to sleep undisturbed."

"You could tie me up or something."

Again, that air of mock surprise, those carnivorous teeth.

"Tie you up? Well, well. You do have some funny ideas!"

"But there are windows here as well!"

He looked at the three windows with closed shutters one at a time.

"So?" he said. "Do you think I'm a half-wit or something?"

So saying, he pulled the mattress and pillow off the nearest bed and threw them into my arms.

"Carry those."

He pushed me toward the staircase. I dragged the mattress down behind me. He made me walk the whole length of the hall, to the front door. I no longer understood, unless he was going to make me sleep in the garden! Apparently not. To the left of the front door was another, smaller door, which led to a tiny closet with no light, no window, absolutely bare. A former cloakroom. When I saw him turn the key that was still in the lock, it was too much. I dropped everything—my patience, the pillow, the mattress. I screamed, "You're not going to make me sleep in there, are you?"

"Why not?" he said in a gentle voice, his eyes spiteful. "You lock poor kids up in there, don't you? What have they done to deserve it?"

Seeing him play the Good Samaritan made me see red. I screamed even louder, "They look up my skirt!"

His reaction was so sudden, so violent, that it took my breath away. Before I had finished my sentence, he had grabbed me by the shoulder—I lost my balance, and was dragged with no more consideration than he'd had for the mattress a little earlier. He made me walk back along the whole length of the corridor to the classroom. There, he literally threw me against the teacher's rostrum.

"Sit down!"

He suddenly switched on all the lights. I put the high-heeled shoe I had lost on my foot and sat at my desk. I don't know if I had started to breathe again. I was the plaything of a madman.

He sat down in the front row of desks, just opposite me. The lock of hair on his forehead, his arms crossed on his desk, he said in a no-nonsense tone of voice, "Cross your legs!"

Of course, I didn't. His gaze was already under the desk, riveted on my knees pressed together. My heart began to beat faster. Was I so silly as to think that he would abuse me as soon as I was snared, roughly, like a nobody? His cruelty, I had been warned, was much more refined. Before the final sacrifice, humiliation for humiliation, he wanted to see me degraded, broken, submissive to the point of losing all my dignity. What was that expression of Captain Malignaud's that had struck me? "Degraded for hours on end."

I know that in a similar situation, many women, all as honest as I, rather than provoking the monster, would have thought: My goodness, let's hope he keeps the ordeals he wants to inflict on us as childish as this. By playing the schoolboy excitedly looking up his schoolmistress's skirt, he's making a fool of himself. He wants to see our legs? Let's show them to him, then he'll be satisfied.

But there you are. I couldn't see anything puerile in what he ordered me to do, it was just another link in the chain of humiliations in which he had been enclosing me since the start. His ingratiating smile mocking my loneliness. The knife blade lifting up my blouse. The fork bent in two. The rush to my bedroom. His provocative display of nudity. The locking up. And now this: forcing me to provoke him myself!

Besides, I'm not made of that stuff. I say this so that you will understand the painful memory I have of that moment, in my own brightly lit classroom. It was torture enough showing myself on the beach in a bathing suit, my thighs naked, impossible to conceal the slimness of my waist, the roundness of my buttocks, the arrogance of my twenty-four-year-old breasts. I only went swimming by the last rays of the setting sun, and not even ten times during the season, but there were always enough bathers on the sand to watch me coming out of the water when the wet material clung to my skin and left few secrets about me. Their gaze went straight to the bulge of my pubis, I could feel it like a burn. Prissiness, you will say. I can't help it, I was brought up to be self-respecting.

I won't dwell on moments that seemed interminable to me, but that were only degrading for my jailer. I should say that he threatened to force me if I didn't obey him. I crossed my legs cautiously. It was not at all what he wanted. From right to left, from left to right, I repeated the same movement, higher, always higher. I watched, helplessly, as his gaze became fascinated with my bare skin, above my stockings, and I could not stop myself from pleading, "You mustn't. . . . You'll get yourself excited, then you won't be able to . . ." My voice trailed off.

He feigned amused disdain. "Well, who on earth do you think you are! Do as I tell you!" he shouted.

I obeyed once more, but closed my eyes. That protected me from seeing the vile delight in his. Several times, in the dark, I complied with his commands: slower, further apart, I don't know what. I still felt his avid gaze probing between my thighs, taking possession of me. I was overcome by giddiness, my whole body felt weak, I no longer knew what I was revealing to him. A tear ran down my cheek. I opened my eyes.

He was leaning against the back of his seat, his hands behind his head, contemplating the ceiling with an ecstatic look.

"Shit," he murmured, "those were the days."

Well, it's beyond me. I've got my own ideas on the subject. For a moment I was incapable of standing up. I was ashamed of myself. I thought, If you get into such a state over him just seeing your legs, what will you be like when he goes into action? You're going to crawl, old girl, you're going to grovel at his feet like a prostitute. I promised myself that from then on I would keep calm, that I would submit, perhaps, but I would be rigid, inflexible, even indifferent. For I did not think that his perverse sexuality, perhaps quiet at that moment, would spare me much longer.

I was not mistaken. No sooner had he taken me back to the tiny closet, with no more protest or reaction than a shrug on my part, opened the door, and thrown in the mattress and pillow, than he said, "I need some sleep. I want to be sure you won't go and wake up the whole town."

He sounded almost apologetic, he looked at me with idiotic embarrassment, but I was wary. What better security could he have than locking me up in this closet? Suddenly I understood. Once again I felt this strange weakness in the lower part of my body.

Straining to control the quaver in my voice, I cried, "You don't mean . . . you want me to give you my clothes as well! Is that it?"

He was a bad actor. And I had already seen that smile of false shock.

"Oh, Mommy Long Legs!" he said. "Who asked you to give them to me?"

"No doubt you'd rather rip them off me!" I retorted, outraged by such cynicism.

I concealed my confusion as I had promised myself I would, with another shrug, and I entered the closet. He let me half close the door. Even though he would be perfectly able to open it wide when I was naked, this concession comforted me a little. I would have been incapable of undressing in front of him after the shock my nerves had just suffered; he would have had to kill me first.

And so I began removing my clothes in the gloom. First my blouse, then my shoes, my stockings, my garter belt. I passed them

— *121* —

to him through the doorway, without being able to see any more of him than his hands and the flat wedding ring he wore. Another question that I wouldn't have asked him before for anything. There, as I removed my skirt, I felt emboldened.

"Are you married?" I asked him.

"I told you, I'm sleepy."

I didn't insist. I had touched on a problem that had greatly perturbed me as I leafed through my hairdresser's trashy magazines: if you were forced to get undressed in front of a stranger, which item of clothing would you keep until last, or something along those lines. Perhaps the idea had never crossed my mind that you could get undressed like that. Perhaps, on the contrary, it had tormented me only too often. All that remained were my panties and slip. If I took off the latter, nothing would be hiding my breasts. And so I abandoned my panties. Today, I describe that moment with the detachment I wished I could have had at the time. I am sure that a woman will understand what an ordeal it was, even in that situation, even if he was only a swine, to hand over to someone else what I had been wearing over my most private parts all day. I won't dwell on it.

In any case, if he insisted on nudity, that would prevent me from running to town more effectively than any chains. He wasn't going to stop at my slip, even though it was made of transparent silk and perhaps even more immodest than nothing at all. What was the use, having gone so far, of running the risk of exacerbating his desire in a hand-to-hand struggle where he would obviously get the better of me and I would lose what was left of my underwear? I also removed my slip without a word and handed it to him.

Then, hiding my breasts and belly as best I could, I stood waiting for what was going to happen to me. If he raped me now, I was resolved not to resist him. He would make me lie down on the mattress, I would submit, motionless, I wouldn't cry, I wouldn't complain, I would let him do as he pleased without feeling a thing: a corpse, a wooden doll. I had only one dread, that I would experience what I had heard my assistant talking about—I can't remember how she came to be talking to me of that—that certain very sensual women, or women who are very sensitive in a particular place, cannot stop themselves, no matter how hard they try, from succumbing to pleasure, and that is in fact why a rape, in the eyes of the law, even if the victim has agreed to everything, remains a rape. But too bad, if he discovered where I was sensitive, I wouldn't give anything away, not a thing, I would keep my shame to myself, he would never know what he had wrested from me.

He did not budge for a few long moments, proof that he was of two minds. Then he closed the door. It half opened again a second later. So that I should be lacking for nothing, he held out, without showing himself, a bucket.

He said, "I've put your things away neatly. Good night. I advise you not to wake me up; I'll be very, very nasty."

This time he locked me in for good. I heard the key turn in the lock, then I heard his footsteps in the hall and going up the stairs. He switched off the light from upstairs; I saw it go out under the door. Then, nothing. I remained standing in the dark for a good while, listening. Even naked, I was hot. The clock struck half past; half past what, I don't know. I had kept my wristwatch, but how could I see the time?

I placed my mattress and pillow between the walls and curled up, my face turned toward the door. Then I wasn't sure if it was the door. I got up to grope my way around the closet. It was the door, all right. I went back to bed. I avoided thinking about what I had just gone through so that I could concentrate on the possibilities of getting out of there. I couldn't see a single one. I dismissed the haunting image of the escaped prisoner, his black eyes, his hands. I must have dozed, not really slept, for I could hear the clock strike every quarter, but sometimes I came to again after a nightmare that seemed to have lasted for hours. Why should I keep it a secret? It was about nothing but sex, of my own body being penetrated, consumed, crushed. I was bathed in perspiration. At last, I fell asleep.

When I opened my eyes, a pale light filtered under the door. I lay there motionless, listening. Not a sound. There was a fanlight above the front door; the light on the floor was the dawn. I got up to look through the keyhole. I then realized that this man who thought he was so clever had left the key in the lock.

I listened again, long and hard, my ear to the wood. I could hear the faint ticktock of the clock, that was all. I went back to the mattress. In the dark I began unpicking the stitching on the pillow and emptying out all the feathers. I tore two sides, as quietly as I could, to make one strip of material. I carefully slid it under the door, gently, gently, until half, more than half, was on the other side. Then I pulled a hairpin out of my hair and I attacked the key in the lock. The clock struck. I stopped, so gripped by fear that I didn't think of counting the chimes until it was too late. Seven, probably—at eight o'clock it would have been broad daylight.

When all was silent again, I set to work once more. It took me less than a minute to push the key out onto the floor, but the noise, although muffled by the pillowcase, sounded terrifying. I lost no time in pulling it under the door. I was overwhelmed with hope and the sensation of victory while holding my breath. I had to control myself. I wrapped myself up in the cloth as in a sarong. I cautiously turned the key in the lock. One click. Two clicks. To avoid a prolonged creaking, I threw the door open suddenly.

As the rush of air made the feathers from the pillow fly around me, like a fluttering cloud of white birds, I choked on a cry of terror, I felt as though my heart would burst: the escaped prisoner was sitting in the hall armchair, just opposite me, wide-awake, calm, a scornful smile on his lips. The pale morning sun shining through the fanlight illuminated him like a devil.

"Well, look at that," he said in a honeyed tone. "Look at this hypocrite."

I saw him get up slowly. It didn't occur to me to lock myself in the closet, I didn't retreat, I didn't move. I was paralyzed. He looked me straight in the eyes, and when he was quite ready, with one hand he removed the cloth covering me, neither hastily or roughly, and threw it over his shoulder. I didn't make any attempt to stop him. Feathers floated up toward the ceiling. Motionless and naked, my face turned toward him, I could only utter a sort of hiccup. Then he placed the same hand on my hair and let it down. It was feeling my hair suddenly fall on my shoulders that triggered off my fit of hysterics. I began to scream like a madwoman, flinging myself against his chest, hitting him with my fists, at the end of my frustration, at the end of my strength, at the end of everything.

He did not return my blows, he merely held me in check. I could no longer see him through my tears, but even with my arms pinned to my sides, I was still screaming. I would have screamed until the end of time, without being able to stop, if a terrifying voice outside, you couldn't tell from where, had not stopped me dead.

It was a bullhorn. It said, *"Be careful! The house is surrounded! Stop torturing this woman, you swine, or I'll storm the place!"*

The escaped prisoner let go of me at once to grab the knife he had left on the chair. His astonishment and the anguish I saw in his eyes avenged me for many a torment. Still panting, my cheeks wet, I could not suppress a snicker of triumph.

Another ordeal was beginning.

Outside the garden gates, Captain Malignaud was perched on the running board of a military truck, surrounded by armed infantrymen. Local residents had gathered on the pavement in their pajamas and dressing gowns. He shouted into his bullhorn at them.

"Get back! Get back! Let the soldiers of the Republic do their duty!"

My attacker and I saw these things through a half-open shutter in the kitchen. He had dragged me there naked, my back to him, one hand clamped over my mouth. It was his turn to give in to panic. He murmured, as if in prayer, "No, it isn't true! It isn't possible!"

A second truck hurtled to the scene in the morning sun. Several soldiers burst out without waiting for it to stop. Then you could count ten, fifteen, twenty. Malignaud rushed toward them cursing that it was about time.

"Surround the place!"

They took the heavy parts of a machine gun out of the vehicle and put it unattached in the road. The fugitive repeated over and over against my cheek: "They're out of their minds, those idiots! They're crazy!"

He closed the shutter. For a second, held close to him, I saw that he didn't know what to do, and then he removed his hand from my mouth and said, "They'll never run the risk of shooting, neither with that or with their guns. If you play fair, we'll get out of this."

"We?" I exclaimed. "You're the one they want! Just you!"

"Machine-gun bullets aren't choosy. If they start shooting, there won't even be anything left of your place. I know old Malignoble well, I do!"

He realized that I was upset.

"Listen to me, Caroline. They haven't seen me. They don't know for certain who I am, or what my intentions are, or whether I am armed! You're going to go to the window and tell them first of all that everything's all right, that you were having an argument with a friend, nothing more, and tell them to go—"

I didn't let him finish. I yelled with all my strength. He violently clamped my mouth shut, knocking me over again, and I could neither struggle nor bite him. I know today that my fate had just changed course and that in refusing to listen to him, I had made the silliest mistake of my life.

"I'm going to have to take a different line with you!" he said in a menacing tone. "If you are that stupid, scream as much as you like!"

He only removed his hand to grab his knife and hold it to my throat.

"Go on, scream!"

I shook my head to show him that I wouldn't scream anymore. Then, without further ado, he took me back into the hall. He kept me in awe of the tip of his blade while he unlocked the front door.

"Please," I stammered, "don't let them see me like this! I beg you!"

He picked up the torn pillowcase from the floor and tossed it to me. With both hands I used it to cover my front.

Then he opened the door and pushed me onto the doorstep in a flurry of feathers, the knife across my throat. I was gripped by the sudden coolness, more exposed than I had ever felt before; the light hurt me. A long murmur rose from the crowd of curious onlookers. I saw with despair that it had quickly swelled and that soldiers had to keep people back from the gates. And then silence fell.

"Take a good look at her, Malignaud!" the escaped prisoner cried. "Look at her. If a single one of your muckworms—do you hear me, a single one—dares come into the garden, it's the last time you'll see her alive!"

After that, the only sound was the waves on the beach, far away. All those silent stares gazing at my plight made me close my eyes. I felt myself being pulled backward, into the warmth of the house. The door closed again, the locks clanged, the escaped prisoner let me slump to my knees on the tiled floor, and I began to cry until I could cry no more.

The closed shutters in the kitchen.

Midday perhaps, I have lost track.

He had allowed me to put on my slip and my shoes and to put up my hair. I had washed at the sink. He had looked away, but he needn't have bothered; I didn't care anymore.

When he needed to be alone, he had locked me in the closet. I think he checked every window in the house. What stupidity! Everything was happening outside the gates, on either side of the entrance. He half opened the shutters from time to time to glance outside, but I didn't even look anymore. I could hear them. They were laughing and calling to each other as if at the theater. They brought an accordion, then a barrel organ. The road was full, they were penned in behind a series of barriers like dangerous animals. It looked as though the whole town was standing outside my house, every single person—the men, the women, the children, the old people—even the dogs. The bathers coming back from the beach gathered in their bathing suits. There were vendors selling snacks and ice cream.

In a way, it was reassuring for the escaped prisoner. The crowd was only interested in itself. Malignaud was shouting himself hoarse, vainly trying to move the show, while I was so sickened that I saw the "monster" as no more than a companion of misfortune, my only solace.

I cooked what was left in the icebox. I had eaten nothing since the previous day. When we were at the table, I saw that he had bent my fork in two. I watched him eat with his fingers for a moment, then I couldn't hold out any longer, I did likewise.

"You see, Mommy Long Legs," he said with his mouth full, "it isn't difficult."

He had found a bottle of wine in a cupboard. Usually my assistant was the only person to drink it. He poured us each a glass.

"I wasn't seven years old," he went on, "and I knew it already: apart from the flicks and aspirin, everything that is called progress is slavery."

"Don't call me Mommy Long Legs."

"Caroline. Will do. Have a drink, it'll make you feel better."

Later, as we were finishing our meal, he said softly, "I would never have believed things would turn out like this. I'm sorry for what I've done to you."

I shrugged. Even in the sweet shade of the kitchen, I was hot. He had shut the windows to keep out the noise of the crowd. He said, "You are beautiful, Caroline. Despite what you have been told, I have never taken a woman by force, but I almost did last night."

"You were a fool to deprive yourself."

It was, of course, out of bitterness that I said that. The entire town must have been telling each other with mournful faces that he had done so, ten times rather than once, and with gusto. And I bet that little gossip of a hairdresser was the first to supply the details.

I saw that of the pair of us, he was the more embarrassed. He averted his black eyes and began rummaging in his pockets. He took out a crumpled pack of English cigarettes. I got up to fetch the box of matches. When I came back to where he was sitting, one of my slip straps fell off my shoulder, by itself, but I helped it a little.

I gave him a light, standing up, my breasts at eye level. I could feel my heart in my mouth. My breasts rose and fell with every breath. I remained like that after he had blown out the match. I wouldn't have moved, even if it had burned my fingers. I couldn't speak either; otherwise I don't know what crazy things I might have said to get him into the bedroom.

Finally, it was he who drew away. And his words were to give me a completely different argument from the one to which I was ready to sacrifice myself.

"I'm going to wait patiently until tonight," he said. "In the dark, I'll find some way of getting out of here."

I stared at him for a long time, pleased, of course, that he should throw me such a good line, but sad as well, sad to see, through the fault of others, only one possible outcome to this escapade. Believe me, if he had raped me as often as the crowd outside wanted to believe, if nobody had known he was in my house, I would have let him leave, and I would never have complained. And even then, if only I could have gone back a few hours and made good the mistake I had made that morning, I would have shouted through the window to all those people that I was with a lover—yes, even that sly old headmistress had one!—I would have told them to go to hell. Then, I'm sure, he wouldn't have hurt me. I can no longer believe that he committed the crimes he was accused of. He would have waited for a few hours until the incident had blown over and then he would have continued his long flight. Perhaps even, considering the situation, I would have given myself to him without remorse during that wait. But you can never repair mistakes.

I adjusted my strap and said, "You could escape at once if you wanted to. I know how. Come, I'll show you."

He watched me open the kitchen door, a little surprised, no doubt wary. I gave him a friendly nod to encourage him to follow me. Before doing so, he threw the knife onto the table.

We went up to the bedroom, me in front, all embarrassment this time miraculously dispelled. My heart beat with another kind of anxiety. When we reached it, I saw, for a fleeting moment, without recognizing her, the woman I had been the day before, flung against a wall. I merely said, "You'll have to make a bundle of your dirty clothes and take it with you. That way they won't know how you are dressed."

I went to a window and gently opened one of the shutters. "Come and have a look."

He was beside me again, but the man who had knocked me about so often no longer dared brush up against me.

"There, at the bottom of the garden," I said, pointing. "Do you see that big twisted pine tree?"

He could see it.

"And the clump of bushes in line with it? Well, behind the bushes, the wall has crumbled and it is only three feet from the ground. The gap has been stopped with wire, but it won't be hard to pull it away. On the other side is a thick pinewood, just above the beach."

I turned to look at him. He was like an attentive pupil; I realized that I was talking in my schoolmistress tone of voice.

"I'll let you have a look. I'm going to make your clothes into a bundle."

As I drew away from the window, I bumped into his tall body, which was suddenly awkward. He restrained me as best he could, but my strap slipped again. His black eyes were so gentle, full of such gratitude, that I could feel my resolve weakening.

I closed my eyes so as not to see his, and found the courage to say with irritation, "Haven't you groped me enough? Let me go."

He would have slipped off the other strap and caressed my breasts as I had so feared the day before; I was his and he was saving his skin.

He let me go.

I went to the wardrobe. I caught sight of myself in the mirror, my hair all over the place, disfigured by the horror of what I was going to do.

"There are bound to be soldiers there as well," he said, looking out the window.

I had no voice with which to answer him. I knelt down, keeping an eye on him in the mirror. I gathered his dirty clothes, one hand groping under the bottom of the wardrobe. I felt the gun stuck to the wood with two strips of insulating tape. My husband had put it there on purpose so as to have a gun within reach in the event of a break-in, and I had laughed at him. I pulled it away easily. Without seeing, I wiped it with the fugitive's shirt.

That was precisely the moment he chose to look around.

"That corner where you've got the swing is so beautiful!"

He was smiling. Unfortunately for both of us, he didn't really see me, he only glanced in my direction to corroborate what he was saying, and he looked out the window again.

"I've got to tell you something," he said.

I stood up, the gun hidden behind my back. My heart was beating so fast that I still wonder that he didn't hear it.

"The woman I loved most, the only true love, the very first," said this young man on the threshold of eternity, "was in Marseilles, when I was at a Jesuit school.

"One May evening, as I came out of school, instead of walking as usual toward the Saint-Giniez station to board my bus, I set off aimlessly on foot, having too many things to say to myself to go straight home.

"In the street I was walking down, there was a huge crucifix at the foot of a flight of steps leading to a square where spring was bursting forth in all the gardens. Right in the middle of this square rose a white villa with Baroque corbeling, surrounded by a park and high gates. It was there, on a swing, in a profusion of oleander, that I saw her. I was going to say 'at last,' for I was at the age when one waits impatiently for the impossible, when one never doubts that it will happen.

"She was swinging gently to and fro, languid in the twilight calm, in a dress of white muslin, and the air was of honey. She was perhaps sixteen, and I already appeared the same age. I paused to watch her, fascinated by her graceful neck and her fair hair in an urchin cut, and even her solitude, far away from the silent house. She looked in my direction. Her eyes were flecked with gold, in the light of the setting sun, and so calm that I was intimidated. I walked away but I walked all the way around the park to see her again, my schoolbooks under my arm.

"When I walked past the same spot for the sixth time, she had found my little game so entertaining that the swing was empty. I returned home, my heart bursting with a mixture of happiness and sorrow. I loved her. I loved an angel with short hair. I did not imagine Joan of Arc otherwise.

"The next day, as you can imagine, I went back, and she was there. And the following day, too, and all the other days of one wonderful week. She was waiting for me, I was convinced, but we never spoke a word to each other. The furthest we went was on the last occasion. It was raining. At the time when I usually began my walk around and around the park . . . nobody. I stood at the gates for a moment, in a tight raincoat that was a raincoat only in name, with dripping hair covering half my face, and then, sadder than a stray dog, I set off home in the rain. That was when I saw her appear in a doorway of the house, in a sky-blue summer dress, with nothing to protect her but a sweater, which she held over her head. She ran to sit on the swing, built up speed, and she was away. That evening we did not speak any more than we had before, she only stayed for a symbolic couple of minutes, but she was really someone, don't you think?

"And then there was a Sunday, and after the Sunday, there was that lousy Monday. It was a fine evening, but the swing had been taken down and all the shutters were closed. I can't tell you what a blow it was. My heart in my boots, I mechanically walked around the park and I found myself once again at the spot where I had seen her for the first time. A sheet of paper was rolled around one of the bars of the gate, with a good yard of string around the paper. She knew how to roll things tight, I swear. It took me almost thirty-two years and all my nails to unravel her bandage.

"Do you want to know what she had written? I can recite it better than the story of Theramenes:

We've god to live in Dottingham, by a big pod full of woda-lilies. It's too far frob here, but we were bord to meet again sub day. I dough dot where or how, dor on what swing, but if we speak to each other this time, I will surely scold you for delaying so long.

Jeanne

P.S. I must have caught cold the other day, or it's frob saying adieu to you, my dose is like a lobster.

— *131* —

"I never saw her again. At least, not so far. I've taken my time rather, I must say, but when I think of her, my heart contracts as it did then."

So saying, he turned to me, his eyes misty with melancholy. He probably didn't see the gun pointed at him. Without knowing whether it was loaded or if it was still working—I left that up to fate—I squeezed the trigger and closed my eyes.

The report was terrifying, the recoil flung me against the wardrobe. The panes from one of the windows, pushed against the wall, shattered. The escaped prisoner remained as if suspended in the smoke from the shot, blood all down one side of his torso, then he took two steps forward on legs that could no longer carry him and fell across the room.

There. It was done. My mind was numbed by a great silence. I stared at a white mass spattered with red at my feet from which I had to step back, which I slowly skirted to back out of the door.

I was saved, I could run away, when suddenly a hand appeared in front of my eyes, clenched, already dead, and grabbed the front of my slip. My cry of horror was nothing but a gurgle; I toppled over on top of my victim. Despite my horrified writhing, despite his wound, the man was climbing on top of me and pinning me to the floor with roars of pain and rage. I saw his face smeared with blood. He wanted to say something, but couldn't. He fell back again, the full weight of his heavy body on top of me.

It was then that I heard Malignaud's voice outside, on the other side of the garden, amplified but far off.

"Caroline! Caroline!" he shouted. "Are you alive? Answer me!"

I couldn't say if he had shouted earlier, or how many seconds had gone by since the report. I don't remember exactly when I let go of the gun, either. Probably as soon as the shot had been fired. During the investigation they found the gun under my chest of drawers, on the other side of the room.

The escaped prisoner rose to his knees, then to his feet, his mouth twisted with pain. He made me get up, too, all disheveled, grabbed my arm, and pulled me into the corridor. He said in a strangled but gentle voice, with no trace of animosity, "You're going to talk to them, Mommy Long Legs."

We opened the window in my assistant's bedroom, which overlooked the avenue. I hid the blood on my slip with my crossed arms.

I saw the mob outside my house, their festivities spilling over the barriers, I heard his relief that the show was going on. I made myself shout.

"Captain! Whatever you do, don't move! You can see I'm alive!"

The escaped prisoner looked over my shoulder. He whispered what I should say. I shouted again.

"Captain! He wants to speak to someone who is in the crowd! In a quarter of an hour, not before! She's known as Zozo, she's one of the girls from the Queen of Hearts!"

Malignaud turned to face the crowd, looking flabbergasted. A woman yelled, "The colored girl, Captain!" I then saw a young black girl with a great frizzy mop of hair and wearing a red striped beach dress make her way to the front of the crowd. The soldiers half opened one of the barriers just long enough to let her through. She walked toward the officer, with an ungainly step in her high heels, her eyes raised toward our window. Even through the gates I could sense the anxiety of a girl in love.

I was tied to a chair in the kitchen in my torn slip, my hands behind the back of the chair, my ankles bound. He kept one eye on what was going on outside. He pressed a towel to his wound over his shirt. Beads of sweat ran down his forehead.

Shortly after the clock struck two, I heard the gate creak. He shouted, "On her own, Malignoble! Nobody else!"

The gravel in the drive crunched under the young black girl's footsteps. The escaped prisoner took the time to close the shutters and windows again, then he went out into the hall, dragging his legs.

I heard the door being unlocked and right away the same sounds in reverse. Then her terrified voice.

"My God, you're injured!"

I gathered she was trying to support him. He said hopefully, "Zozo, you've got to get me out of this mess! You were right, I no longer know what I'm doing!"

Like all men when they have to admit their weaknesses, he must have had tears in his eyes. Then he walked in front of her as they came back to the kitchen. I heard his feet scraping the tiled floor and it sounded as though he was leaning on the wall with his hand. When she saw me, his friend froze in the doorway: all that blood on him and on me, the rope tying me up, my loose hair!

She shouted, "It's not true! How is such a thing possible?"

She pronounced it "pothible," "thuch." She was about my height, my age, and with fine, childlike features, but tall and slim as a liana under her dress, sinuous as a snake. Her skin was the color of chestnut, and at first her face seemed to be all teeth and huge, innocent eyes.

She was in such a state that she, too, had to sit down, while he slid down the wall by the door and slumped to the floor.

I said at once to the woman, "I want everybody to know: he didn't rape me! He didn't do anything to me at all!"

She shrugged one shoulder revealed by her dress and replied, her expression instantly hardened, a scornful sneer on her lips, "Why would he rape you? If he wants to make love, he's got me!"

"You?" I retorted in the same tone. "It doesn't bother you, that's your profession."

In the ensuing silence a tear ran down her cheek, and down mine. I spoke first.

"I'm sorry, that's not what I meant. I meant that people are malicious, they'll take any opportunity to invent all sorts of horrors. All the horrible things that a man like him could have done to a woman like me!"

The escaped prisoner let out a sigh of impatience, his back to the wall, gazing at the ceiling. Zozo stood up, wiping her cheek. She said gently, "Francis isn't who you think he is."

"Francis? He told me he was called Edouard."

"It doesn't matter what he told you. Do you want to know the truth? He's a student who passed himself off as the escaped prisoner from the citadel!"

At the time, I confess, I was taken aback. She seemed so sincere, so sure of her facts. But clearheaded, I asked her, "Have you known him long?"

"Not long, no."

"So," I retorted, "how do you know he's not the escaped prisoner who passed himself off to you as a student?"

It was her turn to remain speechless. For a few seconds she continued to meet my gaze, with a sort of incredulous despair, then she turned to the man on the floor to beg for an answer. Her pathetic determination to believe him moved me, but he, obviously, had other worries.

"Listen, Zozo," he said wearily, "even if she were right, what difference does it make? I've got to get out of this place!"

He raised himself up against the wall with difficulty. When he was on his feet, he said, "There's a gap at the bottom of the garden. Unfortunately, I saw two sentries."

They stood facing each other, him clutching his towel in a wad against his chest to stem the bleeding, she stunned by what she had just learned. Her whole body upright, mustering her love for him, she said, "I'll take care of them."

That was what happened. People have said all sorts of things, but they're not true. That I gave him an injection, for example, to give him strength. My bag, since I had returned home the previous evening, was still on the Chinese console table; nobody touched it. Zozo cleansed his wound with disinfectant and bandaged his torso. I merely told her where our medicine chest was. My husband's gun, I found out later, was an old one-shot Simplex. The bullet had gone through my attacker's chest below the right shoulder, before shattering the window behind him and lodging in the bedroom wall. I was told that if it had perforated his lung, he wouldn't have had a chance of survival.

They slipped into the garden by the side door from the classroom. They left me tied up in the kitchen. Zozo was the first to leave the room.

Before going out, the escaped prisoner leaned over me and said, "I won't gag you, Caroline, but you must tell them I did it. If you don't scream before Zozo gets back, I'll know that you've forgiven me."

He placed a kiss on my mouth and left.

Zozo came back a quarter of an hour later; it seemed interminable. She freed me. I went into the hall to pick up my skirt and my white blouse. While I was getting dressed, she told me that the hunted man had escaped over the broken wall, at the bottom of the garden, while she had distracted the soldiers in her own way. At the last minute, while they panted over her like seals, at a corner where the walls met only fifty paces away, she and he had exchanged a farewell glance. She had seen him stumble into the pinewoods that led to the ocean.

Sitting on the same chair to which I had been tied a little earlier, she told me again, before I opened the window to call the captain and suffer the hell in store for me, "I will continue to believe, contrary to what anyone may say, that he was a student. If he was telling me the truth, I'll see him again, won't I?"

As you know, neither of us ever saw him again.

During the investigation I didn't breathe a word about the help she gave him. She had urged him in vain to give himself up and he had bound and gagged both of us. The sentries she had so graciously dragged from their duty weren't going to broadcast the fact from the rooftops.

As for the rest, those long hours when I had been locked in with him, I learned that there are no depths to which people will not sink. At first they felt sorry for me. Then they laughed. Nobody would believe me. Worse still, when nobody could remember who had said what, they attributed all the slander to my own confidences. Ostensibly urging me to be more discreet, a spate of anonymous letters revealed at what precise moment during a nonstop orgy I had been raped, beaten, sodomized, or reduced to compliance, in which existing or nonexistent room of the house, and in which unlikely position my sensuality, heightened by widowhood, had met its match.

And then other letters arrived, those from my pupils' parents, to inform me that much to their regret, there was a war on, etc. I protested and declaimed my indignation in vain; my assistant herself did not return.

All I could do was sell the house and the furniture and leave the country.

Frou-Frou

I'M A MOVIE STAR.

I'm a lousy actress, but I don't lose any sleep over it. I do what Jicks tells me. I hassle everybody. I stamp on my glasses. I'm sort of color-blind. My famous screen look—that's my contact lenses. For the sad scenes, all I have to do is take them out and everything starts swimming. Then they gave me an Oscar. Twice in a row I got it, like Luise Rainer. Once for *Lips* and once for *Legs*. They made good bookends but weren't enough to put my name up in lights. Another year, at the Biltmore, I had to present Hepburn with a vase. I fell flat on my ass as I was climbing onto the stage. I came off all right there. That wretched photo was on the cover of all the magazines. When I did a tour for the GIs, I even came across it in Korea, pinned on the walls of the john. If they do a Hollywood festival after the bomb has blown everything up, I bet they use it for the poster. All the same, I hassle as many people as I can. Not because I enjoy it. I do what Jicks told me.

At the time we're talking about I wasn't a star yet. I'd shot four or five B-movies in France, in black and white. Once I was taken to a private viewing of one of them. Everyone was snoring by the end of the first reel, even the projectionist. Even me. As I had never understood what was going on while we were filming this turkey, I didn't come out of there any the wiser. I never wanted to see the others.

I must say they go to great lengths to complicate things. The way they insist on filming scenes in the wrong order, for example. When it's a story involving three generations, you never know if you're getting your rocks off with your fiancé or your grandson. The only clue is the wig they stick on your head. And even then you can't be sure. From the start I've always refused to let them age me. I can picture myself dead already. I chuck everything I can lay my hands on at the makeup mirror.

In short, I'd have a rough time telling you the story of the turkey in question. *Toulouse to Whatsit*, it was called; I can't remember the name of the station of arrival. Unless they gave me the synopsis of the wrong film at the end, I play a dancer who flashes her legs in an old-fashioned Parisian dance hall. My costar is a bowler-hatted dwarf who paints pictures. Of course, he takes me to his place to paint me in the nude. Then they write all my rotten lines on a board for me and I tell him all this stuff about my past—ditched at eighteen with a kid on my hands—they take out my contact lenses for the closeup, and he realizes that it's mean to make me freeze to death for a stupid picture. In any case, as he's too little to screw me—unless they decide to make it a comedy—he's even given up on marriage, and he makes me a present of his family fortune so that I can buy up the dance hall. Violins. I become the queen of Paris and all that rubbish, but we never see the train to Whatsit. Or they got the second crew to film that. The worst thing is I'm a lousy dancer. And as for my costar, he couldn't paint to save his life. But he had a stand-in. All that by way of telling you what a load of shit it was.

All the same, it was in that film in the first reel that Jicks's flunkies noticed me. They made me cross the Atlantic. As for him, he's never been near a set, or read a script, or seen one of his films. Jason Ivanhoe Christopher Kelly Santacallas is his real name. A great producer, very shrewd, very rich, but a dreadful man. Not that he deprived me of my beauty sleep; he never laid a finger on me. He said that I'd make money, that's all. But what a leech. He had to choose everything. In my contract he gave me seventy-seven pages spelling out the things I was forbidden to do without his consent, from marriage to what brand of toothpick to use. If I got the urge to play with myself in bed, I would have to ask his permission. So you can imagine the sort of character he was. I spent my life thinking up tricks to scatter the army of muckrakers he set on my heels across L.A. I thought of nothing else. For whole afternoons I would leap from one taxi to another for a quick thrill in all sorts of places, each one seedier than the last. A men's changing room, a car in a wrecker's yard, the washroom in a gas station, the elevator in a foundation for public morality—I've done it all. Motels, out of the question. The one time I tried, they nabbed me in midbattle by kicking in the door to the room. I was so terrified I tensed up, or it was the guy's fault, and they couldn't get us apart for at least an hour. I thought I'd go crazy.

Well, that's what Jicks was like. All the same, he gave me a part in *Neck*, a Technicolor musical comedy that was the biggest box-office success of the year. That's what really launched my career. I'm a lousy singer, but the screenwriter was a genius. When the story opens, I'm an *ex*–singing star. The bastard who ditched me at twenty with a kid on my hands twisted my neck a bit too hard in an argument, and now, when I open my mouth, people run to buy an umbrella. A genius, I tell you. I didn't want to work with any other screenwriter, but he joined the strike that nearly killed Hollywood and Jicks struck him off his list. Anyway, the poor girl, that's the only thing she knows how to do, go onto a provincial stage and sing them "No Use Trying, It's Possible." To feed her kid she gets herself thrown out of every honky-tonk joint in every godforsaken place in America. In that film you do get to see the train. I'm forever rushing from the East Coast to the West with the brat, who's always asking for a bit of pie with a ton of cream on top, until I lift one from the restaurant car. Luckily the young sheriff who interrogates me in deepest Alabama always carries a photo of me in his wallet and recognizes the wonderful singer who gives him a hard-on every time he listens to his record player. And now you get to the really brilliant bit, the one they've copied in the hundred and fifty *Neck* imitations: I continue opening and shutting my mouth on the set, but it's the wretched phonograph that's playing behind the curtain! At the premiere, at the Chinese, even I applauded. Then I tour all the little honky-tonk joints that threw me out, except that this time, in the restaurant car, the kid squashes the whole pie in the face of the headwaiter who turned me in. I become the queen of New York and so forth and it all ends with a wedding with two thousand extras and nearly as many firemen to make the rain, because I want to have a laugh and sing with my real voice. In fact, it's in that last number that they predicted I'd land an Oscar soon. Nobody would believe that I could sing that badly.

It was Jicks, too, who taught me my profession. "When you don't feel a scene," he used to say, "tell the screenwriter it's shit, tell the cameraman that the lights are burning your eyes, the makeup artist to do a repair job, tell all the others they're assholes, tell me to get more dough out of the insurance people. But don't say anything to the director. Sulk until he apologizes and sends you six dozen roses. Give a dozen to your dresser and throw the rest back in his face. You can even crack him over the head with the heel of your shoe, bite him or kick him in the balls, that's what he's paid for. The vital thing is that he keeps his trap shut. You must always make *your* film," he would say, "it's not your job to make it theirs, and don't you ever forget it."

Besides, there was something wonderful about Jicks. He never pushed me into showing myself in public, he didn't pay for tutors for me to forge my personality, none of that rubbish. When it comes to personality, I'm hopeless. The only thing I like is being left alone where I am. Even fucking, I can do without it when I'm not being made to think about it constantly with don'ts. And, in a way, Jicks understood me. After *Neck* he made me do *Eyes*, another one where I didn't understand a thing, but I was pleased. I played the part of a deaf and dumb girl, I didn't have any lines to learn. Then, enough. He promised me I'd be on vacation for two years.

On my last day of filming, I gave the crew their farewell presents between takes. When I kiss my kid, crying, in the barn, because his swine of a father has ditched me to marry the cotton planter's daughter, we'd already gone a bit overboard with the champagne, and I couldn't stop laughing. Even removing my contact lenses, everybody thought it showed. Like heck! Laughter, tears, it's all the same. "It's not your mug that tells them whether to laugh or cry," Jicks would say. "Otherwise, how would Buster Keaton manage? And Rin Tin Tin, dammit!" He had never even seen the mutt on screen. He had heard that he earned more money than Crawford, and that was enough.

All the same, he kept his word. As soon as the scene was in the can, they didn't even waste time taking off my makeup, they whisked me to the airport and put me on the plane to Miami. The same night, I was sleeping on Jicks's yacht, the *Pandora*, and when I woke up, we were already in the middle of the Atlantic.

Picture one of those big white things with engines of I don't know how many thousand gee-gees, full of gangways and bathtubs and copper lanterns. Jicks wanted to sail around the world. That was the only thing he was really interested in: sailing around the world. Europe was at war, and we flew the Swiss flag. When I said that, a long time afterward, the journalists rambled on about my devastating sense of humor.

There were twelve men in the crew of the *Pandora*, plus two girls in T-shirts that came down to their bottoms who acted as stewardesses, a French chef, and a Chinese launderer. Jicks brought his personal psychoanalyst, who he dragged everywhere, a tall, nutty smartass who liked to be called Esmeralda. He didn't touch her either. She claimed, in fact, that no man had ever touched her. And then there was me. I spent my time doing nothing. I sunbathed, I slept. I played gin rummy with Jicks. He won fifty-three dollars and twenty cents off me during the two and a half years we were at sea. That shows how well I play. Checkers, too. Chess, I've never wanted to understand. He played with Esmeralda. As for her, her greatest pleasure, after the three hours of daily blah-blah in Jicks's cabin, was to swim around the boat. Even the sharks didn't touch her.

Anyway, I was very glad to be a long way from the studios and all those hassles because of one hair out of place or because of my French accent or because of one word rather than another. When it comes to languages, I'm hopeless—I ask you—and how are you supposed to tell the difference between one word and another when you read the infernal story of your bloody life *written in phonetics* on a blackboard? "Aye kannot." Fifty lines in a row, sometimes. Besides, without my contact lenses or my glasses, I see all the colors back to front. For the board to be black, it has to be white; to write on it in white, you need black ink; everybody gets confused and nobody gives a damn. And I have to do the shot again. And again, and again. And they put another layer of paint on my face. And they undress me and dress me again because I'm perspiring. And they do my hair again because my wretched platinum blond hair frizzes all by itself. And they add a ton of light bang in the middle of my face because bags are beginning to appear under my eyes. And they encourage me with malicious eyes, they say "darling" as if they want to eat me alive. And by the end, I can't take any more, I do what

Jicks told me, I scream in French, I stamp on my glasses, I want to go home, to Montrouge in the Paris suburbs, and take the metro every day to Nation and go back to being a manicurist. By the way, I did Jicks's, Esmeralda's, and the two stewardess's nails on the boat. Jicks always said to me: "You were born to do this. What a pity that the cinema was born for you." And I saw a glint in one or the other of his eyes that was almost sincere pity.

After a detour via Ireland and a stop in Cork, where he was supposed to meet someone about a plane without a pilot, we wanted to cross the Channel to go to Deauville, but in the end we weren't able to, the sky was full of swastika'd mosquitoes machine-gunning the sea to make us change course. We sailed down the Brittany coast, our only worry being to stock up on fuel, and in La Baule we took aboard an Austrian director and a French actor who Jicks said would make money. The actor had played opposite me in one of my first dud films. They had their wife—joint—with them who they called Heads-or-Tails. She was massive and spectacular from both sides. She only opened her mouth to say intelligent things. For at least a week, at the table, she bored us to death with some bloody place in the Morbihan where, if she had understood correctly, they fished for shrimps that were ready-peeled. In the end even the engines deep in the bowels of the old tub couldn't stand the sound of her anymore; they broke down. That's how it all happened. When it comes to mechanics, I'm hopeless, but the sailors on the *Pandora* appeared to be even worse. Two and a half months we lay at anchor, just taking to pieces the bits that didn't work and waiting for the spare parts that didn't arrive. When they did, they were the wrong ones. Jicks sacked the chief mechanic and cabled for them to send him one by hydroplane who wasn't so dumb. The machine was brought down by a German submarine. They saved the guys, but Roosevelt's ambassador made a stink, Hitler's minister apologized, and the L.A. newspaper's headline read: THREE MEN RISK THEIR LIVES TO SAVE FROU-FROU FROM HELL. And then a second hydroplane landed effortlessly beside us. The new chief mechanic waited for the new parts to arrive. Unfortunately, the factory that made them had been bombed. Luckily, the new chief mechanic, unless it was the Chinese launderer, noticed that we didn't need them. In short, we hung about for a whole summer, like a cork bobbing on the ocean, without being allowed to land, off a peninsula called La Pointe des Amériques between Oléron and Royan.

Jicks said that if he could persuade a writer to come and join us, we would have everybody we needed to make our own film, which would be cheap to produce and would make a fortune, but it was a joke, of course, none of those death-defying writers would have agreed. Even with such a well-stocked cellar as the *Pandora*'s, even with two ultra-sexy stewardesses and Heads-or-Tails as a bonus, they would wire: "Sorry Jicks, it doesn't feel right. But I'm in the middle of adapting *The Three Musketeers*, Selznick isn't the right producer, and if you like . . ." And a hundred to one, they would keep the advance check. They're all like that.

I have to admit that seen from afar, our situation wasn't brilliant. The ship's radio was on the go round the clock. For the world between Sunset and Wilshire we were lost. We were starving in the middle of a storm as well as contending with floods and arms. The fact was that nothing was happening at all. We sheltered in a pretty creek, the Couronnes de la Mer, and every day two sailors went off in a rowboat to fetch everything we needed. We could see the merrymakers on the rocks in the distance. At first they gesticulated at us, waving handkerchiefs. Then they no longer took any notice of us. The radio said that my compatriots and their allies had taken a licking, but it didn't show, not even with binoculars. Anyway, nobody on board listened to the radio anymore, except Jicks, who monopolized it to carry out his business.

When *Eyes*, the film I shot before leaving, had been edited, they made me record a message for that big family, the American film industry, and they blasted it over the air up and down the country on the night of the premiere, with the national anthem and the "Marseillaise," all the trimmings.

When he signed me up, Jicks had forbidden me to talk about myself other than in the third person. I was always to say to people: "Frou-Frou doesn't give a shit," or "Frou-Frou can't remember where the hell she put her goddamn right shoe." Even to my best friend, Rachel Dee, who sold Arrow shirts in Westwood. Even to Jicks himself. This time, for the famous speech, he allowed me to talk like everybody else. Terrifying. With all that crackling from one side of the planet to the other, my voice was like "a glimmer of hope in the gloom of a dying world"—that's what they wrote in all the papers. I told them what Jicks's publicity people had come up with in phonetics, and it was such a nightmare that I tripped over all the words that had more than one syllable. I could have cried, so you can imagine the others. I told them that *Eyes* was the film I was most attached to, because my role as a deaf and dumb girl, in the tragic times the free countries were living through, took on a significance that went beyond my own humble self. I told them how sad I was to be unable to be with them that evening and that perhaps I wouldn't for a long time, but to cherish the memory of the little French girl they had adopted as a symbol of the unshakable friendship that had united my country with theirs since Lafayette. I think I also spoke about Charles Boyer, Edward G. Robinson, and Annabella. Shit, without mentioning any names for reasons that escape me, I even talked about a director and an actor, both talented and fleeing the Nazis, whom Jicks had given sanctuary to. I still wonder why they didn't give me anything to say about Heads-or-Tails and her peeled shrimps.

Anyway, before we set out to sea, *Eyes* made even more money than *Neck*, even though I didn't sing in it. Every morning Jicks received figures that he checked over breakfast. Then he would give me a strange look and say, "If I had Ben Hecht on board, or even one of those little assholes from Harvard who shat a best-seller and who farts away every day in an obscure office at Fox, we'd make a killing."

But I was delighted that the people he talked about weren't there. It was the best vacation I'd ever had. As we couldn't set foot on land, I didn't even have to find a bloody ruined church of breathtaking beauty, or dress, except for dinner, or talk about illness and politics, or kiss a load of snotty brats in their mothers' arms or old people who smell of piss, or listen to crap, or speak in the third person or whatever. I just had to lie in the sun on the deck at the back of the tub, with a huge canvas screen to avoid embarrassing a sailor who had never seen a naked woman before, and believe me, I had everything I needed: my soda, my chocolates, my California oils, my pack of cards for solitaire, my Camel cigarettes, four pairs of glasses designed from fifty centimeters to infinity, my book on houseplants, my bowl of ice cubes, and my mother's latest letter, addressed to Germaine Tison, Postbox 424, Saint-Julien de l'Océan.

I've never felt such nostalgia for any other period of my life, except my childhood in Montrouge, when they used to stuff licorice in my mouth every time I opened it. Until the age of four, everybody's a star. Then they're forever getting up your nose. I know the secrets of happiness like the back of my hand, and they'd fit onto a postage stamp. I'll have a daughter one day, when they've squeezed all the films they can out of every inch of my body. Whether she cries, shouts, rages, even if she catches jaundice, I'll make her into a manicurist. Even if I have to take her there every morning using my Oscars for crutches, and kicking the last title of my filthy career. Let me be struck down by lightning if I lie.

So, to resume the situation, I'm lying on the beach at the back of the *Pandora*, naked as the day I was born, platinum blond like the new Harlow, dozing on my air mattress like a good girl after a whole afternoon of sunbathing, not thinking about anything, and that is when it all began. I can't remember exactly what year it was, or which month. I think it must have been in '40, in early September. If you tell me it was in August, I won't contradict you. If you tell me it was in '39 or '41, I won't contradict you either, I don't care, but I would think you were mistaken.

In any case, it was blissfully quiet. It was the hour when the sun is round and green above the horizon. A plop-plopping in the water made me suddenly open my eyes and sit up. I saw, framed in a *Pandora* life preserver hanging from the ship's rail, a man in black from head to foot who was swimming toward me in the red sea. I picked up my number-three glasses and put them on as I leaped to my feet.

The guy was exhausted. I could tell from his tense hands, from his gurgling, which sounded as though he was drowning. I threw him the life preserver, ropes and all, and two other ropes that were lying around. If I didn't throw him the bridge, it was honestly because I didn't have one. He floundered around in all that for a good two minutes, and all the time that he was climbing out and falling back into the water with crazed eyes, I could hear him moaning, "Gran! Gran!" Unless he was saying "ran" over and over again, which didn't make any sense.

Anyway, when he had managed to get the top half of his body over the guardrail, I tipped him onto the deck like a bag of wet laundry. I knelt down beside him. I saw that he was a tall beanpole of twenty-eight or thirty, and that his Lacoste sport shirt was pink from blood he'd lost. For a minute, all he could do was spit and cough and pant like a boxer down for the count. And then he opened his pitiful big black eyes and looked at me, murmuring between hiccups, "Please, don't call anyone. I've escaped from a fortress, I'm wounded."

I didn't know what to do. At the time, it didn't even occur to me that I had nothing on but my glasses.

He said, frightened by the astonishment reflected in them, "I swear, I was sentenced for a crime I didn't commit."

He was dripping everywhere, but he wasn't bleeding anymore. Under his shirt, he wore a makeshift dressing. He repeated, "Please."

He must have been so desperate to be friends and for me to believe him, his hand caressed my shoulder and wandered over my titties. I gave him a little tap. I asked him, "Can you stand up if you lean on me?"

He squeezed his eyelids in gratitude. I got up, slipped on my bathrobe, and leaped headfirst into trouble. It would be dark before long. The least I could do was hide him somewhere until then.

We struggled down to the deck below and then lower, to the hold. At the end of a corridor full of grease, between the engine room and the fuel tanks, there was a little room where bags of I don't know what had been piled and other bits and pieces: cans of paint, an old fairgrounds horse, old deck chairs. There wasn't much light, the ceiling was made for dwarfs, but it was the only place I could think of where nobody on board ever went, unless Jicks's shrinky-poo decided to get it on with the Chinese launderer and couldn't find anywhere more romantic.

I lay the poor boy down on the bags. I left for a minute to go to my cabin for a blanket and something to dress his wound with. When I got back, all he was wearing was a wedding ring on his left hand; he had put his clothes to dry on a pipe and arranged two burst mattresses in a corner. He was lying on them as he must have lain in his mother's stomach. It was hellishly hot in that hole, but he was shivering.

I took off his hopeless dressing. He had a wound on the front of his shoulder, far above the heart, luckily, and the same behind, only bigger. The ocean had already cleaned them thoroughly, but I still dabbed them with disinfectant. He closed his eyes and let me get on with it. He didn't complain. I stuck two bandages on, with ointment, beautiful as blinis with fresh cream, and I bound his torso, evenly and tight, as I had learned to do in the girl scouts in Montrouge. I love nursing people almost as much as doing their nails. One of the two stewardesses, Toledo, well, her first profession was nursing. We talked about it all the time. She taught me lots of things, but sometimes I floored her, too. Cupping glasses, for example. If they awarded Oscars for cupping glasses, I'd have a whole windowful.

When I had finished, and he was nice and warm in his blanket, I asked him his name.

He said weakly, "Frédéric. You can call me Fred if you like, but that reminds me of prison."

"Were you there long?"

"Six years."

"How did you escape?"

"I can't tell you. You understand, it might come in handy again if they catch me."

He closed his eyes again.

"You rest. Nobody will come and disturb you here. Are you hungry?"

He shook his head on the mattress.

"Tomorrow, after a good night's sleep, we'll decide what to do."

He didn't answer, he was already asleep.

I went back to see him during the night, after dinner. He looked all right, except that he talked in his sleep. From what I could understand of his babbling, there was a swing, a tomato, and the ship's bell. He distinctly said, "You're not going to swallow your bell, you pain in the ass?" And he clenched his fists to strike.

The next day he was really delirious.

I had to tell someone on the *Pandora*, I didn't feel capable of deciding anything on my own. As I later had to bribe almost everyone to keep quiet, I may as well tell you one thing right now: you can publish my testimony where you like, you can write a book, you can make a film with a two-bit peroxide blond actress playing my part, it bothers me less than my first diaper, but I'll never tell you who, aboard the tub, helped me hide Frédéric. Some people are still working for Jicks and I don't want him to strike them off the payroll or worse. I'll just tell you that you can count out Esmeralda, Heads-or-Tails, and the two stewardesses, Toledo and Bessie—that is, everyone of the female sex on that shitty cruise. I'm only a dumb movie star but I've got enough common sense not to trust a woman. Even my best friend, Rachel Dee, who sold her Arrow shirts in Westwood, pulled a fast one on me. A dirty trick. For no reason, just like that. To get attention.

So *someone* went down that afternoon with me to see the injured man.

Lavergne, the French chef. He said so himself, in any case, and he hasn't worked for the producer in question for a long time.

(From the notes of Marie-Martine Lepage)

We decided to wait another twenty-four hours. I changed the dressing on his wound. I added two more blankets. Frédéric had a temperature. He said, in his moments of lucidity, "We must cast off at once. We must leave. Otherwise, I'll never make it. The bell will toll again and again, I won't have any more time."

The next day he was better. I brought him a meal. He ate a little and drank a lot of water. He perspired heavily but was still cold. I had dressed his wound again. He looked at me with unseeing eyes. He confused me with a woman he had known, I could tell, but he never uttered a name. He called me my darling, my pet, my love, my sweetheart, my baby, my chick, and my pretty. I don't know why I was so certain that they were all addressed to the same woman. In any case, he was well smitten.

And then, another two days, and he had recovered. I tell you it was a miracle.

First, at sunset, I went down to see how his wound was, his temperature and his mood, it was beginning to become a habit. He was standing in the passage in the hold, in front of his open door. He said, "I needed to walk. In this rat hole, I can't even stand up."

His temperature was 37.2 degrees. His wound, a bad dream. But you should have seen his tears when I told him we'd be casting off that night and that, as he was fit as a fiddle, his presence on board was no longer welcome. He could even take a lifeboat to reach dry land, there were so many that nobody would notice. I had been very nice to him, like in *Eyes* when the cops give me a pen and paper and, in the end, I don't denounce the bastard who gave me my kid. Now, another person on board knew, I wanted him to go.

"Go where?" he asked. "Please, if you're leaving tonight, let me stay just a little longer. You can put me ashore wherever you like in France, you'll never hear of me again."

I remember we were both in the lumber room, him lying on his moldy mattresses, me sitting on the floor near him, in my Saks Olympic swimsuit, the white one with red and blue stripes, and my specs. That was when he suddenly asked, "Could you take your glasses off for a second?"

I did. I knew beforehand that he would raise himself up on his elbows and look at me with that expression of a guy who can't remember which lousy taxi he screwed you in one Christmas.

The next question, I had heard it more often in one day than hello-how-are-you in my whole life: "Hey, haven't I seen you in a movie?"

I replied as usual: "No kidding, which one?"

The scene is in black and white in a hotel room, simple but clean.

The young woman with platinum blond hair leans up against the door to close it. Her eyes are full of tears. In her cheap rain-soaked dress, she is very seductive.

The young truck driver who is in the middle of packing his suitcase turns around, both surprised and thrilled at her bursting in. His vest, worn but clean, emphasizes his muscular shoulders.

GIRL [*in a pathetic voice*]

I'll tell you the truth! My husband has abandoned me and my little boy. I've had to send him to boarding school so that I can work. But he can't, he can't stay locked up. He escapes! He hides at his grandmother's!

[*Close-up of the young truck driver. He's very moved. He holds out his hand.*

The camera follows the young woman from the front as she comes toward him, distraught.]

GIRL

Oh, he really isn't a bad boy! But he keeps getting into trouble. He throws burning paper out of the window. He walks on the roofs of houses and doesn't care if he breaks the tiles.

[*Indulgent smile from the young man, who is holding her by the shoulders. He makes her sit down on the edge*

~ 151 ~

of the bed. You can sense that he'd like to kiss her but doesn't dare.]

GIRL [*despondent*]

People say I should send him to a Jesuit college. He's intelligent, he'd do well, but I can't afford it!

[*She cries.*
The young man, his face set, walks across the room, his hands in the pockets of his overalls, faded but clean.]

MAN

Listen to me, sweetheart. I'm only a poor truck driver. I was raised in a foster home. But I can tell you one thing: I've never been afraid of hard work.

[*He goes down on one knee. A shot of their two profiles in silhouette against the window. Gradually the music of their first waltz is heard.*]

MAN

My love, marry me! Your son will be mine. He'll go to the Jesuit college. I'll drive my truck down any road, in any weather. . . .

[*She flings herself into his arms, in tears, mad with joy.*
As the music grows louder, they gently draw apart, and there is a shot of the little elephant cymbal player, on the bedside table, which they had bought for the kid when they first met.]

END

A profoundly moving moment.

I told the escaped prisoner that it was indeed me, in one of those timeless masterpieces of my early career. I couldn't remember the title, but I was playing opposite Mathieu, the actor who was on board. As the story is supposed to be set in Marseilles, we filmed it in Nice, during the carnival. We lost the kid who was playing my son in the crowd and never saw him again. That's why you don't see him in the movie. The screenwriter was rushed back and he got rid of his scenes and bundled him off to boarding school. I'd rather not know where they'd have sent me if I'd gotten lost.

Frédéric fell back onto his mattress with a huge sigh, his hands clasped behind his head, and said, "They showed us the film at the citadel. I confess, I cried."

He looked away with that air of not knowing which way to look, but I knew he was trying to get me to take pity on him so that I would keep him hidden until our next port of call. Jicks had decided that we wouldn't cast off until midnight. Why he decided that, I don't know, even now. Anyway, I had the whole of dinner to think about it.

I stood up so cleverly that I gave my head a good crack against that damn ceiling. Every time I went down into that lumber room, I saw stars; I never left the place without banging my bump. I said "Shit," and told Frédéric I had to go and get dressed and that I'd think about what to do with him later.

Give someone your little finger and look what happens. That farewell dinner, I hardly dare remember it. I've never been ashamed of anything, but now, to have to tell you about it, I haven't got the guts, I'd rather move straight on to the next scene. Let's get this clear: it's not the fact that you can publish this in *Confidential* that bothers me; today it would just double the box-office takings if *Time* reported it. It's having to *say* it. I'd almost rather act it, except that it'd take a hell of an actress to convey, without getting her bloomers in a twist, all the nuances of baseness to a poor old woman and her great-granddaughter who came there because there was a line across the street for *Lassie*.

Oh well, too bad, I'll stop up my ears so as not to hear myself.

First of all, the set. It's the dining room of the *Pandora*, mahogany and copper everywhere. The big oval table, covered with a white cloth and English china, is lit by candlelight. It's hot. The portholes have been opened and the flames from the candles flicker languidly in the draft.

Then, the cast: the men in dinner jackets, the women in evening dress. Jicks is sitting at one end of the table, with his white hair, his disgruntled expression, his walking stick within reach, and his fifty little bottles of medicines in front of him to ward off all illnesses. I'm sitting opposite him, at the other end of the table, in a filmy black dress, with my contact lenses, my diamond necklace, my jade heart on my ring finger in memory of my beginnings, my nails and eyelashes immaculate, my lips desirable, and my famous platinum hair shining in the light.

On either side of Jicks: Esmeralda, in a white dress, her shoulders and throat magnificent, her skin golden, her hair elaborately piled on top of her head, crowning a pair of eyes almost as green as mine, with the haughty air of a two-hundred-dollar-a-session shrink, and Heads-or-Tails, six-foot-one and 154 pounds of pink flesh in a bullfighter-red sheath dress, blond with a blue gaze, her mouth ingenuous and her breasts puffed up like globes, the most terrifying breasts you've ever seen, heaving, overflowing, irrepressible, obsessional—in any case, too much bliss for one man. That's why there are two husbands on either side of me: the director, Franz Stockhammer, his single hair brushed back, a sporting fifty, a Gallic mustache, rapacious features, and Mathieu, the actor, twenty-five, a nose job and a teeth job, with Grant's smile, Gable's muscles, Raft's velvety eyes, Boyer's voice, and despite all that, a charming boy. It would be unfair to leave out the two stewardesses who served us in *Pandora* T-shirts and sailor hats, bare feet and legs. The brunette is Bessie, and the blonde Toledo. I've already told you I was friends with Toledo because she had a nursing diploma. I liked Bessie, too, but the feeling wasn't mutual. I really couldn't say why. Unless, without intending to, I have just explained it.

So we're all there, eating God knows what in silence, washed down with champagne. I only drink soda or champagne. It was Jicks's idea. Secretly, when I can, I treat myself to large glasses of ice water. It's supposed to be bad for the stomach, the liver, and the arteries, but I've got an iron constitution, water will never do me any harm. The reason we're not talking is because we've already spent the whole summer together, anchored in the same place, and we haven't got anything left to say to each other. Perhaps Heads-or-Tails, as she cuts her triple slice of rare leg of lamb, makes a clever comment on some idiocy, but I stopped listening to her ages ago.

And then, suddenly, I say, "Excuse Frou-Frou, Mathieu. What was the name of that film you did with her?"

He swallows a mouthful, his forehead all furrowed. He replies,

"A *Mother's Ordeal*? No, wait, they changed the title when it came out. It was . . ."

"*The Beauty and the Truck Driver*," Stockhammer let out peremptorily without even looking up.

"Did I produce it?" Jicks asked from the height of scorn. "Then that is not its title."

It was just then, while Jicks was talking, that I jumped in my seat and opened my eyes wide. Something had grabbed my ankle under the table. I heard Mathieu exclaim, "I've got it! It was *The Abandoned Woman*!"

Now I'm sure, a hand is slowly climbing up my leg, the silk of my stocking is like an electric tingling. I drop my napkin on purpose and bend over to pick it up. I hear Stockhammer say, "No it wasn't! It was *The Abandoned Mother*!"

I lift up a corner of the tablecloth, and what do I see? My stowaway on his knees under the table, near an open trapdoor leading down to the bowels of the ship. His hand is on my knee, already under my dress. Stuck in a space that is too small for his large body, he is twisting his neck, his face upside down. He smiles sheepishly at me, tragic and proud of himself.

I straighten up again, dumbfounded. Jicks bawls at everybody: "The mother, the woman, what does it matter! If that's what the film's called, it doesn't even cover the cost of the prints!"

I can feel the escaped prisoner's hand climb even higher. I open my mouth to say so. I want to leave the table, to get away from him. I don't do anything at all. Firstly, I can no longer feel one hand, but two. They push back gently, very gently, the frills that made me famous. They caress my thighs above my stockings. It's unbearable. I'm sure that the fool is going to get caught. Jicks would have him thrown into the sea. Jicks wouldn't talk to me for twenty years.

And Mathieu says, "I wonder. Wasn't it *For My Kid*? Something like that?"

My dignified expression. Keep my dignified expression. I can't utter a word, but a sophisticated smile stretches from ear to ear. I'm a rich bitch on a two-million-dollar motorboat. I can feel my dress and petticoats being hitched up around my waist. The hands are attacking my panties. They're trying to pull them down. I hear myself beg: "Oh no!"

"Frou-Frou's right," says Jicks. "Never put a brat in the title or on the poster. Except that chubby-cheeked Shirley Temple, it'll never work. And even then, you have to give her a poodle or a tap dancer for people to go and see her."

I keep as still as I can, but I'm forced to move about. Whether I want to stop the bastard from removing my lacy chihuahua pussy-cover or help him get it off, or even both at the same time, I have to lean on one buttock or the other, and I can't tell you what a state I was in while all this was going on.

Afterward, a long time afterward, a colleague of Esmeralda's explained what had been going on in my innermost self that evening. He said, in a weary but polite voice, that he heard the same damn story year in and year out, that it was the most common female fantasy, number one in the shrinky-poos' hit parade. Sometimes it happened in a pizzeria in Palm Springs, sometimes during a neighbor's birthday party, sometimes at the White House because your husband dreamed of being a senator before becoming an insurance broker or a flunky for Universal. In short, it's all the fault of that lousy Christian hypocrisy that dogs us all. According to him, I had dreamed of getting laid like that all my life, in front of everybody, but without anyone knowing, if possible with a guy *on his knees* between my legs to cream all the more at depriving him of his virility. What's more, I had sneakily taken advantage of a poor escaped jailbird. To let myself go like a bitch, I had given myself the excuse of not letting him get nabbed. Apparently, if Esmeralda or Toledo had done that, or any other chick, I would have hit the roof and demanded instantly that he be taken to the gas chamber. Let me be struck down by lightning if that's not what that nitwit dinned into me for a week. Then, seeing that his time and my patience were at an end, he wanted to screw me on his couch, and I damaged his virility with a good swipe of my stiletto-heeled patent-leather shoes and the blessing of the entire Catholic, apostolic, and Roman Churches.

"I think we're completely mistaken!" Stockhammer suddenly exclaimed, flinging his knife down across his plate. "It was a single-word title!"

My panties are around my ankles and come off. I can feel my knees being pushed apart and a cool mouth touching the skin on the inside of my thighs. And then, what he did next, I don't want to tell you, you can just imagine it. Too bad, I give in. I rested my elbows on the table, my chin in my hands, looking as engrossed as anyone else in the conversation, but I know that my eyes are rolling, and a moan escapes me.

"Is something the matter, Frou-Frou?" Esmeralda asks suspiciously.

I reply as best I can with halting breath: "Yes . . . It's the heat! She can't take any more . . . she can't take any more. . . ."

"You can't take any more what?" the silly cow persists.

Everybody's looking at me now. Mathieu gallantly picks up a bottle from the ice bucket. "Some champagne, perhaps?"

I can hardly make him out through my misty lenses, I can't even see him anymore. I murmur, "Yes! Oh yes! Oh yes!"

He pours champagne into my glass.

I must stretch out my legs. I'd like to stop Mathieu pouring. I can feel myself sliding off my chair. I can feel everyone's eyes on me. I know that nothing can stop me now. I beg, "Oh yes! That's it! That's it!"

"More?" Mathieu inquires, concerned, shocked, miles away.

I let go. The champagne overflows onto the tablecloth. Somebody says something. I hear my own voice—a groan, an endless *yes*—and I fall back, my legs outstretched, tense, and it goes on and on, I don't want it ever to stop—well, you know what it's like.

When I collect myself a little, I'm slumped against the back of my chair, my body half under the table, my arms drooping, broken like a rag doll. They are all staring at me, a little puzzled all the same, and so as to show them I'm alive, I make an effort, I grab my glass, I spill half the champagne again as I raise it to my lips. Not a word while I drink. Not a word while I pop out my contact lenses and wipe my eyes to give myself a look of composure.

And then, carrying on with his meal, Jicks concludes, "Bah! If the film was a success, what does it matter what it was called!"

No need to tell you what a dressing-down I gave my vile attacker a little later when I went down to his lumber room to take him some food. As soon as the door was shut behind me, bent double to remain standing, I said to him firmly, "Aren't you ashamed of yourself?"

He was lying on the mattresses as usual, his hands under his head. Perhaps he was ashamed, but not very. He replied, without any conviction, "I haven't had a woman for six years. Six years!"

"And do you think that's any reason to behave as you did with me, while to save you I couldn't say or do a thing to defend myself?"

But just try lecturing a starving hulk who is even taller than Heads-or-Tails. All he was interested in was the tray I was carrying.

While he wolfed down a whole chicken, canned pears, and a bottle of Médoc, I sat down beside him. I couldn't believe, looking at him, that he had treated me in such an abominable fashion. His movements were very refined, even if he did eat with his fingers.

While he finished his wine, a vague look in his eyes, I said, "I come from Montrouge. What about you?"

"Marseilles."

"What did you do, before you were sent to prison?"

"Nothing. My military service."

"Are you married?"

He hid his wedding ring behind his back and looked disgruntled. He said in a tone that meant don't answer back, "Don't talk about her! That's my business and mine alone!"

I didn't insist. I picked up the tray to leave. He caught my wrist. Not aggressively; on the contrary. He sighed, looking away.

"I'm sorry. But she's a saint. All these years, she has waited for me. I'm sure she's still waiting for me. She is constancy itself. In fact, her name is Constance."

He remained like that, plunged in the melancholy memories of his other half, for a good two minutes. We're all funny people. Seeing him think of another woman with such longing, I felt the pit of my stomach churn. With me, that's how you get me. Of course, what he did to me under the table was very naughty, but in a way it was selfless and no doubt even quite frustrating for him. Anyway, I undid the zipper down the back of my dress. Without intending to, since all I wanted was to let him screw me so that we were quits, I had just discovered the wretched secret that mechanical whizzes had been trying to find for months: everything on the *Pandora* started working again! The machines roared, the bell rang, the hull creaked, and we suddenly heaved from one side to the other.

I stood bolt upright in my agitation, I gave my head a hell of a bang on the ceiling again, and I said, lost in the stars, "Shit! We're leaving!"

I teetered over to the door. Before going out, zipping up my dress, I said to Frédéric that fate had decided for me and that he would wait until our next stop before leaving the ship.

Earlier, having accomplished his crime, the rat had disappeared from the dining room in as underhanded a manner as he had entered it, not giving a damn about leaving my behind exposed. Gratitude made him take my lacy chihuahua panties out of his trouser pocket and he held them out to me, hanging like a trophy from the tip of his forefinger. I slipped them on, using the whole range of modest wiggles and getting my pins caught up on purpose to give him something to dream about until the following day.

I don't know if I drove him wild, but I certainly couldn't wait that long. At three o'clock in the morning, mooning about in my night-dress on the main deck, I told myself I was pretty silly wasting my life contemplating the desolate herring pond by the light of the moon and I went down and woke him up, stark naked under the blankets, and of course, we played cards.

There, now you know more or less everything except the end.

You think I'm joking, because between that first time when I wallowed in turpitude with Frédéric, on the burst mattresses off the coast of Royan, and the last time, on the other side of the world in the vicinity of the Christmas Islands, quite a number of days, nights, weeks, and months had gone by. If it were a film, all you'd see on the screen would be the dates being peeled off a lousy calendar at high speed, superimposed with the white bulk of the *Pandora* cleaving through the waves. For fear that people hadn't quite understood, they might perhaps go so far as to add, for no extra charge, a dotted line growing longer and longer across an old map of the world, but nothing else. Jicks used to say, "In a love story, when they know how it begins, all they want to see is how it ends. As for the rest, it's so the dumb director can wank with the camera and so the film can pile up." I puke over films as much as he does—the shorter they are, the sooner we can go and have fun—but this wasn't a film, it was my bloody life, and I'll at least try to tell you a bit more about it.

First, I've never been able to put ashore a stowaway who didn't want to go. Our first port of call was Lisbon. Instead of appealing to my emotions, saying he was madly in love and all that, Frédéric asked me to let him stay because he didn't speak Portuguese. Virile modesty. The furthest he ventured with tender, misleading words was, "Good old Frou-Frou," "Poor old Frou-Frou," and most often, "Good old, poor old Frou-Frou." Once, in the turbulence of a really low moment, he said that if he lost me, he'd miss me. I'll tell you about that when the time comes, but there's no harm in your knowing right away that when he filled his glass that evening, there were no half measures.

I'm a very unique sort, there are only five or six billion of us in the whole world: my dream, once I got used to the idea that they snore at night, is a man, it doesn't really matter at the end of the day which one, tall or short, handsome or ugly, rich or poor, dumb or not, as long as he's mine, and doesn't get on my whatsit too much, and is very, very kind. When I've let him do it to me once, I don't want any others. I know there are two hundred and ninety-three women of all races and creeds, including the concierge of 486 Boulevard Pisse-Vinaigre in Paris, France, who don't share my views and who will tell you, what's more, that I'm lying, that I've lost count of the men who did it to me only in the broom closet on the third floor of the Beverly Hills Hotel, but let them all die with their open mouths full of cockroaches, that's the way it is. If I didn't stay with the first man I knew, or with the last one to date, it's because they were all pains in the ass, whose only concern was to get their rocks off, and as reliable as a weather vane in a storm. To be honest, there are also some who find it hard to put up with my shortcomings and fears of the big screen and who sent me back where I had come from without any mercy, despite the huge snow-flakes falling outside. I've taken a few knocks like any other woman. Have I cried! Until the next jerk comes along!

As for Frédéric, just talking about him makes me sick. He was the best thing that had happened to me since Pinko, my furry bear. I was given Pinko for my third birthday and I kept him until I was eighteen, when Jicks's flunkies threw me onto the *Normandie* to go to America to see if I had the makings of a star. When I arrived in New York, I lost him in all the luggage, forms to be filled out, and all that customs nonsense. Jicks paid I don't know how many detectives, I'm sure he did, I asked to see the checks, but they never found my teddy bear. At that time I was disgustingly pretentious. First class everywhere, the scent of farewell bouquets, and dinners at the commander's table must have gone to my head. It's all very well me going to sleep like everyone else during the first reel of the dud movie that brought me such acclaim, I kicked up such a fuss that people thought he'd been kidnapped. Jicks promised a fortune in the newspapers to anyone who brought Pinko back safe and sound, and his friends in the Senate had a hard job persuading him to abandon his idea of a campaign for the extension of the Lindbergh law to teddy bears. During the first weeks, I received a ton of Pinkos every day, every color under the sun, but never mine. We gave them all to the Philippine Society for the Prevention of Cruelty to Children. Anyway, that's just to say that I was ever so happy with Frédéric.

In Gibraltar the English searched the *Pandora* as thoroughly as if it were the Great Pyramid. My beloved was hidden in a ventilation pipe. Afterward, it took him three days to recover from being shut in. Believe me, I couldn't have gone wham-bam with him in an elevator. I wonder whether he's ever been in one, actually, even to see how different it is from a staircase.

In any case, I mentioned the Great Pyramid on purpose. Jicks wanted to visit them, the Great Pyramid and all the little pyramids, to reproduce them in the studio and do a film with Stockhammer. I would play an adventuress in shorts who would unearth a mummy stuffed with diamonds, to feed her kid, but John Carradine or Basil Rathbone would try to get their hands on my booty by fair means or foul, and with the time it takes Ray Milland to repair his old kite that's come down in the desert, I'm not likely to see daylight again, you know the sort. Luckily, the Mediterranean had become a shooting range for warships; we had to turn back. Over the radio, everyone advised us to go home to America, but Jicks replied that no little jerk of an Austrian corporal was going to stop him from doing something when he had made up his mind, and we prolonged the cruise by six months to sail around Africa.

Now don't go thinking that Frédéric spent all this time bent double in the depths of the hold. After a week, when I had gotten myself sorted out, he practically lived in my cabin or, to be precise, in one of the three cabins I occupied on the main deck, opposite Jicks's cabins. He only went back to his lumber room in the mornings, to let Toledo clean up. On discovering men's things lying around in my cabin on one occasion or another, she must have thought I was getting it on with one of the sailors on board, or perhaps all twelve of them, who knows, but she never said anything or showed it on her healthy face, the color of Ohio apples.

And yet, except for the usual little tips, I hardly showered her. The sailors in comparison were carnivorous plants. At every port I had to find an American bank; they only wanted my blood in cash. Except the Chinese launderer. He didn't want any money at all. He made me promise that one day I'd show him my pussy and the rest for an hour. He wouldn't touch me, he'd just look at me. For an hour. I never saw him again, and for a very good reason when you know how all this ended, but if I ever bump into him in some Chinatown somewhere, I'll drag him right away into a room full of clocks so that it's clear that I'm honest. I mention him because he's no longer on Jicks's payroll and he didn't even ask *why* I wanted to bribe him. I simply told him to keep his mouth shut. If he had swallowed a fly just beforehand by mistake, you'd see it flying out of his coffin.

So, after a while, the whole world, or almost, knew that there was a stowaway on board, except Jicks and the girls. It's the dumbest of the four who ended up realizing it, after months at sea, and who ruined everything.

At the onset of winter, we were anchored in Casablanca. It's a mysterious town with people from all over the place who sing the "Marseillaise" in the nightclubs every time a Kraut uniform walks in. I saw that in a movie on my return to America, otherwise I wouldn't have anything to tell you. Frédéric didn't want to go ashore, for fear of getting nabbed by Pétain's soldiers, and I'm not a tourist. As with all our stops, a load of flunkies and lawyers came aboard and shut themselves up with Jicks for whole days at a time, sometimes even at night. He was busy selling his automatic planes or some other aeronautic crap, I don't know. Besides his movies, he rarely talked about his business. At first I asked Frédéric what he thought about it. He didn't. Nor did the others; they saved all their brains for Scrabble.

We saw the year out in the port, nice and peacefully, except for the last day. During our New Year's Eve preparations, French marines came on board to search the *Pandora* and Frédéric just had time to go back to his ventilation pipe. Which was lucky, because this time they were looking for him, there was no doubt. I was ashamed of my fellow countrymen. I don't mean the marines, who were doing their job without getting unnecessarily worked up, but an officer from the Armistice Force, a tall loudmouth, persnickety and obtuse, and they themselves must have wondered what the hell he was doing on a ship, and even better, a Swiss ship: Major Malignoble. When I described him to Frédéric, afterward, it was Frédéric who told me his name. On hearing that this moron had pursued him from the other side of the Mediterranean, he began to tremble even more than he had in Gibraltar, but it wasn't from claustrophobia, it was from rage. He said: "If I ever find myself face-to-face with him, and even if it's my last good deed on earth, I'll mutilate him."

The scare over, we joyfully celebrated New Year's. I kissed the others, in the dining room, on the dot of midnight. Then I removed my contact lenses, and my cheeks wet with tears, I told them to carry on without Frou-Frou, that she preferred to go and think in her cabin, she wanted to remember her mother and her schoolfriends in occupied France and all that, and for a shitty actress, it was some performance. Even Esmeralda looked away to hide the emotion scratching her heart of stone. Even Heads-or-Tails realized that it was me. Even Stockhammer's single hair stood up on end, as lively and rigid as in the days when Garbo was silent and he directed Gish and Gloria Swanson. So, I'd rather keep quiet about good old Mathieu's fit, or you'll think I'm exaggerating.

I should add that they were playing "Auld Lang Syne" during my act, and that helped. We could still hear it when I was locked up in my cabin, my devouring lips glued to Frédéric's. I had ordered everything we needed in the lounge to be prepared by I-can't-say-who of my accomplices: caviar, foie gras, lobster, turkey with chestnuts, champagne, and a 1928 Pomerol. Frédéric had presents like everyone else, in particular a navy blue, sky blue, and white Fair Isle sweater, imported from the big city, hand-knitted, which looked wonderful on him. Unfortunately, he couldn't wear it, he only dressed as a member of the crew, with "Pandora" well visible across his chest, in case he met Jicks or one of the twits on a gangway. I only saw him wear the wretched sweater twice: that night when he tried it on, saying that it reminded him of his childhood at the Jesuit college, and another night that I'd rather forget about.

Obviously, he couldn't give me anything other than himself, but I was dead happy. So was he, I think, but with the help of the wine, things were spoiled toward the end. He was thinking about his wife. He was planning to return, how the hell I don't know, to the village in the Seine-et-Marne where he'd left her, to contemplate once again her Madonna-like profile through the window, without telling her he was there, to disguise himself as a tramp so that she wouldn't recognize him, not to mention other hairbrained schemes. I had a lousy role, but I did my best to make him see sense. At his trial, his life had already hung by a thread. If he went back to the slammer, it would only be to await the horror of a pale dawn.

In the end, he said sadly, "You're right, Frou-Frou. In any case, I only brought her unhappiness, it would be better for her if she forgot me. She can't be lacking for admirers."

You probably think that made him feel better, imagining the poor girl abandoning her embroidery to leap into another man's bed. Not at all. The only thing that made him feel better was the Pomerol. And I'll pour myself a last one, and I'll pour myself just one more. At four o'clock, sobbing haphazardly, he poured out his youthful memories: the Place Dauphine, where he had met Constance, a typist, when he had just arrived in Paris to enroll at the Sorbonne, a hotel room in the rue Chevalier-de-la-Barre, under the steps of the Sacré-Coeur, and the vile lampshade that they cut stars out of to make it prettier—then, hey presto, as soon as they'd got their undies off, the two hypocrites were in paradise. I told him I understood. I told him that I really understood, and that I was almost as unhappy as he was. I told him I had some nice cool water in the fridge. I told him everything. It was that night that he uttered those wonderful words, that if he lost me, he'd miss me. Shit, I was crying, too, real tears into my champagne, I couldn't remember where we were and I wanted to call a taxi so that we could go, once and for all, to Seine-et-Marne, and if the saint didn't want to share him, I'd give him back to her and return to Montrouge and do myself in with butane gas. Anyway, we'd reached rock bottom, the pair of us. We woke up on the floor, at dawn, lying across each other; I can't even remember who was on top and who was underneath.

It's understandable that I have emotional memories of Casablanca, but was delighted when we weighed anchor. Next, it was the Canaries. Six weeks. There, Frédéric went ashore every time Jicks turned his back. The Canaries are wonderful. A load of hotels closed for the winter, and empty swimming pools. A load of shops that sell the Apostles in plaster of Paris, you can start a collection. Palm trees, dustbins, and everyone speaks Spanish.

Dakar, in comparison, was like the exodus. We weren't allowed to drop anchor anywhere, except by this island opposite, and I'll give you three guesses what it was. A penal colony. Then you wonder why Frédéric looked unhappy. All the same, it was in Dakar that I was able to buy a sound projector to watch films in my three adjoining cabins. Jicks picked up all the B-movies wandering around Africa. In a Bentley that he had had painted white, with his name on the doors, they each brought me back at least thirty cans; after that I couldn't have a pee, or open a cupboard or get out of my bathtub without breaking three legs, they were everywhere. Don't talk to me about *Chicago*, the *Conquerors*, *Gunga Din*, *The Little Princess*, *Mr. Smith Goes to Washington*, nor do I want to hear about *Mr. Deeds*, *Mr. Chips*, or *Mr. Bébé*, wherever they are, and for the love of God, especially not that old woman they're forever losing in a train, I tell you, and it's the honest truth, that still today, I don't give a damn. Even myself, in *Eyes*, I can't imagine myself otherwise than cut up and heaped in a washbasin.

As for Frédéric, he was in seventh heaven. He would watch the same picture projected onto a sheet ten times in a row. And as I was already asleep during the first showing, ten times in a row he described the scene where Dietrich gets herself killed to protect Stewart, who has picked up his six-guns, and how she kisses him before she dies, and her sublime movement as she wipes her bloody lipstick off. If I happened to point out that a sheet had other uses, he clammed up for an hour. And when he opened his mouth again, it was to tell me what an ungrateful little so and so I was to be successful in the finest profession in the world and to turn my nose up every other minute, and that for one, I was a lousy actress, he could see that, but I had a hell of a screen look and tits to puncture the film, and legs you wanted to strangle yourself with, and the best ass ever seen under a tight dress, and as for the rest, if they were going to continue to give my films titles of my best parts, I would die before I finished just shooting what was permitted by the legions of decency, and that it was an act, and this, too, was an act; in short, I was dumb.

Then I was the one who kept my mouth shut for minutes on end, and he regretted what he had said. He would adopt a very, very weary, very, very gentle tone to confess with deceitful humility that he was ignorant on all subjects—music, art, literature, and houseplants—and that his culture was purely cinematographical, that he couldn't help it, it wasn't his fault if he had been born after the arrival of I-don't-know-what-damn-train at the station of La Ciotat.

What could I say to that? For fear that he would think I was even dumber, I didn't even dare ask him what La Ciotat had to do with us, but it was Mathieu who explained it to me. At least I know the name of the asshole who invented all the torments of my life. Let's be fair. In this jumble of old movies that Frédéric wouldn't have thrown into the sea for anything, or allowed to be piled up anywhere other than in our living space, there was one consolation: the scene in the second reel of *Eyes,* where I'm supposed to get laid in the barn and I defend myself more and more feebly against my seducer, without being able to scream or anything. Every time he projected it, I couldn't avoid having to play the scene again with him, exactly as in the film, with the same lost, round eyes. After that, I promise you, I had it coming to me.

In Libreville, Gabon, in addition to our Swiss handkerchief, we hoisted the tricolor with the cross of Lorraine, purely in my honor. It stayed there until the end of the voyage. You're bound to have seen the photo where I'm kissing it as if I wanted to eat it, with a pom-pom beret on my head and a striped sailor's jersey revealing the beauty spot on my right buttock, in your dentist's waiting room or at the hairdresser's. All the magazines use it each time they do my life story again, almost as often as they use the one of my acrobatic number with Hepburn's prize. Well, in the porthole you can see in the background, just above the Chinaman who's laughing his head off with his lips painfully closed, there's Frédéric. He's fuzzy, it's hard to recognize him, but it's him, always poking his nose in where he shouldn't.

I've often asked myself why it is that men have that crazy habit, even the brighter ones. If you count up all the times I went into my cabins unexpectedly, because I'd forgotten my nail file or something, let's say it comes to a hundred. That means that a hundred times out of a hundred, Frédéric had his eyes glued to his favorite porthole and that ninety-nine times, not even a yard away from those same eyes, there was Toledo's or Bessie's behind, in a pair of tight, flimsy panties, stretched to the splitting point because they were on their knees washing the deck. The one time they weren't there, washing the deck, I didn't see what he was looking at, but I'll bet you my shirt against yours, and you'll go home with no clothes on, that Esmeralda had just bent over to pick up her wretched earring. I've never met anyone who lost her earrings so often in my whole life. If one day you're climbing the most inaccessible peaks of the Himalayas, and you find one in the cactuses, don't go to any trouble, put it in an envelope and send it back without an address.

Just from the feel of it, even the dumbest postman will know that it's for Jicks's shrinky-poo.

All the same, men are sex maniacs. Even a bitch my grandfather wouldn't have been interested in, and he was someone who'd run after a frying pan, they've got to see her chubby cheeks, they can't help it, it's their nature. In fact, I never held this mental aberration against Frédéric. I took it upon myself, I contented myself with telling him, reluctantly, that he was just a poor idiot, a bent screw-driver, a depraved shithead, and would hurt my hands on his fore-arms, raised in cowardly protection of his hypocritical mug, and try to thump him one where it hurts with my patent-leather stiletto heel, and would always end up trampling on my glasses.

The most preposterous thing is when you know what he was ogling in the famous photo. *My ass!* Honestly! He had it entirely at his disposal twenty-four hours a day, I could remove my little pant-ies and present it to him at any favorable angle he chose before he had even finished asking, I consented in advance to whatever he wanted to do, except perhaps blowing in it—but no, that wasn't enough, he had to crane his neck behind his porthole to spy on me in secret, burning with impatience for the lousy jersey to ride high enough up my body so that he could glimpse my beauty spot on my right buttock. Do you understand what men are about? I don't. It's a bottomless pit, and I get lost in it.

Luanda, Angola. Ugly. Palm trees, dustbins. We crossed the Cape of Good Hope for Independence Day, I remember because it was also Frédéric's birthday. Thirty years old and his eyesight intact to look up skirts. I gave him a present when we reached Port Elis-abeth: ten more movies, including *Marie Antoinette*, which he already knew by heart, and *The Women*. For days and nights on end, he talked of nothing but Norma Shearer. He was crazy about her. I had met Miss Shearer the year before, at a party where I had only stayed ten minutes and she had said a couple of kind words to me. Big deal. I wore myself out repeating the two words so many times, imitating the voice of his beloved as best I could, I filled the ten minutes with so many harebrained details that I still have night-mares about it sometimes and wake up bathed in a cold sweat. What's more, *Marie Antoinette*, with the head and all that, isn't short. At least fifty tons of cans. Bessie did her back in just trying to make room for me in the bathtub.

I'm skipping East London, Durban, Lorenzo Marques. Palm

trees, dustbins, only the name changes. I can't remember on which far-off shore it was that the others decided to go off on a safari, and Jicks took the opportunity to fly to America and back. Frédéric and I stayed on the *Pandora*, with just the crew, and those were the best moments of that infernal voyage. He could walk around on the deck to his heart's content, talk to the guys, go fishing with his buddies. In the time that was left for me to see him, we swam, went water skiing, and went ashore for dinner in a hut where there wasn't even any electricity. I've always liked dinner by candlelight and candles in churches. When I was little, I thought it was what rich people did. I would have been more intimidated in that cheap joint with its hundred candles than at Maxim's. The Wheel Turns, it was called. The boss was a Frenchman with his neck imprisoned in a metal cage, like Stroheim in a film, except that he had a mustache and was dressed like a tramp and lived in some far-flung corner of the earth.

The fright I had, the first time we went there, I can't tell you. The minute he saw him, the guy took out a big revolver from under the bar to kill Frédéric. He chased him all around the place, shooting at him—well, I assume he wanted to shoot him—and each time they reappeared, galloping across the room like lunatics, Frédéric shouted to me, "Watch out! Watch out!" and he shoved me under the tables, my gams waving around, until they next passed. When the revolver was empty, they changed direction. It was Frédéric who chased after the guy, who was even more aggressive because he was afraid, and it was the guy who threw me on the floor, giving me just enough time to act as a shield for him. That evening I realized all the grief and the sense of injustice of the poor slices of ham that are made into sandwiches.

In fact, I was the only one who was crying. If I've got it right, the guy was a former gamekeeper. Frédéric had met him in Charente, in the days that followed his escape. After their performance, they had a drink together and fell into each other's arms. What had happened between them to make them wreck my white linen suit and give me bruises all over, they never told me. Men's business. I'll gladly believe that they got into some dispute about poaching or something. When it comes to hunting, I'm hopeless, I couldn't hurt a fly, unless it had stung me, but I'm not as dumb as people think, and given their bright and breezy air when I brought the subject up, I sort of suspect that the quarry they had fought over for a while had been a female and wore silk stockings. They would never have made it up for a rabbit.

In short, they were good times all the same, as long as we were anchored there. The guy, I can't remember his name, or the place, it was the bay of something or other in Mozambique, but the metal thing holding his chin is called a surgical collar. When he felt like going ashore, Frédéric would say, "Shall we go and see Giraffe?" And when they had an argument about, shall we say, the war, de Gaulle, and all that, the guy would say to him, "You're a pain in the neck, you're a pain in the neck," and they would both laugh and slap their thighs as if it was the funniest joke they'd ever heard. They had another one and that was quite something, too. When I sat down, I had to keep an eye on my skirt and my blouse, because old Giraffe never missed an opportunity to slide his filthy hands into the place politeness forbids me to mention, exclaiming each time in a high-pitched voice, "It's as soft as down there!" And Frédéric, instead of reminding him of his manners, roared with laughter with him, and both of them held their sides and slapped their thighs even harder, gulping so loud the place shook, I was afraid they'd choke. An abyss, I tell you.

Jicks came back after three weeks, for my birthday, on August 11. I'd been stuck at twenty-one for three years, as he had insisted, but I was twenty-four. Today, with all that crap, I've lost count, but I've got the impression that the twenty-five years I boast, I've been there for some time. All the same, Frédéric was in a regular state, I'll give you three guesses why: Norma Shearer! She was born on August 11 as well, in Westmont, Montreal, he didn't want to tell me what year. Destiny really is fatal, isn't it? With the money he'd scraped together from beating Giraffe at cards, he bought me a baby marmoset that we called Sheeta, even though it was a boy, but the beast ran away the minute it tasted the food on board and realized what a bunch of primitives we were. He disappeared before our hunters returned, and I was relieved for him.

In fact, he wasn't in much danger. They descended one evening, in single file, from a hydroplane, chug-chug, pooped, grimy, bitter, with drooping shoulders and long faces. In a month's safari in the heart of Tanganyika, they hadn't shot anything, except for Bessie.

What happened exactly, I don't know. They didn't know themselves. Apparently they had used up all their cartridges to drive off an antelope that they weren't allowed to shoot. They had found

Bessie with buckshot in her legs after the rodeo. They had taken her to the nearest civilization in a tent canvas that Toledo had sewn herself. At that moment, the poor girl was lying in a hospital bed in Dar es Salaam, far away in the north, and Stockhammer had left her two thousand dollars for her flight home to Florida, when she recovered. Jicks said that was exactly the right thing to have done. Toledo wanted us to go up to Dar es Salaam and wait until Bessie was well enough to leave with us, but he took her aside, and she came out of his cabin with red eyes, and after that, she gave up the idea.

So we took another stewardess on board, a young black girl, very obliging, with only her head poking out of a multicolored *boubou*, the billowing dress worn by Muslims. She didn't open her mouth much more than I did in *Eyes*. She only spoke Italian, or rather the sort of Italian that an Abyssinian girl can use in Mozambique. She received lots of love letters from the crew and I was the one she asked to translate them. I tried to make her understand with signs what each of them wanted from her. I use mime sparingly. Luckily she understood, all the more because it was always the same old story. She would shake her head with a wistful little smile, a tender sigh, and she would indicate what I should reply. There, too, it was always the same thing. At first I would tell them politely, on the ship's embossed notepaper, to stuff it under their armpits, or to try their luck with the launderer, but the propositions she received were becoming increasingly urgent and specific, and in the end I simply wrote "shit" across the page and she traced "Didi" underneath it.

I can't swear that she didn't give in under the pressure of numbers during the crossing of the Indian Ocean. Her vocabulary began to include a disturbing number of American curse words, and her greatest concern, together with wanting to know who was on watch, was to take over cleaning my cabin from Toledo and filching my underwear that went with her skin. She put it back in my drawers, always clean and beautifully ironed, that's not the point, but I can reasonably dismiss the idea that Frédéric was getting it on with her. For one, I'd have recognized his writing. Two, he spoke American as well as I play the trombone. Three, the only black woman he'd ever known, I'm not kidding, he used to scrub with carbolic soap to get the dye off.

So, we fled Africa like thieves and made for the Seychelles, the Maldives, and India. No longer any question of going to see the pyramids. Jicks said that it was just as good, if not better, to shoot Stockhammer's film in the Hindu temples, the sets wouldn't cost any more to build and might even cost less, and all that. I would be an adventuress in shorts who profaned a statue of Kali stuffed with diamonds in order to feed her kid, but Rathbone or Carradine, unless it was Bickford because of difficulties with dates, wants to steal my booty and stupidly triggers off with his dynamite the sacred volcano's anger. While poor Ray Milland rebuilds his kite scattered in the heart of the jungle, there's every chance I'll be buried alive under the lava. Suspense. They can't decide whether I live or die, so in the end they shoot two versions. Frou-Frou says that Frou-Frou doesn't give a shit and goes off to live her secret life with Frédéric. Every evening, the others have brainstorming sessions in the big lounge to find a title.

Of course, they look for one between the top of my head and my toes. Stockhammer says that the wretched bone, or muscle, or limb they choose has got to be relevant to the film. Jicks doesn't see why. Nor does Heads-or-Tails. Esmeralda is torn. So is Mathieu. In the end, let me be shot like a stewardess if I lie, they tore up my whole body into little pieces of paper, they threw them into the boatswain's cap, and what came out? *Lips*. Brilliant. They all thought that it would be next year's hit, they congratulated one another like little old ladies who've just won the church's baking contest. Frou-Frou says that Frou-Frou doesn't give a shit, except that she's fond of her lips, and that they'd better not come up with some warped scheme to make them fit the story.

I know the movie business inside out, it isn't difficult. With a title like that, the hack they're going to hire will be paid according to the number of kisses I can give in eighty minutes. Starting with Milland, Carradine, Rathbone, Bickford, Peter Lorre, and Boris Karloff, not forgetting the statue of Kali to make her spew out her stones, and then the whole village of Indian extras who saved you when you escaped from the burning plane, including the priestess with weird customs, and you end up slobbering with a crocodile. What am I ranting about? The bastard who makes you kiss the *lava*, the fucking symbol that engulfs you, and it's never realistic enough, they make you retake the shot until you become a carnival freak, the Woman with No Mouth, how does she eat, there's an explanation on the cage.

You know what saved me, thanks to what stroke of my destiny I managed to escape those horrors? Well, I'll tell you. It was the last thing we expected. The Japanese bombed Pearl Harbor.

I've never seen Jicks shed a tear, or stand there gaping when overwhelmed by the situation, or lose his head to the point of talking to Hollywood for an hour and forty minutes without worrying about the previous day's take—except that day. The tear appeared in his left eye at around nine o'clock in the evening, local time, when a sailor leaned toward him, at dinner, to whisper the news. Then he called L.A. Then he shut himself up in his room.

He had recovered by breakfast the next day. He told us all that the Japs were assholes but that our aircraft carriers had fortunately not been in the Hawaiian Islands at the time of the attack and that in the future, even if the war was to last ten years, he was sure of victory. We entered the Bay of Bengal. He told us we'd have to forget Calcutta, which in any case was filthy, noisy, and of no interest. We headed toward home via Singapore and the Philippines.

I think that everybody was pleased with the decision, even if no one dared show it at that time of morning. I asked Frédéric what he thought. He didn't think anything, he didn't know how he'd be greeted in America. He had no passport and no papers. He couldn't see what he would gain, after such a long voyage, by ending his days in an American prison rather than a French one, surrounded by poor devils who wouldn't speak the same language. Especially as he had his doubts about American food.

It just goes to show how dumb it is to worry about things in advance. Nothing ever turns out the way you expect.

First of all, Jicks refused to shelter under the Swiss flag any longer. He said: "Switzerland is for protecting money, not cowards. I'm a Greek-French-Jew naturalized American citizen, I'm proud of my origins and my country." Everybody gathered on the upper deck to watch the star spangled banner being raised. Jicks said that we'd keep the cross of Lorraine, too, because there were four French people on board and it was the least we could do. I'm a bit slow at math, and for an hour I got my fingers muddled up and was worried stiff that he'd discovered Frédéric's presence aboard, but along with Mathieu and me and the cook, he was also including Esmeralda, who had been born in Roquefort, which she was rather sheepish about, and here I thought she had come from a penthouse on Washington Square and had come into the world clutching her degree from Vassar.

All I can remember next was a hopeless race against the Japanese. They were going a hell of a lot faster than us. The time it took us to get to Singapore, they were sweeping down on Hong Kong, Thailand, Burma, Malaysia, and attacking the Philippines. We had to move out of the way fast and head down south. Jicks had put up a huge map of Asia and the Pacific in the lounge, with little flags on pins. I'm hopeless at strategy, but it wasn't hard to see that an anthill with slanting eyes was growing bigger every day to block our path east, and at this rate, we were going to end up in Australia.

That is in fact what happened. We saw the New Year arrive in Darwin, but our hearts weren't in it. We loaded all the fuel and food that the *Pandora* could hold, we armed the fore and aft decks with big machine guns, and we set off again for the Pacific, dodging around New Guinea. It was a close call and the ants nearly landed. In the Coral Sea, it was worse. There wasn't even any room for an inflatable canoe. The U.S. Navy asked us to go away and play somewhere else, and we had to head south again.

We stopped off in New Caledonia to have the I-don't-know-what damage repaired, and there, too, everyone was ready for action. After that, we sailed for weeks on end, following the Tropic of Capricorn in a straight line, and I saw on the big map in the lounge that the Japs would never go down that far, unless they wanted to occupy the Antarctic to attack the Eskimos from the rear. From time to time, one of their Zeros strayed in the blue vastness and came to see if it was worth him ending in a kamikaze dive to hit us. We raised the general alarm, we spat out a volley of machine-gun fire, but he always gave up before we could catch him.

Anyway, I've seen Tahiti once in my lifetime. We stayed there for the whole of May 1942 and the thirty days of June, because of the engines once again, and Frédéric agreed to go ashore on French soil, but only at night. If I can recommend one thing in Papeete, it's the night life. I soon got tired of coconut palms and dustbins in the moonlight; I preferred to stay at home and watch a lousy movie out of the corner of my eye, or yak about our youth and the good times we'd had in Mozambique.

Nobody on board, in fact, felt much like sight-seeing anymore. Jicks was completely preoccupied with the war. He had had Mac-Arthur's and Nimitz's photos framed in the dining room. Before every meal, he would raise his glass to their health, his eyes full of an emotional but unfaltering confidence. Esmeralda told me one day that in these difficult but exhilarating times, Jicks had found in Doug, with his pipe and his dark glasses, the father he had never had, and in the admiral, the great sailor that he would like to have been. It was so obvious that I should have been ashamed of not noticing it all by myself. But I wasn't ashamed at all, firstly because I was used to her treating me like an idiot, and secondly because I had in fact noticed a long time ago that craziness was getting hold of people's minds, starting with hers. As we were sailing along the coast of Sumatra, she had made me swear not to leave her alive in the hands of the Japs, merciless rapists, if through misfortune they inspected us. I was to put a bullet through her brain. She had lifted up her hair to show me exactly where. She had dragged me to her cabin to show me her little pistol with an ivory handle and explain how to use it.

Even Heads-or-Tails had become hysterical. She never used to speak to me much before, but now she kept her trap shut completely. Do you know why? Because she had suggested to me that we should wear helmets and take turns keeping watch day and night over the machine guns, in case there was a spy among us. Of course, you'll have to translate my reply into polite language.

Before setting sail again, Jicks assembled us and warned us gravely that we were going to face the longest and hardest crossing of the entire voyage. We would sail nonstop until we saw the beam of the lighthouse at San Diego, California. Thousands of miles of deep water with no other assistance than our own courage and God's mercy. He reluctantly conceded a stop at Honolulu to have a look at the shops. In any case, we never got that far.

Now for the end. Before telling you, I've got to explain quite a few things, little arguments between Frédéric and me over trifles, about an afternoon when he stayed shut up in his lumber room in the hold and I went so far as to throw cans of film into the sea, about a night when he threw me out of my own bed so he could sleep alone and when I slept on the floor like a dog, and a load of other incidents that were as pointless as they were painful. I must also tell you about time passing and gnawing away at love, and that boredom was for our love an even more formidable enemy than the Japanese. But what's the use? Everybody will have realized that he fucked me less and less.

When a man who has loved you in every possible way, for months, begins to get bored, don't rack your brains trying to find a reason. There are only two: either he's gone off with someone else, or he hasn't done so for too long. Naturally, I suspected all the girls on board. As there were only four, it wasn't difficult to guess which one of them had borrowed Frédéric. I had to exclude Didi; I've already explained why. As for Heads-or-Tails, what with Mathieu in front, Stockhammer behind, Scrabble in her hands, prawns in her mouth, her helmet over her ears, and the barrel of the machine gun waiting to be of use, I really can't imagine that she had any room for my man's dick. Esmeralda; it was unthinkable. He would have come back castrated. Which left Toledo. Poor Toledo, how I regret now my murderous thoughts, the tortures I made her suffer in my imagination. She wasn't my rival, but on following her trail, as fiercely as I had been taught in the girl scouts, I came across the vile truth.

One night when there was a full moon, after a spate that gave Frédéric every reason not to come and join me, I went up to the upper deck and knocked on the stewardess's door. Toledo was asleep; so was Didi. I pretended that I'd come up the wrong stairs and apologized. They probably thought I was drunk. I wasn't one bit drunk, despite the two bottles of champagne that had consoled me in my loneliness. I was perfectly in control of myself and I decided to comb that lousy boat for the bastard and to do in whoever was with him—woman, man, or beast.

With those intentions, I walked all around the deck, in my black nightdress, stumbling a little because of the rolling of the boat, trying to peer through the portholes. There was a light in only one cabin. Before I reached it, the door opened. I just had time to dive into the shadows. It must have been two or three o'clock in the morning. It was Heads-or-Tails's cabin.

The great cow was also in her nightdress, but hers was white. In the dual light from the moon and from the cabin, she looked like a ghost. I saw this ghost enfold Frédéric in her arms, swallow him with her mouth; I almost fainted it was so disgusting. The whole time the kiss lasted, I bit my fist to stay alive, to stop my screams and my tears. At last, she spat him out. He was wearing the white Fair Isle sweater I'd given him. He walked past me without seeing me. I saw him disappear down a staircase.

When I had the strength to emerge from the shadows, Heads-or-Tails had closed her door again. I thought of going to Esmeralda's cabin and borrowing her pistol. She would yell and wake up the whole tub thinking that the Japs had invaded and that her hour had come, but too bad. Before anyone could stop me, I would already be at the foot of the other bitch's bed, I would take a great delight in telling her to burn in hell, and I'd shoot her in the sheets where she had sprawled with my lover. Six bullets in her dairy cow's body. Blood everywhere. She wouldn't escape even if she slept in her helmet.

When I reached Esmeralda's door, I was crying, I couldn't see a thing through my glasses, except that I'd lose Frédéric forever if I behaved like that. He would be arrested and he'd get his throat slit, and it would all be my fault. I didn't want to lose him. I wanted him to come back to me and in one piece. I had to talk to him, and tell him that I forgave him, that it didn't matter, except that his bitch was carrying a disease, that contagious one, I'd disinfect him, we'd never talk about it again.

Or, said Frou-Frou to herself, so pissed that she slid down the stairs on her pretty ass, I'll give him a scare, it'll be me or death, but I need a gun. That was how I broke a window in a gangway and grabbed a huge thing that looked like a pistol, with a huge thing that looked like a cartridge. I cut my right hand. I've still got the scar. One thing's for sure, I'd already lost my head.

When I pushed open the door of the lumber room, it was suddenly just like at the beginning of our voyage. Frédéric was lying there in his Lacoste shirt and white pants on his burst mattresses between the fairgrounds horse and an empty magnum of Côtes du Rhône which he used as a lamp. He was reading a book, one cheek resting on his hand. I loved him so much that I couldn't say a word.

He exclaimed, his eyes bulging with horror, "Frou-Frou! Please, drop that! It's a rocket launcher! And it stinks of gas in here!"

I replied, crazy, "I don't give a shit! What are you reading?"

He didn't get it. He looked at his book.

"The Narrative of Arthur Gordon Pym."

I knelt down beside him. I swear before God who knows me that I no longer intended harming anyone, especially him. He was handsome in the light of that crappy lamp, handsomer than ever. Unless you find anyone inaccessible handsome. I said, "Who wrote it?"

"Edgar Poe. It's translated by Baudelaire."

"You see how you keep everything from me. I've never seen you read."

He took me in his arms. He kissed me gently, so gently that I began to cry again like the fool that I am. Neither of us knew that we were in the last minute of our life together, and that we would never see each other again.

He said sadly, hanging his head, "It's not my fault if I cheated on you. She makes me. Otherwise she'll tell all. And you know what they'd do to me? Either I return to the citadel for the rest of my life or I'll be thrown into the sea."

He looked up at me with black, shining, naive, and anxious eyes for the last time. He said, "Frou-Frou, have you seen all those sharks following us?"

I had seen them. I stroked his hair. I asked him—and I'm dumb, dumb, dumb, I'll never forgive myself for going on about it: "How long has it been going on?"

"She saw me coming out of your cabin."

"When?"

"I don't remember. When we left New Caledonia."

It was as if he had thumped me in the stomach with his fist. I'm not fast at addition, but all the same. I shouted, "New what? You lied to me for all that. . . ."

In astonishment, rage, grief, I leaped to my feet, and of course the bloody ceiling hit me again. I moaned, my head crushed with pain: "Shit!"

And a deafening salvo was fired from the weapon I was holding. Two seconds, perhaps three, perhaps four, Frédéric sitting there, me standing, we watched speechlessly as the wretched rocket zigzagged all over the lumber room, rending the air with burning flashes, and then the world exploded.

When I came to, I was lying in the bottom of a canoe, wrapped in a blanket, my head on Toledo's knees. I felt as though I had been beaten up. Jicks was beside me. He watched the *Pandora* recede as she lay burning on the ocean. The silence was terrible. From America to Australia, all you could hear was the regular splashing of our oars. Two other rowboats followed us in the milky mist, as night seemed to my naked eyes.

And then Jicks put his arms around my shoulders and said, "We're lucky, if we'd been sunk by the Japs, the insurance wouldn't have paid up."

At lunchtime we were picked up by a convoy of cargo ships on their way to Colombia. They lent us sweaters and trousers. We counted up everyone on the three boats. In the shipwreck, we had lost two people, including Frédéric. They gave me needles to make me sleep.

There. Back in America, via Bogotá, I convalesced for several weeks by the swimming pool, at Jicks's mansion. I didn't have a burn, not a scratch, except the cut I'd given myself on my right hand when I broke the sights of the rocket launcher. I wasn't well, I wasn't ill, I was empty. Now, I don't care, you can do what you like with this story, I won't even deny it, but you're the first person to know how the accident happened. Not even Rachel Dee, my friend who sold Arrow shirts in Westwood, knows. There's another one who steals her friends' men for you.

In September I went back to the studios. I wasn't sorry, at least at first. Of the movie they had thought of doing during that wretched voyage, they only kept the title, *Lips*, in the end. I was that nurse in Bataan who kisses the brave GIs on the lips before they succumb to their injuries and who is reunited with her kid when MacArthur gives her a medal. Then I did *Legs*, and all those slushy Technicolor movies where I never stop changing my clothes and smoking long cigarettes and laughing like a madwoman at jokes like "Are they all yours?" They may as well have used a talking doll, she would have acted better than me and cost less in glasses.

Jicks had a new yacht built twice as big, the *Pandora II*. Since I refused, two years ago, to set off on another world cruise, we only have purely professional relations. Since I married, last year, the boss of the biggest international chain of beauty salons, he only talks to me through my agent. For the two months that I've been a widow and richer than him, he's broadcasted all over the place, so that it gets back to me, that he's unearthed another dizzy platinum blonde, even more devastating than you know who, and who'll make a fortune.

But I know him. Before he's exhausted all the possible titles using my body and stuck my ass on a poster as a last resort, I'm not likely to hire myself at one of my salons and go back to being a manicurist.

YORO

I'M NOBODY, NOBODY AT ALL.

I spent my childhood, very happy, with my parents, in Yoko-hama. My father is very strict Japanese gentleman and manager of the port and my mother is born in Talcahuano, Chili, and she sing all day and she laugh. My father say, "Enough, woman with no brain!" But he laugh, too, hiding his mouth, and he is full of happiness with her because she cook good food. That's why my eyes aren't half-shut like other Japanese. At school, stupid girls call me Little Doe Eyes, but I am not full of hatred, I take with grain of salt.

I learn French and English and Spanish and especially drawing, very modestly. When I am seventeen, my father gives in to my mother and I go for a year to the Beaux Arts in Paris, France, and I live very happy in the middle of the Louvre and the Boul' Mich', as they call the Boulevard St.-Michel in the Latin Quarter, and the Seine and all those places of unparalleled beauty. I am in love with a friend from the Beaux Arts and with another who is very beautiful, shh. I never have such a good laugh as in Paris. I am very sad to leave and to leave my friends and I cry shamefully when I get a postcard sometimes, but that's life, isn't it?

Two years later, when I have my diploma in drawing, my father gives in to my mother and I go for a year to Melbourne and Sydney, Australia, becoming acquainted with English language. Very unfortunately, it's the war. I am taken on Japanese ship to come home. *Boom!* Torpedoed!

For many days and nights there are many of us on a piece of ship in the big ocean, eating the little fish easy to catch and drinking rainwater. We throw overboard two old women, three men, and a baby without milk who are dead. And still many men are weak and the big waves carry them off. I often cry in my corner, thinking about my family, and I'm not full of hatred, but I hope the Americans will be punished for their wickedness.

Luckily, I have good health like my mother, whose grandmother's grandmother is still alive in Talcahuano, Chili, and is a hundred and twelve years old. We run aground one night, and in the light of dawn I see with my eyes that I have come ashore in a land with big green trees, but I don't know how you call them in your language, and with me are six sailors from my country lying on the sand.

It is the season of the burning sun. Our clothes are torn. I have my dirty kimono with only one arm. My companions are even more rotten and sad at our fate. I tell you their names: Yoshiro, the boss, Tadashi, Akiro, Nagisa, Kenji, and Kimura. For many hours they are painful in the shade of the trees, and they wander in the water, looking at the end of the ocean, and they raise their fists and shout bad words.

The next morning, Yoshiro make them all stand in front of him, talking with good sense, and together they put on the beach all the things from the poor ship that the ocean doesn't want. We walk in single file along the beach in the direction of the rising sun. We walk for a long time. We find drinking water several times. We see birds and fish easy to catch and crabs living on land and climbing trees. I don't know their name in your language but they are plenty tasty to eat. We see with our eyes nobody on this beach and no trace that anybody ever live here. There are lots of giant bamboo and Yoshiro laugh because we can build a roof over our heads and wait for help. It's not his advice to build a boat, although Tadashi, Kenji, and Kimura want to build a boat. He say we are too far from another shore inhabited by Japanese. He say, "We are soldiers now, and we keep for our country this land given to us by fate."

We are still marching beside the big ocean, and when we see with our eyes again the things from the poor ship lying scattered on the beach, the sun is shining behind us. Then we know that we have beached on an island big as it take half a day to walk around. In the middle, we see no mountain but only the green jungle with birds' cries all the time, even at night.

The morning after that, I stay in this place with Nagisa, the youngest, and the others go in single file into the big trees. Nagisa and I look carefully at all the things from the poor ship and we put to one side all the things that are good and to the other all the things that are no use. Among the good things, we have a rocking chair and a box full of clothespins, and lots of silly things like that, but no guns for hunting and no food and no material to dress ourselves in. Things of mine, I only find my sketch pad and I dry the pages on the sand, and Nagisa find his little sailor hat.

Our companions come back before dark. They see lots of rodents easy to catch and fruits and drinking water, they are happy. They climb up the big trees, and no sign of other men. Yoshiro congratulate us plenty for our work, me and Nagisa, but he carefully look at all that is good and after he say *kuso*, which is "shit" in English, and he kick the rocking chair.

The next days, they make tools with the iron from the poor ship, especially Yoshiro and Tadashi, who are very good with their hands, and they cut down the hard trees and the big bamboo to build the house. All the time they build, it's three weeks. I carry the little things, and the water for their thirst because they are very hot, and I cook with the fish and the crabs, and often I swim under the ocean to catch shellfish, and everybody congratulate me much because I make good food, relatively speaking, of course. The house is built in the place where we land, just at the edge of the jungle. There is a spring of drinking water close by which comes into the bamboos that Kimura, the cleverest, hollows out and puts one inside the other, and we are in the shade of the trees until evening, and a lovely spit of yellow rocks stop the waves coming too noisy on the beach. It is a very practical house and very strong, although it look a bit of a mess. It is as long as ten of my strides, seven wide, and big enough for everyone to sleep, with a fine balcony in front and little steps down to the sand. Under the house it's as tall as me for when the ocean swells, and now I laugh because the ocean is never angry enough even to wet our feet, but it's practical for the rainy season and to keep the useless things from the poor ship.

At night we make light in lamps with animal and fish fat, but it smell horrible, and after a while we make it with Kimura, the cleverest's, wood alcohol. Kimura know how to make alcohol from anything and plant anything and find water anywhere when he need it. Me, Yoko, I make mats to sleep on, and the branches decorated with little bits of paper to honor the gods of this island and our deceased fellow countrymen from the poor ship. I make the window and the door with tracing paper and lots of utensils for eating and drinking, and I sing when the sun goes down and when we are all so sad far from our homeland. I sing songs from my childhood and songs my mother used to sing, and also dirty songs that my friends at the Beaux Arts in Paris used to sing, and I translate the words and we all have a good laugh.

All the time we live together on this island, my companions never say anything hurtful or scold me. They praise me for my work and they give me flowers and shells, and they are all mad with desire for me, but very respectfully. After a while I see they are very unhappy with this desire when I walk on the sand or when I swim or when I am lying on my mat. To avoid quarrels and to satisfy my strong desire to be fucked, I give one day of the week to each of them, and on the seventh day I rest. My companion who satisfy me the most, I don't tell you, I make a promise before the big ocean, at the end of the yellow rocks, to never tell anyone.

Every day, when they are in the jungle, I dive into the water which cleanses and I wash my worn-out kimono and I fix my long hair with sticks to make myself beautiful, relatively speaking, of course. They don't want me, Yoko, to go into the jungle, because of the snakes and evil spirits that might take me. They are sailors and only trust the big ocean.

Yoshiro, the boss and the engineer for the machines on the poor ship, sharpen a tall tree trunk and they plant it in the sand on the beach to raise our flag made from scraps of shirt sewn together and the blood of an animal, but the blood turns black, and Kimura, the cleverest, make the red from little crushed shells. When they both stand in front of the flag and me behind them on the sand, Yoshiro say, "We are in rags like beggars, we have no guns, but we are alive and our lives belong to our revered emperor to fight for victory."

We live many days under the burning sun, with hunting and fishing and laughing, and shameful tears sometimes, and I go into the house when the sun set, hand in hand with my lover, and our other companions stay outside, sitting on the beach, silently drinking Kimura's alcohol or telling of their happy lives when they are sailors. After, they come inside when it's dark and they sleep. And me, Yoko, when my happiness to be fucked is over, I think of my family and of our beautiful house in Yokohama and I dream of being there during all the time I am asleep.

Then, just before the rainy season, come that day that will never leave my memory. My companions go in the jungle to catch a wild pig they see several times, and Yoshiro walk ahead with the spear he make with his hands and the others are armed with knives and grass ropes. Nagisa, the youngest, walk last with his little sailor hat. He is twenty years old like me.

They are far, for one hour, not more. I wash the food utensils in the ocean. Then I hear *bang-bang-bang* in the jungle and I stand up, and I hear *bang-bang-bang* again, the noise of that gun that spit many cartridges, and after I don't know how you call it in your language, the tommy gun. For a long time I hear nothing and I walk aimlessly along the beach, very fearful and calling on the spirits of the island for my companions. Then I see with my eyes Yoshiro coming out of the jungle shouting, "They're all dead! They're all dead!" And me, Yoko, I run to him and soon we are together, fallen down on the sand, and Yoshiro cry like a woman and he say, "All, poor wretches! All dead!" And I see he is holding the gun that spit much.

The truth is that they go in single file down a narrow path in the jungle to catch the wild pig, looking at their feet because of the tracks. Then, Nagisa, the youngest, looking elsewhere, suddenly pick up a ball of red and white paper in the grass that leap out at his eye, and when he put it flat in his hand, I tell you what it is: a Lucky Strike cigarette packet. Nagisa, very fearful, look everywhere, shouting, "An enemy! Warning! An enemy!" And Yoshiro, the boss, see the paper in his hand and say, "Shut up! Fool!" At same time he look everywhere like Nagisa, and the others, too, and I tell you what they see above their heads: an enemy airman hanging in the branches of a big tree with his parachute, and he is rotten but still alive. So my companions want to hide anywhere in the long grass, because the enemy is holding in his hands the tommy gun pointed at them, and very unfortunately they can't, that's when I hear the *bang-bang-bang* while I wash the cooking instruments, and they all fall down, hit without arms to defend themselves. Fate protect only

Yoshiro, who throw his spear very hard into enemy's body, like he learn with Hokkaido whale hunters, and he shout "Victory!" taking the tommy gun that fall into the grass for himself, and he make *bang-bang-bang*, too, he is so pleased, because all the time this massacre, it's just a handful of seconds, and he see after with his eyes all our dead companions.

That is Yoshiro's painful story as I hear it from his mouth when we are on the sand. We lie there a long time, defeated and sorrowful, and I think that never again I can stand up and walk on this island and continue my life. But Yoshiro get his courage back and say, "Come, we must go back to that place and bring back the bodies before the animals eat them."

And so I enter the jungle for the first time with Yoshiro. When we arrive before this massacre, I cry helplessly, touching with my hands the faces of my unfortunate companions. Only the day before, I caress Kenji on the mats and he have much happiness in my mouth and in my belly and he tell me poems he make up when he is alone. And the day before, Nagisa, the youngest, who make me promise to marry him when we are safe and home again. And Kimura, the cleverest, who want to see if the little paddy field he plant give food when the rainy season come. And Tadashi, the harshest, who fuck me very energetically and for a long time to satisfy himself. And Akiro, the oldest, who is forty-eight years old and who is known as Popeye, I don't know why, and who have a good laugh with me all the time. All, all, they are lying on the ground, covered in blood and earth and still warm from life. Shh.

Yoshiro and me, we drag each body by the feet out of the jungle and onto the beach, and when Yoshiro arrive, he run to me, because I am not strong enough, and he drag the body for me. After, he climb the tree where the dead enemy is and he cut the branches to make him fall down with his parachute. He tell me he think this man blown onto the island by the wind during the night and that his plane is shot down far away by our fellow countrymen, because we are woken by the noise if it is hit here.

The truth, I find out later, is that the plane isn't hit at all, but its engine done for, and it fall not far away in the ocean. Only the birds and the beasts that cry in the jungle at night stop us from hearing, very unfortunately.

The enemy is an American lieutenant and his identification plaque say Howard J. Fairchild. He is thirty years old, we think, and tall with yellow hair and not married because he has no ring. I am happy, relatively speaking, of course, that his death doesn't make a loving wife and perhaps children suffer. Yoshiro say that we drag him to the beach, too, even though he kill our companions, because death make no distinction between the poor soldiers and it is a sin for us to abandon his body to the animals. So that is what we do. Before leaving this cursed place, Yoshiro take two belts filled with cartridges that our enemy is wearing across his chest, and he look carefully under the tree. He find a good knife in the long grass and he say, "I understand why this man cannot escape and kill us all while we sleep."

After, on the beach, I take our enemy's clothes and boots, and Yoshiro go to cut the wood to light a big fire and give them all proper funeral rites. I cleanse our companions' and our enemy's bodies with drinking water. I immerse myself in the sea to cleanse myself, too, and I fix my hair with sticks, and I put red on my cheeks and black around my eyes to honor the dead. Under the setting sun, Yoshiro place the bodies on top of the carefully built pyre and he sweat very much and he cry shamefully, and then I see with my eyes that his courage and his reason are failing him. He stay like a ball on the sand, crying and banging with his fists, and he say, "It is too much to have to burn my good friends and the young and turbulent Nagisa, it is too much for me and I can't go on anymore."

So I comfort him with gentle words and I lead him into the house, and here I say that it is woman's destiny to be always mourning men, that he already build a good and fine pyre, that he rest now. I give him Kimura's alcohol on his knees and I say to him, "If you want to honor our companions, get drunk and think of the good times you had on the big ocean and in the arms of your young ladies, from China in the north to Australia in the south." He cry and laugh at the same time, shaking his head, and I go outside, and nearly all night I run backward and forward putting wood on the fire and the flames are very high and I cry to all of them, "I don't forget, I don't forget, let your spirits return to the mountain!" Sometimes I fall over. And sometimes I have sand and ash on my face. But I ask forgiveness and I get up and I rush about all the time, and I make them good funeral rites, relatively speaking, of course.

After, for another two weeks, or perhaps three, I live all alone with Yoshiro. He sit until evening in the rocking chair, with the tommy gun on his knees and the cartridge belts around his chest, thinking about the massacre, and he speak only to ask for food or drink. As for me, Yoko, every day I go to the end of the yellow rocks and I throw the wreaths of flowers I make into the ocean. This is where I throw the ash from the pyre, and I carefully clean the place on the beach where our dead burn and no stain remains on this island.

I walk alone in the jungle, looking everywhere for flowers for the wreaths and rodent tracks to put down traps. My kimono is completely without arms and only come down to my bottom, and for underneath I sew panties with the material from the parachute. I am very hot on the beach and in the jungle, and when the sun go down, I have the American's big fur jacket. His boots are too big for my feet and Yoshiro refuse to wear the enemy's things. I must tell you that all the time we are cast away on this island, we go barefoot. So I cut out a good pair of sandals from the boots to go in the jungle.

And so I continue my life—"you just have to make the best of things"—and I still laugh, and I cook good food for Yoshiro and keep everything nice and clean in the house. Very unfortunately, Yoshiro is sad and silent, rocking his body all day on the balcony, doing nothing, and at night he stay a long way away from me on his mat, despite my strong desire to be fucked. After, he doesn't remember that Nagisa and the others are dead and their ashes in the big ocean, he sometimes talk to Nagisa, who doesn't obey his orders, or to Tadashi, whose advice is to build a boat, and he say, "I think it is a good idea, Tadashi, we must build it tomorrow and go home." All that is very painful, and again, after a few days, he is like a child of forty, because I have to scold him and lead him to the edge of the jungle to empty his stomach.

Then come the rainy season. The day I tell you about, the water pour down everywhere on the jungle and on the beach, and Yoshiro is on the balcony, gently rocking his body, his mind turned inward, and as for me, Yoko, I wash the floor in the house and I can see Yoshiro through the open door. Then Yoshiro moan and I see him with my eyes fall out of the chair, and he is dead on the balcony floor with an ax stuck in his bleeding back, and the chair is still rocking, and I am so full of horror that I cannot scream. I just stand up and I see with my eyes a man who is very tall and he is standing in front of the door with his filthy soldier clothes and red hair and beard. And after, I see another western soldier, who is smaller, with a yellow beard and a hat on his head like the Australians I see in their country.

Then I go back quickly against the wall and they both stare at me for a long time in silence and they see that I haven't got the weapons or the strength to attack them, and they lose their stern look and bow their heads to greet me respectfully.

I tell you who they are: the Australian infantry soldier William Collinson, twenty-five years old, he's the redhead, and the Australian infantry soldier Richard Benedict, twenty-seven, with the hat and the yellow hair. The day I tell you about, they ask for food before anything else, and I give them food, crying to see poor Yoshiro dead. They take away the ax but they leave him lying on the balcony floor. Then they drag his body out of sight and they close the door and tell me to take off my kimono and that they will spare me my life if I let them do what they want. I say that they can do what they want after I can cleanse my poor companion and make him proper funeral rites. They are pleased I speak English, although not well, but they must wait for the evening and for the rain to ease off for the funeral rites and they want me very badly, not having a woman for many days. I also ask for their word and they both give it to me and I let them do what they want. I suffer from being fucked like I never suffer before, especially with Redhead, who is very big to come inside me, and he fuck me vigorously, with my legs up on his shoulders, and I am ashamed to be miserable in front of the other soldier who is watching.

After they are well satisfied, they carefully inspect the tommy gun and the cartridge belts they take from Yoshiro, and I tell them how we have the massacre, and they tell me in detail the airplane accident. The truth is that they are five men in the plane, going to Hawaii from Australia, two Americans and two Australians and an injured British colonel, but the engines stop and they try to land on this island. Then, seeing that they can't, the colonel, injured in a game of polo, order them to jump with parachutes, and they do. The plane fall into the ocean on the other side of this island and it is night and Bill and Dick lose their companions. In the morning they look for them in the jungle and on the beaches. Then they see with their eyes our house and me and my six fellow countrymen, too many to be attacked with only an ax, and they go back and hide in the place they landed with their parachutes.

During the next days, they eat roots and fruit because they are not quick enough to catch fish, and the crabs that go on land turn their stomachs over. They build a shelter with branches, afraid they will be seen by my fellow countrymen, and one time they decide to swim in the ocean to find the place where the plane fall. After many swims, they find it under the water, deep as two minutes without breathing, and they can't touch it. In everything, they are less skillful than my fellow Japanese sailors, even Nagisa, the youngest. All the time they didn't know about the massacre, it was until today. In fact, they don't want to attack us but to steal arms and food. So they make the most of the noise of the rain to come very close to the house and they watch for a long time and they realize that Yoshiro is all alone with me, and they kill him with the ax.

This is what the two enemy soldiers tell me. They are angry that the American airman is killed, but not full of hatred for me; they just shake their heads, saying "Shit," and after, they say they help me for Yoshiro's funeral rites.

It's true that they do. When the night is black, the rain stop and we take the alcohol lamps onto the beach to give us light. Bill and Dick cut the wood with the ax and build the pyre, me telling them how to do it, and while they build, I wash my unfortunate companion all over, and I talk to him gently so that his spirit rest always happy with the other dead members of his family, or with his sailor friends if he prefer, and to soothe his fear, I give him many messages for Nagisa and Kimura and our other companions.

After, Bill and Dick lift his body onto the pyre, with the spear he make with his hands and a big bowl of Kimura's alcohol, and as for me, Yoko, I cleanse myself in the ocean and I paint my face red and white and black all around my eyes and I do all these very painful things. For a long time the pyre refuse the fire, because it is wet from the rain, but after, the flames rise high and I run all around, making sure the wood burn well. The two enemies sit on the stairs, in front of the house, silent and respectful for the funeral, and after they go to sleep, and when the fire die, it is almost day and I can run away, but where?

The morning I tell you about, Bill and Dick help me carry the ashes to the end of the yellow rocks, and I carefully wash the beach and the balcony to wipe away the stain. After, they want to take down my country's flag, which is on the hewn tree. I say, "Me, Yoko, I cannot stop you, I am a woman of twenty years and alone in your hands, that's why I let you fuck me and I don't bite or scratch and I am not full of hatred, but if you take down the flag, you lose a good arrangement." They talk far away from me and at last Bill, the redhead, say, "All right, the rain will come back, we don't care about this thing that look like women's period towel." He say it differently and with rude words, I don't know the words in your language, but my country's flag stay on this island all the time I live with them.

After, it rain for more than one week, and we stay in the house, or bungalow, without going outside. Even though they are enemies, and less intelligent and peaceful than my fellow countrymen, they are good company. Never they say hurtful words to me or hit me. We have plenty of food and I teach them the games I know with little shells, and sometimes they have a good laugh and sometimes they are grumpy like animals in a cage. I am fucked by each of them, day and night, and also by both of them together, and I am ashamed to have pleasure like that, but after, I shrug it off. The truth is that after a few times, they are angry and they don't want to do it together anymore, and when I am fucked by Dick, the other one go onto the balcony, banging the door and saying bad words in his beard, and when Bill fuck me, Dick watch us and laugh and he keep saying, "You fuck badly, I bet she get more pleasure on her own with her little finger."

Then come the first day without rain. I walk with them in the wet jungle, with cold droplets falling from the trees, and Bill and Dick in their filthy soldiers' clothes and me in the dead American's shirt and Nagisa's sailor hat on top of my hair, and we go to the place where their shelter is. It's a beach the same as ours but without yellow rocks, and the waves are very big. We cut and tie together the parachute cords, which are made of modern fiber and very strong, and they tie this thick rope around my body and I go into the ocean. They swim with me into the middle of the very big waves and after, the ocean is calmer, and they show me the place where the plane fall. I swim alone under the water, and then I see the plane, and I dive down sharply toward it, which has one arm broken, and all this time I look carefully all around. The ocean isn't as deep as the two Australians say and I am a good diver, relatively speaking. I cannot see with my eyes this time where I can tie the rope, but I see that the water is in the plane and that it is a matter of pride for Bill, whose idea it is, to pull it out.

When I come back out of the ocean, I say this and they are very angry and pensive because they hope to salvage the radio and tell their fellow countrymen where they are. After, I go under the ocean again and I go inside the plane through the hole in its broken arm. I see with my eyes the dead pilot and the colonel, too, and I chase away, screaming loudly underwater, the many fish eating them, and I see they are eaten down to the bone, and I see things from the plane that might be useful but not the radio, and I need air. So I come up again very fast, and when I am out of the ocean, I spit the food I eat before, I still see the fish together on the bodies of the poor enemy, and I stay a long time unable to tell about it. After, I only say that the pilot and the colonel are dead and that I don't see the radio. Then a third time Bill and Dick encourage me to go back down to the plane and Dick draw on the sand where I find the radio, and I go back again. I see with my eyes all the equipment that fly the plane, and it is possible to take the radio, with three dives perhaps, but I think fast and wisely, relatively speaking, of course, and it is my opinion that I must not help our enemy contact their fellow countrymen.

After, I tell Bill and Dick that the radio is with the other equipment and that I can't get it, even going under the ocean more times than there are hairs on my head. So they say "Shit" and are angry, and finally they want to go back to the bungalow and think up a scheme to bring the plane up. The truth is that they think only about food and sleeping and arguing over little things and each one fucking me with enjoyment, and all the time they are doing this, life go on and the rain fall. As for me, Yoko, I don't want to say anything hurtful about anyone, but I see many times that men from the West have big noses and little patience. You blow with your mouth and they are afraid of the wind and change their minds. Although not always, I meet one after more stubborn than a mule.

For more days and more nights we stay in the house, going out in the rain only to empty our stomachs, and once Dick see with his eyes that box full of clothespins under the house. So he laugh and he say to Bill, the redhead, that he must go onto the balcony because he want to fuck me very bad. As for me, Yoko, I am fucked before by both of them and I make a bad face, although I prefer Dick because he isn't so big and his skin is softer and he smell better and Bill fuck me hard with no respect for my body. So Dick encourage me and wheedle me, and in the end I want to. He make me take off my shirt and my panties and lie on the mat, and then he give me very violent and very long enjoyment, many times, with a secret he learn in a bad place in Borneo, and all the time he do these things to me, I forget to be ashamed and I shout out and my body shake, but perhaps you know it, so I won't say. It take seven clothes-pins.

After, Bill come back and he is full of hate against his companion because he hear my enjoyment, and for everything I say, he shrug and call me "little bitch" or "Japanese whore." So Dick say to him, "Stop being nasty to Yoko, she is good for you when you are crying out to put your big prick anywhere you can!" And Bill say, "Do you want me to tell you where I put it? In her Japanese ass, yes, and deep enough for it to come out of her mouth and you can suck the tip!" So Dick punch him in the head with his fist, and after, they fight in the house and I shout at both of them to stop. Very unfortunately, Bill is stronger and Dick is covered in blood on the floor. After, Bill say to him, "Poor son of a bitch, I show you how I fuck your geisha's ass!" And after, he fling me on my knees and hold me down by the shoulders and he want to fuck me like that, like he do before, several times, but this time he must kill me dead first, and I shout, full of hate and crying, "A curse on you and all your family and all your fellow British countrymen!" Then he become calm and ashamed, and I can finally stand up and wash poor Dick. After, they never say another word to each other, and as for me, Yoko, when Redhead is too close behind me, I say, "Yes, try to come in my mouth, I want to show you how strong my teeth are!" So Bill stay on the balcony, angry, but never he fuck me again, I make a promise.

Then come that day without rain, and they both go outside the house, on the sand, and I cook the food and I hear their voices full of hate. I go onto the stairs, telling them not to fight, but their faces are angry and without color, and they circle each other in the sand, looking at each other and both holding knives, and they don't listen to Yoko. Then they try to kill the other one with hate, and I scream, and after I cry, sitting on the stairs, not wanting to see with my eyes and not wanting them to die, especially Dick, the weaker one, and finally Dick is dead and Bill covered in blood because the knife go in his stomach.

All the time Bill is alive he is with me in the sand and I say to the gods of the island to let him live and that we've had enough dead bodies now to pacify them, although we still put them to a lot of trouble by being castaways here. I am with Bill in my arms as long as the night is black and the rain falls and at last he say, "Poor Yoko who is good to me and I am always bad to her. And my poor friend who I kill in my madness, how can Christ forget my sin?" As for me, Yoko, I gently rock his head in my arms and I invoke Christ and I tell him that he must forget his sin because we are all far away from our mothers and only war is bad, but perhaps the rain make too much noise for Christ to hear, I don't know.

On the next day I can't make funeral rites for my two Australian companions and I put them under the sand to protect their bodies, and after, I cry for a long time and I think of their faces and I scold myself a lot because I don't let Bill have his enjoyment with me and he become full of hate.

At last, the day after, the rain isn't so heavy and I build the fire and I make the funeral rites. In the night I finish, I am cold and sick. And after, I am ill for many days. And sometimes I see with my eyes Yoshiro or Kenji or Nagisa, the youngest, and I ask them to forgive me for keeping them waiting for food, I say I am going to get up. And sometimes, too, I see myself with my eyes alone on this island, lying in the house, listening to the rain outside, and I am afraid of dying like this, in the food that I spit and the filth from my empty stomach. But I don't die, and after, I know that I never die.

That is the end of the first part of my story on this island.

When the dry season come back, I am happy and I walk on the sand and I take all my clothes off to feel the sun on my naked body and cleanse my body in the big ocean. I catch fish and crabs and shellfish for food, and I hollow out bamboo like Kimura to repair the attacks made by the rain and bring back drinking water into the house. There is everywhere plenty of drinking water, and I arrange the channels of water in Kimura's little paddy field nicely, and I build two good water tanks in the Australians' parachutes.

So I work to forget that I am all alone during these many weeks, with the burning sun and the birds in the jungle. Sometimes I go in the jungle with the tommy gun, but I am afraid to displease the spirits even more with the noise and I prefer to put down traps for the rodents. And also I clean the bungalow every day to make it nice and tidy, as if waiting for my fellow Japanese to come back from the jungle and congratulate me much on my work. And also I draw each one with pieces of burned wood on my white paper, as my memory see them, and always I cry stupidly and my tears make blotches on the drawing. And often I make wreaths with flowers and I go to the end of the yellow rocks and throw the wreaths into the big ocean to honor all my dead lovers.

Then come the day the big ocean choose to give me a new destiny. I am standing on the yellow rocks, dressed in Dick's shirt, and I close my eyes and bow my head to invoke the spirits, and I hear noises that make me look around. Then I see with my eyes things moving in the water, going toward the beach, but too far for me to see what. After very little time, I am at the foot of the rocks and I see that they are two swimmers, one ahead of the other and a better swimmer. Then I think that I leave the tommy gun on the balcony of the house, and I must run to take it before these strangers, and after, I see if they are fellow Japanese or enemies.

That is what I do, and I say without pride that I run fast, being tall for a Japanese girl. Unfortunately, there are many steps between the bungalow and me, and the first swimmer is nearer. Although tired, he stand up and I see with my eyes that in fact it is a European woman and she is going to the house, too. Then I think stupidly. I don't run straight to the house to take the gun from the balcony, I go to the edge of the jungle so they don't see me with their eyes. I never forgive myself this stupidity. After, I am still running but the woman walk with determination, picking herself up each time she fall on the beach, and she reach the steps. The other swimmer is a man with no strength after the swim and he make his way over the sand on his hands and knees. And then, while I run, looking at him, this woman take the tommy gun and fall into Yoshiro's chair, and I see that I have lost the gun and I throw my body into the tall grass to hide.

That is how these things happen, and it is less time than two minutes. As for me, Yoko, who live on this island many, many months with my fellow Japanese and the Australians and then alone, in less time I lose the house over my head, and the American's sheepskin jacket, and the reserves of food and water, and my sketch pad, and the weapons, and all my belongings, and I am like a tramp running not fast enough, and thinking *idiot*, and *kuso, kuso, kuso*.

The woman, I tell you what she is like, because I see her with my eyes every day for a long time: very tall, a stern face, her eyes the color of the jungle, dark hair, long below her shoulders, a beautiful body, very intelligent, very active in everything, a fast swimmer like me, a fast runner, a good cook, good at washing the house, very clean in her body, and French.

The man, also French, I tell you very quickly what he is like because you see him with your eyes before me: he is more stubborn than a mule.

Of course, when I see the two strangers for this time, angry and afraid in the grass, they are rotten. The woman is dressed in a torn nightdress, down to her feet, wet from the ocean, showing her breasts and her stomach and all her body as if naked, and her hair hang all over the place. And him, his clothes are in shreds, and he move across the sand with his arms and knees like a big cat fallen in the soup. Then she say sharply, pointing the tommy gun at him, "Stay where you are!" And after, she say, "If we have to live here for a while, don't forget that I'm the one who is holding this thing!" I can't remember her exact words, but then she make the tommy gun spit, *bang-bang-bang*, and I see the sand jump in several places in front of the man. And he, in his terror, he point with his arm to our flag on the hewn tree and shout, "Shit! Can't you see? There are Japs on this island!" She shrug and reply, talking to him like a worm, "I am very surprised if it's true. When there are men somewhere, every woman knows it, just by the smell." And she say to him, full of hate, "You stink!"

The poor swimmer wipe his hands on his clothes and look at her like a scolded child, but he can't find a word to defend himself. Then she look everywhere, sitting in Yoshiro's chair, and she say, "It's too clean here. I think a woman live in this house and at this minute she is hiding and watching us. And if she is only watching us, it's because she isn't armed." She taps with her hand on the bang-bang, and she say, pleased with her sharp mind, "The only one she have when we arrive, is this one!"

Since that day, our flag is no longer on this island, and as for me, Yoko, I go into the jungle. I throw behind me the bungalow and all the good useful things inside. I have with me only Dick's shirt, and panties from the parachute material, and another piece of material on my forehead to tie back my hair. I am on my bare feet and careful where I walk because of snakes. Then I go to the other side, where the Australians' shelter is, and I tidy it up and put fresh leaves to sleep. This first night, I think carefully and my opinion is not to attack the two French people together without a gun. My opinion is to wait until I am confident that the gods of this island are on my side because I live here longer.

I can't remember if the French are enemies of my country or not. When I leave Australia on the poor ship, I don't care about the war in Europe, I think only the Americans and the English are our enemies. But I think this evening that the French are, too, because of the way the man speak about the Japs. I am, of course, very sad that they are, I prefer the French to all the others, because of the Beaux Arts in Paris and all my friends and the nice ladies from the overseas students' hostel, in the rue Soufflot. So I promise that if the gods of this island give me victory over the people who steal my house, I never kill them, I find a ruse to trap them.

The day after, I walk on the Australians' beach and I think that I go back to the plane and I find another gun. But I am afraid of the dead men eaten by the fish, and that I see their bones and their heads, and that I greatly offend the spirits of the ocean. I'm not sure, having little knowledge of these things. Then I invoke the big ocean and I say if it is offended because I come into its depths and disturb the dead, it show me with a sign. I say that I dive, near the edge, and I take a shell, and if there is a pearl in it, I mustn't go, but if there is no pearl, it give me permission to search the plane. That is what I do, swimming for very little time, and I take a shell. After, I open it, banging it with a stone, and there is a beautiful pearl shining in its flesh. So I thank the ocean for giving me this sign and I forget my idea.

The day that I tell you about, and many others, when the sun is low, I go to the edge of the jungle on the other side of the island, and I watch the French for a long time, carefully hidden in the grass and silent, and I listen to their words, becoming familiar with their language. I don't learn much because they always say the same thing. This man, whose name is Frédéric, has his hands and feet tied up with the parachute cords, and his footsteps on the sand are too short to run, but he act as though it is nothing to be tied up and he laugh and say, "Stupid bitch!" And this woman, whose name is Esmeralda, is standing in the shallow water, with the lower half of her nightdress hiked up between her legs and tied like undershorts, and she make the tommy gun spit out fire anywhere, or to kill fish, and after, she come back to the beach with maybe three fish, in shreds, beside her and she say, walking far from the wretched man, "Stupid bastard!"

At night, in the house, I don't know what she do with him, but I think she keep him tied up to sleep. Once, I see her tie his feet to a big piece of our poor ship, and now, when he want to walk on the beach, he must drag the weight. And another time she tie the material from the parachute around this man's eyes and she say, "That'll teach you to look at me like that." After, she leave the tommy gun on the beach and take off her nightdress to swim with enjoyment and she say: "It is a very pleasant thing, my dear Frédéric, to swim naked!" But the other days, he is only tied up like the first time, and she scold him without anger. She say, "It make me sad, too, to keep you like this. If you are good and don't want to take the gun from me, and if you promise, you may be free very soon." But he spit on the sand with his mouth to show his scorn and he say, "I am free one day all by myself and I tie you up, and I do to you a hundred times what you do to me once." The truth is, I think, that you can't ever put two French people together and they agree.

During all these long days, the bad woman doesn't go more than a hundred paces from the house, and she swim on one side or the other, but she doesn't go far out into the ocean. Often, she look at the edge of the jungle, turning her head quickly, and she hope to see me with her eyes. She make food only with fish and shellfish, and once, too, with a rodent with no common sense that come out of the jungle. And always her food smell very good and I want very much to eat it.

After, Frédéric work in Kimura's little paddy field, on the other side of the house, and he is clumsy with his hands tied in front, but he gather the rice and carefully make the little water channels. Now his hands and feet have little bracelets and anklets that this clever woman make with wire from the poor ship because once Frédéric burn the parachute cord tying his hands, and he can almost escape.

Often, this man sit on the sand with the bowls and the bamboos and the lamps with which Kimura make the alcohol, and I see that he cannot understand what Kimura do with all these things, and he say to himself, "Bloody machine! I lose my days and my nights if need be, but I find out your secret!" And it's true that he find it after much time, and he make alcohol with the wood for the lamps and crushed rice to drink. After, he drink a little, still hot, and I laugh inside because his face show that it is bad, but this woman come not further than ten paces, curious and scornful, and then he make a satisfied sound with his mouth and say, "Very good! I never tasted better."

One day at last, coming to hide in the grass to watch the French, I see with my eyes that this woman is bold enough to stand up on the yellow rocks, and I say to myself: Ah! Just you wait, my dear, you go faster than me once when I am on these rocks, but we see now who get their own back. The man is sitting on the beach, his back to me, and I go behind the house like a snake. After, I am out of their sight and I climb silently up the bamboo with my hands and feet, and I go in through the window that look at the jungle. And then I know that I am brainless and proud because this cursed woman put everywhere in the house little bells made of pieces of tin can hanging from wire like a spider's web. When you are in this trap, you don't get out without making even more noise.

I take, of course, everything I can carry in my hands before the Frenchwoman, running and shouting, come to kill me. I take the American's sheepskin jacket and his iron and cloth bottle marked "U.S.," and instruments that I make when we land on this island, and I quickly look around to see the soldiers' knives and the ax, but it isn't there or it is carefully hidden. Then I am close to my death, because this woman come into the bungalow, or shack, just as I escape through the window and I fall from my height, and she shout, "Stay! Stay or I kill you!" And me, I fling my body in the tall grass, with my possessions, and she make the bang-bang spit fire anywhere in the leaves of the jungle, many times, and my heart is wild, and I promise myself that I never come back in this house if they don't invite me. Even after, when I am far and peaceful, I still shake all over my body with fear.

But the day I am telling you about, before the sun set, I see my death again. The bad woman is full of hate that I run away and she walk in the jungle for more than two hours, looking at my tracks, and she come on the Australians' beach. I don't believe my eyes, and nor do you perhaps, but it's true. She is standing there with the tommy gun in her hands and the cartridge belts crossed over on her body, and I am lying in the shelter I make with leaves, and very luckily for me, she doesn't see me and doesn't walk on the side where I am. But she see the beach in front and the sand often churned up by my feet and she shout, "Why go on like this? We French don't kill women! If you show your hands on your head and come to me, I give you good food and plenty of water and you are treated with respect as a prisoner!" And this is what she say with gentle words, but I know that if I show just my nose, even though it is short like my fellow countrymen, she kill me in blood with perhaps a hundred cartridges, and she leave my dead body for food for the animals after she spit on it with her mouth. Also I am afraid but I don't move more than a stone, and I invoke the spirits of this island not to let the Frenchwoman tread on my shelter.

She stay a long time, looking everywhere on the beach and in the jungle, and she turn around on the spot, speaking French and English, saying: "Are you here? Answer me! Are you here?" Finally, she lose patience and say, "Japanese mule, I show you what I do with you when I catch you!" And she spit out *bang-bang-bangs* full of hate anywhere into the leaves. Luckily, I am not dead, and she shrug her shoulders and go into the jungle from where she come and go home. Ayayay, this woman have a nasty character!

After, it's the season of the burning sun, the two French stay in the house nearly all day. When they go outside, I see with my eyes this man even more pathetic than a dog in the street. His beard grow and also his hair and he have only his pants for clothes, even though they are cut above his knees, and his skin is dark from the sun and his hairs are yellow. He sit, a prisoner on the beach, watching the end of the ocean, and sometimes he sing to himself, very softly, but I can't hear the words. I prefer him and I am afraid he lose his reason like Yoshiro, but once he show me that he have common sense.

He is on the beach, his feet tied up to make little steps, and his hands tied up, too, in front of him, and he start doing something in the sand. I don't see what he is doing from where I am in the grass, and this woman on the stairs can't see either, because she say, "Frédéric, what are you doing?" And he answer, "If someone ask you, say you don't know." And then, before the sun go down and she shout to him to come back in the house, he work very hard and carefully, and he walk to find stones and a stick useful to make the sand clean and nice and flat, and I think I understand a little, and my heart beat faster because I am afraid that the woman understand, too.

After, when they are both inside the house lit with lamps, I go like a snake to this place on the beach. Then I see with my eyes that he make what I understand, a very little garden like in my country, and sure, if my fellow countrymen see this garden, they laugh, but

I don't. I think that this poor man say to me, "I know you are watching me from the jungle and I make this humbly for you." Then I write "YOKO" on the sand, with my finger, just next to the little garden, and I also put a tasty fruit to eat that is in my shirt, and I run away quickly.

The day after, I come to the grass before the sun, and when Frédéric, tied up, walk out of the house, he go and look at the garden as if he doesn't know what to do. Then he see my name and pick up the fruit. He wipe out my name with his foot, with his back to the bad woman, and after, when he is sitting far from her, eating the fruit, she say, "Well, well, where do you find this fruit you are eating?" And he doesn't look at her and he answer calmly, "It's not a fruit, it's something I cut off from between my legs."

Another day, when they are in the shade of the house, during the long burning hours, I forget fear and I come like a snake to listen to their words. And after, I stand up silently and look through a hole in the bamboo to see them. They have two beds, or mattresses, like Europeans, made from the material from the parachutes and dried grass, and now Yoshiro's chair is inside the house. Most often, this woman is sitting in the chair, the bang-bang slung behind, and he is lying flat on the mattress tied up. They talk to kill time and it is about things I don't understand, but it is more enjoyable for me than to live alone in the jungle. Also, the next days, I come again and all the other days.

I don't say I am unhappy. I build a bigger, more practical shelter deep in the jungle where there is plenty of drinking water if you dig the earth, and I eat fruit, fish, and shellfish, but not rodents or crabs because if I light a fire, the bad woman know where I am because of the smoke. This woman wear the airman's jacket before I take it and I find in the pocket the comb that Nagisa, the youngest, make for my hair and also a very pretty necklace she make from shells. Now I always keep this comb with me, and I put the necklace around my neck. I also have Tadashi's cutting tool, no good for killing a Frenchwoman but very useful for food, and a bamboo spear for catching fish. Around this island, I know all the beaches and all the places where the tasty fish hide, and once I quarrel with a shark who want my fish, but he and his brothers are not very skillful near the beach and very afraid of noise. The most dangerous are snakes, but they are afraid, too, and if they don't have their nest near where you live, you can chase them away easily. If they have their nest, you can live there, too, but only if your life is too bitter and you are fed up.

As for me, Yoko, when I am fed up, because I am always alone, I go and see the French in the house, in the shade of the bamboos. For more than four hours, I am like at the theater, living only to breathe. After a few days, I understand why the woman tie up Frédéric when they arrive on this island. The truth is that they don't know each other before. He is a criminal who run away from a prison in his country and hide on a ship, and the first time she see him with her eyes is when the boat burn and sink to the bottom, and he cling to a piece of wood in the night with her. After, they are three days in the big ocean and they see this island, and they swim, and Esmeralda take the gun of a stupid girl.

Several times Frédéric say that he is in the prison for a crime he doesn't do, but she shrug her shoulders. She prefer apologizing when they are saved than to suffer the same fate as a twenty-year-old peasant girl in the south of France. If I believe her, this peasant girl kill herself because Frédéric fuck her and she is ashamed. Frédéric say, "Never!" As for me, Yoko, I am nobody to judge these things, but I think Frédéric speak the truth, because this story doesn't make sense. I am fucked many times by the Australians, only to save my life. Even if I am ashamed that I can't stop my enjoyment with them, never the idea enter my mind that I must kill myself. If I must kill someone, it's the two Australians, and especially Bill, the red-head, but they always hide the bang-bang and the knives from me, and in the end I cry even though Bill is going to die and I scold myself painfully for this massacre, because if I agree to be fucked by him, he doesn't become full of hate. But perhaps the French peasant girl, although the same age as me, has less years of the tragedy and madness of war. Or perhaps, I must believe Bill's opinion, I am a Japanese whore.

Very fortunately, the two French often speak of other things than this mix-up. Esmeralda not much, and I tell you after what about, but Frédéric talk about moments of his childhood and his life before he go to prison, and the beautiful women he love. And he say that his grandmother is very good, and his mother abandoned by a coward when he is only six years old, and his wife, Constance, very good, too, and very beautiful, who never forget him. And also the time he fight for this Joan of Arc, and as for me, Yoko, I am afraid the wretched English kill her, and I stop myself showing my big happiness when Frédéric save her life. I am not *baka*, which mean stupid in English, and I understand that it is a story maybe not true, but who know? One day I ask the big ocean and it reply that nobody know. It make me think that if the English burn another, it is not the first or the last time that they lie.

Often, in my shelter, when sleep is a long time coming, I see in my memory the moments Frédéric speak about, especially the moments of laughter. Then, when he is a young student at the University of Paris and in love with a student who is learning law and perhaps you know her. And even if I replace in my mind this French student, whose name, like yours, is Marie-Martine, by me, Yoko, living in Paris, I tell you the story.

One day, when I want to go with my lover, Frédéric, and it's night and the door is closed in the girls' hostel, my opinion is that I go out by the window, but very unfortunately, it is high and I can't, and my lover call to the rue Soufflot the big red fire engine, with that big ladder. And the chief fireman say, "But I can't see the fire, boy!" And Frédéric say respectfully, "You cannot see it. My Japanese darling and I keep it hidden, but it is a very strong fire that we want to put out." So the chief fireman understand and say, "Poor France! It's all right this time, but tomorrow you buy a ladder with your own money or you tell your Japanese darling to live on the *ground floor!*" After, everyone in the hostel know that I hide the fire under my dress, and if the head doesn't write to my parents, it's because she is afraid that my father's heart explode.

I don't want to trouble the big ocean again to find out if this story is true like the other one, the fire not being of equal historic importance, but if you have the power of fate to give me the reply today, I am very happy and respectful.

It would be easy to sidestep the question, for there were probably countless Marie-Martines in the Paris law faculty during the years I studied there, but it would be an unjust reward for my Japanese respondent's frankness. I shall confirm, therefore, that the story is true, if not altogether exact. The hostel I lived in was in the rue de Grenelle, the fire engine was not called out but was passing by, and I found myself in such an awkward position on a narrow third-floor window ledge that the good men had no choice but to intervene, and as for my father, had he been informed of my escapades, he would certainly not have lost his appetite or any sleep, as he was already far too preoccupied with his own worries. All that detracts nothing, of course, from the incendiary qualities of the man who drove his beloved from the Sologne to such aberrations.

(From the notes of Marie-Martine Lepage)

There are many other very interesting moments in Frédéric's story, especially when he is running away from prison with another man's new wife, and when he play the piano in a luxurious house full of women, all perfumed and dressed in beautiful clothes, and when he frighten the bad schoolmistress to punish her. One of the moments that always stay in my memory when I am alone in my leaf shelter, with a little lamp I made that is well hidden so it can't be seen from outside, is when after he live almost one year with the two sisters born the same day who sell ice cream, and he is exactly like me with the two Australians, although it's hard for a man to be able to satisfy two women, relatively speaking, of course. And also, I often think, without being able to stop myself, of the time when that actress called Frou-Frou, whose beauty is unparalleled, is eating in the big dining room, on the boat, surrounded by everyone in fine clothes, and Frédéric secretly under the table, and then she is very afraid that they see her enjoyment. But I am with no one on this island for many long months. Even though in my mind I replace the woman with Yoko, and I caress myself, this thought makes my desire to be fucked too painful. Also, when I want, I chase it away, saying hurtful or mocking things to myself.

The fact is that I find Frédéric's stories very beautiful and Esmeralda find them very ugly. Esmeralda is twenty-seven years old. Before being with her friends on the boat that I speak about, she look after people's reason and she is very proud to know how to look after this. So, while she rock her body in the chair, looking stern, Frédéric lie on the mattress speaking about his childhood with his friends in Marseilles, France. And then, with his friends, he climb on the roof of that house where mothers take their baby and they all look through the window in the roof. In this big room, the mothers are sitting down, and when a baby cry sorrowfully, the mother open her dress and give it something to drink. Then all the other babies want it, too, and all the mothers show their beautiful breasts full of milk, and Frédéric and his friends like very much watching, even the little girls who are with them. I understand Frédéric very well, being little myself once, and I like to watch the baby sucking tastily its mother's beautiful breast. Then Frédéric say, forgetting the years that go by since, "And they suck, the bastards, they suck as if it's a matter of life and death!" And even through a tiny hole in the bamboos, any Japanese idiot can see from his face that he is very happy at this thought.

Unfortunately, Esmeralda stand up, in her torn nightdress that is mended many times, and she walk from one side of the shack to the other, her face scolding and not at all, but not at all happy. She say, "Yes, that's exactly what I think since the beginning. You are like most men, a retarded child, a voyeur, and"—here, a word I learn later—"*a misogynist!*"

Then Frédéric sit up on the mattress using just the strength in his back, and he say laughing, "Me? A *misogynist!*" And she say, "Yes, you! All voyeurs are misogynists! They are only interested in women's bodies, because they represent nothing but corporeal nourishment for their appetite. Even as children!" Frédéric shout louder than her, "Don't baby girls suck milk then? What are you talking about?" She stay standing, tall above him, and she say, "Idiot! I don't mean the appetite for milk! But that unhealthy and vicious appetite that women always see in your eyes!" And louder still, Frédéric shout, "It's not true! Do you know what Shakespeare wrote? *The eyes are the window to the soul!* And he's no two-bit psychologist!"

As for me, Yoko, not liking quarrels and feeling like a voyeur sheltering from the burning sun, I certainly favor Shakespeare, even though he is English, but I see this woman turn around sadly, weak and exhausted, she take the bang-bang and just go to her bed, or mattress, and when she is completely lying down, she say, "I hate voyeurs, you understand? They terrify me."

She doesn't speak for a long time and Frédéric respect her silence. After, she say: "Listen. When I am younger, my most beautiful dream is to be a tennis champion." And again, she doesn't speak for a long time. Frédéric get up and walk with little steps because of his wire bands and careful not to disturb Esmeralda's thought. Then she say, "The day that put an end to my dream, I am playing in a tournament in a luxury hotel on the Riviera. . . ."

Very unfortunately, I can't tell it like her, because I forget the words in your language; also, I tell it in my way, but think of her speaking modestly with a soft voice.

So, she is eighteen years old, a good player, often congratulated, dressed in a pretty white tennis dress, above her knees, and on the court is her Swedish enemy, or Norwegian or other nationality. Before the match, they both throw balls up in the air to warm their bodies, and Esmeralda bend her body to pick up a ball on the ground, and she hear laughing. There are many people from this very smart hotel on the Riviera to watch the match from the sides of the court, and a very wise judge sitting on a very high chair. Then Esmeralda hit the balls with her spoon and every time she jump in the air or bend her body, the people laugh, and they even clap their hands to show their enjoyment. Then she ask herself why all these people see her so interesting, and a crazy idea come into her head. So she touch her body with her hand and it isn't madness at all: when her dress go up, she has her bottom completely naked! How this thing happen, that she forget that day to put on her panties, she can never explain. Of course, it is a terrible shock for her mind. She want to carry on playing, because she is proud and very determined, hiding her dignity with her free hand, but the people laugh loud and all the time, even her enemy, and then she run to hide in the hotel, very ashamed and her eyes full of tears, and never she set foot again on a tennis court.

That is Esmeralda's unhappy story when she is lying on her mattress in the shack. She stop talking with her arm over her eyes, and Frédéric, very thoughtful, and understanding her sadness, walk with little steps on the noisy floor, his hands tied behind his back, and finally he say, "So what, so what, so what? Why you stay unhappy with this moment in your memory? You make a *block* about nothing at all. Life is long and helpful. You show your behind once to all those people, so what? You are *forgetful*, so what?"

Then, although crying, Esmeralda make with her nose a mocking snort and she say, "Forgetful! Imagine forgetting to put on my panties!" And she can't stop herself laughing noisily with Frédéric, and as for me, Yoko, I laugh, too, hiding my mouth. After, they are quiet for a very long time, and Frédéric sit in the armchair and rock, and it is very hot. At last, she dry her eyes and sit up, and she say modestly, "Thank you, Frédéric. I feel that it is a good relief to tell you my confession and that you talk to me."

That evening I tell you about, and the next days, they are peaceful together and good friends. She shave Frédéric's beard with the American knife rubbed hard against a stone, and he look younger and handsomer. He is thirty-two years old. When the sun go down and they go outside, she sometimes let him go free without the wire around his wrists and ankles and he swim in the ocean and throw the water in the air and laugh. She watch him from the beach with the tommy gun, but he doesn't try to attack her or to run away, and when she tell him to come back or to turn around so she can tie him up, he shrug his shoulders and do what she ask without anger. She tie him up, too, when she want to go in the jungle to kill a rodent or pick fruit. She stick in the sand two big bits of sharpened wood to tie him up and keep him lying down, but she also put wood to make a wall against the sun with the material from the parachutes.

Unfortunately, I must run from my shelter when she go in the jungle, because now she is bold and skillful with the bang-bang, and if she see me with her eyes, I am dead, and perhaps with a single cartridge. Once, she kill a wild pig, big enough for many days' food, and I hear only one shot. My opinion is that she think to leave Frédéric on the beach, tied to the wood, and look as if she go deep into the jungle, and then come back quickly when I am there to free him. I'm not more *baka* than this woman.

One morning, too, from the grass I can smell the smoke of her food and it is the very good smell of fried eggs with belly of wild pig. After, I carefully look where she walk in the jungle, because I know where are all the birds' eggs of this island, and I make where she go traps with holes and bamboos and rope and trees that bend easily. I need many days to make the rope and build these traps. If I have Bill or Dick's knife, of course I need less time, but then perhaps I am a liar in my promise not to kill, I jump out behind the Frenchwoman and cut her throat. I say this joking, of course, although only just. The truth is, I don't want to kill this woman or for her to kill me. I want to take her prisoner, to take the gun and the man from her.

So I see days being born and dying, and each one is full of work to ward off loneliness and moments when I watch the French live. But each day also bring the rainy season closer, and I am very afraid to have to live under a flimsy shelter made of leaves and that I lack food and after Esmeralda will find me dead in the mud and eaten by the beasts.

Then, one day, I am swimming in front of the Australians' beach, and the sun say it is morning, and it come into my head that the birds are many and high above the jungle, and complaining, too, like when they are disturbed by a hunter, but I don't hear the bang-bang before, and as for me, I am in the water and Frédéric is certainly tied up. So I just put on Dick's shirt and I run quickly into the jungle. Before long, I hear a lot of noise in the leaves of the trees and shouts full of hate, and I go in that direction. Then I am trembling with happiness, seeing with my eyes what I see, and I shout my triumph. Esmeralda is hanging by her feet from the top of a young tree that I bend perhaps three days before, and she shake her body in vain to escape from my trap. I put the rope for this trap, made with the fiber from strong grasses, in front of a bird's nest, and certainly this woman want to take the eggs, and now she is up in the air shouting, she is well and truly caught.

So I go calmly up to her, without fear of her bang-bang because it is not in her hands. She has her face all red and upside down, and her upside-down eyes look at me very big, and she stop shaking her body. She say, "Who the devil are you?" I say with enjoyment, "Yoko." And I quickly pick up the gun from the grass. After, I say, "If you stay quiet, me, I don't kill anybody. Nobody!" I go behind her and I unhook her cartridge belt and I leave this proud woman to think carefully about changing her character.

I run through the jungle and at last I reach the beach where the house is. Frédéric is lying in the sand, his hands and his feet tied to the wood, and he is sheltered from the burning sun behind the cloth wall, but he is very hot. When I am in front of him, he look at me with astonishment, and after, he close his eyes and say, "Shit! It isn't true!" Then I say, "I make the bad woman prisoner!" He open his eyes, even more astonished that I speak his language, even modestly, and he say, "Be a darling, Yoko, free me quickly from these bracelets." I think carefully when I run through the jungle. So I answer, "My opinion is not that I must free you. You are French like her, and after you free her, I am the prisoner. I must hold you and her, too."

Then he speak softly to me, promising that never he do anything against me, and he beg me very often to free him. Never, since I am born, I see such beautiful eyes in a man and his face, too, but I force myself not to change my mind. I go into the house to get water in a bowl and I give him a drink, and after, I put water on his neck and chest to make him cool. Then I can't stop myself kissing his mouth.

And I kiss him for a long time and finally he kiss mine, too, mistakenly for sure, thinking that I free him, but after, I am without breath and my cheeks are burning and my brain is all mixed up. Then I say, lowering my eyes modestly, "Forgive me but I am without everything since the rainy season and I have too strong desire to be fucked." Then I open my shirt in front and I come naked on top of him with my knees each side of his body. I open his short pants, too, and he pull on his bracelets, saying, "What on earth are you doing? Are you mad?" I listen to nothing he say. Sure, he want to run away from me and hurt me with mocking and stop himself from getting big, but I know how to make a lover grow big, shh. Then I hollow the sand out under my knees to feel this man deep inside me and I move like on a pretty horse and I have much enjoyment several times. And sure, I say in my desire for enjoyment words of madness, but in Japanese, he cannot understand. Even when he is defeated, I enjoy for a long time more and fuck him vigorously. Finally, I have no strength left and I lie on the sand, across him, and all my body is wet with sweat, even my hair on my face. Ayayay! I never do it before with a lover tied up, but it's so good!

That same day, when I free Esmeralda from the trap, she has no spirits and look almost dead from hanging by her feet for such a long time. And sure, I scold myself for being so unthinking, but I drag her to the beach and into the house, and after one night she is fully alive and still bad-tempered.

After, for very many months, seeing the rainy season twice, we are together on this island, sometimes good friends and sometimes less, and never we see with our eyes a ship on the big ocean or a plane in the sky. We know nothing of the war and perhaps it is finished and my compatriots victorious or perhaps not. I raise my country's flag on the beach, nicely done with red because it is ruined by Esmeralda, who use it to wash the floor, and I carefully look after my prisoners, watching over them with the tommy gun.

The truth is that after the first rainy season, I am very sorry that I am not the prisoner. Both of them, although still tied up, they rest on the beach, and go in the water, and eat my food with appetite, and they play with the cards they make from my drawing paper, and as for me, I must cut Frédéric's beard, and I must always run from one to the other when they are apart, only because Esmeralda want to do a wee-wee, and a hundred times a day they both ask me to free them from their bracelets to do something like scratch their ear, and a hundred times a day I free them and a hundred times a day I tie them up again. That's not all. If they quarrel, I don't know where to run or what to say or do. And every moment I must run. To go in the jungle and look for food, to give the fire wood, to wash my body in the ocean before they wake up, to take the slops outside when they are asleep. And I must also clean the house and dig for drinking water and cut down trees with the ax. The days aren't long enough, and the nights I sleep with my left eye or my right eye but never with both.

Frédéric often want me very, very much and I take him under the house so that Esmeralda doesn't see us with her eyes, because one night she wake up and see us, and she shout that we stop. But I am very close to my enjoyment and I don't want to stop. And then she say, "Dirty slut, is it so nice to be knocked around by your pig?" And many other hurtful things that make Frédéric laugh, and I lose my enjoyment. Even under the house, when she hear my cries, because I am noisy and when I show Frédéric the seven clothespins, she bang with her bracelets on the floor, calling, "Yoko, are you still alive? Is he cutting your throat? Answer me! I am afraid when I hear your terrible cries!" I promise that never I give her food or drink if she hurt me again, and after she leave us in peace.

I don't know if before I make them prisoners she let Frédéric fuck her. My opinion is that she allow him sometimes, because there are days when they are good friends, but I don't see it with my eyes. So I ask Frédéric and he say, "The Geneva Convention forbid making prisoners talk." So one day, when I see Esmeralda alone on the yellow rocks, I ask her and she reply, "What do you think? That a man and a woman can be together for so long, day and night, and nothing happen? Do you believe that?" I say no, if the woman is me, because I often have a strong desire to be fucked, but I don't know about her. Then she say, "I let you make up your own mind whether I am a woman, too, or something else." After, she look at me for a long time and see that I am silent and not happy with her reply, and finally she turn her eyes to the big ocean and say, "I let him several times, and the first time is also the first time I go with a man. Perhaps you want to know the exact number, and how, and who ask the other one first, or is that enough for your curiosity?" Then I see that there are tears in her eyes and I stop.

After, when I go in the jungle, I am afraid even more that Frédéric listen to the Frenchwoman's soft words and that she agree to let him fuck her so that he run far away with her, and then they free each other and they are two against one. So I tie them up together, standing, facing each other, prisoners by their legs and their arms, and they can only move on the sand taking great care. I am fairly pleased to see them like this, because they look like stupid idiots as they say, but do you think they forget to argue? Esmeralda make a face that her body touch Frédéric's body through the thin material and she say, "I want to see you dead! Do you hear me? Dead!" And he say, laughing, "But why don't we lie quietly on the sand until Yoko come back?" Then she shout: "You know very well why not!" And he, looking unjustly scolded, reply, "But it's not my fault! It's *uncontrollable!*" She turn her face far from his, full of hate, and when I come out of the jungle, perhaps one hour later, they are fallen on the sand and she is red and accusing that he rub his body on purpose against hers, and she beg me to separate them.

Then, one day when the sun is burning, I can't go on. I put the gun, the cartridges, the knives, and the ax, all the weapons in the parachute cloth, and I go and dig a hole in the jungle. After, I come to them and I say, "Now, that's enough. If you kill me dead, I don't care." And I free each of them, their hands and their feet. They are both very silent with round eyes, and as for me, I can at last lie down on the sand and rest. Then Frédéric say, "That's good. You see now that if I promise something, nothing can change my mind." And he go and swim very happy in the ocean, and Esmeralda come to me and give me her hand, and she go, too. After, we swim together and we laugh very much. Me, Yoko, I swim the fastest, and Esmeralda not far behind and Frédéric always last. But he say, "I'm not used to it like you, one day I am not so lazy." In the evening, leaving Esmeralda behind in the house, I walk with him and he carry me sitting on his shoulders, and we go to another beach. The sun is all red on the big ocean, and he take off my shirt, kissing all my body, and he fuck me in the sand without his wretched bracelets scratching my skin.

The day after, I see that my opinion to hide the weapons is not good, because they are useful and there are plenty of others enough to kill me. So I take Frédéric to the place where I dig. Then we divide the weapons in three. A knife each, the American airman's one for me, the ax, too, for Frédéric, and the bang-bang for the one who go hunting. Although there are not many cartridges left in the belt and we keep them only for the wild pigs.

What can I say about these long days? I am very in love with Frédéric, but Esmeralda is, too, a little bit, and I understand that it's the cause of her little quarrels with him or with me. Certain things that I must not see, I prefer to confront them. So I say to Esmeralda, "If you want the man, you know that you can have him behind my back. If we cut him in half with the ax, we don't gain anything. If I kill you or you kill me, we don't gain any more, because he is sad that the other one die for love of him and all the time his mind is preoccupied. Don't you think we must have a good arrangement?" And Esmeralda say, "I am happy that you speak like this, because I want to speak the same but I don't dare." Then we both think how to share Frédéric fairly. I tell how I share the days with my fellow Japanese when we land on this island. She is very astonished that I can satisfy a different man every day and she laugh, hiding her mouth, saying, "I don't believe my ears! But how can you?" I say that only one touch my heart, but the others are poor men, too, and I think, being the only woman, that I must not refuse them enjoyment, no more than food or drink. After, they lose their minds and kill the only one who give me enjoyment and sure I am fucked against my will.

But Esmeralda and I have the same opinion, that this arrangement to share the days isn't good. If Frédéric is tired after three days with one, he doesn't touch the other one, and after, three days, if he has a good rest, he give enjoyment to the other one. We laugh very much, thinking of these things, and after, we are sad, I don't know why. Then Esmeralda say, "Perhaps we mustn't speak like this. Perhaps it is enough to agree that Frédéric go with you and with me and we stay good friends in our misfortune."

That is the arrangement we promise and we touch our hands, and after, when I see they go together, I find work and I try to forget that they enjoy each other, and Esmeralda is the same with me for a long time. Only little things change. In the house, or on the beach, she doesn't care about taking off her clothes if Frédéric is there. And sometimes, when he is busy in the little paddy field, or making alcohol for the lamps, she come to him and speak softly to him and give him a quick kiss on the neck. And sometimes she cry when she look at me and all three of us are eating our meal, and I don't understand why and I don't want to ask.

Very fortunately, there are other things than this to-do to occupy us. We go to the Australians' beach and all three of us swim under the big ocean to go inside the plane. Now Frédéric swim the fastest and he is a good diver, with a big reserve of air in his breast, and he isn't at all ashamed to disturb the dead. We pull out of the water many things from the plane, but not the radio. Frédéric quickly see that it is kaput. We take the soldiers' bags with clothes, more cartridges for the bang-bang, and bottles, and a crateful of cans, another with cigarettes and chewing gum and biscuits untouched by the water, and a hammock to sleep in, and cans of oil, and more parachutes and tools for mechanics. Frédéric's opinion is that we must take the fuel from the plane's tank, and we make a long pipe of hollow bamboo, and all the time that we hollow them and fit them together, it's more than three months, but never in our lives do Esmeralda and I see a man who is more patient and who work harder for his idea than Frédéric. He say, "If I want it for long enough, I can." That is what the priests of Jesus teach him in Marseilles, France. Then I say, laughing with Esmeralda, "And if you want to bring up the whole plane, can you?" And he say, "You can laugh. One day, that is exactly what I do."

He do it just before the second rainy season that we see together.

First, he take the fuel. To hold it, we dig tanks in the sand and put parachutes in the bottom. After, he take the plane's engine, with the parachute cords, and all three of us pull, and Frédéric is five weeks to take it all apart, clean it well with gas and grease with oil, and make a smaller engine that doesn't work any better. Then he start all over again, like for Kimura's alcohol, and often I come and watch him work, his arms and upper body filthy with black grease, and I don't know his idea at the end, but I invoke the spirits of this island, if Christ perhaps isn't enough, that they consent to help him.

At last, one day, we two women are near the house and we hear a big noise of an engine far away, and it stop and start again, and we run to the Australians' beach. When we arrive, the sun is red behind the trees and its beauty unparalleled, and amid a terrible din, we see with our eyes the whole plane, water running everywhere from it, coming out of the ocean by the nose and its good arm. And it is Frédéric's smoking engine that pull it to the shore, with a wheel and chains and the parachute cords, and Esmeralda and I jump with happiness and cry victory.

I like the thought of this day. I like seeing in my memory Frédéric on his knees in the sand, his face filthy with grease and uncontrollable tears, thumping his fist on the ground of this island, shouting, "Shit! I do it! I do it!" And to see Esmeralda and me falling on him and kissing him, and after, we are as dirty as him. Then we look at this big iron thing that is beached in the shallow water and I say, "Perhaps Frédéric want to make this go up in the air now?" And they both laugh and pretend to beat me in the sand, but not really. After, we go back to our house, and we all wash each other's bodies with the soap from one of the soldiers' bags. We eat together and drink the rice alcohol to congratulate ourselves, crying, "To the devil with the war!" And Frédéric tell, very proud, that he know just a little mechanics from his second father, a truck driver, and how he quarrel for a long time with that stubborn engine, and how he replace the fuel with air in the plane's tank. After, he take off Esmeralda's soldier shirt and forget his shame, in front of me, and I watch all the time he fuck her, so different and sorrowful, and again after, he fuck me, too. I like the thought of this day.

Very unfortunately, we have a bad surprise when we wake up. A big smoke is rising in the sky on the other side of the island, and when we arrive at the Australians' beach, everything is destroyed by a very high fire. It is still too hot to go close, but we stop it eating the jungle, and all day we take water from the ocean and throw it on the trees. In the evening, when the fire is out, the plane is only twisted metal and we lose everything, the fuel from the engine, everything. Never we know how the fire is lit. Perhaps Frédéric throw his Camel cigarette when we leave. Perhaps the hot engine set light to the cord or a piece of wood. As for me, Yoko, my opinion is that we disturb the dead in the plane, and the spirit of the big ocean, which give me a sign before, light the fire.

All night the three of us talk, and Frédéric is very despondent that he lose the fuel and the body of the plane because the day before, he think of building with it a motorboat and run away from this island. When Esmeralda ask if we flee with him, he say, "No, because if I die, you both die, too. The sensible thing is for me to reach the Christmas Islands, and after, help come to you. And if I die in the ocean, you are still alive."

But Frédéric is never despondent for long. His opinion is that the Christmas Islands are two thousand kilometers to the west, because it is the last position of their boat when it sink. Perhaps he can reach them another way. As for me, Yoko, my opinion is that my fellow Japanese are good sailors, especially Yoshiro, the boss, when he still have his reason, and if Yoshiro say that we can't go with six experienced men, how can Frédéric go by himself? But Frédéric reply, "You tell me before that Yoshiro doesn't want to build the boat because there is no land inhabited by your fellow Japanese. Never you say he think it's impossible to reach the Christmas Islands." And me, never I say it is possible to reach Japan. I must confess this is true. Then Frédéric say, "We see this project after the rainy season. All the time it keep us in this house, let's be content with our fate." That is what we do, eating the food and playing with the stones and the cards and speaking of our lives. Esmeralda make a musical instrument with bamboo and we sing songs we make up. I teach my two companions Japanese, but they think it is too difficult; after, I stop teaching them. At night we sleep together, usually with the rain making a noise. We show Esmeralda the seven clothespins and she go wild, and is very ashamed after, but when we wake up, she whisper to me that she is happy. She know very well the days to make babies, I don't know so well. She often make joke and say, "Today, Yoko, you mustn't allow Frédéric to do anything." But she is also very good for him and for me, and never looking at the little things, and very willing to look after the house. Frédéric has a livelier, more changeable character. Sometimes he is laughing and very gentle in his words. And sometimes he stay in his corner and sulk, and Esmeralda and I don't know what we say before to make him angry. The truth is that he doesn't know himself, he feel things stronger than he understand. Sometimes, too, drinking too much of this alcohol that he make and forgetting his unhappiness at being far from home, he tell proud and muddled dreams, that he go across the big ocean and is successful, that he put all his patience and courage to do a thing so good that everyone see with their eyes that he is very, very capable and he always end up with, "Fuck the lot of you!"

When the sun come back to this island, we swim again and live our days, but the best of us is far and all that remains is the sadness of being forgotten. I don't want to tell how Esmeralda lose hope first, and me, too. I only want to tell the last moments that we are three companions on this island.

Before long, Esmeralda speak very much about this fire on the Australians' beach, because she is afraid that Frédéric and I think that she light it, and she say no, she doesn't light it. After, she say that perhaps she want to light it so that Frédéric can't run away across the ocean and then no one will know what she do with us that night after we pull up the plane.

Then Frédéric say to her, "I know very well who light the fire and why. So rest in your mind." And of course, my opinion is that he think it is me. I say, "But how can I? I stay all the night in your arms and not once do I go outside the house." And he reply, "Did I say it's you? Do you still see me as a *téki*?" That's enemy. I say no, and I run far from them not to hear idiocies that are painful for all of us.

After, Esmeralda want us to bring inside the material from one of the Australians' parachutes, properly hung from a cord. That way, she is separated from us when I am with Frédéric. He say, "Let's do what she want," and we do.

After, she doesn't want Frédéric to come over to her side and see her naked. He raise his shoulders and reply, "When you feel like it again, you say." And he never go to her side.

After, on the beach, she is alone and sad and she sing softly, like him, before, when he is tied up. For each thing that I say, she answer, "I am not displeased with you, Yoko. I am fine like this." And once, Frédéric go and talk with her, sitting close to her in the sand, and she put her head on him and she cry. I don't hear their words, being far away.

After, in the night, when she sleep on the other side of the parachute material and I have a strong desire to be fucked, the time it take for me to be on top of Frédéric or for him to be on top of me, she have nightmare. She scream to disturb us. I know she do this on purpose, because bad dreams I have, too, sometimes, but never I tell them so well with my mouth while they are coming, and as precisely as this: "My God, I am at a big reception! And all those men looking at me! My God, my beautiful dress is caught in the door and I forget to wear any panties! They can see me! They can see my bare bottom!" I am angry and I say to Frédéric, "Don't listen, don't listen, please." But you try and fuck like that, you'll see what fun it is.

Another day, Frédéric is tastily eating the shellfish that I catch under the ocean. And like he often does, he find a pearl. We are all three of us in the house, Esmeralda lying in the hammock. Then he say, "Yoko, do you catch many of these pearls?" I go to the place under the floor where I hide my treasure, and I lift up a plank and I take out the bag I make with Akiro, known as Popeye's sock when we land on this island. And I shake the bag vigorously to show how heavy it is, and after, I open it in front of Frédéric and he see with his eyes all the beautiful pearls that I have for my parents, or for a good husband, or anybody, I don't know. Then he say, very astonished, "Shit! It's perhaps as valuable as my grandmother's inheritance!" And me, I say, "I give you three pearls for each time you kiss my mouth so well, and five for each time you kiss the tips of my breasts so well, and ten for each time you consent to be the pretty horse, and all of them for once when you want them without doing anything to me because they are yours." Then he laugh and so do I, but Esmeralda say, "What's this business of your grandmother's inheritance? You never speak to me of this." There is silence, and Frédéric reply, "That is none of your business." And he eat the shellfish without another word.

At last come the night. Frédéric fuck me on our side of the material, and Esmeralda talk in her sleep to stop us. He act as if he is the man without ears, and she understand from my noisy enjoyment that she can dream all the idiocies she like, I don't give a damn. So she make up this, even if the words aren't exact, "My God, here I am in the country house and my parents gone to see the village fete! This blue soldier tear my dress with his hands and throw me on the floor! Ah, now he touch my breast and my bare bottom! My God, he enter my body and take satisfaction with me! I am too painful! My flesh is too sullied! I want to die! My God, forgive me, I throw myself!" And all the time that this crazy woman scream, Frédéric shout, too, "Stop! You have no right! Stop or I get up and shut you up!"

Of course, he separate from me, and he stay sitting on the mattress, his head in his hands, while Esmeralda pretend to wake up and say, "Oh, what a terrible dream!" Then me, Yoko, I say to Frédéric, "What an idiot you are. You know very well this woman not dreaming, she talk on purpose to disturb us!" And he answer, "Even in her dream, she have no right!" And to her, he shout, "Do you hear, you have no right!" Then she laugh and say on the other side of the material, "Come, come, my dear man, that is *uncontrollable!*"

That is human stupidity, on this island or anywhere else. Frédéric stand up, his face white, saying, "Bitch!" And after, never, I mean this, never he talk to anybody again, not one word, not for her, not for me.

I tell you what he do, as silent as the man without a tongue, every day, every week: he cut the bamboo and the trees with the ax. When he is tired, he smoke a cigarette, and he drink water or fruit alcohol. Sometimes he swim in the ocean, alone.

I go to him. I say, "Me, Yoko, I do nothing against you and I am unhappy that you don't speak to me. I beg you to talk to me." Nothing. And Esmeralda ask him to forgive her and I hear with my ears what she say, even far away, and her words are modest and beautiful, and make tears come into my eyes. Him, nothing. He cut down bamboo.

The memory of a wound in this man is as long as his patience. Often, I go to him while he is cutting with the ax, his face and body dripping with sweat. I put the food on the ground, but he doesn't eat. He make his food with fruit and roots and shellfish, and sometimes eggs from the jungle. He sleep in the sand under the house. His beard grow and his hair. Then we see that he tie together bamboos with strong cords and that he build the wall of another house near the yellow rocks. After, he build the floor. After, a big mat of grass, nice and tight. I say to Esmeralda, "When he finish his house, we go inside every night, showing him our bodies and dancing like in films, and he is loving like before." But I live a long time with Frédéric and I don't know him.

One evening he is also pensive on the sand, smoking his cigarette, watching the red sun at the end of the ocean. I go to sleep. The morning after, I go into the jungle to catch a bird or a rodent. I come back when the sun is higher. I can no longer see with my eyes Frédéric's construction on the beach. But also I see, raised on the hewn tree, together with my flag, the French flag, blue, white, and red, with the cross with four arms, and I am happy that Frédéric tell me in this way that he make peace. My legs are weak and my heart turbulent when I run to the house.

I climb the stairs. I go in. Esmeralda is alone, dressed in her soldier's shirt, her eyes red but her hair tidy, standing by the window. She say, "Poor Yoko, poor fool. He doesn't make a house, he make a boat with a sail. And he is far now."

Then I run outside and I look everywhere on the big ocean. And I don't want to believe. Then I walk on the sand and I shout. I shout to Frédéric to come back. Then I run again into the house. Esmeralda is still by the window. And I move my head to say I don't believe. She say, "Look!" And she point to the place where I put the pearls and the open floor.

So I go to the balcony, my mind lost, and I shout to the big ocean to bring back my Frédéric. And after, I am sitting in the chair, crying without being able to stop myself, and Esmeralda come behind me and put her arms on my shoulders and say softly, "Don't cry, don't cry, Yoko. We'll survive. Women always survive. Later we can think about him calmly and we only have in our memory that he love us and that he go to look for help."

That is the end of my story on this island.

There is, of course, another part, but I think it isn't interesting for you. So I tell it quickly. Esmeralda and I live together for four weeks more, and then a U.S. cruiser come and take us. When we ask who send help and where is he, the captain say he doesn't know. The cruiser is on the way to Hawaii and the order come over the radio to go and get us. The war is lost for my fellow Japanese and my poor country wounded, as everyone know.

After, I am interrogated for a long time in San Francisco for the death of the American airman and the two Australians, and I say what I see with my eyes. I sign many papers and I live free in Los Angeles with Esmeralda, who looks out for me. The time I am with her, it's almost four months, and she is always very kind and treat me richly and stupid people say behind her back that we are lovers, but she doesn't give a damn.

After, I am declared innocent of the massacres, leave this wonderful friend, promising to come back quickly, and I go at last to my country by plane, and I am almost twenty-five years old.

I have the good fortune to still have my mother and father alive, and also this grandmother of my grandmother of my mother, who is now a hundred and sixteen years old. One day I write a letter for her, in Talcahuano, Chili. She answer, using someone's hand, because she never learn to write, "I see all my friends from my childhood die one after the other. Nobody know anything about them anymore. Nobody even put a flower on their graves. So, I'm no fool. I don't die."

Toledo

O N MY RETURN TO FLORIDA, AF-
ter the absurd shipwreck of the *Pandora*, I met up with Bessie again,
now recovered from her African wounds. For a while, we tried to
run a fish restaurant together, in Key West. Unfortunately, that also
foundered. We parted company, still good friends, and I joined the
marines as a nurse.

On the last day of the war, I happened to be in a hospital unit in
the Gulf of Bengal, about sixty-five miles from Rangoon in Burma.

I was twenty-seven and I was equal in rank to an ensign.

Before that, I'd always been in the Pacific. I had followed the fleet
in the retaking of the Philippines and to Iwo Jima. I had seen the
wounded and dead coming back by the truckful.

In Burma, after that, it felt as though the war was already over.
The British had taken Rangoon and cleaned up almost the whole
country. Of our five big hospital tents, in the Irrawaddy delta, three
were empty. The remaining convalescents were mostly American
airmen or marines who had come to bring fresh supplies to our
allies during the winter offensive. They were just waiting to be
repatriated.

Japan's capitulation made them shout for joy, but did not hasten their departure; quite the opposite. By now, there were a lot of combatants to be repatriated all over the world. We were told to be patient, that it would only be a matter of days. The least pessimistic reckoned a year to be three hundred and sixty-five days.

It was mid-August, right in the middle of the monsoon season. Whether it rained or not, our clothes clung to our skin. Even the rain was warm and cloying. Around the camp, the arms of the river brought the yellow mud down from the mountains and sometimes there were drowned buffalo floating in the water.

That was when a man was brought to us on an IV. We knew nothing about him except that he was completely exhausted by his ordeals and that he was delirious, in French.

Dr. Kirby, who was in command of the unit, examined him and had him taken to one of the empty tents, the one we called the Carlyle, like the New York luxury hotel. The other tents were known as the Plaza, the Delmonico, the Pierre, and the St. Regis. As I was the only one who spoke French, I was detailed to look after him.

We settled him under a mosquito net, in a deep sleep, and I installed the IV at the head of the bed.

When the two stretcher bearers left us, Dr. Kirby said to me, "Until we have some information about this man, don't let anyone approach him, Toledo. And raise the alarm immediately should he try to escape."

"In his condition?"

"He's a tough nut," said Kirby. "According to his delirium, he crossed the Pacific on a raft."

I followed him to the door of the Carlyle. He then gave me a khaki canvas bag, the size of my hand.

"It was hanging around his neck," he said. "There was another bag inside it. Apparently it's an old sock full of pearls. Count them when you've got a moment. They are accompanied by a certificate from the U.S. Air Force on Jarvis Island, and those jokers have written down the exact number."

Before going out, he turned to look in the direction of the sleeping Frenchman and added, "You name it, we've seen it, in this war."

Later I counted the pearls. It took a long time. There were 1,223 of them. The air-force figure was 1,224. Maybe I had made a mistake, but perhaps the sergeant called J. K. Dawn who had counted them before me had made a mistake. In any case, I couldn't imagine anyone so low that they would give their girlfriend a necklace made with just one pearl.

For five days I nursed the stranger in accordance with my instructions, which mainly consisted of prolonging his sleep and keeping an eye on his IV. At night I also slept in the tent that was the farthest from our barracks so that I wouldn't have to keep running backward and forward. The rest of the time I worked with the other nurses, and between downpours we would go and swim in the sea, but were unable to refresh ourselves.

One morning, as I was having breakfast in the mess, Dr. Kirby came and sat opposite me with his coffee. He said, "We've received some information about the Frenchman. On Jarvis, a cargo plane was in transit, en route to Rangoon, and as nobody knew what to do with him, they sent him to us. A chopper had just picked him up from a raft in the middle of the Pacific. He was drifting unconscious around a desert island."

"And nobody knows who he his?"

"Perhaps he'll tell us. We'll let him wake up now."

The man continued sleeping until late afternoon. The big fans inside the tent halfheartedly stirred the heat. I had abandoned my uniform. I was perspiring in a white coat, the lightest I could find.

When he opened his eyes, I was leaning over the next bed sorting out medicines in order to tidy up the medicine cabinet, and had my back to him. I suddenly heard his voice behind me. It was weak but perfectly clear.

"Toledo!"

I turned around with a start. He was watching me through the mosquito net with an astonished smile. But his astonishment was nothing compared to mine.

"Do you know me?"

"I saw you on board the *Pandora*," he replied.

I parted the mosquito net to see him better. I couldn't recognize him.

"Stowaway," he said, still grinning. "Shh!"

So it was him. On board the yacht, I had cleaned Miss Frou-Frou's cabin every day. I'd have had to be blind not to notice that she was granting her favors to someone in secret, but I suspected the crew, or that actor who was with us. In any case, I don't like sticking my nose in other people's business. I might get it dirty.

"Well, talk about a surprise!" said the Frenchman. "You know, Toledo, you haven't changed a bit!"

He sat up without thinking and I made him lie down again. Then, stuffing a thermometer in his mouth, I told him that it was disturbing for someone to be recognized by their bottom, and that he would have to explain that to me one day. And also that my nickname was because I was born in Toledo, Ohio, but that my real name was Jennifer MacKeena. As his temperature was as good as it could be, I asked him his name.

"Maurice," he replied. "You can call me Momo or Riri, like when I was a kid, but I don't like being called that anymore."

"Maurice what?"

"Maurice Maurice. That's the clever bit. You can say Momo Riri or Riri Momo, I know that you still mean me."

"Are you French?"

"Free French. General de Gaulle and all that."

I pointed out that the whole of France was free, that Germany had capitulated in the spring and Japan the day of his arrival.

"Where are we?" he asked.

"In Burma. One of our planes brought you in from the Pacific."

Then I saw a glint of anguish in his eyes. He grabbed my arm and cried, "Dammit, how long have I been here?"

"A week."

"There are two women out there, alone on an island! I've got to tell someone so they can be rescued!"

That was how I learned that evening that Miss Esmeralda was still alive. Dr. Kirby had two officers come from Rangoon and they interrogated Maurice for more than an hour.

On leaving the tent, one of them said to me, "Either this froggy is completely off his head from your injections or the world's spinning the wrong way and nobody's noticed. Apparently you were on this goddamn tub yourself when it sank?"

I confirmed that the *Pandora* had indeed gone down and that we had lost a young psychoanalyst from Los Angeles.

"Where?"

"About a thousand miles south of the Christmas Islands. We were on our way to Honolulu."

"Jesus!" exclaimed the officer. "It's the most unlikely story I've ever heard! Clothespins!"

And he and his companion left, looking confused.

When I brought him a real meal—steak, puréed peas, canned fruit salad—Maurice ate with a hearty appetite. He had slept enough over the last few days and did not feel sleepy anymore. He talked to me at length, but said very little about what had happened to him after the disaster. He only told me that he had seen Miss Esmeralda alive, in the company of an extraordinary Chilean girl, a former pupil of the Beaux Arts in Paris and an accomplished French speaker. As for the rest, his tongue would be burned with a red-hot poker if he revealed anything about his affair.

And so he talked to me about his childhood in Marseilles, France, and about his grandmother, whom he adored, and the Jesuit school where he was a pupil. He also talked to me about the wedding ring he wore. He had been married to the kindest, most beautiful woman a man could wish for, but they had been apart for twelve years, and it was too painful for him to believe that she was still waiting for him. He did, however, want to send her something, and that was when he started worrying about his pearls.

I showed him the bag and told him straight that there was one missing. He hadn't counted them himself, but he agreed that a thief, while he was being transported from Jarvis to Rangoon, would have taken the lot, or at least a good handful. I put the bag under his mattress and we agreed that the incident was closed.

Then I went to sleep in my usual bed, by the tent entrance. I slept naked, the other nights, unable to stand anything other than my mosquito net, but of course I couldn't remove my white coat in his presence now that he was awake. I promised myself I'd have a screen brought in and went to bed as I was. I could hear him talking for ages afterward. He asked in the dark, "Are you asleep, Toledo?"

"Fast asleep."

And he was off again. All the films he'd seen with Miss Frou-Frou. The heat. A place called the Wheel Turns in Mozambique. A marmoset that had run off into the trees.

In the morning he was sleeping peacefully. I went and had a shower and a coffee. When I came back, he was no longer there. I began to run, to raise the alarm, when I saw him, or someone who looked exactly like him, except that he was vertical, and I joined him on the beach. He had brought a sheet to conceal his nakedness. His long hair was plastered down by the obstinate drizzle of the monsoon, and all that was visible was one eye.

"Are you mad?" I asked.

"I must be to end up in a place like this! Is this what Burma's like? It's like Saintes-Maries-de-la-Mer the morning after the Flood."

I made him go back to bed. I could already tell that threatening him would have no effect. I pointed out that if he didn't behave until his compatriots came and explained his situation, I was the one who would be blamed. I would be finished, thrown out of the marines. He remained speechless for a few moments, and then his wary eye noticed that I was in uniform.

"How can a woman wear that getup?" he asked disdainfully. "You're cute, and you've got a good body all the same!"

That evening, when he saw me in my white coat, he let out a little sigh, nothing more.

The screen had been set up. I placed it in front of my bed. When it was time to go to bed, after countless games of checkers, I switched off Maurice's light. Over in my corner, I removed the little clothing I had on.

Then I heard him say, "Switch off your light, too, Toledo. I can see you in silhouette and that's the worst."

In the dark, we went on talking for hours, him in his bed, me in mine, separated by about fifteen paces. He made me laugh, but it's a very strange feeling, being naked and laughing with a man in a huge, dark tent. I mean, even if he can't see you, you can't relax, and at the same time, you laugh louder than usual and at just about anything.

The next day, as I drank my coffee, I caught myself staring at my reflection in a windowpane in the mess. No doubt I often did, without realizing it, but I was aware that I was falling in love with him.

I'd had three lovers since I had been in the marines. The first, a doctor-captain, during my training in San Diego. I was in awe of him. The second, an ensign straight from school who broke a leg doing God knows what with a gangway. He was forever saying, when I used to try and position myself on top of him in his sickbed, "Be careful! Be careful! You'll screw up my meniscus!" As officers were decidedly not for me, and I was already going downhill, the third was a Texan recruit, and it was just a one-night stand, before the landing at Leyte, to copy the nurse I'd gone out with and to forget the war. But I hadn't forgotten that strange empty feeling that weighs on the heart when you're in love.

So you can imagine my frame of mind when I went to the Carlyle that day. As for Maurice, he had decided to be more of a pain in the ass than usual. The soup was no good. The fish was inedible. He wanted me to cut his hair. Then it was too short. The whole time I was shaving his beard, he kept his fists clenched as if he were enduring torture, or perhaps to punch me if I cut him. After that, I figured that for a Frenchman, he wasn't bad at all, but he had never seen such an ugly guy, but of course, he pointed out, he had never set foot in America. In the end, I had had enough.

I said, "What is it you want from me? Nobody here would dare talk to me the way you do! You can manage on your own if that's what you want!"

I was standing at the foot of his bed. I began to cry foolishly, not that there's any such thing as crying intelligently. I ran away, convinced that he could read me like an open book. I did not go back all evening. I asked someone else to take him his dinner, preferably with something in it to rid us of him, and a nurse's aid looked after him during the night.

I went back to our barracks to sleep, enlisting my friends' warm sympathy and gamboling about naked to my heart's delight. What's more, after a few more tears to accompany the inner ramblings that are customary on these occasions, I slept like a queen.

The next day, same punishment, same reason. It was Paddy who took him his midday meal, a small round brunette with braces on her teeth and the temper of a Doberman that's just had its tail stolen. She couldn't speak a word of French, probably not even the words on a restaurant menu.

When I asked her how Maurice was, she replied, "Pleasant to look at, but nothing between the ears. No matter how much I threatened, begged, called him a son of a bitch, he insisted on writing 'Toledo' on his top sheet with the ketchup."

I don't need to tell you the effect that had on me. I promised myself, however, to keep him waiting until dinnertime. I busied myself with everybody and everything except him. Then I immersed myself in soap, toothpaste, and shampoo. I polished my finger- and toenails. I put on a clean white coat, nurses' cap, and panties. I changed my sandals and brand of deodorant.

As the sun went down into a sea of mist, a ravishing blond doll, just out of her box, took a naughty boy the best the kitchens could come up with for a Frenchman: soya soup with peppers, buffalo steak, macaroni au gratin, apple pie, and a beautiful orchid to make things pretty and intimate.

If you could have read this doll's mind, assuming that she had one, this is what you would have seen: she enters the tent, he is captivated by her beauty, he implores her forgiveness. After that, too bad. Despite all their differences and although she had heard "The French They Are a Funny Race, Parlez-Vous?" sung a thousand times when she was knee-high in Toledo, Ohio, she gives herself to him on the disheveled bed in the cloying humidity of the monsoon.

Nothing ever turns out as well or as badly as you think it will, as he himself would say.

When I went in, he looked around, his arms folded, propped up on two pillows behind him. He was sulking. I acted as though I didn't care. I tried to place the tray in front of him. He pushed it aside. Much good would that do him. I left that lovely meal on the next bed and went away again.

During the night, I went back. I was no longer a doll. I was a nurse dripping with rain, incapable of understanding men, making her rounds. I turned on the light above his bed. He hadn't touched his dinner. He wasn't asleep. He watched me with sad eyes, his ketchup-stained sheet folded back just high enough to hide the fact that he was past the age of capriciousness.

I said, "The head cook will be furious. He's a black guy from Washington, very straitlaced, very jealous of his prerogatives. He is even taller than you, and when you're up and about, I wouldn't be surprised if he punches your head in."

Maurice shrugged his right shoulder, or his left, I don't remember which. Not a smile. He said, "You don't know what it's like, Toledo. Years of war without setting eyes on a woman!"

"Every man I've nursed has already said the same thing."

"Oh no! You don't know what it's like."

"But you weren't alone on that island?"

"What island?" he asked. "I didn't even stay there for an hour. I just had time to meet Esmeralda and promise the pair of them that help would come. A typhoon was threatening."

He held out his hand for me to come closer. I took it. His other hand slid under my uniform. I pushed him gently away.

I said, "You're not being reasonable, Maurice. Why didn't you eat?"

He sat up a bit and I saw anger and derision in his eyes. "Eat? What for? You know what's waiting for me when I get out of here? A firing squad!"

He regained his breath and declared flatly, "I'm a deserter!"

The shock made me sit down. I placed my behind on the edge of his bed, about level with his knees. I said, "But that's impossible!"

"A de-ser-ter!"

I was speechless for a long time. I looked at him. He hung his head. I took his hand again and asked him very softly, "Why did you desert?"

"Exactly. Because I couldn't even remember what a woman looked like!"

Of course he was putting on an act, but his hand was squeezing mine, I could see tears in his incredible black eyes, with longer natural eyelashes than I have ever seen. Pathetic, that's what he was. He was pathetic and my heart swelled with concern and pity.

I whispered, "What do you want?"

He sadly shrugged his left shoulder, unless it was the right; in any case, it wasn't the same one as before. "You know very well what I want," he said, looking away. "I won't even try to touch you."

As I asked him, I had my own ideas as to what would make him happy. Now I was at a complete loss to understand, except that I must be stupid.

I got up, just in case. His gaze returned to me. It wasn't difficult to see from his eyes that I had begun to do what he wanted and that he was waiting for what came next, but I didn't feel any the wiser. After a few long moments of gazing at each other without moving so much as a little finger, I was so embarrassed that I said, "Do you find this amusing? Well, I don't!"

And I ran outside, getting caught up in the flap that served as the door to the Carlyle. I turned around and blurted out, "Have you told our officers that you're a deserter?"

He shrugged both shoulders at once this time.

I ran through the rain until I reached our barracks. Two soldiers and a doctor were chatting under the porch. They inquired as to whether the froggy was in good spirits. In a little camp like the one I'm talking about, everybody soon knows what's going on. I said in passing, "Fine, fine." Just ask them whether they believed me.

The next day and the day after that, I was a sphinx. I went to see Maurice in uniform, duty-duty. I rammed a thermometer in his mouth. I didn't say a word to him. His temperature was normal, his blood pressure wasn't bad, the whites of his eyes were as white as his teeth, his virility was modestly hidden beneath a sheet. When I tried to pull back the sheet, glaring at him, merely to change it, he yanked at it as if the honor of Eternal France depended on it. I didn't care. I took the clean sheet away with me again.

But at night, Lord, you made it too long, Armstrong sang, I wept a little. I reproached myself a lot. In particular for not having understood what Maurice was asking me for when I was beside him. And yet it was perfectly obvious, and thinking about it, hardly any more difficult than when protected by a screen. Hadn't I resolved, a little earlier, to give him plenty more?

Perhaps it isn't absolutely essential to tell you what happened on the third night, but I will anyway.

After having firmly secured the tent flap, I placed his dinner on his lap once again. I said, severely enough to have the courage to look at him, "Will you eat if I do it?"

He looked up at me with trusting eyes. He nodded that it was a promise.

I took three impeccable steps back, my gaze riveted on an imaginary horizon, as I had been taught in San Diego. Upright as an admiral's sword, I removed the belt from my white coat and undid one breast button, then another. I had already acted out this scene a dozen times in the space between my ears where there should be a brain. But shame got the better of me, I couldn't go any further. I turned to look at him. He picked up his plate and enthusiastically swallowed a mouthful of mashed potatoes.

I could hear the fans wheezing. I was clammy. He was looking at my breasts, through the opening in my white coat, as if they were the softest, most beautiful breasts in the world. I bravely undid a third button with trembling hands, and the last one hastily, forced to lean forward.

You'll never guess what he said when, speechless and probably crimson, I let my white coat fall to the floor. He didn't beg me, as in my nocturnal imaginings, to remove my remaining clothing, a pair of panties I had borrowed from another nurse because they were trimmed with lace. He murmured: "Be quiet!"

And he flung himself back onto his pillows, his eyes suddenly elsewhere, and all he needed to do to complete the Garbo act was to place the back of his hand on his forehead and cough a little.

That relaxed me. On my own initiative, I slipped my friend's panties down to my ankles with a newfound grace, and though I lost my balance getting him over the hurdle of the shoes, I took it all in stride. I insisted, of course, on keeping my shoes till last because heels make the legs look more shapely, but I must say that hardly encouraged Maurice to keep his promise not to touch me. I was completely his and I still had them on. My little nurse's cap, too, in fact.

I was really and truly in love. And that was nothing compared to how I soon felt. I loved his mind, his sensibility, his soul, anything you like. But what he did to me, what he did to me, there's no name for it.

Until then, I'd always been a girl who was at peace with herself, safe from frustrations and from frenzies—in other words, fairly calm. I don't know if the others in the camp were aware of the revolution, whether they were surprised, amused, or shocked. Nobody made any comment. All that I know is that my cries were enough to rouse the entire navy.

The second of September, the day peace was signed, Maurice was given a uniform, some clean underwear, and shoes. He had a long conversation with Dr. Kirby. Until orders came from above, he decided that the Frenchman would remain in my care, on the condition that he did not leave the Carlyle, other than for a daily walk as far as the barbed wire surrounding the beach. To me, he said, "Do as you wish, Toledo, but I don't want to hear another word about him until we leave."

Another day, news came from Jarvis, via Rangoon. They showed me the message. I ran to see Maurice. He was thumping a duffel bag full of sand that he had fixed up inside the tent. He was wearing khaki long johns and was sweating profusely.

I said, "They've found your two friends in the Pacific. They're on their way to San Francisco."

He was pleased, but too breathless to speak. He picked up a towel and mopped his face and torso.

I added, "Miss Esmeralda claims that you lived on that desert island for three years."

No answer.

"You said the other girl was Chilean. The telegram says Japanese."

"Chilean, Japanese, what's the difference?"

I stretched my eyes with my forefinger to show him.

"Listen," he said, "she's a wonderful girl. I didn't want her to have any trouble with your fellow Americans."

He sat down and untied the bandages he had wrapped around his hands to punch the duffel bag. "Besides," he added, "she hasn't even got slanty eyes. I assure you, she looks strangely Chilean."

"Did you sleep with both of them on the island?"

He looked at me, saw that anything was better for me than silence, and replied, busy with his bandages, "It was hard to catch them, you know."

That night, when we were together in his narrow bed, another question came into my head, "If you lived on that island for all that time, after the shipwreck, what army can you have deserted from?"

"So why do you think I hid on board the *Pandora*?"

"To do your dirty business with Miss Frou-Frou."

"No," he said. "I had escaped from a military fortress. That means I was still a soldier."

Then he told me that he had been sentenced for life for a crime he had not committed. When he told me what the crime was, I knew very well that he could not have committed it.

I consulted the regulations of the American navy, but I found nothing similar to Maurice's case. As soon as I had the opportunity, I asked an airman from the Delmonico, wounded over the Arakan, what would happen in the States to a military prisoner who had escaped in wartime.

The airman was called Jim or Jack Forsythe and came from Virginia. He said, "They'd have his hide. If they didn't want to waste bullets, they'd send him to the front line and that would be the end of him. Either way, they'd have his hide."

"Are you sure?"

"Sure as I'm my mother's son."

"Supposing they only find him when the war is over?"

"They'd have his hide. No longer need to worry about the bullets."

Luckily for my morale, since I had been all his, Maurice no longer tried to make me feel sorry for him by reminding me of the cruelly short time he had left.

"I've got plenty of time before they remember my existence," he said. "Anyway, there are enough dead already, everybody's tired."

He made the most of the bright intervals to take his walk on the long, empty beach. Beyond the camp fences, there was nothing but flooded paddy fields, and far away, the green of the trees. Not a village in sight, not a pagoda, nothing to remind him that we were in Burma.

He looked at all that and said, "Water is the same everywhere. Do you know that we are probably descended from strange beasts that came out of the sea? I'm a Cancer. It's a water sign, the only sign of the zodiac governed by the moon. What about you?"

"Pisces."

"I like you," he said.

In fact, his favorite sign was Taurus. His wife was a Taurus, and past friends of his. I'd never thought about it before.

We walked aimlessly along the beach. Sometimes we swam. Unfortunately, the branches of the river brought down lots of debris and filth. I was less tanned than him, and my behind was even paler than the rest of me; I was ashamed of it. I'd never thought about that either.

Then there was the famous night of Chou-Yang. It was still the beginning of September. Everything I'm telling you happened very quickly, in fact.

I took Maurice his dinner at sunset, as usual. While he ate, sitting at the teak table I'd had brought in, I kissed his neck, I slid my hand inside his khaki long johns, I excited him in lots of little ways. His shoulder and back muscles were very big from having thumped the sandbag, and he was in a conciliatory mood. He said, "Stop it, Toledo, for heaven's sake!" but I couldn't make him really angry.

Suddenly we heard the kitchen bell ring, far away outside. Maurice stopped eating, his fork in midair, listening with a sort of terror, his eyes glazed as if waking up from a dream.

"What is it?"

I was surprised to see him like this, but it's true that we rarely heard that bell. It must have been used when the British occupied the camp before us. I said, "Nothing. It's a code. It means that Chou-Yang is coming from Rangoon to play cards."

"Who?"

"Chou-Yang. Known as 'The Chinese Who Fleeces Us.' Nobody has ever managed to beat him."

Maurice had gotten up and was looking at the door. He was

breathing hard, perhaps to get over his momentary anxiety. He asked, "Does he play for high stakes?"

I had no idea, having little interest in these games during which our soldiers got fleeced. I saw his gaze shift to the mattress under which he hid his pearls. I murmured, "Oh no! Not you!"

Now I'll tell you what the Carlyle looked like six hours later. The light was engulfed in a haze of cigarette smoke. Outside, the rain fell and it was the only sound that could be heard. The fans had been switched off so as not to disturb the players. An attentive audience stood around the table in the center aisle, their mouths buttoned. There were two off-duty nurse's aids, three nurses, American and British convalescents, and at least fifteen sweaty people in various states of undress sprawled in chairs or on the nearest beds.

On one side of the table was Chou-Yang, his head shaved, his eyes like dark slits, in the uniform of a Chinese general, his features rigid with Chinese impassiveness. Standing close to him was the woman who always accompanied him when he came to take our money, Chérie-Chen, a young, haughty, and very pretty Chinese girl, in an evening dress with a very long slit, who only moved, not even batting a false eyelash, to raise a long Chinese cigarette holder to her mouth.

On the other side of the table, in a pair of beige pants and a Hawaiian shirt lent by a sailor from the Plaza, Maurice delicately poured the pearls into the bowl of a little pair of golden scales to equal his opponent's stakes. At the beginning of the game, Chou-Yang didn't have any pearls. He paid eleven dollars for one. Now it was he who had the most, and he was raising the stakes each time.

They were playing a very subtle game: the pack of cards was between them, and each took the top card in turn. The one who had the highest card won.

It became even more complicated when they both drew cards of the same value. Then Maurice would shout triumphantly, "Snap!" but Chou-Yang didn't say a word. He never showed his emotions. Then they would each take another card, very slowly, to tantalize their opponent and show how crafty they were, and Chou-Yang would turn his over and grab the pearls, without even bothering to see what Maurice had drawn.

By three o'clock in the morning, Chou-Yang had not lost more than six rounds. He had a reputation for never losing more than seven, no matter how long the game lasted. When they reached the end of the pack, they began all over again, so there was no shortage of cards. It seemed reasonable to suppose that this game would last until Maurice had run out of pearls. Between bids, he would wipe the sweat from his forehead with the back of his hand, drink a sip of rice alcohol, draw on his cigarette, and look inside his old sock to see what he had left.

At dawn, he had nothing left. He put his last three pearls in the scales and Chou-Yang matched their weight and drew a jack. Maurice played a seven. A murmur of disappointment rippled through the tent. It was even worse when the Chinese, playing for the old sock against its weight in pearls, won that, too.

As the hours passed, many had gone off to bed. Those who had held out till then got up to do likewise. There were two British and two Americans, one of whom, Sergeant Wilkinson, was supporting my colleague Virginia Cosentino, who was asleep on his shoulder. I was close to Maurice. Drunk with alcohol, tobacco, and exhaustion, he stared fixedly at Chou-Yang's delicate Chinese hands as he poured the pearls into the sock.

Suddenly he straightened his shoulders, tears of pride in his eyes, and shouted, "Stop that! I didn't say the game was over! I've still got my grandmother's inheritance!"

I put my arm around him and said, desperately, "No, Maurice, please! Don't do that!"

He pushed me away. He looked at Chou-Yang with bitterness and defiance. But Chou-Yang's eyes were nothing but two unfathomable slits.

Then Chérie-Chen leaned forward to whisper a few words in her companion's ears. The two slits became even narrower, but Chou-Yang sat back in his chair and asked in French, "The honorable ally did say 'inheritance'?"

Even without understanding the words, those who were leaving came back to the table. Maurice poured himself a drink and gulped it down. He lit a cigarette. He blew out the smoke in a long sigh. He said, his face miraculously relaxed, "When I was a little boy in Marseilles, my grandmother was always dressed in black, even in the summer, because she wanted to wear mourning for my grandfather until the end. . . ."

For my fellow Americans and the two British, I translated: "He was a child. His grandmother was a widow."

*   *   *

"She was poor, too," added this young man far away from home, "and to earn a little money, she went from door to door, all over the Belle de Mai district. She would bravely climb the stairs, one hand holding the banister, the other holding the shopping bag and the black umbrella that never left her side.

"She would ring a doorbell. As she regained her breath and her heart began to beat less wildly, she would see the door open to reveal a man in his vest and, behind him, a woman in a bathrobe. And the man, disturbed while reading his newspaper, would say to my grandmother, 'We don't need anything!'

" 'Just as well,' she would reply, 'because I haven't got anything to sell you. But if you have everything, perhaps you've also got some empty toothpaste tubes? I work for the reprocessors.'

"Sometimes the man would claim that nobody cleaned their teeth in his house, but his wife would nudge him with her elbow, and whether he liked it or not, he would go and see. And while she was alone with my grandmother, who leaned against the wall and looked straight at her, the woman in a bathrobe would say, 'If you like, instead of throwing the tubes away, we'll keep them for you. Just drop by from time to time.'

"That way, after a few weeks, my grandmother filled her shopping bag more easily. Then she would sell the lot for the price of lead. It might not sound much, but wait a bit.

"She boldly climbed more stairs, and more doors opened, and one of those revealed a retired man in a dressing gown who was already holding some empty toothpaste tubes. And while she was stuffing them all into her shopping bag, complimenting him on his excellent hygiene, the man shuffled from one foot to the other and, finally, said timidly, 'We are alone in the world, Madame Isola, and I've got a good pension from the railways. Why don't we get married?'

"My grandmother shot him a withering look, her cheeks red, and retorted, 'Who do you think I am? I am the wife of one man alone! Nobody can accuse me of ever having looked at another.'

"And she went back down the stairs to get away from this base person as quickly as she could, but the old man, sorry for having insulted her wifely honor, called her back.

" 'Please, don't leave like that! I have something that might interest you.'

"He showed her two empty wine bottles and pointed to the strips of lead around the necks. My grandmother tore off the lead and stuffed it into her bag, saying, 'I'm interested in everything, I work for the reprocessing people.'

"Gradually, her hunting ground extended to the Boulevard Longchamp, the rue Saint-Ferréol, to the Prado, to the whole of Marseilles. She now pulled a small cartful of scrap metal along the middle of the road, in and out of the sun, using both arms, a strap around her chest. She went about her business, toiling, taking no notice of anybody else, staring straight ahead, her black umbrella dangling from her load. My grandmother was an ant.

"When I ran away from the boarding school they'd had to send me to, because my monster of a father had left home," continued this young man after clearing his throat to hide his emotion, "I went to her for sanctuary.

"At that time she lived on the Boulevard National, on the first floor, in the little apartment that had been my mother's for a long time and in which I was born. There was a kitchen, a bedroom, and a very narrow little room where there was still the bed I had slept in as a child.

"The kitchen was where we lived by day, with a big filter over the sink for drinking water and a window overlooking the boulevard. It was from this window that I used to throw flaming balls of paper before I was sent to boarding school. I don't know why I did that sort of thing; you know as well as I do how hard it is to explain to oneself the powerful urges one felt at the age of five or six, and they are impossible to express in words. In my case, that was precisely it, the only language I had found was that of terrifying passersby with burning paper.

"I remember that the afternoon I arrived at her flat, having come on foot from Trois-Lucs, which was quite a distance for me, all she saw at first was a dirty, ravenous grandson. She washed me from head to foot in a basin, wrapped me up in a big towel, and sat me down at the table covered with an oilcloth. While I dug into the polenta with lots of meat sauce and Parmesan, she sat down beside me and said, after looking at me with heartbreaking tenderness for a while, 'Poor little thing, whatever are we going to do with you? What will become of you?'

"I replied truthfully, 'I don't know.'

" 'What would you like best?'

"I thought for a bit and replied without conviction: 'A doctor?'

"She made me a crushed banana with sugar.

" 'That's no life,' she said. 'People call you out day and night, you end up being a slave. No, that's not what you should do at all.'

"We looked at each other in silence for a good minute more. There was something that I would have liked to do perhaps and that was to be a boxer. The big boys who taunted me because my family were wops would have been afraid of me, and I'd have given them what for without her having to come and rescue me with her umbrella. Unfortunately, I couldn't say a boxer: if I had so much as a scratch, the whole neighborhood heard about nothing else for a week. So, I said, 'Oh well, never mind! Tell stories!'

"She was already old. She didn't understand right away. 'What do you mean, tell stories?'

"I said, taking the plate with the crushed banana, 'Yes! You know! Like at the movies! That's what I mean.'

"My grandmother hadn't been to the movies since Pearl White, but she saw the posters in the street, she wasn't stupid. She asked me, puzzled, 'And can you make money doing that?'

"I replied truthfully, 'I don't know.'

"A sigh. She got up and opened the cupboard next to the stove. She came back with a cheap cardboard sugar box, put it down on the oilcloth, and opened it in front of me.

"The box was full of bank notes, carefully arranged in wads, and each wad had an elastic band around it. It was more money than I had ever seen in my life.

"I whistled loudly and asked, 'Say, Grandma, how many boxfuls like that have you got?'

" 'Nine,' she said proudly. 'And if I live long enough, I'll have twice as many! And that will be your inheritance!'

"She leaned over and kissed me, and she smelled of that lovely perfume she always wore, I don't know what it was called.

" 'That way,' she said very softly, for it was a secret between the two of us, 'you can tell all the stories you want and you will never be anybody's slave!'

"I can picture her exactly as she was, in her little black everyday dress, her gray hair in a bun, pleased that we had decided so satisfactorily what was to be done.

" 'Now, I'm going to give you a piece of advice,' she added after closing the box again. 'When you are grown up and you start chasing women like all men and like your poor grandfather, take great care before choosing one. Your inheritance must only go to the woman who will bury you!' "

Maurice fell silent, staring sadly at his glass. Everyone around the table was very moved by his story, even those who had only heard my translation.

And then, Chérie-Chen leaned forward and whispered a few words in the Chinaman Who Fleeces Us's ear. He said gently, "Perhaps my brave opponent would be so kind as to tell me where the contents of the sugar boxes are today?"

"In a bank," replied Maurice. "Swiss, of course."

Chou-Yang raised the slits of his eyes to look up at his cursed soul mate. She lowered her endless false eyelashes as a sign of approval.

"Very well," he said. "We'll play double the inheritance of the revered grandmother's savings or quits."

And he put the old sockful of pearls in the center of the table.

Maurice took the first card. I was behind him and my heart leaped in my breast when I saw it: it was the ace of diamonds. He thumped it down triumphantly in front of Chou-Yang. There was a murmur and Virginia Cosentino could not help clapping her hands and expressing her delight out loud.

Only the Chinese man and woman remained impassive. Chou-Yang carefully placed his card on top of Maurice's. It was the ace of spades.

"Snap!" he said for the first time.

They each drew another card. I saw Maurice's when he looked at it, and everyone could see from our faces that it was a bad one. He threw down a seven, in despair, and the general threw down a ten.

Chou-Yang did not waste any time in unnecessary Chinese consolation. He took a notebook and pen from his tunic pocket. Outside, it was daylight and it was no longer raining. I saw Maurice, exhausted, begin to write an IOU. I couldn't contain myself any longer.

I cried, "No! The Frenchman still has something left to bid!"

I stepped forward, tearing off my nurse's cap, my eyes full of tears and defiance, and went to the general with the shaved head.

"Me!"

I cannot describe the astonishment of the others. Virginia Cosentino clung to my arm without being able to utter a word. Maurice got up to restrain me. I fiercely shook myself free and looked the Chinaman in the eyes. Reclining against the back of his chair, his hands flat on the table, he said, "Not interested!"

I ran to the medicine chest. I came back and I threw down seven clothespins. Seven ordinary wooden clothespins that I had taken from the clotheslines behind the kitchens where the sheets were hung to dry. And don't ask me to tell you what you do with seven clothespins.

The spectators' astonishment gave way to panic, except for Maurice, who sat down again, his head in his hands, and Chérie-Chen, who was leaning over and whispering in her companion's ear once again. While she spoke to him, the Chinaman's eyes, staring at me, narrowed even more, until they were just two black lines on his marble face.

Finally, Chou-Yang gathered the clothespins with both hands and pushed them toward the center of the table, without a word.

I went back to stand behind Maurice. My hands gripping his shoulders, I gradually felt him regain his courage and sit up. The silence was so absolute that you could hear the cries of the birds above the paddy fields.

There weren't many cards left in the pack. Four, in fact. The Chinaman made as if to pick up those that had already been played, but Maurice, whose forehead was bowed, raised his hand to stop him.

Then his shoulder muscles suddenly tensed and he said calmly, "You first, it's your turn."

The Chinaman took a card; Maurice took his and looked at it from underneath so that I couldn't see it. The Chinaman turned over a ten. Everybody held their breath.

Then, instead of showing his card, Maurice placed it facedown. Looking his opponent straight in the eyes, he said softly, with a sort of cruelty, "My card is better than yours. I've already won back my inheritance. But if you like, you can take another one, and it's all for all."

There were only two cards left in the pack now. Chou-Yang was listening to what Chérie-Chen was whispering. He wagged his chin several times. Then he said, "My opponent, I am sure, would not use such a childish threat without being aware of the consequences of his words. May I ask if he did indeed say, 'All for all?' "

"You heard," Maurice replied.

Then Chou-Yang slid a long black lacquer object from his sleeve into his hand. Before placing it on the table between them, he unfolded it and we saw that it was a razor.

This time the spectators instinctively moved back, except me, who hadn't understood yet, and I clung even harder to Maurice's shoulders.

"All for all," Chou-Yang said slowly. "Money and the pleasures of the flesh of our wretched existence are nothing compared to the beauty of gambling."

I begged, "No, Maurice, no!" but I was pulled away from him. He signaled to me to trust him.

Placing his nails on the back of his card, he said to Chou-Yang, "I find you very talkative, General, what's stopping you playing?"

The Chinaman moved his hand forward and took his card. He looked at it for a moment without revealing his feelings. Finally, he turned over the jack of spades.

Now everyone was watching Maurice, and nobody could tell what he was feeling either. He had the look of a man who was looking his destiny in the eye. Supposing he had been bluffing? That's what we were all wondering, while Chou-Yang and Chérie-Chen were convinced of it.

He flipped over his card. It was the queen of hearts!

Everybody hugged each other with joy. Sergeant Wilkinson began to play a tune on the harmonica. Virginia Cosentino danced with one of our men and I danced with a Britisher.

Maurice remained seated, in his sweat-soaked Hawaiian shirt, his chin in his hands.

Without a word, General Chou-Yang stood up. He put on his kepi, picked up the razor from the table, and left with the same gait as usual. He barely paused for a couple of seconds at the entrance to the tent and took a deep breath of morning air.

Nobody ever knew what became of the Chinaman Who Fleeces Us. Perhaps he committed suicide, perhaps he didn't. There are some, in the Irrawaddy delta in Burma, who say that it was he who denounced the French fugitive.

The last image I have of that horrible night is of Chérie-Chen, motionless by the table, as if indifferent to everything. Rigid in her silk dress with a deep slit, her large enigmatic eyes resting on Maurice, she was content to draw on her long cigarette holder.

*   *   *

During the days that followed, people spoke of nothing but going back home. Everybody had their own sources of information and spread rumors, but one week went by, then another, and then another, and there was no indication that anyone even remembered us, except that I and the other nurses received forms to fill out.

Paddy was the only one who wanted to stay in the navy. She had no family and no boyfriends anywhere and she told me in confidence that at one time she had been posted on board a mine sweeper after Guadalcanal, and that for three weeks no man aboard had bothered about details like the size of her behind or her dental braces. Later I was to receive a postcard from her with the stamp of an occupation unit in Tokyo. She had only written one sentence: "I'm wallowing in debauchery."

As for me, before seeing my own debauchery arrive on a stretcher, I had been planning to go back to Florida and attempt a fresh commercial venture with Bessie Duncan, my friend from the *Pandora*. With my savings and my demobilization bonus, we would have been able to obtain a loan to buy a nice yacht and cart tourists around on fishing trips. We could have opened a nightclub with Cuban music, or published a classified-ads magazine, or sold hot dogs on a beach. But now I had no idea what I was going to do.

I couldn't see myself going back to America and abandoning Maurice to his fate. I broached the subject with Dr. Kirby, despite his repeated refusal to discuss it. What were we going to do with the Frenchman in the event of a sudden departure? Was it not our duty, since he was in our care, to take him home with us?

"The French are going back to Indochina," Kirby said. "If he is going to be sent home anywhere, it should be to Saigon."

And then, seeing that I bowed my head and was holding back my tears, he burst out, violently sweeping the papers that were on the table aside, "Shit! Have I ever stopped you from doing what you wanted during this entire damn war? Put him to sleep, mummify him, slice him up and put him in your bag, disguise him as a midshipman, a nurse, or a chimpanzee, do what the hell you like with him when we leave! But I don't want to know about it!"

That evening, in the Carlyle, I devised a complete plan for taking Maurice back to America. The scars on his torso weren't the scars of war, but nobody would look too closely. He would be called MacKeena, like me, Jeremy MacKeena, so that he could use any document with only the initial of my first name. He would be a good American, wounded during the Japanese withdrawal. I could even put a fake cast on his left leg, covered with as many messages and signatures as any real cast.

"Nothing ever turns out the way you think," Maurice repeated. "Leave my leg alone. I didn't learn to run on one leg."

The day they came for him was a Sunday in mid-September, in the late afternoon.

Despite the heat, I had put on my summer naval uniform to satisfy his whim. I think that everyone will understand. I had packed all my belongings in a bag and brought them into the tent. He had kept his back to me all the while I was getting dressed. It was the first time in a year that I had attached a pair of nylon stockings to a garter belt and that I wore our confounded little hat. I even wore the tie.

After studying me with his eyes and his hands, kissing and stroking me, he crumpled my uniform and stripped me of my white jacket and all my pride, and wanted me standing up in my high heels, leaning over the teak table, which happened to be covered with pharmaceutical bottles that day, and the bottles clinked to the rhythm of my sighs. I had closed my eyes, and felt I was about to sink, body and soul, when Maurice stopped dead in the middle of our lovemaking. It was too cruel, and I don't know what entreaties I uttered, but he stopped my mouth. I, too, then heard a car come speeding across the camp.

I don't know how I did it, but I pulled my skirt back down and I marched toward the door just as a vehicle screeched to a halt outside the tent. I haphazardly did up my blouse before opening the door of the tent.

It was a jeep with a pennant sporting the cross of Lorraine, and a tall French colonel jumped out. There were two men with him, a driver and a corporal. All three of them were wearing combat uniforms.

The colonel flung his helmet into the jeep and came toward me. His hair was white, his features rugged. His gait could have been mistaken for John Wayne's, if John Wayne had been born bad. I could tell from his expression that it had not escaped his notice that I had emerged from activities other than my duty. I was disheveled, my tie was crooked, and my cheeks were burning.

"Colonel Malignaud," he said.

His voice was as harsh as his way of bursting into people's lives.

"Excuse me, Colonel. I had dozed off for a moment."

He slapped his cheek hard to squash a mosquito. How I spent my days was of as much interest to him as the life of that poor insect.

"I have come to arrest the man who is inside this tent."

"Arrest him?" I cried. "But that's impossible!"

In my panic, I spread my arms to bar his way. Luckily, the canvas and plastic door had closed behind me. I continued in a tone that was more appropriate to my position, "It's impossible, Colonel. He's in a coma."

"So?"

He made me lower one arm and tried to get through. I planted my whole body in front of him and stood my ground.

"Colonel! Please! We are desperately trying to save him! He is growing weaker every day! Let him die in peace at least!"

I was speaking rather loudly, but it was so that Maurice would hear. The two soldiers had jumped out of the jeep and were standing a few paces away, looking dumb.

"I want to see him," the colonel said calmly. "Out of the way, miss. That's an order."

"I only take orders from the doctor in command, Dr. Kirby! You'll have to go and get him!"

But he pushed me roughly aside and went in.

Maurice was lying in bed, motionless under the mosquito net, the sheet pulled up to his chin. His eyes were closed and he looked as if he'd received his last rites long ago. His breathing was nothing more than a heartrending rattle. The tube from the IV bottle above his head disappeared under the sheets.

I barred the colonel's way again in the central aisle.

"You see!" I whispered. "Have you no pity? Please leave."

He contemplated the dying man for a few seconds longer; I sensed a hatred mingled with profound joy, then he turned around. I followed him outside and hastily closed the door.

The colonel squashed another unlucky mosquito on his cheek. He said flatly, without looking at me, perhaps to himself, "That's the monster, all right! I've got him at last! I've covered thousands of miles and taken five years of my life to find him. Because of him, I, who was under oath to Pétain, even became a Gaullist. Now he won't get away from me again!"

Turning to look at me, he added, "We'll come and get him

tomorrow at dawn. Even if he has to be dragged to the execution post unconscious, I'm going to have him shot!"

He went off toward the jeep. As soon as my legs would move, I caught up with him, my hair all over my face, terrified. I said, "But why? Why such relentlessness, Colonel?"

He signaled to the two others to go back to their seats. He replied in a voice that was barely audible but quivering with rage, "You want to know? In France that bastard raped and murdered a young girl on a public holiday!" He buried his head in his hands, overwhelmed by an inexpressible emotion.

"She was eighteen . . . she was pure . . . and the evening before . . . the evening . . . she had consented to marry me!"

He couldn't say any more. Even John Wayne has tears, and I saw one running down his cheek.

The young soldier at the wheel of the jeep then spoke up softly and compassionately. "Come, come, Colonel, don't get yourself in such a state!"

Colonel Malignaud wiped his face on his sleeve. Making a tremendous effort, he found his commanding tone to say to me, with a flick of the chin, "Do your buttons up. I hate slovenliness."

And so saying, he got into his jeep and they drove off.

I had done one blouse button up wrongly. I undid the lot. I went back into the tent and locked the door as if sleepwalking. Still dazed from what I had just heard, I walked past Maurice without seeing him. When I reached the table, I hitched up my skirt and automatically took up the position I had been in when the dreadful man had interrupted us.

Maurice came up behind me and kissed my neck and caressed my breasts, but his heart wasn't in it either.

"Were you listening?" I asked.

"He's lying. You know very well I've never raped or murdered anyone. It's a dreadful miscarriage of justice."

"I'm not talking about that. You can't stay here another night."

I felt him enter me. I let out a moan.

"There's an ambulance outside. Can you get me the keys?" he asked.

"Yes, of course."

The bottles on the table gradually started to tinkle again. He murmured: "Could you run away with me? This minute?"

"I'd never let you leave alone."

"I don't even know where to go!"

I wanted to tell him that we could get on the road to Mandalay and try to make for China, that I knew a shrewd American in Chungking, but I wavered. I simply breathed, "I do know."

"All right."

When I climaxed, he had to support me in his arms to stop me from falling over. As it was the same moment for him, and there was nobody to support him, we both fell over, taking all the medicine bottles with us, because the table toppled over, too. We reached heaven in a pretty mess, me underneath, him on top, and nobody will ever know how, face-to-face. My skirt, done for. My blouse, for the garbage. No, not for anything in the world could I have let him leave alone.

I took all my clothes off after making love, not before. I was drenched. I rolled my torn stockings into a ball and put them back in the packet I had taken them from. That was when he saw the brand name: *The Queen of Hearts*. He found that amusing, because he had beaten Chou-Yang at cards with a queen of hearts and he had once lived in a holiday villa of that name.

We were lying on a bed, the nearest one after our antics. He asked, "Does the navy supply your stockings?"

"Lord no. Not usually."

I tilted my chin toward five or six piles of wooden crates that had always been there, in a corner of the tent.

"All those crates," I told him, "are full of stockings. It's supposed to be powdered milk."

He sat up to see them better. Then he went and touched them. Then he rummaged in the one I had opened to satisfy his fetishistic instincts.

Knowing him as I did, that means in kinder words that I had never met anybody, I only had to look at his eyes, when he looked at me, to know that I had missed yet another marvelous opportunity to keep my mouth shut.

He said, "Shit! You know that's a gold mine, all that?"

At nightfall, I came back from the barracks with my bag. It contained underwear for him and for me, and about twenty marching orders of all sorts bearing our unit's stamp.

When you've been a thief once, the second time costs nothing. I drove the ambulance parked outside the Delmonico to the door of the Carlyle. We loaded the crates of nylons into the back. Maurice carried a lot of them, but so did I. We were in fatigues, and I was steaming.

I sat at the wheel. I stopped behind the kitchens. I told Big Henry, our black head cook, that I needed supplies for one or two days, that I was going up into the Arakan Yoma to pick up a patient. He showed me where there were daily-ration tins, saying, "Take what you want, pretty Miss Toledo, nobody will be wanting them anymore." When I had loaded my tins into the ambulance, I went to the lean-to that served as a garage and Maurice helped me in the dark to stow several jerricans of gas. Then he went back to his hiding place behind the crates of nylons marked MILK.

The nurse's aid on duty at the camp exit was Barry Nolan, a redhead of Irish extraction, like me. Everybody thinks I'm of Scottish origin but it isn't true. My father, at the age of twelve, was still knocking around the streets of Limerick.

Barry only switched on his flashlight long enough to recognize me. He said, "You're leaving? You're going to miss a hell of a bash tonight! And without any offense, we haven't got enough girls as it is!"

I told him I was going into the Arakan to pick up a patient and that I'd be back in two days at the latest. I knew that Dr. Kirby, having interrogated him, would be reluctant to report my disappearance before then. He would probably think I was driving the Frenchman somewhere safe and I would be back.

Having got past the camp gates, I followed the narrow road along the shore for a while. I stopped to let Maurice get in beside me. With his navy camouflage cap on his head and the "J. McKeena" badge on his fatigues, he looked as American as any Brooklyn immigrant's son.

We picked up the road to Mandalay in Pegu, north of Rangoon. We were often slowed down by long British convoys, but we were only stopped once. I showed the orders I had written myself. At the last minute, Maurice nearly ruined everything. When the soldiers, who were from an Indian regiment, let us go, he couldn't stop himself from saying, "Cinq you," showing, as was his wont, one hand with his five fingers spread to ensure he was understood.

We drove all night, each taking a turn at the wheel, seeing nothing in the beam from the headlights but a long ribbon of mud, cracked in countless places from skirmishes, with the rain coming down in sheets.

After Mandalay, in the brightness of a dry, sunny day the likes of which I hadn't seen since my arrival in Burma, we continued toward Lashio and the Chinese border. The jungle disappeared. We were gradually climbing up into the mountains. We only stopped to eat and to empty the jerricans into the gas tank.

By late afternoon, we had reached Kutaki, a large village outside of which a milestone informed us that we were right on the Tropic of Cancer and less than sixty-five miles from China. There was a prison camp full of Japanese there and a group of them were working on a bridge to secure it. Maurice slowed down and drove alongside them and asked in his halting English if anyone was from Yokohama. They pointed to a young man, who came up to the door, a headband around his forehead, dressed in rags. While he walked alongside us, Maurice gave him a tin of rations and asked him, when he returned to his country, to try to find a certain Yoko, the daughter of a port manager.

"I think there are many Yokos in this town," the Japanese replied, "but you give me food, so I'll look for this one. And what I say when I find her?"

"Tell her you saw the man who saved Joan of Arc; she will understand."

The Japanese knew who Joan of Arc was, and so did I, but I still didn't understand. So, while we continued our journey, Maurice told me, in his own way, the story of Joan of Arc and also that of a teenage girl with identical features whom he had seen on a swing. This brought out my Irish persnickityness, unless it was an obscure form of jealousy.

"There aren't two identical people in the world, and you know it."

"Precisely," he replied. "That proves I'm right and that it was the same girl in different eras."

I huddled up against my door and didn't speak to him again for at least five minutes. Then he had the nerve to put his right hand where he shouldn't, and light my cigarette for me when I was rummaging for a match in the depths of a pair of fatigues, and act like someone who wants to fling an American ambulance over a precipice to put an end to it all once and for all.

Suddenly we saw pine trees on the plateau, whole forests of pine trees, and, in the distance, we could make out the mountains of China and snowcapped peaks. A little later we went down into a valley where vines were growing, with a little lake in the bottom and a village called Kalegaw. An Australian garrison of about thirty men was there and we stopped to ask them for gas. We had enough left to take us a few hundred miles farther, but it was a long way to Chungking and we didn't know if the Chinese would let us have any.

The air was pure and it was a pleasure to walk on the dry earth, with all those vineyards around us. In the end we stayed there for more than an hour. Most of the soldiers had arrived at the end of the war and luckily had not had to fight. They had built a volleyball court and showers that were much better than ours. Maurice and I took a shower. He was very wary, he kept his bag of pearls around his neck. Afterward, he drank the local wine with our hosts. Of course, he couldn't help telling them he was French, more intelligent than anyone else, and a great connoisseur of wines and all that. He clicked his French tongue and said, "Not bad, not bad. Rather young, a deceptive color, but it goes down easily." And I translated his enlightened opinion.

When we left, with five of our jerricans filled up again, the sun had disappeared behind the mountains. Maurice was driving. We had gone barely a mile. He stopped the ambulance beside a vineyard. He said it would be better to sleep there and cross the border during the day, and that at least if they made things difficult for us, we would be able to call our Australian friends.

We ate in the back of the truck, sitting on the floor, watching the lights go on one by one in the village below. I don't know if Burmese wine induces melancholy, but that evening he fretted over his wife, on the other side of the world, and over his daughter, whom he wouldn't see grow up.

I said, a little surprised, "You've never mentioned a little girl."

"What's the use." He sighed. "I'll never see either of them again."

"How old is she?"

"Eleven. I was already in prison when she was born. I'm sorry, Toledo, I shouldn't have told you. I just felt a little down; it'll pass."

It passed. My chances of keeping him much longer, after that revelation, seemed slimmer, but I forbade myself once and for all to think about what would become of us. I'm not a masochist, and the war, among other things, teaches you to enjoy the moments God gives you without tormenting yourself unnecessarily about the future.

Later we opened up a canvas bed in the ambulance. He kissed me and I took off my fatigues, and we made love, in the back of beyond.

Later still, he opened the doors again and he stood there, inhaling the air. He said, "It's funny, all these vines, in an ambulance like this, except that it was from before the last war . . . there was a girl who danced to an old record and whose name was . . . was . . . I've forgotten. I had escaped, I had taken a young bride as a hostage . . . I swear, a real bride, with a wedding dress and everything."

He laughed, a slightly forced laugh. He came back and sat down next to me. I could only see his silhouette in the moonlight. He was silent for a long while, then he said: "We will never be able to stop for good anywhere, Toledo. I'll have to keep running away, and running away again, until they catch me. I had no right to drag you into all this. I'm a bastard."

I snuggled up to him, squeezing him tight between my arms. "Don't say that."

"Right now, you would be calmly packing your things to go back to America."

He took me by the shoulders. "Toledo, please. You must tell them I took you as a hostage, too, that I forced you! Promise me!"

"So that you can forget me? Thanks a lot."

I couldn't make out his expression, but his voice gave me a delicious thrill when he said, "No, I'll never forget you, Toledo. And don't you forget either. Don't forget, whatever happens, that I love you: it's true! And that I wish I could have several lives so that I could give you a whole one!"

"If you had several lives," I said cheerfully, "I'd want them all!"

Perhaps my face was better illuminated than his just then, for his mouth came and glued itself very precisely over mine, and we tumbled onto the canvas bed. He kissed me again, for ages, naked in his arms, and I enfolded my legs around his waist and wiggled gently to bring him back to more intelligent matters, but he moved aside, one hand clutching his right shoulder, with a sort of stifled groan.

I asked him, worriedly, "Are you in pain?"

"It's nothing. My old wound . . ."

I let him lie down on the bed. He breathed deeply two or three times to relieve the pain. Since he had woken up in the tent, five weeks earlier, he had never complained. I hadn't brought any medicines with me, except perhaps some aspirin. There was always a bottle in the bottom of my overnight bag.

I opened my bag to look for it, but Maurice stopped me.

"No, I don't need anything. Leave that alone."

I came back to sit beside him.

"You know what I'd like," he said after a moment. "To eat grapes."

"Did you see some?"

"I don't know."

I rummaged through my bag and put on the first shirt that came to hand. It was a man's shirt that I had brought for him. I went barefoot and bare-assed toward the door, saying, "I'll be back. You rest."

I got out.

"Jennifer," he said.

He was half sitting up on the canvas bed. He was looking at me affectionately. In the light coming from outside, I could see that he was smiling at me.

I walked through the vines. I felt all funny, without knowing why. There weren't many grapes, only shriveled little bunches that had escaped the harvest. I was looking for them under the leaves, bent double, when the sound of the ambulance engine made me stand up. The headlights went on as it lurched away from the ground, where my bag lay, and sped toward the road.

I don't think I moved a muscle, or let out a sound. I watched it grow smaller, that was all. I watched it grow smaller and disappear into the night. Everything was fuzzy through my tears, which were tears of incredulity, of refusal to believe. I hadn't realized right away that Maurice had called me by my real name. And it took me even longer to realize that he was dumping me there, between Burma and China, like some poor dumb bitch from Toledo, Ohio.

Marie-Martine

I AM WRITING BY THE GLOW OF A red light on my ceiling that stays on all night. It was a hard battle before they let me have a pencil and paper. They claim my condition deteriorates when I delve back into this affair. But who else could tell the rest of it?

I pretend to be cheerful.

I pretend to be good.

At first they thought I was going mad. They gave me injections. I could no longer tell the difference between night and day. I cried. I stamped my feet. I hit a so-called doctor. That doesn't get you anywhere. So I pretend.

I sometimes find it difficult thinking an idea all the way through. It's because of the injections. And then I complained. At night, male nurses used to come into my room and torment me. Sometimes there were two of them, sometimes three. I think it was in Le Mans, in the first establishment I was in. I was drugged, I honestly can't remember where it was. Of course, nobody believed me. They all stick together.

Evelyne Andreï, my former assistant, comes to visit me the last Saturday of every month. She is keeping the seven accounts I collected and annotated last year, in the hope that I would be better able to defend the man I loved. I want to add my own testimony to the others. But that is no longer of any importance, because today everything has been said: I am the one who is in prison, disbarred, rejected by everybody, and he is no more than a shadow accompanying my misfortune.

There are nights, as I am about to drift into a nightmarish sleep, when I imagine that his trial is reviewed. At last they realize he is innocent. Not that I am absolved as a result, nobody recognizes my qualities, but it doesn't matter; they were really and truly taken in.

His real name was, in fact, Christophe.

I met him in Paris, long before the war, when I was a student. The girl at the top of the fireman's ladder, remember? He was my first lover. I was seventeen. He was at the Sorbonne. We used to make love in a sort of attic he rented near the Observatory. He would take off my clothes and caress me in front of a big oval mirror. At night, in my girls' hostel on the rue de Grenelle, I would write my diary. I used code words for the most intimate passages. In the end, even the most insignificant terms sounded perverse to me. Even my law textbook made me yearn to be in Christophe's bed.

I burned that notebook full of my thrills when he announced that it was over, that we wouldn't see each other again. He had met a young secretary under the chestnut trees in the Place Dauphine, he wanted to marry her. Our love affair had lasted eleven months and nine days. I was so shattered that as I fled I slipped on the polished stairs of his apartment building and broke a leg. As the hospital was down the road, within half an hour I found myself ditched and confined to bed with my leg in a cast. And I was the only one who couldn't see the funny side of it.

I know nothing of his movements after that, about his departure for military service, and even less about his being sentenced for a crime he obviously didn't commit. My grief passed, so did time.

I was fortunate enough to be born into a rich family. A lawyer at twenty, my heart was free, as I was in everything, except that Christophe had accustomed me to pleasure, and as long as they were discreet and didn't tie me down, I had affairs rather like a man. When love waned, I left.

In the law firms where I did my articles, then in my own practice, people probably always saw me as a cold career woman, a workaholic. My own mother only caught me once in the company of a lover. And that was during the occupation, when she came back unexpectedly to our country house, and perhaps she imagined some shady meeting of soldiers out of uniform, that expression alone being able to justify why I was so scantily clad.

The morning that Christophe burst into my life again, at least I was wearing the bottom half of a bikini. Bright red. It was last year. I was born in July, like him. I was a few hours beyond thirty.

I say last year. Too bad if I've got it wrong. It doesn't make any difference whether it was the year before or the year before that. It was only in September that I started mixing up the days and nights and the places I was transferred to. As for the rest, and despite what all the shrinks think, I can remember the minutest details. I know that it was the morning of my thirtieth birthday. A little earlier I had lost one of the screws from the frames of my sunglasses, and I had damaged the nail of my left index finger trying to fix it with a hairpin.

I had been following a mindless rest cure for two weeks, in a club exclusively for women lawyers. I didn't know anyone there. I spent my days lying on a lounge chair, front and back, beside an incredible figure-eight-shaped swimming pool, with ornamental bridges, rocks, and waterfalls. I swam little, did not read any newspapers, didn't smoke, didn't drink, didn't open my mouth except for a few vague hellos. I could feel myself becoming a vegetable.

A shadow suddenly fell across me. I instinctively opened one eye. At first all I could make out in the sunlight was a long feminine shape wearing something transparent. I heard this apparition say, "I'm Constance, Christophe's wife."

As I grabbed a bath towel to cover my breasts, she stepped out of the bright sun and sat down beside me on the edge of a deck chair. I then saw that she was my age, and despite the suppositions I had made in the past to console myself, she was beautiful, with curly blond hair, classic features, and an expression of touching gentleness. If the word "angel" can be used to describe a human being, it was invented for her.

I raised myself up to a kneeling position. I was speechless with surprise. Future luminaries of the law courts and ex–future luminaries roasted around us or splashed about energetically in the turquoise water, but in my disarray, the shouts and laughter were magically silenced.

"I came to find you," said Constance, "because Christophe needs a lawyer to save his skin, and you're the only person he trusts."

Out of the blue.

I stammered, horrified, "What? Christophe? Save his skin?"

I had a huge frog in my throat. I was overcome by a fit of coughing that brought tears to my eyes. Constance smoothed her silk skirt over her knees, staring at the ground.

When I was in a state to listen, she explained simply, in a melancholy voice, "Yes, he's done a lot of stupid things, for the love of women, but he's been wrongly accused."

She looked at me again and her eyes were clear, attentive, and calm. She then opened the huge white handbag that was sitting nearby and took out a brown paper envelope, which she held out to me.

"Read this. I think that everything I have to say to you is written here."

"What about him? Where is he?"

"In a fortress from which he once escaped. Now he's the only prisoner there. Nobody can see him, except his lawyer, and so far, he's even refused to have a lawyer. At least, that's what I've been told."

"You haven't seen him?"

"No. Nor has our daughter, who is twelve, and only knows him from what I've told her. She ran away for over a month last year, in the wild hope of finding him."

She visibly tried to suppress the memory. She was already getting to her feet, picking up her handbag. Our conversation had not lasted five minutes.

"Please," I said, "do stay."

A hint of a smile, so as not to hurt me. She shook her head. "I've got a taxi waiting. I've just got time to catch my train."

She stared at me with a calm gaze, standing upright over me. "When you see him," she murmured, "tell him simply that we will always wait for him."

I can't remember if she held out her hand. She walked off into the sunshine as she had come, unreal and mysterious, and I remained kneeling, incapable of moving. It took me a moment to become aware of the world around me again.

I ran to my room. Without wasting time getting dressed, I opened the envelope on the bed. There were twenty or so typed pages, relating what Christophe wanted to disclose of his travels since that afternoon in Arles on a certain public holiday, so many years earlier. There were also addresses, notes on an aberrant procedure, as only special tribunals are.

I telephoned to Saint-Julien de l'Océan to reserve two rooms in a hotel that had just been completed, then I called Evelyne Andreï, my assistant, asking her to come and join me there that evening.

What's the point of encumbering this account with my uncertainties. No sooner had I hung up than I was locking my suitcases, even though, as usual, I was carting around enough luggage to survive until the end of my days, equipped for all seasons and circumstances, from Africa to Alaska.

The next day, eleven o'clock.

The all-powerful—or nearly all-powerful—magistrate in this case is Judge Pommery, whom I am meeting for the first time.

Tall and corpulent, with big, kind eyes and a spectacular nose, he talks he wanders around the office of his family apartment in Rochefort, done up in plum velvet and dark wood, with a view over the quays of a deserted canal.

He has decided to give up smoking. A huge tin of candy is open on the table, and behind this table, on the wall, is a gun rack. The choice is clear: kilos or suicide.

"In short," he says, "we have reached the point when your client abandons an American marine nurse in nothing but a shirt, in the middle of a Burmese vineyard. It's not very nice, not very nice!"

He has a smooth, booming voice, an actor's voice. I retort, sitting bolt upright in a Second Empire armchair, my heart proud under my new blue dress, "He did it out of self-sacrifice! He didn't want to drag an innocent young girl into his wild adventure!"

"What!" exclaims the least excitable judge of the Liberation trials. "Taking eighteen thousand pairs of stockings with him! Ten denier nylon, top quality!"

I hold my tongue, I turn away.

"What became of him over the next five months," he goes on, "nobody knows. The clues he has given are as scant as they are evasive. Apparently, in K'un-ming, in China, he met up with a young Eurasian girl he claims he won at cards."

"If that's what he says, then it's true. Christophe never lies."

"He only tells the truth that suits him," the judge corrects. "The priests taught him that."

"You're not going to hold the school where he was educated against him as well!"

He laughs, helping himself to a candy. He undoes the wrapper with the same jealous care that he no doubt uses to employ in stripping a cigar.

"Please, child." He sighs. "Don't try to delude me into thinking you stupid. And stop contradicting me every time I open my mouth."

He has already offered me a jawbreaker; he doesn't offer again. He sucks and chews for a moment, pacing up and down. Suddenly he stops in front of me and waggles a pudgy index finger under my nose, in a somewhat obscene way.

"And last February, where do we find him?"

I have no idea. According to Constance's notes, from China Christophe followed by air, land, and sea, a line that is more or less that of the Tropic of Cancer. During almost the entire expedition, a devoted girlfriend called Chérie-Chen accompanied him, but by the time he reached Arabia, where he made his way up to Cairo, he was alone.

"Vienna, Austria!" the judge cries triumphantly. "The center of all European trafficking after the war!"

I went to Vienna, a few months ago. I can picture the snow-covered ruins, the Big Wheel/Ringsträsse, number 16 Wohleben-gasse where my friend Reya lives; I recall the sound of a zither playing.

"The son of a bitch sells his nylon stockings for a mint, he makes a fortune. He's wanted by the police in all the Allied countries!" Leaning toward me, his big eyes looking deep into mine, Pommery dramatically lowers his voice as he gets to the important part.

"One night, in the British sector, they manage to entice him into a trap and track him to the depths of the sewers. He flees from one underground passage to another, surrounded on all sides . . . and just as they are finally about to catch him, guess who appears?"

He raises his voice.

"His grandmother! His own vociferous grandmother, who beats back his pursuers with her umbrella! By the time they've got her under control, he's escaped again!"

At that, I burst out, thumping the arm of my chair. "For heaven's sake! That's madness! Christophe's grandmother died years ago!"

He sighs, he paces up and down on the rug. He says, waving his hand, "Granted that there's something fishy about this Vienna incident. It's somewhat implausible! *But!*"

Again, his enormous index finger is aiming between my eyes.

"Six weeks later, the police picked up his trail again thanks to an informer. And you'll never guess where he turned up this time."

Oh, yes, I will. It's mentioned in Constance's notes. Pink roofs, as if faded by the sun, the Old Port, the hill of Notre-Dame-de-la-Garde. I reply halfheartedly: "In Marseilles, the town where he was born."

The indecent finger drops. As he walks, the judge stifles his disappointment.

"Now he's involved in a different kind of business. He's now operating a sort of warehouse where women wait their turn, like at the dentist's. One by one, they climb up onto a table and lift up their skirts. Then your Christopher, with a brush and some mixture he's concocted, paints stockings on their legs going halfway up their thighs, with a nice straight seam, more genuine than the real thing!"

He bursts out laughing and so do I. He goes over and sits at his desk, rubbing his eyelids with his fingers, his body racked with guffaws.

"Lord!" he says. "The seam nice and straight and lace at the top! It's written in black and white in the police reports!"

A secretary comes into the room at that point, forcing him to be more serious. She herself is very serious, and very young, her breasts full under a blouse buttoned up to the neck. She asks the judge to sign some letters, and while he does this, he keeps one arm around her waist, heedless of my presence, with the thoughtlessness bred by habit.

As she leaves, her gaze meets mine and she flashes me a butter-wouldn't-melt-in-my-mouth smile. I'd say she was seventeen. I learn later that she's nineteen.

"Isabelle!" the judge calls before she leaves the room. "Would you prepare Maître Lepage's visitors' pass . . . Marie-Martine, I believe?"

I nod. Once the door has closed behind her, he tells me he saw a film during the Occupation called *Marie-Martine*, with Renée Saint-Cyr in the lead part.

"How beautiful and moving that woman was! What a melodious voice! What class!"

He is lost in his reverie for a few moments, then, his huge eyes staring blankly into space, without altering his expression: "This time, once again, your client escapes a positive siege, he disappears. . . . Do you know what I can't help admiring in him?"

He looks at me solemnly. "That obstinacy, the courage he has in always escaping, always running further."

A sigh.

"And to finish up where, when all is said and done? Do you know where we caught him? In one of those establishments where he hid in the past, and which Marthe Richard had shut down. So that, he got his just deserts, you could say that it was a woman who betrayed him!"

He flips through an open file and takes out a sheet of paper. He says, after glancing over it, "One dark Sunday, darker for him than for anyone else. It was the Queen of Hearts."

Wandering over my knees, his gaze fills with such nostalgia that I dread some embarrassing confidence—great student escapades, first sexual exploits—but I am wrong.

He murmurs: "He's quite something, your Christophe! The soldiers who threw out the girls with their suitcases and their bird cages found a closet on the first floor hidden behind a painted canvas, and inside, a young boy who had been locked up in there. Listen, these are the words of the corporal who found him: *He was huddled in a corner like a terrified child.* . . ."

After another sigh, the judge stands up and paces across the room with a heavy step.

"My dear," he says, "you've arrived on the scene rather late. Arrested in April, sentenced in May by a military tribunal, saved at the last minute from the firing squad by a government ruling, handed back to the civil courts thanks to his wife's efforts, but the army still won't let go of him, your client is a legal can of worms."

"Precisely. I'm amazed—"

He waves a weary hand.

"Whatever you do, please don't interrupt me. It's already hard enough for me to keep track. A court of competent jurisdiction will be held in five weeks' time, in Saint-Julien de l'Océan, at which I shall preside, with seven jurors picked at random from the inhabitants of the peninsula. The court's decision will be final."

"But how can—"

"It can!" Pommery curtly interrupts. "That's the way it is!"

Despite himself, he thumps the table.

"I'm sorry," he says. "I would rather lose an eye than bow to a procedure that holds everything I have learned up to ridicule. Sometimes I wonder if I'm dreaming."

He falls silent, looking away, parting one of the curtains, giving himself time to get a grip on himself.

"No doubt it's the times," he says at length, "but what is more, there is a precedent: Georges-Marie Dumet, in 1919, sentenced by a special tribunal in Martigues, in the Bouches du Rhône area, and shot. A conscript sailor, tried in 1908 for the murder of an adolescent, he escaped from jail and was recaptured eleven years after his crime. If I were to sentence your client to death, he would also have a choice between the firing squad or the guillotine."

Aghast, I can only reply, with burning cheeks, "But Christophe is innocent!"

"My poor, poor child. Innocent of what? In the time you have left, you won't even be able to unravel a fraction of the accusations against him! The list alone of the crimes he is alleged to have committed takes up twenty-three pages! The least of these are desertion, the taking of hostages, attempted murder, rape, torture, arms dealing, handing over information to the enemy, espionage—"

"What?"

"Espionage! The army wants his hide! And unfortunately for you, your bitterest enemy will be a war hero, medals down to his navel, Brigadier General Malignaud! Who will the jury believe?"

I get ready to leave, my throat aching from swallowed indignation, carrying the file he had set aside for me. It is enormous, three fat volumes strapped together. On saying good-bye, all he can do is pat my cheek with a sad hand.

I say, "I'll find all those women that Christophe knew. The jury will believe them."

He does not reply. He shuts himself up in his office with his skepticism and his sweets.

In the hall I meet Isabelle, his secretary. She gives me my safe conduct to go and visit Christophe in his prison. One hour every Tuesday and Friday until the trial, between three and six in the afternoon. Today is Tuesday.

"I saw you pleading a case in Paris," the girl says to me. "I've got photos of you on my bedroom wall. I cut them out of magazines. You're the most beautiful and the best. I'm sure you'll win."

She's probably a bit cracked, but she makes my desire to burst into tears unbearable.

I walk along a quay, haughty as a modern Mathilda clutching my lover's head to my breast. I fling the file into the back of my car, a fiery Renault 11, the color of my thoughts. No matter how often I tell myself that in a few hours' time I'll see, I'll kiss, I'll touch the man who has always filled them, alive and well. I have a good cry, my head resting on the steering wheel.

A year after the war, the Pointe des Amériques has not regained the lively atmosphere of the past summers. Here, the Germans only surrendered the day after the Armistice, like in Dunkirk. Shells fell everywhere. There are still some unexploded ones, buried in the dunes.

That's what the grumpy fisherman whose services I've hired to take me to the citadel tells me. A mischievous genie has whispered to me to dress smartly for this first visit, tight-fitting dark gray suit and high heels, the perfect outfit for sailing in a leaky motorboat that stinks of fish. The crossing, luckily, only takes about ten minutes; the sea is calm and the sky blue.

Christophe's prison is one of those things built under Richelieu, with a few improvements from the Wehrmacht period. We draw alongside a rusty iron dock at the foot of high walls with a sheer drop down to the sea. A soldier, who has spotted me from miles away, is waiting for me. He is very sorry, but I can't set foot on the island before the dot of three o'clock.

So I wait in the boat for four minutes, caressed by a warm breeze. The fisherman says to the soldier: "The army will never change. It's still as stupid as ever."

"I'm not so sure," replies the soldier. "It was obviously much stupider when you were in it."

At last, one holding my top half, the other my bottom half, they both help haul me up onto the dock, comfortable as you can imagine in a skirt that rides up above my garters, and the fisherman even rescues one of my shoes before it falls into the water.

Informed of my visit or not, the soldier wants to see my pass. I show it. He cries, "Ooh!" A heavy door in the wall creaks open.

Another soldier takes charge of me. There are thirty of them altogether, so I've been told, to look after the sole prisoner, including three kitchen staff and two nurses.

I cross a quadrangle that had once been paved in stone. It is cracked, with grass growing over it. Perched at intervals on a covered way, grinning, silent sentries follow me with their eyes.

In front of the building that seems the least run-down, my guide cries, "Ooh!" A sergeant opens the door and he, too, wants to see my visitors' pass. He puts on his glasses and reads each word twice, his lips twitching. Then he memorizes my identity card. He consults his watch.

"You must be gone by four o'clock," he says to me.

I go down a corridor that smells of disinfectant. The sergeant walks ahead of me until we reach a gate with thick iron bars. He unlocks it with a key dangling from his belt and locks it again behind us. We go down a spiral staircase with iron steps, making more noise than a whole battalion.

At the foot of the stairs, another iron gate, identical to the first, and on the other side, another guard. This one is no ordinary soldier. All that remains of his uniform is an old pair of pants cut off at the knees and a washed-out, sleeveless shirt, his only badge one of Snow White's seven dwarfs—Sneezy, I think—pinned to the flap of his breast pocket. Twenty-five years old, he looks delighted to have company; he is barefoot and is wearing a headband emblazoned with the Nippon sun.

The NCO having left without saying a word, I plunge into the bowels of the fortress in the wake of this strange character. My heels clatter along the endless corridors. I despair of ever getting anywhere when an armored steel door with more locks than the door of a bank opens and a corporal in summer uniform with a khaki tie shows me into what seems to be the anteroom to the cells.

"My respects, pretty lady," he says.

And to the one who has led me there: "That's all, Jitsu, beat it."

When all the locks have been secured again, he turns to me, grinning from ear to ear, but—how shall I say?—his ears are not symmetrical. He is small, stocky, approaching forty, getting a bit thin on top, and his beady little eyes aren't symmetrical either.

"They call me Beau Masque," he says. "You'll get used to it, you'll see."

He doesn't ask for my visitors' pass but for the leather brief-case I'm holding. I protest. Since when was a member of the bar obliged . . .

"Since when, I don't know," he interrupts. "My orders are from this morning. I must satisfy myself that you aren't giving the prisoner anything I don't know about."

I shrug and hand over my briefcase. He glances at the contents, closes it again, and places it on the rough wooden table, which, together with a low cupboard and two chairs, constitutes all the furniture.

"I'm very sorry," he then says, "but I must also search you."

"What?"

"Perhaps they thought it was a male lawyer, not a woman. It's not my fault."

"In that case, have a woman brought here!"

"I'd be quite happy to," he says slyly, "but it would take a few days."

I restrain my urge to swear at him. He can damn well go and search himself, and so on.

"Very well," I say flatly, "but hurry up."

"Raise your arms, please."

He feels my front from top to bottom and from bottom to top without rushing particularly, and then he feels my back, turning me like a pancake. I had been searched several times when I had crossed the demarcation line along the river Cher, during the war, but no gray mouse had ever been so thorough.

Straightening up, he rewards me with his most hideous grin. "You see," he says, "it's not as bad as all that! Show me that you're not hiding anything in your stockings."

My cheeks red with indignation, even redder with shame, I control the urge to slap him. But he's got all day, I haven't. I do as he asks and pull my skirt down as quickly as possible.

"Where is my client, please?"

Three solid steel doors stand in a row along the wall on the far side of the anteroom. He walks over toward the middle one with little mocking steps. While I adjust my clothing and pick up my briefcase, he turns the keys in the lock.

"You'll see, it's all been redecorated," he says. "Christophe is well treated. I'm like a brother to him."

He opens the door. In the middle of the cell, in army shirt and trousers, stands a tall young man, a little older, a little stronger than before, but whose eyes and smile have not changed.

I've prepared a speech, imagined gestures to ease the difficulty of the reunion. I thought of Constance. I had made up a dream in which I would remain the faithful and loyal friend, in which Christophe and I would only exchange words relevant to his trial. A dream. The minute I cross the threshold, I am in his arms, my mouth glued to his, and on our first kiss I feel weak to find the taste, the sweetness of my only true love.

Beau Masque stands rooted to the spot, watching us. As Christophe draws slightly away and glares at him over my shoulder, he coughs and displays a charming tact.

"I shall tiptoe out of the room."

The heavy door does, indeed, close. Christophe kisses me long and hard. And then . . . and then . . .

What's the use of going into detail? It's not hard to guess that we don't talk much during the short forty-five minutes we have that day. It is only during the last few minutes, while I am getting dressed and tidying myself up as best I can in the mirror of my compact, that we touch on the subject of his defense. What's more, it is then that I notice in the cell door a spy hole and that the upper or maybe the lower eye of the disgusting corporal is perhaps glued to it, and I am in a total state.

I rush over to cover this vile hole with my hand, shivering with belated horror, and wearing nothing but my slip.

"It isn't possible! He's been spying on us all this time?"

Christophe has no more idea than I do.

"If he has, which of the three of us is worst off? But in the future, bring some chewing gum."

I slip into my suit. Enfolded once more in his embrace, on the edge of the narrow bed, I no longer have the heart to question him about the events that have brought him here. Besides, he informs me: "If I asked for your help, it was only because I wanted to see you again. We can't pin any hope on this trial, it'll be as phony as the others. And justifying myself before those creeps is the last of my worries."

I beg him not to lose hope. I'll help him with all my strength, I'll devote every minute of my time to saving him. I'm considered good at my profession. I'll be even better when it's for him.

He places a finger over my lips.

"I'm not losing hope," he says. "I'm convinced I'll get out of this."

He has the same lively expression as before, the same face, which suddenly reveals how he must have looked as a child.

I ask, "What do you mean?"

"As I always have, of course. What's more, I've already escaped from here once, I'm used to it."

In spite of myself, I laugh to see him so calm, and he laughs to see me happy.

I can't wait for Friday. Other than chewing gum, what else can I bring him? He doesn't need anything. He is given as many cigarettes and as much food as he needs. He devours movie magazines and stories of films, which Beau Masque and Jitsu bring him when they go on to the mainland. They are both General Malignaud's henchmen, and he'd have them shot if he knew, but he doesn't know, and all you have to do is grease their palms. Besides, Christophe bribes them with their own money; he filches it from them at cards or checkers.

The cell walls are painted satin pearl gray, not bad, and on the wall facing the bed are pinned photos of actresses: Norma Shearer, Giselle Pascal, Gene Tierney, others whom I don't recognize, and Frou-Frou, of course, her sensual mouth parted in *Lips*, showing her perfect thighs in *Legs*, the films for which she won two Oscars.

"I cut them out as best I could," Christophe says. "I'm not allowed a knife, or scissors."

"Is it true that it was Frou-Frou who carted you off on a yacht at the beginning of the war?"

His face clouds over. "I don't want to talk about it."

I don't press the matter, this time. In any case, the door opens. Beau Masque declares, shifting from one foot to the other, " 'Scuse me, but it's four o'clock, and if the young lady doesn't leave now, I'll get a roasting."

"Come back soon," Christophe says to me.

On my return from the Rattrap that day, I find my assistant, Evelyne, sitting in my car parked at the harbor of Saint-Julien.

She joined me last night. We sat up some of the night working on Constance's notes and talked for hours.

She is a woman of forty, with a generous heart and figure, a fraction too fond of Gauloises cigarettes and beer, but her eyes sparkle with mischief and she is more industrious than an ant.

During my visit to Christophe, she has done a thorough tour of the peninsula and gleaned some information. She tells me all this as we drive back to the hotel.

Madame, the former owner of the Queen of Hearts, is currently running a marriage bureau in Bourges. Evelyne has phoned her. Obstinate reply to three separate pleas: "Professional secrecy is as vital for whores as it is for lawyers. Sorry."

A Dr. Lauzey, who treated the girls of this establishment for many years, is lying in the cemetery of his native town, in the Dordogne. His housekeeper, although deaf and fairly senile, states that she remembers "as if it were yesterday" a certain Tony, or Francis, a tall lad, all legs. He lived, she said, with two twins who sold ice cream on the beach. The doctor removed some bullets from his body on two separate occasions, before mobilization and afterward. Worth following up.

Madame Bonnifay, the hairdresser, lost her husband during the occupation and her hair at the German surrender. She has since emigrated to Germany to marry the garrison soldier with whom she collaborated most closely.

Séverin, Emma's unfortunate husband, divorced, a militiaman, also died, leaning too far out of the window in an obvious state of inebriation. His words, before breathing his last, were to hold his own brother up to public obloquy and to state his legitimate cause in an old and very obscure quarrel about a horse.

The former cook of Saint Augustin's Boarding School is today in the kitchens of an old people's home on the Ile d'Oléron, where her mother, aged eighty-three, is quietly ending her days in the sun. Evelyne will go and visit her if I think it is necessary.

I think that's a good haul given that I had only left her alone for just over an hour, all the more since the weather is hot and you have to include the beer breaks on the terraces of the cafés in the harbor, but the dear ant saves the best morsel till the end. The most amazing revelation, which she makes to me as we turn into the hotel grounds, is that I myself have just met in the citadel two witnesses of Christophe's tumultuous past, the dreadful Beau Masque and the eccentric young soldier nicknamed Jitsu. If one is to believe a Saint-Julien skipper who, over a drink, makes no secret of having been a regular customer at the Queen of Hearts and knew all the girls who passed through that establishment, the former was the pimp of the tall Belinda and the latter the handyman.

I am driving. In my astonishment I almost hit a palm tree.

That night, like the previous night, we hardly sleep. The papers from the file given to me by the judge are scattered everywhere on the carpet of our adjoining rooms, with the Grand Richlieu motif on it, among the remains of the meal we had brought up, full ashtrays, empty beer cans.

Wearing just our underwear, we kneel on the floor patiently reconstructing Christophe's itinerary after his escape in August 1939. Through assiduous cross-checking, we try to find out where the women who took him in, loved him, hated him, and so often bumped him off might be living today.

Contrary to what one might expect, the ones living farthest away are not the hardest to contact. The file itself gives us Yoko, Esmeralda, and Heads-or-Tails's addresses. An agent in Paris gives us Frou-Frou's address in Los Angeles over the telephone. We subsequently locate the places of residence of almost all the others. By the time the first rays of the early-morning sun steal in through our open windows, Evelyne has typed, sealed, and stamped all my SOS letters to those whose names I have mentioned, and also to Emma, Zozo, and Toledo. Later that day it will be Belinda's turn. The next day, Caroline's, thanks to her former cook.

Much to my regret, I will probably never know, nor will anybody else, what became of Vanessa and Savenna, the twins from the Queen of Hearts. It is a pity, because the file corroborates to some extent the ramblings of Dr. Lauzey's old housekeeper. Apparently, they left prostitution and hid Christophe for a whole year, from the time when, wounded, he fled from the besieged Saint Augustin's Boarding School until, still in bad shape, he sought sanctuary on board the *Pandora*. As he was no more able to tell the difference between them than their own mother, even in lovemaking, he was never able to say which one fired a gunshot at the other, unfortunately at the very second he had chosen to put himself between them, in a beach hut where they made vanilla and pistachio ice cream.

Nor will I learn any more about the fate of Salomé, of Chérie-Chen, Yasmina, a certain Gertrud whom he met in Vienna, who denounced him to the British and about whom he obstinately refuses to say a word other than: "Women betray us, too, when they have lived too long among men."

I remember that July and August as a period of violent contrasts, of sun and shade.

The refreshing shade was Christophe's cell. The bed and its khaki blanket. The table, riveted to the wall, completely filled with a model of the *Pandora* that he was building with matchsticks and paste glue, to while away the time. The forgotten smell of that glue. The very high barred window, looking out onto a quadrangle, the one where he took his walk. A single chair, a magnificent, incongruous chair, like something out of a brothel from the roaring twenties. It came, in fact, from the Queen of Hearts, brought to the citadel by a sentimental German gunner who had exchanged it for a crate of margarine.

The photos pinned to the wall changed almost as often as republics, but Christophe was uncompromisingly faithful in his affections, the actresses remained the same: Norma Shearer, Giselle Pascal, Gene Tierney, Frou-Frou, and another who appeared in the sky bursting with starlets, Martine Carol.

The sun was my night, my solitude, my battle against time. Evelyne Andreï went back to Paris. I rented an outboard motorboat, which was like driving a car, for my trips to and from the Rattrap. As Belinda had done for Beau Masque, I climbed to the top of the lighthouse and contemplated the high gray walls that imprisoned my lover.

Beau Masque. I could have killed him. I promised myself I would when it was all over, when Christophe was free. If possible, over a gentle heat, like the Apaches in Westerns. I would delight in watching him suffer slowly. I don't think I've ever hated any man so much in my whole life, but he was so dreadful that it can't be a sin.

After my first visit and the humiliation he made me endure, not least of all having to be engraved forever on the back of his retina in the most excessive nakedness and abandon, I decided, first, to complain to Judge Pommery. But on second thought I changed my mind. What would I gain by admitting that I offered my client in his cell the pleasures he was deprived of? At best, they would have fixed up a visiting room and we would have talked to each other in front of soldiers armed to the teeth. And then, Beau Masque, all powerful in Christophe's detention area, did have one advantage for us that another warden might not have: he was bribable. And nobody knows how far people who are bribable will go to serve you.

In short, I gave up the idea of being a tattletale and making a fool of myself in front of the legal profession, at least until the trial. As for the judas hole through which that Judas could spy on us, I took Christophe's advice. On my next visit, I brought some American Dentyne chewing gum, which is also said to prevent tooth decay. All I had to do was chew a piece on my arrival and stop up the hole in the door for the situation to be reversed: Beau Masque couldn't complain without admitting that he had violated the defense's right to secrecy. Sentences have been overturned for less than that.

I decided to be pleasant to the odious creature in order to have him on our side. Even without stockings, for the heat obliged me to wear light dresses, I always slipped a garter on my right thigh when I went to the citadel, and tucked a carefully folded crisp new note inside it. Before he even expressed the wish, the minute we were alone in the anteroom to the cells, I accommodatingly lifted up my skirt, stopping at the limit of what was not for him, so that it was up to him to stoop to snatch the price of his discretion. The first time, he wasn't exactly shocked, but at least he was pretty surprised. But he got used to it. One day he was bold enough to compliment me in his own way.

"You know, if ever things turn bad and you want to learn a new trade, one with a future, ask me. The two of us could make a team."

I realized that I didn't even feel like hitting him anymore. I shrugged, and replied that we would see.

We live in a world that's gone crazy. Not surprising that I'm mad. The only part of me that more or less makes sense is the memory of the sharp snapping of locks being turned in the bowels of an island in the middle of the ocean, of a door that opens onto one of the best hours of my life, onto a face, a voice, a skin, and what is commonly called, quite rightly, one wonders why, moments of madness.

The first to reply to my appeal, contrary to all expectations, was Esmeralda. I received a telegram from her in New York, written in French:

> *If Frédéric is indeed Christophe, I believe him*
> *capable of all the crimes he is accused of, except, of*
> *course, the first. I testify on my honor to having had a*

sexual relationship with him, without either of us being
able to claim that we were raped. If he does so, on the
pretext that the first time I tied him up by his hands
and feet, may his head roll. I will open a special
account at the First National Bank to enable fresh
flowers to be put on his grave twice a week. With my
most anxious best wishes and regards,

Esmeralda

When I showed this message to Christophe, he burst out laughing.

To my subsequent questions, he replied, as he generally did, "Please, all that was a long time ago, I don't feel like talking about it."

Yoko's telegram arrived next. It said that a long letter was in the post and also that she was engaged to a "very nice agricultural engineer" whom Frédéric-Christophe knew, since he had entrusted him with a message for her "when he is Japanese soldier prisoner in Burma and the good Frenchman and the good nurse give him food."

About this incident, Christophe was a little more forthcoming than usual, but I had to wait for Toledo's account before the picture became clear.

Then a wild letter from Heads-or-Tails landed on my desk, and Evelyne Andreï translated it for me with amusement over the telephone, as her English is much better than mine. Broadly—and you can say that again—the fright she had during the shipwreck of the *Pandora* had completely upset the poor woman's metabolism; she now weighed more than two hundred pounds, which enabled her to envisage a fruitful career as a female wrestler, very popular in the States, but which had lost her the affections of her two husbands, whom she had taken to court, one of them—Stockhammer—because he was indeed her husband in the eyes of the law and was guilty of mental cruelty, the other—Mathieu, the actor—because he had run off from their home in Beverly Hills with a black maid and a painting by Henri Rousseau that was only a third his. She also accused them jointly of having pushed her into the immoderate consumption of alcohol and into sexual depravities such as fellatio, flagellation, and sodomy, and she demanded the sum of one million dollars as compensation, in addition to the return of a third of the painting and her maid in full, as well as a few other trifles such as the replacement of a filter in the swimming pool, a hunting cap given to her by Patton, or perhaps his orderly, on New Year's Day in 1943, and the payment in full of her weekly sessions with a psychiatrist who was treating her for memory blackouts. Frédéric-Christophe, in fact, had been obliterated by one of these blackouts, as had all the passengers and the shipwreck of the *Pandora*. In any case, she wanted to make herself clear, if something or someone should surface again one day, she reserved the right to think about what good she might derive from her memories. So far, she remained the sole proprietor, and should I use her name, she threatened to use me, too.

I told Evelyne to throw the letter from that paranoiac into the wastepaper basket.

When I related the relevant passages to Christophe, I saw his eyebrows knit together in a frown. I thought for a second that his male pride could not stand being forgotten by a former conquest, even though it was after a shipwreck, but he made the following comment: "The picture she mentions, I saw it on board, it was a country wedding, with lots of green and little yellow flowers. It was done by a set decorator for one of Frou-Frou's films, *Eyes*, the story of a deaf and dumb girl. Unless Henri Rousseau has ever worked in Hollywood, the poor woman sounds completely off her rocker."

Then, emerging from a long reverie, he said with a curt dry laugh, "A wrestler! That's the effect she had on me, all right, when she locked me in the cabin with her!"

I gave him a good thump, but I'm not even half Heads-or-Tails's size and he easily got the better of me.

At the beginning of August I started receiving the testimonies that will have preceded mine if I have succeeded in my task.

First of all, I learned of the Caroline episode, from a long handwritten letter, composed on paper from a school exercise book, in a refined, rather pointed hand, with upstrokes and downstrokes that betrayed long years of using quill. There were few deletions, the teacher having quite obviously executed her essay as she had taught others to do, with a plan and a rough draft. I won't comment on the style, not being fully conversant with the finer points of grammar myself, but as I noted at the time, this paragon of virtue's hypocrisy often makes me see red.

Be that as it may, she is presently exercising the noble and completely new profession of airline stewardess and her bulky letter was postmarked Stockholm. Such are the upheavals caused by the war.

As for Belinda, she had long since left the address where we wrote to her. My ant found her in a Parisian cabaret, Les Quatre Drapeaux, in the rue de la Gaîté in Montparnasse, where between two numbers by a student quintet, she performed a turn that had been a success during her last days at the Queen of Hearts.

One Friday evening, after my visit to Christophe, I took the train from Rochefort and went to see her. Wearing a black dinner jacket, a bow tie, and top hat, she sang a medley of Dietrich's hits in French, in a honeyed, drawling, curiously childlike voice. She was about my age and lived alone in a small flat in the rue Delambre from which she could stare from her window at the streets where she had begun her career.

She no longer prostituted herself, she told me, and why should she be lying? She had the calm impression of having come full circle. She was no Dietrich, but she was very beautiful, in an entirely different way, much more so than I had expected. She had never received the money she had earned—when Madame did her accounts, there was nothing left—but she had forgotten about it. She had, after all, come full circle. Under the spotlights, every night and matinees on Sundays, she was what she had dreamed of being at seventeen, "cigarette holder and all."

I had a dictaphone. She talked to me for three days, for almost the entire time when she wasn't on stage. I have faithfully transcribed what she said, retaining her words as far as possible, as I have done for all of them. I should just point out that she did not seem that surprised to learn that the man she called Tony was still alive.

When I said good-bye to her, after our last meeting, it was in the empty cabaret theater, illuminated by a single light. She had kept on her dinner jacket. She had had a few drinks. Tears of tiredness filled her eyes. She wanted to give me a message for the prisoner but didn't know what to say. In the end, she shrugged and waved her hand in a way that meant, "To hell with that, too." She kissed me and I left.

On my return to Saint-Julien the next day, I found Yoko's long letter waiting for me. Forty-five single-spaced typed pages. I didn't have the heart to correct her grammar, firstly due to lack of time, but also because the little Japanese girl had probably gone to a great deal of trouble. And then, even if the judge only glanced at her efforts, they would be more convincing of the sincerity of my testimonies than beautifully constructed sentences, and he would be less reluctant to put them all into the file.

A few days later came Emma's holiday homework. She had remarried. Her husband was a doctor from Draguignan and she was the mother of two little boys. Her handwriting was small and precise, that of an artist. She hoped that I wouldn't ask her to be a witness at the trial.

Here I must confess to an error of judgment on my part, the night I had asked these women for their help. The prosecution, among other wild accusations, reveled in the fabulous sums of money that Christophe was said to have accumulated from shady dealings and which were hidden abroad. I had deemed it essential, and even, to use a word that is even more appropriate here, capital, to emphasize the inheritance he had received from his grandmother. He himself had signed a settlement before a lawyer in February, in Marseilles. He refused to discuss it. It wasn't difficult to guess that Constance would be the beneficiary in the event of anything happening to him, but I had thought it shrewd to question the women on the subject, firstly to find out more, but also, I have to admit, to tempt those who might hesitate to contact me.

Emma, on ending her letter, found my question on the subject "insulting" and made the most of the opportunity to put me in my place. As for Christophe, when I told him, he called me a dummy.

Then, later in August, Jennifer MacKeena, known as Toledo, wrote to me, from New Mexico. After spending three months in prison in that state for "gross negligence" toward the U.S. Navy, the ex-nurse had married the boss of a freeway restaurant, the Twin Oaks, where she worked as a waitress. It was less than a year since Christophe had ditched her in a vineyard in the north of Burma— although not far from a British garrison—but she talked of it as though it were a lifetime ago. And no doubt, time being different for everybody, that was true.

And to finish up, Evelyne Andreï managed to find Zozo, who was unknown at the address and in the town mentioned in the file. This exotic flower now ruled the streets in Deauville. More sensible than Belinda, she had left the Queen of Hearts before Madame paid her off in her usual way, leaving her savings of the last ten years to buy herself back from the man who owned her, and it was up to him to retrieve the money from the brothel keeper, and free from all obligations during the last months of the occupation and the liberation of Normandy, she had earned her bread and slabs of butter among the German officers as well as among their American counterparts, giving both the priceless pleasure of maintaining a perfectly clear conscience when they gave in to their irrepressible penchant for black girls.

Evelyne jumped onto a train and had a three-hour interview with her, under a large beach umbrella, on a rain-drenched hotel beach. She was obviously astonished beyond words at finding herself face-to-face with a darling whose complexion was lily white. She was to tell me, later, over the telephone, with such circumspection that I nearly imagined the worst, that my mother was dead. Due to an aberration alas more common than one suspects, nothing in the fat case file gave reason to believe that Zozo was white. Of course her role was no more than accessory, but what about Caroline in her letter, what about Belinda, who had mentioned her name several times?

Evelyne Andreï, perhaps not yet recovered from the shock, informed her of her former friend's statements before recording her lisping account, and it may have been a mistake, we shall never know. Their versions of events being contradictory at this point, we had no option but to conclude that one of the two prostitutes was making it all up. But which one?

I didn't see Zozo, I saw Belinda. I know that Belinda was telling the truth, at least where the essentials were concerned. Besides, painting oneself black from head to foot, every day, for eons, frankly does not seem to me to betoken honesty. But Evelyne saw Zozo. She is convinced that she, too, was speaking the truth. And I have to admit that on listening to the recording, despite the irritating patter of the rain on the beach umbrella, the voice of the fake black girl sounded so sincere and, at times, betrayed such passion that I no longer know what to think.

People will tell me I'm making a mountain out of a molehill, that Christophe is there to settle the matter, for heaven's sake. But he merely replied: "Zozo told you what she had to say to you, so did Belinda. If one or the other or even both of them have taken the trouble to rack their brains, it is certainly not in order to harm me and it's not up to me to contradict them. No more would I contradict Mommy Long Legs, or Toledo, or any of the others if you asked me to! They all came to my aid when I was most in need. And that for me is sacred!"

I remember I was sitting on the edge of his bed and he was on his feet in the cell. He saw my eyes fill with tears. He took me in his arms and said softly, "As for you, I hate you, you know that."

And we hated each other so hard during the time we had left that day that I'm still making mountains out of molehills.

On another occasion, on leaving, I held out my hand to Beau Masque, who was choked. I let my hand rest in his until I was beyond repulsion. I asked him kindly: "Is it true that you, too, have been a prisoner in the citadel?"

"Never!"

"Your ex-girlfriend Belinda told me about it."

"I don't know any Belinda."

"But everybody knows you were her lover."

"Everybody's lying."

I wiped my hand on my dress and left.

On reaching the gate guarded by Jitsu, I tried my luck again. This boy doesn't seem bad at all. He was even rather helpful.

"You saw Christophe often, didn't you," I said, "when you used to work at the Queen of Hearts? Who was he closest to, Belinda or Zozo?"

His eyes, with their expression of a beaten dog, avoided mine. He shifted from one foot to the other. Was it the fear of General Malignoble? Had he received orders? Not a word.

"Please, Jitsu," I insisted. "It's very important for me to know."

I tilted his chin with my forefinger to make him look at me. He recoiled as if I had the plague. I gave up. I must have looked a sorry sight, for as he opened the gate with his big key, he said by way of farewell, in a sympathetic voice, "Come, come, Miss Lawyer, don't get yourself in such a state!"

But that was all he said.

Of course I have my own ideas as to the veracity of the confessions I've read, reread, analyzed every which way, I have cross-checked the subtlest details, I know their most capricious twists and turns. I'll tell you for what it's worth. In the end, none of my correspondents was satisfied with being a witness or worried about being contradicted. They all went to great lengths to leave a red herring across the trail in order to extricate from a tight corner a man who had shattered their lives to varying degrees, but whom they could not help loving, including Caroline. Woman's heart is like the ocean. God knows, when the most frenzied storms stir it up, stubborn survival, the Cancerian immutability of its depths.

However, two weeks before the trial, there was still one person I hadn't heard from: Frou-Frou. She was surrounded by so many barriers that Evelyne and I despaired of reaching her in time. She was no longer just a movie star, but also the widow of a cosmetics and beauty-salon magnate; no one ever knew which country she was in or what plane she was on.

It was Christophe himself who told me. One of the film magazines I took him each week, *L'Ecran Français*, mentioned that she was in Monte Carlo at a gala dinner in aid of something or someone or other. Evelyne rushed there.

If Frou-Frou was, indeed, on the Riviera, so were the barriers. At first my ant couldn't even gain the sympathetic ear of the boyfriend of the assistant secretary of her third chauffeur. But she doesn't give up easily; that is the least of her faults. Since she could not contact the actress, she tried to get at the industrialist. I should have thought of it: the trump card she held was my own father.

Lucien Devereaux-Lepage, the last of the line, is before me, and long may he be so, the sole heir to a vast fortune built up by nine generations of perfumers established in Grasse. Secondarily, factories belonging to the Devereaux branch of the Devereaux-Lepages manufacture in Vierzon, Romorantin, and a few other places in the Sologne region, beauty creams and makeup, which I have always used myself with complete satisfaction. The kid from Montrouge, who had often seen the two intertwined *L's* of the family motto when she was a manicurist, was flattered to speak to my father over the telephone. He passed her to Evelyne, who told her what was happening to a tall beanpole of a chap she had thought dead in '42, alive in '45, and dead once again since.

The sky opened, that's no exaggeration, for Frou-Frou never did things by halves. An army helicopter came to pick me up the next day from a field on the peninsula, dropped me at an airfield somewhere near Périgueux, from where a twin-engined private plane took me to Nice. At one o'clock on the dot, I was having lunch face-to-face with the star of *Lips* and *Legs*, in a fifteen-meter-long van, at the Victorine film studios.

She was finishing a film called *Elbow*, in which she plays a tennis champion, let down by her right elbow, who tries desperately in secret to become left-handed so as not to sink into oblivion, alcohol, and decrepitude. In the end, she wins. The star-spangled banner is raised over the courts of Monte Carlo and she can at last be seen openly with her kid, fatherless of course, whom she was also keeping hidden, having sent him to a private school in Switzerland.

"In short, crap," said Frou-Frou.

Behind the sort of glasses worn by mousy librarians, delightfully outmoded, her eyes were the green of a watercolor. It was common knowledge that she was twenty-five but close friends knew she was twenty-eight or twenty-nine, depending on whether it was an odd or even day. She was as pretty as on screen, although she smiled less. She exercised her rapid humor, which was nearly always directed against herself, although she spared nothing and nobody. She had kept her working-class Paris accent. Her delivery would have put a submachine gun to shame.

They only came to get her for the shoot at the end of the afternoon. I accompanied her to the set. I watched her act the scene where, if you see the film, her coach, Agnes Moorehead, slaps her in the empty dressing room. It was she who asked Moorehead actually to slap her. By the second take, the slaps were in the can but she said, in English, "Tell that bastard of a screenwriter to take a trip to Bikini. If he comes anywhere near Frou-Frou when she's got her glasses on, he's dead."

That evening she put me up in her lounge at the Hôtel de Paris. She went on talking late into the night, wearing a black terry-cloth bathrobe, her face smooth, free from all makeup and without her glasses. The light from a lamp made her golden hair shine. When I fell asleep, we were cruising off the coast of Mozambique.

The next day was a Sunday. I followed her onto a tennis court, where she trained for two hours a day, before or after the shoot. I watched her listening, attentive and serious, to the advice of the U.S. champion with Indian features. Then a French giant, who had won Wimbledon the month before, came and kissed her. It was he who told me, while she sweated blood and tears opposite a real player, that I shouldn't go by her couldn't-care-less attitude toward her profession. I could see for myself that without ever having touched a tennis racket in her life, in the space of a few months she had reached a level that was sufficiently credible for the close-ups.

She was quick on her feet, her backhand shots were as regular as a metronome, and she wasn't at all bad at volleys. To top it all off, if they reversed the film for the sporting scenes in the middle, when her right elbow was supposed to be acting up, she didn't need a platinum blond stand-in for the grand finale: she was naturally left-handed.

Of course you can't really know someone you only met two days previously, especially when spying on them with a dictaphone, but on transcribing what the actress told me, I often felt like crossing things out and correcting them. Once again, I haven't done this for any of these statements. I simply hope that in hers, more so than with the others, the constant self-deprecatory humor ends up revealing more than it hides.

Frou-Frou had me taken back to the Pointe des Amériques the same way as I had come. She gave me a letter for Christophe. I can't say whether it was the feeling of betraying them or betraying myself that prevented me from opening it during the flight. Despite the din of the engines, the words she had spoken on giving it to me were still ringing in my ears: "I didn't go to school much, he'll have a good laugh."

Christophe read the letter, put it away in his shirt pocket, and remained pensive for a long time. Then he exhaled the air in his lungs and said, "Shit, I could do with a drink."

We had our little habits now. I called our valet with the twisted face and he brought the brandy he kept in his cupboard. This bottle, which I had bought in town, cost more every time we had a drop, but Christophe was allowed a clean beaker for free.

The model of the *Pandora* was finished. On the table riveted to the wall, another model was taking shape. Its creator wanted it to be the exact reproduction of the bamboo raft he crossed the Pacific on.

I asked him that afternoon: "And what will you build after that?"

"If I've got time, perhaps the sampan on which I lived with Chérie-Chen. Or else I'll have to reproduce something, but it's not very artistic and everyone will guess how I got out of here the first time."

"Won't you tell me?"

"I don't want them to be able to accuse you of complicity in anything."

"I'm capable of keeping a secret, you know."

"Secrets are much less of a burden when you don't know them."

He never budged an inch. The same when it came to his plan to escape. To please me, and for the pleasure of loving me twice a week, he had agreed to wait until the sentence was pronounced, but that was all.

"Even if they reduce my sentence to three years, I'm leaving." His kisses smacked of brandy and adventure.

The trial was delayed ten days for technical reasons I can no longer remember. Judge Pommery told me the good news over the telephone before he told me the bad news: he had read the "true stories" I had insisted on giving him, he had even found some of the Frou-Frouesque and Yokotian passages very amusing, but in my own interest and in the interest of my correspondents, he judged them inadmissible.

"Unless, of course," he said, "your phenomenon signed them page by page and asked me in writing to add them to the file. It wouldn't do his case much good, though, and at least four of these women, who have already made statements, would be convicted of giving false evidence, without prejudging the case of Jennifer Mac-Keena, which is primarily a matter for the American courts."

I was devastated. It was a Monday evening. I didn't sleep a wink all night. Christophe had never shown much enthusiasm for reading the confessions of his ex-loves. For various reasons, not the least being that my visits could be put to better use. Which, I admit, I would agree with.

The next day I took him the hundred-and-fifty-odd pages of testimonies. I gave them to him in front of Beau Masque, threatening the latter with hellfire if he so much as tried to glance at them during the two days I was leaving them with the prisoner. I also gave that slippery rat five hundred francs, but he pointed out to me that he, too, had eyes like anybody else, and I had to add another five hundred.

"Blind, deaf, and dumb," he said as he pocketed the money, "that's my motto!"

When I was alone with Christophe, he lay on his bed, absorbed in Emma's story. He didn't even notice me undress. Sitting beside him, I watched half an hour tick by. He laughed several times. He put his head on my thighs to make himself more comfortable. Without thinking, he slid caressing fingers where modesty prevents me from saying.

Then, suddenly, his face clouded over, he gathered the sheets of paper and declared, "You mustn't show this to anybody, I forbid it! I've done this woman enough harm as it is!"

On leaving, I did however leave him the six other women's accounts.

I got back into my outboard. I returned to Saint-Julien. I was close to giving up, which is contrary to my nature. I didn't even have the strength, like Belinda in the past, to go and light a candle at the village church, nor did I believe in miracles. But it was precisely that evening that the miracle happened, and what a miracle it was.

On arriving in the brand-new lobby of the Grand Richelieu, wanting nothing else but to have a bath and go to bed, I spied one of the hotel waiters coming toward me. He seemed very relieved to see me.

"Ah! Mademoiselle! A lady's been waiting for you in the bar for hours. She's on her twelfth brandy."

The merrymakers were still at the beach. In a corner of the deserted little room, behind closed shutters, sat an ageless woman, with wispy hair, her forehead bowed in sadness. I seem to remember she was talking to herself and that she didn't break off when I approached her table. She wore a short, above-the-knee green rayon dress, a tatty remnant from the occupation, gaping to reveal a bra of dubious cleanliness. I had never seen her, but when she looked up at me with mist-colored eyes, when I saw her fleshy features, her blotchy cheekbones, contrary to all expectations, I felt as if I knew her. I don't know how, but it came to me that she was one of the girls from the Queen of Hearts, and my heart began to beat faster. The certainty struck me, in a flash, that I was standing in front of Salomé.

"Are you the lawyer woman?" she said in a drunken slur, blowing away the smoke from her cigarette. "I'm Michou; Ninotchka, if you prefer. Georgette the tall giraffe's friend. Sit down, you're making me all giddy."

I sat down opposite her.

"Call waiter. Doesn't want to serve me anymore."

I ordered her another brandy. She leaned across the table to look at me. Her eyes probably couldn't focus.

"This lousy place hasn't half changed," she said. "I can't believe I wore out my ass here when I was a kid."

I didn't understand. It was she who told me what the whole town was keeping secret: I was staying in a former brothel. In ten weeks, that spring, the Queen of Hearts had become Le Grand Richelieu. They had renovated the facade, put up partitions, added two modern wings, extended the grounds, built two tennis courts and a swimming pool, and drowned the whole thing in white paint, pink asphalt, and Saint-Gobain glass. The bar where I was listening to Michou was part of the big room where the girls' chairs had once been. My room, from the description I gave, must have been Estelle's bijou quarters, Salomé's den of iniquity.

For all my searching around The Crowns during my solitary afternoons, the Queen of Hearts was there, by the pinewood, which ran along the shore just outside Saint-Julien l'Océan. And contrary to its final transformation, as I read the accounts of the establishment's former residents, the image of its splendor deteriorated constantly. What a far cry from Belinda's crystal chandeliers, beautiful clothes, champagne, and grand piano! And a far cry, too, from Zozo's establishment that greeted the lawyer, the chemist, with sparkling wine and the old painted piano!

Michou said, as she lit a cigarette from the one she had just finished, "It was the seediest whorehouse you'd ever seen, and except for a few fishermen who weren't afraid of a bit of dirt, it was a filthy brothel for the military. We guzzled red rotgut, the only music was a scratchy old phonograph that was sometimes stuck all night on 'Go to It, Lads, Show Me Heaven . . . Mummy . . . Mummy . . . Mummy'—shit, you wouldn't believe how much they'd bawl over their old ladies!"

She had found me through an ad in the newspaper. She was living in Saintes now, she had come by bus. If I understood her correctly, she had found a home among some Gypsies, right by the town garbage dump, where she found reading material. Even though she was half-blind, she liked reading, especially the news in brief columns, the obituaries, and sometimes the classified ads. She was the first, and was to remain the only, one to reply to the few lines that Evelyne Andreï, in July, had put into the local newspapers of the southwest.

I promised to reimburse her bus fare, to pay for glasses, and to provide her with a sum of money in exchange for some information which, according to her, would be of great interest to me.

She drained her brandy in one gulp. Having bravely put up with the shudder that racked her whole body as she did so, she launched into a terrible story.

"I haven't always been the person you see in front of you," said Michou. "In those days—it was twelve years ago perhaps, but it feels like twelve centuries—I was a newly hatched chick, I was straight out of my shell, to tell the truth, from a village near Saint-Flour, where I looked after the cows. One little trip to Montmartre, hardly had time to open my peepers, and I get whisked off by a specialist in waltzing on his back.

"I had huge peepers, not much darker than the gray of my life, my flesh was firm all over, I was well padded, with hair down to here, which I bleached with thirty-volume peroxide, and cheeks that made me look like a Russian doll. For a laugh, I claimed I knew the fly-by-night who had tumbled my mother the harvest time before I was born, and that he was a prince from the Steppes, the bastard. That's why I was also known as Ninotchka.

"So, one night I'm with the girls in the room filled with the smoke of the troops who made us squawk, and we're all wearing cotton blouses and stockings, held up with string, our asses bare to make things faster, faces that would bring joy to the heart of an undertaker, and I go up with a sky-blue uniform who I've already screwed twenty times since I've been there, a corporal called Kowalski, drunk like the Pole he is.

"I'll skip the details, and what a struggle it was to get the man up the stairs. In short, once he's in my room, he doesn't want me on top, underneath, standing up, or any other way. He sits on the edge of the bed, blubbering, beside a lampshade decorated with beads that go *ding ding* the minute you wiggle your little toe, and he howls and howls, his eyes staring into space, not a word, nothing. Then I lean over to give him a hand job, but he won't even allow me to let the birdie out, he doesn't even want that. All he wants for his money is to blubber away all his wine, sniffing like a sick dog.

"I didn't mind having a little rest, so I sit down behind him and I get out my nail polish to stop a run in my stocking and I say to him, 'My poor pet, we are sorry for ourselves, aren't we? Tell Auntie, it'll make you feel better.'

"And then he blubbers even more and bawls between sobs, 'I'm a swine! I'm a swine! I've never told anyone this terrible thing, but tonight I can't take it anymore! I can't take it!'

"And as he clams up after that, and he might go on chewing over his memories all by himself for ages, I badger him: 'I'm listening, pet.'

"Then he wipes his face with his hands and he says, gulping back his hiccups, 'It was last year, near Arles, for the July Fourteenth celebrations. . . . A private from our company picked up a girl during the ball . . . the daughter of the mayor of the village where we were billeted. . . .'

"She was eighteen, her name was Pauline," said Kowalski. "She was as fresh as a spring morning. He was a big lad with black eyes, called Christophe, sometimes known as Canebiére because he was from Marseilles, and sometimes the Storyteller, because in the barracks room we enjoyed listening to him when he got carried away about a movie he had seen. Besides, I'm sure he made up movies that didn't exist, especially stories about lost children, runaway fathers, with all the details you see on the screen, and it was as though he was leading us through a labyrinth that got more and more complicated, you really had to concentrate to keep up with him, but he always managed to get out of it.

"It was a bright sunny day," said Kowalski, "and I can still picture the two of them, running through a vineyard where I had come for a nap and to eat a few grapes. He was bare-headed and so was she; she was holding her lace headdress in one hand, and they ran, laughing happily, stopping frequently to kiss, far from the blare of the dance music.

"I soon guessed that he was taking her to the farm where she lived. All her family had gone to the dance. I couldn't help following them.

"Hell, I don't feel bad about that," said Kowalski. "We had all gone through hard times, the sky was like a furnace, and what have I ever had? Girls who are anybody's, whores like you.

"Oh, I'm very sorry," he said to Michou, who was barely offended, 'but you must understand me, you must understand me.

"When they got to the farm, first of all they went into the living room, but it was only to pick up a bottle of good wine; they came out again right away. Then they went into the barn.

"I waited awhile, and then I, too, went in, climbed noiselessly

— 288 —

up the wooden ladder, because I could hear them up there in the straw; they were much too busy to notice me.

"I hid. I held my breath. I saw them. They were naked as the day they were born, they kissed and caressed each other, and Pauline moaned softly as he caressed her, softly. It was the first time she had made love and she stifled a cry when he entered her, but after that she liked it and she murmured her enjoyment louder and louder, and in the end, she cried again, but from pleasure.

"And afterward they laughed and joked again, Christophe drinking from the bottle, and they kissed even more passionately and began all over again. I didn't dare leave for fear they would catch me, so I watched them through tears, because it was beautiful, beautiful, and it hurt me so much to watch them.

"I don't know how long I stayed there," said Kowalski, brushing away his tears. "Perhaps another hour, perhaps two. Christophe, full of wine and healthy exhaustion, had fallen asleep. Pauline tickled his ear and neck with a piece of straw and kissed him gently, but it was no good, he rolled over deep in a heavy sleep. Then she slipped on her peasant blouse and went to stretch by the big hole where they bring up the hay, her back to the light. The noise of the festivities wafted in even up there.

"That's when it happened, that madness, that terrible crime, the memory of which paralyzes my heart. . . .

(*"You leaped on top of her and raped her!" Michou accused, horrified.*)

(*"Not at all!" Kowalski replied. "Wait, wait for the rest."*)

". . . suddenly, crouching behind some bales of hay, only able to see it all through a hole no bigger than my hand, I looked around. Someone was climbing the ladder as stealthily as I had done. I saw the dreaded form, the big brutal body, the boots so ready to kick asses, of our leader, Sergeant Malignaud. He took in at a glance what had just taken place between the private and the girl. He was already mad as he walked toward her. He passed within six feet of me without seeing me; I think I had even stopped breathing.

"He barely glanced at my sleeping companion. He had eyes only for Pauline. He said in a flat, furious voice, faltering with pain, 'Pauline! Why did you do that? Why? After what I said to you yesterday evening!'

"He was holding the young girl from Arles's wrists, shaking her violently, and he's a strong man, but she resisted proudly and stood up to him. She replied in the same tone of voice, a sort of hoarse whispered cry, as if they were afraid of waking Christophe, 'Will you leave me alone, old fool! I love him! I'm entitled to!'

"Breaking free, she beat the sergeant's chest with her little fists.

"Entitled to what?' he retorted, his face twisted with murderous rage. 'To do filthy things? I thought you were different from all the others! Different! And you're the same! A hole!'

"Then he hit her. With all his strength, with his great paws, like a madman.

"And to get away from him, the poor thing retreated, protecting herself with her arms, teetering from one side to the other, already spattered with her own blood. And then, without a cry, she fell out of the opening. When she fell, I heard a dull thud, which was the most frightening thing of all.

"I was sweating profusely. I was shaking all over.

"Malignaud looked down, petrified, suddenly calm, and his breath came in a strange whistle. He looked down, he looked at his hands covered in blood, he looked at Christophe in the straw, knocked out from wine and love, and he went noiselessly back to the ladder and fled.

"As for me, huddled in my hiding place, trembling from what I had seen, my thoughts all confused, I waited a little longer, until he'd had time to get away from the farm, until nobody would see me coming out, and I ran away, too, without looking back, without even having the guts to look at the poor girl's body lying in the farmyard."

"That's what that son of a bitch of a Pole told me," said Michou, "and I'd long since stopped fiddling with the run in my cotton stocking.

"And when he'd finished his story, he just sat there on the edge of the bed, in his grimy sky-blue duds and with his crocodile tears; I thumped him on the back and I scolded him, 'Well, shit! What happened next? Get on with it, you lazy bum!'

" 'Next, what do you think?' he said, wiping his cheeks. 'Sergeant Malignaud had the private arrested, had him court-martialed, and now the poor man is locked up for the rest of his life in the citadel opposite! And when Malignaud was promoted to sergeant major and transferred to Saint-Julien, I was made a corporal and I fol-lowed. . . .'

"As he has begun to blubber again, and clammed up tighter than an oyster, I jump off my bed of sin, thump him again, bang in the middle of his red face, and shout, 'I don't believe it! You didn't say anything?'

" 'What could I say?' he says to me. 'I was frightened! I've always been frightened. Just the thought that Malignaud might find out one day that I was there makes me sick!'

"He bawls, he bawls, and I haven't got the heart to yell at him again, it's not someone's fault if they're frightened. I hear him murmur, gurgling amid his tears, 'Anyway, who would they believe, the NCO or me?' "

That was how I learned the truth about a drama that had happened thirteen years ago, sitting in the Grand Richelieu hotel, from the mouth of one of the former residents of the Queen of Hearts, in the acrid smoke of the cigarettes I had ordered for her and which she chain-smoked.

She stopped talking. I was speechless with emotion. So we sat in silence for a while. In this corner of the empty bar, where the lowered blinds only let through tendrils of light, we stared unseeingly at the mingled circles made by her empty glasses on the table between us.

Then we both shuddered, and I asked her incredulously, "But what about you, Michou? Didn't you say anything either?"

She replied, with a weary shrug of her thin shoulders, "Who would they have believed, a whore?"

"But a young man has been wrongly convicted! And for life!"

Her lips quivered, her eyes filled with tears. She murmured, pathetically, "I know . . . that's why I think I'm a bitch and I've become the creature you see in front of you!"

And in disgust, she swept away with the back of her hand the glass and the ashtray that were on the table.

The minute I had put her on the bus to Saintes, not without her having promised—her word as a woman—to be a witness in court, I telephoned Judge Pommery.

He saw me at his home at nightfall.

At first he remained glued to his armchair, as if he'd had a heart attack. I saw consciousness gradually flicker back into his eyes, which grew rounder with skepticism.

"General Malignaud!" he exclaimed. "Are you out of your mind!

How much did you give that drunk for me to have to listen to such nonsense?"

"There's a very simple way to check that she's not making it all up! Soldier Kowalski, whatever's become of him, can be found! Have him appear in court!"

"I'll do what I have to!" the judge replied, thumping his files with the palm of his hand. "It's not up to you to tell me what to do!"

He immediately regretted having lost his temper. He picked up the gun he had been cleaning on my arrival, stood up, and put it back on the rack on the wall. Throwing the rag he had used into a drawer, he said by way of excuse, or to change the subject, "I'm invited to go hunting in the Sologne next week. That's your neck of the woods, isn't it?"

"I grew up there."

"I'll probably have the pleasure of meeting your father. My hosts are great friends of his. The Delteil family from Beauchamp."

"My father doesn't hunt. And the Delteils are peasants."

He smiled at my offended tone. "Be off with you, child," he said, "before you make me lose my temper."

He showed me to the door, where he touched my cheek as he had done the first time we met.

"Love really is stubborn," he said. "Tomorrow I'll telephone the War Ministry. Unless he's dead, and even then, the jury will hear your witness."

I could not get a message to Christophe that might not end up being passed to Malignaud himself. I had to wait until the following Tuesday to tell him about Michou's incredible story.

After the anger, the rage, the hope that elated him at first, he, too, proved skeptical, but in a very different way.

"Even if that soldier's still alive, he's a dead man. And he knows it. He won't talk." He thought for a minute, sitting on the edge of the bed, his chin in his hands.

"Kowalski . . . Kowalski . . . I can't put a face to the name. But it's true that I was sometimes called Canebiére in that company. It's also true that Pauline took a bottle of wine from a cupboard in the house before taking me into the barn. I must have been in a fine state not to notice we were being followed."

"You were, indeed, in a fine state."

"Not then, it was the bottle that finished me off."

"You said at the court-martial that you hadn't slept for thirty-six hours, that the celebrations had been going on for two days."

"When I see this Kowalski with my own eyes, I'll tell you if things happened the way he says. So far, I can't imagine Malignaud, ignoble as he is, running after Pauline and killing her in a fit of jealousy. Michou's talking nonsense. Or Kowalski is, if there's any such person."

"Supposing they're telling the truth?"

"We'll never know. They won't tell it twice."

I was in a good position to know Christophe well. And I'd known him for a long time. It was when he said the least that he calculated fastest. Afterward, you were left behind, you didn't dare question him anymore. In any case, he puffed out his cheeks, you had no choice but to change the subject.

Kowalski was still alive. He was a grade-crossing keeper in the north, between Pont-de-la-Deûle and Dorignies. He had lost his right leg in '40, when the tanks broke through at Guderian. I know that it's a terrible thing to say, but it seemed to me that in the eyes of the jury, that leg, lost for his country by an obscure corporal of Polish origin, ought to make more of an impression than all the decorations of a general who had joined the Gaullist ranks rather late in the day, and I was far from sorry about it.

Unfortunately, they only discovered the humble lair of this vital witness the day before the trial. By the time they managed to bring him to court, the trial had begun. I was to hear him for the first time when he appeared in the witness stand.

There had been a law court in Saint-Julien, but the final combats of the previous year had not spared it. It was gutted, left to the mercy of the winds and to scoundrels of all ages who did their business in it.

And so the tribunal was held in the classroom of the local elementary school. This school was no other than Caroline's former boarding school, seven years and a bit of graffiti later. The desks and benches were pushed to one side, a trestle marked the place where the witnesses were to stand, and that was all.

On the schoolmistress's rostrum sat Judge Pommery and his assessors. The prosecution, half-civilian, half-military, sat in a row in front of the windows. I was alone in the front row on the other side of the room. Christophe sat behind me, flanked by two soldiers.

At the back of the classroom was the jury. Seven jurors, seven women. I had the feeling they were against us from the start when they were introduced to me in the former kitchen.

"Is it allowed," I had rashly asked the judge, "for the jury to be composed solely of women?"

"My learned friend, this peninsula may have been under military rule since the decree in 1903, but it is nonetheless part of the Republic, and to my knowledge, the law of the land in this matter is random selection. May I remind you, however, that it permits you, and the prosecution, to object to the jurors you find unsuitable without having to give your reasons."

The deputy judges were also women—which shows, to say the least, in the workings of fate a dubious irony. There was nothing for me to do but backpedal and accept the jury as a whole. But that didn't help matters at all. These peninsula dwellers glared at me for the whole two days of the proceedings. The heat was infernal. They rhythmically flapped their skirts under the desks, but as they did so most often while I was speaking, I wouldn't swear that it was to cool themselves down.

I had dressed Christophe up for the occasion. Navy-blue alpaca suit, sky-blue shirt, tie halfway between the two shades of blue. Well groomed and having made the most of the sun during his daily hour's walk, he looked very attractive. Probably too attractive. The jurors easily confused the seductive-looking man with the seducer. Besides, wasn't it a bit monstrous to take so much trouble to look good when he was about to lose his head? They couldn't bear looking at him without feeling uneasy.

The mere reading of the charges took hours. When I raised my hand for the first time—I can't remember whether it was a matter of rape, kidnapping, or procuring—one of my adversaries said in an aside to the audience: "The defense could have come prepared!"

The laughter was so loud that I sat down again.

A black eye never left me: that of General Malignaud, almost opposite me, who was advising the military. His summer uniform did not bear a single decoration, the kepi on the desk in front of him had only the two stars of his most famous counterpart. This man with stern features and the squashed nose of a boxer gave an impression of brute force, barely softened by his white hair, but I confess, the minute I set eyes on him, it was as difficult for me as it was for Christophe to imagine him to be the murderer of young Pauline.

In any case, he never intervened. Even when I let myself go and questioned him personally, which immediately triggered off a protest by his friends and the judge called the court to order, nothing altered his marble expression. He stared at me with his black eye, that was all. He never lowered his gaze.

But what's the use of dwelling on the trial? I was hopeless. I did everything wrong all through the first day, and the next day was worse. I interrupted the jurors when they asked for an explanation. I questioned the sincerity of the tribunal. I giggled like a silly goose at all the arguments to which I had no reply. I kept referring to testimony that had not been given to my adversaries, until Judge Pommery was in despair even though he was well disposed toward me, for it was he who had declared the testimony inadmissible at the start.

In fact, all I could think of was winning by a knockout, on a single blow: the arrival of Michou and Kowalski in front of the trestle that served as a witness stand. I no longer noticed the wounds inflicted on me or that Christophe himself had long since thrown in the towel and was taking an interest in the flies, in his nails, or in the color of the panties of the jurors in the front row as they ventilated their legs. When I turned around to look at him, he gave me a broad smile, he pressed his eyelids to console me: "Don't worry, I told you it'd be a sham."

Michou came. She had certainly found a better use for the money I had given her to buy some clothes with. She reeked of alcohol and the garbage dump from twenty feet away. She said precisely this, "I was drunk when I saw the lawyer. I told her the first thing that came into my head. I don't remember a thing."

Kowalski came next. He made a great impact with his wooden leg. He was a big, ruddy fellow in his tight Sunday-best suit, his beret in one hand, his summons in the other. He gave the general a pathetic salute. He was terrified.

Christophe tapped me on the shoulder and said, "That's it. I'm escaping."

As he saluted, Kowalski dropped his summons. On bending down to pick it up, he knocked over the trestle. As he tried to right it, he tripped himself up. By the time he had sorted himself out, he was crying as usual. His precise words were, "You must understand, you must understand. I was dead drunk when I went with the girl. I didn't know what I was saying. I can't remember anything."

It was lunchtime on the second day. Outside the school gate, as during Caroline's time, the locals and the merrymakers crowded around them in the hope of catching a glimpse of something. The sound of an accordion wafted in through the open windows. The children shouted. Snacks and ice cream were being sold.

I made a brilliant speech.

Christophe was sentenced to death for the second time.

The jury was out for ten minutes. Out of decency or sadism, Judge Pommery kept the jury locked up in a first-floor room for an hour. Not a voice was heard in favor of my client.

As the sentence was read, I burst into tears. Christophe leaned over toward me, kissed my hair, and murmured, "I love you. You were terrific. You're driving me crazy with desire in that dress."

He meant my gown.

I took it with me the next day when I went to visit him in his cell to get him to sign certain documents. He comforted me, cuddled me, and took me without removing it altogether.

Of course he signed everything I wanted, but only to please me. He didn't give a damn about the appeal, about going to the court of appeal, even less about the plea for pardon.

He said, "When I knew Kowalski, he was too dumb to make anything up, especially to believe in it to the point of tears. I'm convinced he told Michou the truth twelve years ago. They were both frightened."

Then, when we discussed what we should do, he said, "You, my pet, don't need to do anything more, except, if you can, get Pommery to allow me to be transferred back to my old cell, on the next floor, where I spent six years of my life."

"Why?"

"Tell him that during my last days I'd like to remember my youth. I'm a sentimental old thing."

When Beau Masque opened the door, knocking no more than he usually did, we were still in each other's arms. I sadly put my black gown back into my briefcase and got dressed in front of the creature. Little did I care if he saw me naked. I should add that he looked away, uneasy, as if he felt something resembling pity.

In the doorway I kissed Christophe passionately, one last time. And yet I was unaware that I was not to see him again.

The minute my hired outboard motorboat was moored in the harbor of Saint-Julien, I jumped into my car and drove to Rochefort to see the judge.

He wasn't there. His secretary, Isabelle, told me that he had risen early in the morning to go off on his hunting trip in the Sologne. She bent over backward trying to get hold of him on the telephone. That was how I found out that I had a dirty mind, thinking she was her boss's mistress. She was simply his daughter, Isabelle Pommery, nineteen years old, a law student who had failed her exams so many times that she had given up.

She didn't know what to say or do to express her sympathy. I informed her of my unhappy client's wish to move back into his old cell. She walked me back to my car, promising that she would get hold of her father before the evening. And then she walked beside me without a word, her forehead jutting out like that of children who think too hard, her cheeks pink beneath her long blond hair. She was tall, a few inches taller than me, even in sandals.

When I was at the wheel, she stood looking at me with big, honest blue eyes. I made a movement to kiss her on the cheek. She leaned forward and received the kiss through the window, and ran off.

I returned to the Grand Richelieu. A letter from General Malignaud was waiting for me at the desk. Pauline's murderer reminded me in military terms that my visitor's pass expired after the trial. Consequently, henceforth it was useless for me to go to the citadel.

That was the last straw. I saw that Christophe was lost. I realized that it had been him, until now, who had been holding me together. I telephoned the general. He refused to speak to me. I went down to the bar. I wasn't thirsty. I walked along the beach. I promised myself that if my lover were to die, I would drown myself.

Proof that I wasn't mixing up the years, the days and nights yet: in the newspaper I glanced through at the hotel, because I no longer knew what to do with myself, there was talk of nothing but a plane crash that had happened the day before on the Copenhagen–Paris route. Twenty-one dead. Now there was another crash that day; the Paris-to-London had crashed on takeoff. Twenty dead this time. It was the third or the fourth of September, you can check.

I took a sleeping pill. I slept a dreamless sleep. It was broad daylight when I opened my eyes. I felt better, well enough at least to fight. I called Malignoble again. I was informed that he was away. I knew he lived in a large villa on the other side of the peninsula. I decided to go there.

I was in the bath when the phone rang. I thought it was Malignoble calling me back. It was Isabelle Pommery. She had tried to reach me twice during the night; I hadn't replied.

Her voice, on the other end of the phone, was so sad that I guessed what she was going to tell me.

"My father won't do it."

"Have you spoken to him?"

"For more than twenty minutes. He won't. The general has already complained about the indulgence you've been allowed. My father thinks it would be going too far, encroaching on his authority in the citadel. Besides, he can't see any valid reason for changing cells."

"When is he coming back?"

She hesitated for a long time. I could hear her breathing at the other end. And then she said, "He won't change his mind, but I don't give a damn."

"I don't understand."

"The order has already been signed."

"What order?"

"I'm afraid someone might be listening."

In any case, I had understood. It may surprise you that I didn't say a word, not a single word, to prevent a girl of nineteen from betraying her father. You may be indignant that I could unhesitatingly encourage her when I knew instinctively that she was the more vulnerable. But like her at that moment, I didn't give a damn. To escape, Christophe needed to be back in his old cell. I was deaf to all the rest, and if I no longer had a soul, it was because love is a thief; it stops at nothing.

I said to Isabelle, "Come, I'm waiting for you."

An hour later, watching from my balcony, I saw her arrive behind the wheel of a black, prewar Matford, probably belonging to the judge. She got out of the car, wearing a beige flared skirt and a white blouse, her hair done like a lady. I let her come up to my room.

To tell the truth, I didn't know what attitude to adopt. She stood before me, her eyes lowered, silent, a little pale. I had never yet kissed a woman, except a friend when we were students, who had dared me to in one of those games where you receive penalties. I kissed Isabelle and her lips were soft and trembling. I told her that I had never yet kissed a woman except a friend when we were students, etc. The color came back into her cheeks.

"Sit down. I'll just run a comb through my hair and we'll go and have lunch."

She was too naive to conceal her disappointment.

"In the hotel restaurant," I said, "downstairs."

It was barely midday. The restaurant was empty. I seated Isabelle opposite me, at the table where I usually ate. We talked across a huge plate of shellfish. She drank a glass of Sauvignon. She said she had sent a letter to Malignaud by messenger and that it wasn't the first time she had forged her father's signature. Of course, on the other occasions, her father knew about it, it was to save time, and it amused him. She also had a letter of agreement for me in the little bag she had left in my room.

I was prepared to bet that Malignaud would not be content with a letter. He would telephone the judge.

"I'm the one who'll answer the phone," she said. "And he knows that I'm fully informed of all my father's business. Don't worry. Besides, I think it's disgusting to refuse a man who's sentenced to death something that costs so little. When my father finds out that I went over his head, I'm sure he'll agree that I did the right thing."

It was very difficult for me, listening to these words, I confess. So I got her to change the subject, to talk about her studies, her mother who had remarried a painter, her love life.

"I haven't got one. I mean, I didn't have one," she corrected herself.

She helped me as best she could to dispose of my crab, she buttered my bread for me. When the first residents came in from the beach, I was less anxious about going back up to the room. In any case, she never knew why I had been in such a hurry to leave it. She thought I was hungry, that was all.

In the light that filtered through the closed shutters, I undressed her, I freed her hair, I pulled her over to my bed. I gave her what no man or woman had ever given her. I caressed her and kissed her as Christophe had taught me. She forgot, I think, where she was, who she was, and as for me, at the end of all things, having ceased some time ago to be the bolder of the two, or the least beseeching, I joined her.

In short.

Later, much later, after making ourselves presentable, getting dressed, doing our hair, we kissed standing up against the door. I made her promise never to try to see me again. She nodded several times, speechless; she didn't have the strength to leave me with a smile.

She looked at me and whispered, "I love you." Then, so as not to give in to her tears, she opened the door and ran out.

I closed the door. I had barely turned my back on it when she knocked again. I opened the door.

She was standing there, all breathless, holding out the letter she had forgotten to give me. "I don't know whether I'm coming or going!"

And she left, as hurriedly as the first time.

I told myself, once I was alone, that she was beautiful and kind and lovable; I hoped with all my heart that she would be happy. How could I have guessed that I had held in my arms, for a whole afternoon, my lover's very destiny?

Winter is wearing on. I have been writing for so many days and nights, under the red lamp.

Here's the end.

At first it all happened as if in a dream. The general, furious, telephoned the judge. Isabelle confirmed that the latter, on leaving, had granted the prisoner permission to be transferred to his old cell to alleviate his grief, and that the judge would be furious if this transfer was not carried out immediately.

Malignaud had to comply. He informed me and added that he was going to double the number of guards, just in case.

I was very tempted, over the telephone, to blurt out all the horrific things I thought of him, but I simply thanked him. I didn't even try to obtain permission to visit Christophe. I'd have had to beg for it.

Two days later, on Sunday, September eighth, at around six o'clock in the morning, the citadel sirens awoke all those who were neither deaf nor already up and about.

During the rest of the morning, I went through every imaginable state of excitement and anguish. At midday, in the harbor, from the mouth of a soldier urged by the people to speak, I found out that

Christophe had not been captured. By the time they noticed his disappearance, he had probably gained several hours' head start. The soldier did not know how he had escaped from his cell. They were in the process of demolishing it from top to bottom to find an explanation. The sentries on the covered way had not noticed anything unusual during the night, other than an old barrel, from Spain or Portugal, floating on the ocean.

And to this day neither the barrel nor any other clue making it possible to understand how Christophe had managed to vanish into thin air has been found, so my opinion is as valid as anyone else's. I remember that mysterious craft that he refused to make a model of, "because there's nothing artistic about it" and it would reveal how he had escaped the first time. I am sure, knowing the way his mind worked, that he wasn't someone who would deny the attraction of an old barrel like that, even the most ordinary barrel. I had time to think about it in my own prison. Either he wasn't talking about a barrel, or what wasn't artistic was the use made of it. At the citadel, perhaps there were some barrels, but I never saw them. All I saw, like many other people, were big metal bins that the soldiers brought back to Saint-Julien, full of garbage. Dustbins.

When I get out of here, if I ever do get out, I'll check where they used to keep the dustbins in the Rattrap. It would be logical to have them somewhere near the kitchens. The kitchens looked out onto the ocean. I'll go back there just once, where there's no prisoner, no guard, but where perhaps there's a trapdoor to facilitate the loading of the dustbins onto the boats. It is through that trapdoor that I'll step to keep the promise I made myself last year—or was it the year before, what does it matter—to drown myself.

The judge was informed of the escape at about the time I was down at the harbor. He immediately realized who had signed the order to transfer the prisoner back to his old cell. Of course, he endorsed everything to protect Isabelle.

I went back to the hotel, convinced that Christophe would find a way to contact me or to get a message to me. But I didn't expect anything for a few days and certainly not on the peninsula. I packed my bags. My wardrobe was still in a jumble on my bed when they came to arrest me.

I was taken to the Rochefort police station. I said, without having to lie, that I had no idea where Christophe might be. I was given a sandwich. I waited in a locked room. I was questioned again in the afternoon. I gave the same answers.

I learned, without batting an eyelid, that unable to contact General Malignaud since lunchtime, they had finally gone to his villa on the peninsula. They had found him in the cellar, sitting on a chair, bound hand and foot, gagged, and half-strangled.

From then on, I lost hope. It seemed to me that Christophe had lost precious hours, that he was stuck on the peninsula, that he would never get away.

I was given a lemonade.

Night had fallen on the other side of the curtainless windows. I remember they gave me a lemonade.

Then Judge Pommery came into the room where I was drinking that lemonade. He was very pale. He had been crying. Two policemen were with him.

Christophe had extorted from the general a letter of confession that at last exonerated him from the murder of young Pauline. He had telephoned the judge, but he, too, had spoken to Isabelle.

Then it was Isabelle who had just told the rest of the story.

She had spoken to Christophe over the telephone in her father's office. She had arranged to meet him, at sunset, on the beach by The Crowns, for him to give her the general's confession. On hanging up, she had taken a gun from the rack. She had loaded it with two cartridges.

Christophe was waiting for her at the agreed-upon place, sitting on the dune, facing the deserted beach. A big red ball hung just above the horizon. He had found some clothes—probably at Malignaud's house, for they were of the same build—a pair of white pants, a white sport shirt, a pair of moccasins.

She descended from the Matford with the gun. He didn't understand; he was holding out a piece of paper that he hoped would settle everything, would wipe out everything.

She had probably cried, "I don't give a damn about your bit of paper! Do you know what you have done? Marie-Martine is going to stay in prison for months, perhaps years! And it won't be long before I'm in prison, too! And the judge will be relieved of his duties, his life will be ruined! And he's my father! Do you hear? My father!"

She fired, and it was as if I myself had been hit, and she fired again, and it was as if my mind stopped dead at the image of